MW01074543

WELLINGTON
REDEMPTION

A Novel

Stephen F. Medici

Wellington Redemption

For more information contact:
Stephen F. Medici at sfmedici@hotmil.com

Printed in the United States

Wellington Redemption
Stephen F. Medici
1. Title 2. Author 3. Fiction

ISBN 10: 1547260939
ISBN 13: 9781547260935
Library of Congress Control Number: 2017910096
CreateSpace Independent Publishing Platform
North Charleston, South Carolina

Other fictional novels by Stephen F. Medici:

Adverse Selection, 2007
A Walk Around Cold Spring Pond, 2011
The Girls in Pleated Skirts, 2014

To the 343 and their families

ACKNOWLEDGEMENTS

I am once again privileged to acknowledge the contributions others have made to my work. First, a sincere thank-you to my wife, Colleen who is always the first one to hear my stories. Her critique of my ideas caused me to rethink some of the character traits and rearrange some of the events. I am confident her thoughtful suggestions improved the final product.

Special thanks to Dr. Ben Smith and Dr. Austin Schenk for their insights into the arcane world of organ transplantation. And special thanks to our daughter, Lauren Ward and her husband, McLain, without whose help I would not have even begun such a story.

Thanks also to my sister, Cathy Colgan and daughter-in-law, Carissa Amsterdam for helping me edit the final proof, and to Jeanette Bruce from Equiline, who kindly walked me through some of the equestrian terminology.

And thank you again to my life-long friend, Jerry DiCola who, once again waited patiently for me to complete the first draft so that he could offer his valuable feedback on character development. As always, his input gave these fictional people greater depth.

CHAPTER ONE

Summer 2001

Joey Martinez could see from his lounge chair, the two children playing on the raft. The afternoon sun was warm, even for September, and the two Bud Lights he'd just enjoyed made his relaxed position even more so. Lonnie, his weekend guest, was reading People magazine in the lounge chair next to his. Both faced out onto Lake Senoa, a small but pristine body of fresh water in northwestern Connecticut.

From their chairs on the dock they could see across the lake to the west and all the way to the northern end where two streams fed the lake and kept the water cool. A young boy and his sister were taking turns diving off the swim platform anchored about sixty feet from the dock. Joey assumed the kids belonged to the young family two cabins to the right of theirs. He'd never seen them before.

Then again, he hadn't spent much time at the cabin since his father-in-law moved to Myrtle Beach back in the spring. Technically, the cabin belonged to Jim Berman, his wife's dad, but after thirty years of vacationing on Lake Senoa, Jim and Lisa Berman decided they wanted to live closer to the sea and Jim's first love- unlimited golf. So, after his retirement, the cabin was entrusted to Joey and his wife Claire, the Berman's only daughter, for safekeeping.

Joey and Claire made the two-hour drive from Hoboken to Lake Senoa several times early in the summer but the novelty of having a "cabin-at-the-lake" wore off after a few Sunday-night traffic jams on the way home. So, they hired a local property manager to look after the place and now visited only occasionally.

On this occasion, Claire was in Myrtle Beach visiting mom and dad while Joey was enjoying a clandestine rendezvous with his high school sweetheart, Lonnie.

"Sweetie, could you put a little more sunscreen on my back", Lonnie asked as she rolled onto her stomach.

Joey was about to say, "It's September. I don't think you need to worry about…" But then he realized Lonnie had pulled the bottom of her bikini down even lower than it had been, revealing a serious tan line followed by two fleshy white cheeks. She was motioning for him to apply the lotion on her lower back and butt; a service he felt foolish refusing. So, he said nothing and applied the lotion generously.

While he did, he reflected on the past two days with Lonnie. Spending the weekend with another woman was something he'd never done before and, before the previous Saturday, something he would never even have thought about. But that's when he ran into Lonnie Rossetti at the Labor Day weekend street fair. He didn't even know she lived in Hoboken. He'd completely lost touch with her since high school but back in senior year they enjoyed a steamy and passionate romance for several months. Then Joey left for college and by Thanksgiving, Lonnie was dating someone else.

When he ran into her last week she was alone. He was with a few friends. They hadn't seen each other in nine years but the flame apparently hadn't gone completely out for Joey because within an hour he'd ditched his friends and was having dinner with Lonnie catching up on most of the nineties. She'd married and divorced quickly and was now working for JetBlue as a PR specialist. Joey explained that he finished college and grad school a year ahead of his peers and had been working for Cambridge Partners, a boutique investment bank for the last three years. And, oh yes; he mentioned he got married four years ago. He implied that he was making more money than he ever dreamed of. What he didn't say was that he was bored with both his job and his marriage.

They both had a bit too much wine with dinner but neither was intoxicated. When they parted outside the restaurant, Lonnie put her arm behind Joey's neck, pulled him in close and gave him an "*I don't care that you're married*" kiss. Then she tucked her JetBlue business card into his hand and said, "Call me. We should catch up some more."

When he got back to his apartment on Bloomfield Avenue, Claire was already asleep. He and Claire moved into the two-bedroom basement unit four years ago, just a few months before they were married. At first, the tiny apartment was their love-cave; a place they had sex wherever and whenever they choose. It was their first home. But lately it had become more of a well-appointed prison for Joey.

He went to the fridge for a beer then sat at the kitchen table, sipping the cold nectar as he rolled Lonnie's business card over in his hand. Seeing her again had rekindled a forgotten passion deep inside; a passion, not so much for Lonnie but for passion itself. It suddenly felt good to be excited about something, or someone again. And he knew if he called her, it wouldn't just be to catch up on old times.

Up to that moment, he'd never even thought about cheating on his wife. Sure, things between them had gotten a bit routine, maybe even mundane; but doesn't that happen to every young, working couple at some point? Being bored didn't mean he no longer loved Claire. Maybe it just meant they needed to fire things up again; maybe work a little less and play a little more. He did love Claire. Things would get better.

But as he stared down at the business card in his hand he thought about Lonnie's kiss. What felt so good about it was that for the first time in months, he felt important to someone. He felt wanted. He felt excited. He tried to remember if he'd felt this way when he first met Claire but …

His cell phone was vibrating in his pocket. As he flipped open the phone he tried to think about what minor disaster must have occurred at the office that someone felt couldn't wait another eight hours. Phone calls in the middle of the night were not unusual for Cambridge Partner employees. Young associates were expected to be on call at all hours. It wasn't an official policy but the associates knew that to gripe about the treatment would mean instant ostracism from the potentially promotable.

But this wasn't a phone number he recognized. Joey left the kitchen and headed for the front porch so as not to awaken Claire with the call. "Martinez here," he whispered.

There was a short pause, then, "Well that's very formal." The voice was soft and seductive. "I hope it's not too late to call. I assumed you just walked in."

"Lonnie? Is this Lonnie?" He was surprised.

"Yeah, I just wanted to see if you were available for dinner any night this week. I thought it would be great to catch up some more. It was so good seeing you."

Joey was caught completely unprepared for this. He was expecting to have a few days to wrestle with the memory of Lonnie's kiss and the moral dilemma it brought on. He thought the decision to take the first step would be his; if there was to be a first step at all. He thought about Claire sleeping in the apartment. He thought about what his calendar at work looked like this week. He thought about what he would tell Claire if he needed to get out for a night.

There was too much to think about. Too much to consider before such a fateful decision. He wanted to tell Lonnie he'd call her in a few days. That would give him time to think it all through.

Instead, he said, "I think I can get away Wednesday night."

"Great. I'll call you Wednesday morning to pick a place. I hope my calling you doesn't cause you a problem. I mean with Claire." Joey thought she said the word "Claire" with some sort of sarcasm but let it go.

"Okay. Talk to you Wednesday morning." He flipped the phone closed and turned it off for fear of another unexpected and paralyzing call.

He was rousted from his daydream and returned to the sunny dock on Lake Senoa by Lonnie. "Hey sweetie; I think that's enough lotion. It's running down the crack of my ass!"

He realized he'd been squeezing the plastic bottle of Coppertone the whole time he was daydreaming. "Oh man; I'm so sorry. I'll rub it in."

He began to spread the white goo over Lonnie's lower back but there was far more than needed. The cream was cool and her skin was hot creating an odd sensation on his palms. Joey scanned the dock for an extra towel he could use to wipe some of the excess from Lonnie. A forest green bath towel was lying on the third lounge chair but it was too far to reach without getting up so he decided to rub the excess onto the back of her legs and outstretched arms. As he did, she spread her legs apart slightly to accommodate his effort. Her legs were even warmer than her back and a bit pink from the afternoon of sunbathing.

As his hand slid up the inside of her left leg she teased, "Watch yourself sailor."

"This seems very familiar." He was referring to their love-making earlier that morning.

"Umm", she moaned. "I could do that again soon."

Joey looked out at the lake. A gentle breeze blew from the south forming the first ripples on the otherwise serene water and causing the Aspen trees on the opposite shore to start a shimmering dance. He couldn't remember a more perfect day. The air was unusually warm and dry for early September, especially in the mountains of northern Connecticut. The lake water was still warm; warmer than he could ever remember. And his two days with Lonnie had been, well they had been unforgettable.

He couldn't believe it had been just four days ago that he'd met Lonnie for dinner in Manhattan. She had called on Wednesday morning and asked if he could meet her at a tiny place on Cornelia Street called Po. She promised exceptional Italian food and it seemed off the beaten trail just enough to ensure his philandering wouldn't be observed by anyone he knew from Hoboken.

Lonnie was already seated at an outdoor table with white linens when he arrived. There were only four tables outside the restaurant and none of the others were occupied but Joey worried that being outside increased the odds of someone he knew walking past. As he approached the table, Lonnie stood and gave him an innocent kiss on the cheek. She wore a white tee shirt with an insignia he didn't recognize and skin-tight jeans. Her dark brown hair was pulled back in a ponytail and it didn't appear she was wearing any makeup.

In contrast to her casual appearance, Joey had agonized about what to wear. He had two meetings at Cambridge in the afternoon so he had to be at least business-casual, but he didn't want to appear as though he'd put too much thought into his clothes. In fact, he had. He made sure to wear one of his custom made button-down shirts with the monogram on the sleeve. He chose a pale blue one. The khakis were a no-brainer but he made sure he had on his newest pair of dark blue briefs in case the evening went in the direction he expected. The final decision was shoes. He'd read that men's shoes were of vital interest to women and although he couldn't understand why that would be, he bought a new pair of loafers at lunch.

"Am I late?" He asked after taking the seat across from her, the one that would hide his face from passers-by.

"Nope. You're a minute early. I hope that means you're anxious."

"If by anxious, you mean a little nervous, then yes." As he said the words he couldn't help glance over his shoulder to see if anyone was close enough to hear their conversation.

"Well, I'm one Cosmo ahead of you so sit down and relax."

Strangely, Joey was able to relax. Lonnie had a way about her that he found disarming. She told him about how she got her job at JetBlue and how she expected it to be the next great airline even though they only had a few routes at the time. She told him about her divorce and how her ex-husband had lied to her about just about everything. She admitted that she was nervous about calling Joey after their chance encounter the previous weekend.

Then she turned the attention on Joey and asked him a barrage of questions but without seeming overly intrusive. She wanted to know all about the accident that had killed his father and mother. She'd heard about it while they were in college and wanted to call him after the events but just didn't think it was the right thing to do.

"How did it feel to lose them both like that? Did you feel like an orphan?" She reached across the table and put her hand gently on his.

No one had ever asked him that before and he thought for a moment about the answer. "To tell you the truth, it did. I mean I don't have any brothers or sisters. My mom was an only child and my dad had one brother who's a priest in California so I really don't have any traditional family."

"That sounds so lonely," she sighed. "What do you do on holidays? I mean where do you go for Christmas, for example?"

"Before I met Claire, it was rough. I became the lost friend that people felt an obligation to take home for holidays. But Claire has a big family and they've adopted me." Mentioning his wife's name reminded him of where he was and what he was doing. It made him feel guilty.

Lonnie picked up on this and quickly changed the subject to his job. "What exactly do you do at Cambridge Partners? I know very little about finance." The transition was obvious and awkward but Joey took the well-intended bait and explained his daily routine.

"Mostly, I do research. If one of the fund managers wants info about a start-up or background info about its owners, I do the legwork and present a report. As a result, I travel a bit, which I like. I also do statistical research, more like analysis, on small cap stocks. So, if my boss needs to know the five-year trend of how a stock performed each time after it runs up five percent, I figure it out. I do a lot of number crunching right now. All the new associates do. It can be really boring but it's one of those things you need to do to be able to get to the next level."

"And what would the next level be?" She wanted to know.

This was a question he and Claire had discussed a lot, especially after he'd get home from work at ten or eleven o'clock and they'd sit in the kitchen talking about the future. She was growing tired of his long hours and their lack of time together. Claire often wanted to know that this wasn't going to be the way they'd be living for much longer; that sometime soon, Joey would get the big promotion and life would get instantly better in so many ways.

But he couldn't promise that, and he wasn't even sure he wanted the big promotion. He wasn't sure what he wanted, but he did know, even though he was very good at what he did, it wasn't what he really wanted to be doing. The problem was, he didn't know what he really wanted to do instead. Joey was analytical and that's what Cambrdige paid him to be, but he felt he had a creative side that needed to break out. A talent that lay yet undiscovered but to which he felt a magnetic-like pull.

"I'm not sure. I like Cambridge and they're very good to me but I feel like I want to do something different, something totally different. Like maybe tomorrow I'll wake up and want to be a farmer or something where you actually create something."

The rest of the evening flew by. Joey and Lonnie both ordered one of the house specials and shared a bottle of Chianti. They talked about everything from the upcoming mayoral primaries that were a week away to the work he'd done last year preparing for the Y2K changeover. They enjoyed listening to each other's perspectives and for Joey, it felt good to have someone take such an interest in him. For the first time in a long while someone was encouraging him to be unconventional and maybe even follow his dream, as soon as he knew what that was.

As dinner ended Joey was surprised when Lonnie said, "I need to get going. I'm supposed to meet my friend Lilly for a drink back in Hoboken. Her fiancée just got shipped off to the Middle East for fourteen months and she's a wreck. I promised her I'd meet her."

She could see the disappointment on Joey's face. What she couldn't see was that he was also relieved that he now had more time to think about what was happening. He played it cool.

"No problem. That's really nice of you." He meant it.

"How about we share a cab back to Hoboken?"

The car ride back to Jersey took less than twenty minutes and not much was said on the trip. When they stopped in front of Lonnie's apartment, Joey got out with her.

"I'll walk from here," he said as he handed the driver a twenty.

"I'd like to see you again. Maybe we could do something different. Sometime soon?" She sounded sincere and hopeful.

"I'd like that too." As he said the words, Joey tried to picture the calendar sitting on his desk at work. What did he have the next few days? Next week? Then he remembered that Claire was going to Myrtle Beach to see her folks that weekend. "Maybe this weekend?"

Lonnie looked at her watch. "Call me tomorrow. I have to go." She reached up to kiss him on the lips. Another one of those "*Don't forget me*" kisses. Joey felt her hand on the front of his thigh.

And then she was gone.

The next day he couldn't get his mind off Lonnie. By noon he'd decided he would call and suggest they do "*something*" on the weekend. When he did, she suggested a drive to the country which, for those from the city, usually means somewhere upstate New York or Connecticut.

"I don't think the leaves have started to change yet but it might still be nice."

Before his brain knew what his mouth was doing he heard himself say, "Have you ever been to Lake Senoa?"

CHAPTER TWO

"They really look like they're having fun." Lonnie motioned with her magazine towards the brother and sister still jumping from the raft.

"It's amazing how much energy kids have."

"Do you ever think about having kids?" Lonnie asked as she turned over on the lounge chair.

"It's actually a big issue with Claire and me. She wants a house full and I'm not sure yet that I want any. I mean it's such an enormous responsibility. Don't you think?"

"I'm the same way." She said with some relief. "I have enough trouble taking care of me. I'm not sure I have it in me to be responsible for another person."

Joey thought back to the last conversation he and Claire had on the subject of children. It was only a few weeks ago and ended in tears, both saying things they regretted soon after. They were in the car driving home from a dinner with friends who spent the night babbling about the amazing things their eight-month-old was accomplishing. Claire kept asking probing questions that only resulted in more inane rambling from the prodigy's mother, while Joey couldn't wait for the check to arrive so they could escape.

It wasn't the first time he and his wife had argued about children. It wasn't that Joey was sure he didn't want them, he just wasn't sure either way. Claire on the other hand seemed sure of everything and that's what made Joey crazy. She knew she wanted two boys and two girls. She was equally sure they would move to the Jersey suburbs to raise their herd and that the public schools would be unsatisfactory. She seemed to have their next twenty years completed scripted right down to the details about future family vacations. What Joey found most infuriating was that Claire claimed to have felt this way her whole life but failed to mention these details to Joey before they were married. She said she had.

Back on the dock, Lonnie said, "I mean it's a huge responsibility bringing kids into the world, not to mention the expense. I've got two nieces and my poor brother-in-law works three jobs to keep them in dance school. The fricking kids are only seven and eight years old. What's it going to be like if they want to go to college?"

"I'm with you," was all Joey wanted to say. He didn't even like talking about the subject, even if they were both in agreement. He knew it didn't really matter how Lonnie felt about kids, not to him anyway. He knew, as nice as this weekend had been, he and Lonnie had no future together. There would be no need for family-size conversations between them. Their future probably didn't extend beyond Monday when he planned on dropping Lonnie at her apartment.

It's not that the weekend hadn't been fantastic. For the first time in years, Joey felt excited about something and that excitement wasn't just the acrobatic sex they'd enjoyed since arriving Friday night. Being with Lonnie awakened a passion in him that had been silent for some time. It was a passion for passion itself, for stepping outside the lines and trying new things. He hadn't done that in a long time. Being with Lonnie was a new thing. Being with

Lonnie represented a departure from his world of "must dos" and into a world of "can dos" and "why nots".

As he looked down at the back of her long tan legs, he reflected on their love-making the past two days. It had been wonderful; lustful yet surprisingly gentle. Lonnie was masterful at making him feel like his desires were the only things that mattered. She stroked his skin softly, stopping along the way to massage any muscle she thought felt tight. "You're so tense," she said more than once. "Try to just relax and let go. Nothing bad will happen. I promise." Then she would gently kiss his skin where she was working a muscle and whisper, "All better now."

Making love with Lonnie was more about sensual awareness than it was about sex. Her focus was touch and until then, Joey had no idea how many parts of his body had been craving touch. Lying naked on top of the cool sheets with Lonnie gave her a canvas to work with, a new body she could explore and stimulate and Joey was happy to be that canvas.

Sex with Claire, while satisfactory, was just sex. Claire was a beautiful woman and Joey still found her very desirable, but now that he had a point of comparison, it seemed that Claire was more concerned with the destination than she was with the trip, more concerned with achieving a climatic ending than with the twists and turns along the way. Lonnie took much time to paint the picture. Claire took a photograph.

But still, Joey knew his weekend with Lonnie was just a weekend, a wonderful weekend, but just a weekend. After tomorrow they would both go their separate ways. The passion she'd awakened in him made him aware not only of his complacency with Claire and his job but also that he wanted more from a relationship than what someone like Lonnie could offer. She was fun but she wasn't his future. He would either work hard to improve his life with Claire or...

His reflection was shattered by screams coming from the lake. He sat up on his lounge, his legs straddling the bench. Lonnie must have heard the screams at the same moment because she was now busy securing her bikini top while twisting around to find the source of the cries.

His attention was immediately drawn to the raft floating off shore. A moment ago, there had been two children, a boy and a girl, standing atop the raft. Now there was only a boy. Joey guessed he was about nine years old. He was screaming, "Dad, Dad, where's Megan? What happened to Megan?" His voice was frantic.

Joey could see that the boy was looking towards the dock about fifty yards north of the one on which he stood. He could see a man on that dock fumbling with the lines that secured a canoe while trying to climb from the dock into the canoe. Clearly, this was not someone who was comfortable with small boats. The man was dressed in khaki shorts and a blue oxford shirt. He looked more ready for brunch at a country club than for a canoe ride.

"Dad, she's gone!" The screams were louder and more desperate.

"I'm coming Sean," the man called back from the canoe, still tethered to the front of the dock.

Lonnie put her hand on Joey's. "What happened? I don't see the little girl anymore. Oh my god. What happened?"

Joey stood and assessed the scene from an elevated vantage point. It appeared the little girl had disappeared from the floating raft. The raft was nearly sixty feet from the end of Joey's dock and much further from the fellow still trying to untie his canoe. It looked like the man, probably the boy's father, was attempting a rescue but wasn't much of a boater. Joey did a quick calculation and figured that he could swim to the raft much faster than the man could paddle there, assuming the man ever got the canoe untied from the dock.

He turned quickly to Lonnie. "Run in the house and call 911. Tell them where we are and that a child is missing in the lake." Then he glanced out at the raft again. "I'm going to see if I can help."

He ran to the end of his dock and dove into the cool water. Lonnie hesitated just long enough to see him surface and begin swimming toward the raft. Then she ran to the house and made the call.

Joey had always been a strong swimmer. In high school, he spent two years on the swim team and was good enough to go to the county finals. So he covered the sixty feet in less than a minute. The water was surprisingly clear and he could see the bottom most of the way out to the raft. But as he approached the wooden raft the lake's bottom abruptly fell off into a dark abyss. He could see a silvery chain extending from the raft and disappearing into the darkness. He assumed that was what anchored the raft in place.

He reached up and caught hold of the raft. With one arm on the platform he asked the boy, "What happened?"

The boy looked back at his father who had now freed himself from his dock. Then he looked back at Joey's face bobbing in the water.

"My sister was doing hand stands and flipping into the water but she hit her head on the edge of the raft and didn't come up! She didn't come up!"

As Joey caught his breath, he did another quick calculation. It had taken him about minute to swim to the raft. And it had been about thirty seconds from when he first heard the screams to when he dove in the water. The little girl had been under water for at least a minute and a half, probably a little more by the time her brother started yelling. Maybe two minutes in total. He knew that after four minutes without oxygen, a person is pretty much dead.

"What side of the raft did she go off?"

The boy pointed to the opposite side of the raft. "Over here. Over here. Hurry!"

"Okay. You stay right here until your dad gets here." Joey didn't want two kids in the water.

He swam around to the other side of the raft. Before submerging to begin the search, he asked the boy a question that, for the rest of his life, he didn't understand why he'd asked it. "What's your sister's name?"

The boy's eyes were popping out of his head as he stared down at Joey. "Megan Minnick. She's eleven."

Joey took a long deep breath and swam head- first, straight down. He was swimming hard and after a few seconds could see the weedy bottom approaching at about twenty feet. Long sea grasses extended up from the bottom several feet and seemed to wave in unison as the lake's currents softly tossed them back and forth. He tried to scan as much of the bottom as he could see without going all the way down into the weeds. He looked to the right and then to the left. Nothing. No sign of a little girl.

He swam a little to the right and realized he needed to surface for air. His lungs were straining already and he cursed his seden- tary desk job for robbing him of his stamina. As he climbed back toward the light of the surface he could feel his ears pop so he swallowed hard. He surfaced ten feet from the raft, checked to be sure the boy was still there, and noticed out of the corner of his eye the boy's father had made it to the raft. He was clutching the side of the raft to steady the canoe but was still in the canoe.

"You check that side. I'll go down again over here!" Joey yelled toward the man.

The panicked father glared back at the figure in the water. "I can't. I can't swim."

The timer ticking in Joey's head told him three minutes had elapsed. There was no time to waste talking to anyone on the sur- face. He needed to get to the bottom again. He sucked in as much air as his lungs could bear and dove.

Again, he stopped a few feet above the tops of the weeds and scanned the area. Nothing. He decided to swim in an arc to the right until he came to the anchor line. This way he could search in a methodical way, hoping not to miss an area. As he kicked his legs and carved through the water with his hands, he thought about what he was looking for. He'd never been faced with death before. The thought of a young child's dead body, perhaps already bloated, scared him. He wasn't sure how he would deal with such a horror. But there wasn't time to think.

This time he stayed down nearly a minute. His lungs were bursting as he surfaced on the opposite side of the raft. He knew the four-minute mark had passed and that Megan, if she was ever found, was probably already dead. But he also knew he couldn't stop looking, certainly not until others joined in the search. And certainly not with the girl's poor father looking on so helplessly from his canoe. He had to keep diving. He had to keep looking even though with each dive he dreaded more and more, what he might find.

Once more he filled his lungs as well he could and dove straight down, head-first. As he neared the bottom he saw something in the weeds. At first it looked like the back of a shirt. It looked white or light grey from his distance but his view was impaired by the grasses. He swam closer and as he did his eyes began to focus on the object entangled on the bottom of the long weeds. As he swam deeper his ears popped again, and again he swallowed hard. He knew he had just enough air to get to the object and hopefully enough to raise it, maybe her, to the surface.

But as he pushed aside the grasses that covered what he'd hoped was Megan Minnick, he realized it wasn't a child's body. It was a large cinder block that had probably been the raft's anchor in prior years. With nothing left in his lungs, he flew to the surface, gasping as his head cleared the water. At least five minutes had now elapsed and the feeling of defeat was overwhelming.

This time he came up right next to the canoe. The man still held tightly to the side of the raft. His son had climbed into the canoe. Even with water in his eyes Joey could see the man was sobbing. Joey put his left hand on the side of the aluminum canoe to steady himself and rest for a moment. He'd been swimming hard for several minutes on just a few deep breaths.

The man looked up from his sobs. "Please. Please find my Megan. I can't lose her," he said so softy Joey could barely hear.

There was nothing to say. Joey knew he had to keep diving. Again, another deep breath, but this time, to avoid the pain in his ears, he decided to go down feet first. So, he made his body as streamlined as possible and began to slip down into the darkness feet-first. He looked up to make sure he was still aligned with the raft and that's when he saw it; a pale little leg sticking out from under the raft. It was so white it might have been from a porcelain doll.

Using his arms for thrust he stopped his decent and swam to the leg. It was the little girl! She must have gone under the raft and her body was now wedged between two large pieces of Styrofoam that acted as the raft's floatation. She was face down. Her eyes were open but lifeless. Her face was already cyanotic, approaching the color of the sky.

He pulled at the leg. It was stuck. Then he grabbed as much of the little girl's blond hair as he could get his hands around and pulled on her head. Again, no movement. Her torso was wedged firmly between the two blocks of moss-covered Styrofoam and Joey couldn't produce the leverage needed to pry it out. He surfaced.

"She's stuck under the raft!" he gasped as he broke water. "Have you got anything sharp?" He knew he needed to cut away some of the Styrofoam.

"Is she alright?" The father had to know.

"Anything sharp?" Joey yelled back.

The man shook his head. Without something with a sharp edge to cut away some of the Styrofoam, he knew he couldn't produce enough leverage in the water to move the small body. His eyes darted frantically along the top of the raft. Nothing. Then he lifted himself on the side of the canoe so he could see inside the metal boat. The canoe tilted severely toward him and the man and boy lunged to the opposite side to avoid tipping. As they did the wooden paddle slid along the floor of the canoe.

"Snap that paddle in two!" Joey screamed at the man.

At first the father of the drowned child didn't understand the command.

"Use your foot and snap it in half!" Joey had reached in and grabbed the paddle and shoved it toward the man.

Under normal circumstances, it might have been difficult to find the balance in a canoe necessary to break the paddle, but this was anything but normal circumstances. The father's adrenaline was pumping and, once he grasped the concept, the paddle snapped sharply over his knee. Joey grabbed the handle end and dove again.

There wasn't much light directly under the raft and Joey was careful not to jab the broken end of the paddle into the girl's body. Still, he needed to strike the block of Styrofoam hard enough to chisel out a few pieces. Perhaps if he could carve out one side there'd be enough space to roll Megan to her right and slide her out.

He grabbed the paddle handle with his right hand and guided the broken end with his left. He found it difficult to exert any significant thrust because, in the water, he had no leverage. As the tip of the broken end sliced into the Styrofoam he pushed forward as hard as he could. A large chunk of the green block broke off. Joey felt a rush of adrenaline. He struck the foam again. Again, a piece came away. He pushed both chunks away. Once more he thrust the paddle into the foam, this time just an inch from the girl's face. Her bulging eyes remained fixed and lifeless.

Joey sensed he had enough air for just one more try. His lungs were exhausted. This time he pushed the paddle into the Styrofoam next to Megan's shoulder and used it as a lever to push her body away from the entrapment. As he did, her body twisted and moved forward. He could now get his arm under her torso and by rotating his body in the water he was able to squeeze the limp child from between the foam blocks.

Joey put his arm around Megan's neck and guided her to the surface. Even though she weighed only 95 pounds, he knew he couldn't hoist her body out of the water onto the raft, not without help. And the girl's father, who was still in the canoe clutching the side of the raft for dear life, was unlikely to be of any use.

Joey did an instantaneous calculation. He knew he needed to begin CPR on the girl as soon as possible, but to do that he needed to be on firm footing. He couldn't do it in the water and he couldn't get her onto the raft. He also knew that time was critical and that the 30-40 seconds it would take him to swim to shore with her might be the difference between life and death. Her life and death. Or maybe, if she could be saved at all, the extra time would result in an irreparable brain damage because he'd be prolonging the deprivation of oxygen-rich blood to her brain.

He swam hard toward the closest point of shoreline, just next to his dock; one hand for swimming and one rapped around the limp body's neck. Swimming like this was much harder than he expected and it took him nearly 90 seconds to make it to shore. When he finally felt the sandy bottom on his feet he stood and carried the girl a few feet up the beach. Lonnie was waiting with a towel which she placed on the sand as Joey plopped the lifeless body down. He glanced out at the raft to see what had happened to her father who, by this time, had figured out how to use the flat end of the broken paddle to get to shore and was just reaching the beach.

Joey tried to remember what he'd learned about CPR way back in the boy scouts. He recalled turning the mannequin on its side. But now it was real. This was a real person, a child, lying in front of him. The consequences of his next actions seemed overwhelming.

He shook her by the shoulders and called out, "Megan. Megan. Can you hear me?" But there was no response. He felt for a pulse, first on her delicate wrist then on her neck. He felt nothing. He immediately began doing chest compressions. He remembered he was supposed to do about a hundred a minute but he had no sense as to how far he was to push down on the child's fragile chest.

After ten thrusts downward he could feel movement. It seemed as though her ribcage was being extended down just enough to convince her heart to move some blood along but not so much as to break ribs or crush her heart completely.

He settled into a rhythm of compressions by counting to himself. The cadence seemed to make sense to him. But then, as his body jerked up and down over the lifeless child forcing blood to circulate, hopefully to her brain, he recalled the second part of the life-saving procedure. Someone needed to force air into her lungs.

"Lonnie!" he yelled. "Can you do mouth to mouth on her while I'm doing this?" It wasn't so much a request as a command.

Lonnie dropped to her knees at Megan's head and covered her mouth with her own. She blew hard into the little girl's mouth. Joey stopped the chest compressions just long enough to see her chest rise and fall with each breath from Lonnie. He knew that was a good sign. It meant Megan's lungs were not full of water.

"Keep doing it." He said as he watched for any change in the little's girl's color. But her face was still blue. "Stop," he shouted. And he began the compressions again. As he silently counted to himself he asked, "Lonnie, did you get through to the 911 number?"

"Yes. They said about eight minutes. That was right after you jumped in the water. Should I keep doing the breathing?"

At this point they were joined by the girl's father and younger brother who had extricated themselves from the canoe. "Is she alright? Is she going to be alright?" The father frantically inquired. He was standing directly over Joey.

"She's not breathing and I can't get a pulse." As soon as the words flew from his lips he knew they were a mistake. It was the truth but her father didn't want the truth at that moment. He wanted reassurance that his precious Megan would be home for dinner.

Joey began another round of chest thrusts then stopped and told Lonnie to breathe again. He waited for her to give three or four deep breaths then began the compressions again. This rhythm seemed to make sense and they carried this on for several minutes as Megan's father looked on helplessly. In the distance Joey could hear a siren.

"That's got to be the ambulance. They should be here soon." As he turned back to Lonnie to request another round of breaths, he noticed the little girl's face was no longer blue. "Hey, her color is better," he yelled.

Just then, Megan coughed and water rose from her tiny mouth as if a geyser was erupting. She coughed again and Joey turned her on her side so the gushing water had somewhere to go. Nothing happened for several excruciating seconds. Then she coughed a third time and vomited forcefully.

CHAPTER THREE

"She's alive!" The little girl's father shouted. "She's alive!" He was leaning over Joey to get a better view but didn't want to interfere in the success this young man had achieved so far.

Joey kept patting Megan's back as she vomited, partly to make sure she didn't roll over onto her back and partly just to offer reassurance. Her color was rapidly returning and through the retching he could make out her first words.

"Daddy?" She said faintly at first then with more clarity. "Daddy, what happened?"

At this point Joey and Lonnie moved back to allow the girl's father to kneel beside her. He helped her sit upright and hugged her as only a father who thought he'd lost his child could. He was crying and kissing her wet hair. "Oh baby. I thought you were gone. Oh, thank God you're okay." He buried his kisses on the top of her head.

Joey was on all fours trying to catch his breath. The ordeal had taken a lot out of him, both physically and emotionally. When he jumped into the water he didn't expect it to end well and now that the girl seemed okay, he was filled with a backwash of emotion. Lonnie was at his side, her ample breasts pressed against his face. "Wow Joey. You did it! You saved her life."

Joey rolled onto his back. He was having some trouble regaining his breath. He was dizzy from the prolonged oxygen deprivation caused by his long dives. It was way more than he was used to. Again, he silently cursed his sedentary office job for causing him to be so out of shape. He saw Lonnie looking down at him with a worried look on her face. There was a flash of light.

The next thing he remembered seeing was a man asking him his name. Joey could feel something foreign over his face, something plastic.

"Just take a couple of deep breaths son. The oxygen will make you feel a lot better." The paramedic assured him.

Things began to come into focus. He realized he must have passed out but he couldn't tell for how long. He felt light headed but the pure oxygen he was getting from the cold bottle lying next to him was helping a bit. He heard a car door slam shut and looked to his right. A red and white ambulance was driving off. Lonnie was kneeling next to him.

"You passed out for a couple of minutes baby," she told him. "The medics got here right after you passed out. They took the little girl and her dad to the hospital. They said she's going to be okay though. Thanks to you Joey. You saved her life."

The paramedic kneeling on the other side of Joey was adjusting the control knob on the oxygen bottle. He said his name was KC. "Hey there buddy. How you doing now? Any better?"

Joey sat up a little on his elbows. He felt the sand rubbing against his arms then recalled that he was on the beach next to the dock. It was coming back to him; the swimming, the diving into the dark water under the raft, seeing the small blue body wedged between the Styrofoam blocks, and swimming with the limp child as fast as he could toward shore.

"I suggest you lay down for a while longer," the paramedic explained. Joey guessed he was about fifty. He had thinning grey hair, ears that were too big for his head and wore a blue cap that said Duchess County EMS. "Just keep breathing the good stuff a while longer then we'll get some info from you."

Joey dropped his head back onto the sand and did as he was told. Lonnie was now holding his hand. The more he breathed the better he felt. The world was coming into focus again.

"Where's the kid?" he asked Lonnie but his voice was muffled by the mouthpiece supplying the oxygen.

"They took her to the hospital just to check her out. They said she'll be okay." She paused then added, "How are you feeling?"

He pulled the mouthpiece away from his face so he could speak. "Yeah. Better now."

KC pushed the mouthpiece back into place. "Keep that on a bit longer." Then he turned to Lonnie. "Maybe you can give me some of the info I need?" He motioned to the metal clipboard in his hand. "Connecticut's got a million questions."

"Sure, what do you need?" She volunteered.

"Let's start with his name, date of birth, and home address."

"His name is Joseph Martinez," she whispered. But Lonnie had no idea when Joey was born or his exact street address. She looked to Joey for help.

The paramedic began filling in his form as Joey rose to one side and slipped the mouthpiece off. "I feel okay now."

"Okay then. Date of birth and address Joseph?"

"January 16, 1974. I live at 1606 Bloomfield Avenue in Hoboken, New Jersey." Joey noticed for the first time that KC the paramedic wasn't the only person leaning over him. In addition to Lonnie, there were several other people and one female police officer taking her own notes as he spoke.

"Are you allergic to anything Joseph?"

"No."

"Take any medications on a daily basis?"

"No."

KC went through his list of questions including the name of Joey's primary care doctor, a brief medical history, and others then turned to the police officer and asked for her badge number and name for his report.

"Let's see how you feel if you sit up." KC said as he helped Joey into a sitting position.

"I feel okay," Joey assured him. "I'm fine now."

"Well you lost consciousness there for a few minutes so I want to be sure. Do you want to take a ride to the hospital and have them check you out?"

"No. I'm fine." He said it and was beginning to believe it himself.

"Yes, I think you're fine too. You did a very brave thing there young man. You saved that kid's life you know?"

Lonnie helped Joey to his feet and steadied him.

"Have you ever fainted or passed out from over-exertion before?" KC wanted to know.

"No, never."

KC asked Joey to sign his form acknowledging he was offered and refused transport to the hospital.

"Okay then. I'm going to get back to the Giant's game." KC shook Joey's hand. "You did a good thing today kid." Then he motioned to the other ambulance attendants standing around to gather up their equipment and load the ambulance for the trip back to the Sharon Fire Department.

"Thanks for your help," Jocy offered. He took Lonnie's hand and began walking back to the cabin. He really wanted to get out of the wet clothes and just lay down for a while. But the police woman stepped forward as the ambulance drove way and asked, "Sir, may I have a moment of your time?"

Joey looked up at her. She was very tall and thin but had a pretty face. Her strawberry blonde hair was pulled back in a professional bun. He guessed she was younger than he and Lonnie.

"Sure. What can I do for you officer… McKeon?" He read from her badge.

"You don't know who that little girl… the one you saved… you don't know who she is, do you?"

"I just know her name is Megan."

"Yes, it is. Megan Minnick. She's Senator Minnick's daughter. And that was the senator in the canoe. He went to the hospital with her. His wife took their son. I assume they were all going to the hospital."

Not being from Connecticut, Joey didn't recognize the name of the junior U.S. Senator. Officer McKeon could tell that from his blank expression. In fact, Joey couldn't name both the senators from his home state of New Jersey. Politics just didn't interest him. He'd only voted once, in 1996 for Bill Clinton. And after the Monica Lewinsky debacle, Joey was completely disillusioned by all things political.

"Well, I'm glad she's going to be okay." He said, hoping that would be the end of it.

"Yeah, that's their summer house right there next to yours." She pointed toward the large log structure just to the north of Joey's father-in-law's cabin. It was at least a hundred yards away with thick brush separating the two properties. He'd never really paid it much attention. But now that he did, he could see it was a magnificent home with a sprawling lawn that led down to the lake.

"Actually, this isn't my home. It's my father-in-law's. We're just here for the weekend."

"Well then," she said to Lonnie, "Your dad's a lucky man to have such a beautiful spot right here on the lake. What's his name? I don't think I know him. I haven't been on the job very long."

Lonnie froze and looked to Joey for help.

"His name is Jim Berman." Joey offered. "But he lives mostly in South Carolina now so we look after the place." He really hoped that would be the end of it.

Officer McKeon didn't seem to notice that Lonnie hesitated when asked for her father's name and began to walk back to her patrol car that was parked in the driveway, lights still flashing red and blue. "Well, like I said, you did a nice thing today. I hope your wife…," she motioned to Lonnie, "…takes you out for a nice dinner in town. You're a hero now."

CHAPTER FOUR

As officer McKeon's car disappeared into the distance, Lonnie held Joey's hand and walked him back to the cabin. Once inside, Joey stripped out of his wet shorts and wrapped a white towel around his waist. He came out of the bathroom and plopped onto the bed face first.

"Are you okay baby?" Lonnie asked.

The term baby was starting to annoy Joey but he let it go. "Yeah, I just want to rest a few minutes. I'm exhausted."

She sat on the bed next to him and began to rub his back. "You did a wonderful thing Joey. That kid was like dead. I mean she was really like blue when you pulled her out of the water."

"You did it too." Joey responded with his face still buried in the comforter. "You got the air into her. I think that's what really saved her. I think you're the hero Lonnie."

"Wow. I never did anything so cool in my life. It was awesome seeing her roll over and puke. That's when I knew she was okay." Lonnie was gently rubbing his naked back as she spoke.

"Well, I think the cop was right. I think we should go out for a great dinner tonight and celebrate."

"Where we gonna go? There's like nothing around her for a thousand miles." Lonnie said.

"Come on. It's not that bad. It's only eleven miles into town and there are two decent restaurants in town. I'm just not sure they're open on Sunday night, especially after the season is over." Joey flipped onto his back and put his hands behind his head.

The playfulness of his motion wasn't lost on Lonnie, still in her bikini. She began rubbing her hands on his thighs. "We could just stay here and eat the leftovers from last night. I think we have two bottles of red wine left too." Her hands were running gently from his knees up to the edge of the towel and back again.

Arousal was the last thing Joey had on his mind but aroused he was. He could feel the hair on his legs electrified by Lonnie's touch. And the vision of her firm breasts hanging from her bikini top convinced him Lonnie had the right idea. Besides, he really didn't want to go into town again and risk being spotted with Lonnie by someone who knew Claire's parents. It was very unlikely, but an unnecessary risk.

He clasped his fingers tightly behind his head and playfully asked, "What did you have in mind then?"

Lonnie reached behind her and unclipped her top letting it fall to the floor. She released the towel from around his waist and slid on top of him. Her legs straddled his. "I've never fucked a hero before," she whispered in Joey's left ear.

"Neither have I." He replied. "And I did say you were a hero, didn't I?"

Joey was awakened on Monday morning by a sharp ray of sunlight screaming mercilessly through the bedroom window. According to the cable box below the TV, it was 6:10 A.M. It took him a moment to realize where he was. After all, this wasn't his typical Monday morning. On a typical Monday, he'd be getting up in his own bedroom, having slept with his own wife and clicking off the alarm at 5:25 so he could be in the office by 7:15, in time for the morning call with the Cambridge office in London.

Today, he woke up entangled in a combination of Lonnie's legs and wine-stained sheets with a rock-hard erection. That meant he needed to take a piss but his entire groin ached a bit from the previous night's carnal experience. He remembered very little of what happened but spotted two empty wine bottles on the floor next to his side of the bed.

He swung his legs off the side of the bed and rested his elbows on his knees for a few seconds before attempting to stand. He definitely felt hung over but he knew from experience it would pass in a few hours assuming he could get a couple of cups of coffee. He glanced back at Lonnie as he walked toward the bathroom. Her ass looked ridiculously white compared to her deeply tanned back and legs.

As he stood over the toilet relieving himself he did what he did every morning as he pissed; he mentally organized his day. Usually that meant planning his day at work. But today was different. Today he had lots of different things to do. He wanted to start the day with Lonnie; one last fantastic half-hour of sex to remember her by. Because he knew that before the day was out, he'd have to tell her he couldn't see her again. His plan was to talk about it in the car on the drive back to Hoboken. He'd explain that he needed to work on his marriage and that he couldn't do that if she was in the picture. It was the truth.

He assumed Lonnie would be upset, that she'd poured a lot of emotion into the weekend. But he wasn't completely sure. It was possible that Lonnie had many such weekends with many guys and that this was just one more. Perhaps it wasn't as big a deal to her as it was to him. That would make it easier. He didn't have any sense how the car conversation would go. It was just something that had to be done. And by the time he dropped her at her apartment, all would be settled and he could really focus on his relationship with Claire and whether it could be salvaged.

As much as he enjoyed the heady feeling of importance Lonnie had provided all weekend, he knew he didn't want to do this again. There'd be no more lost weekends with Lonnie or with anyone else until he sorted things out with Claire. He'd betrayed Claire and he was already starting to feel guilty about what he'd done. This was unusual for Joey, a first. He was seduced by the excitement, by the need for passion in his life. But he knew if one door was to be closed it had to be closed before he opened another.

Back on the bed, Lonnie rolled to her side and slipped under the sheets. "Wow. That was some night! You were like the Energizer Bunny. I'm a little sore in places I didn't expect."

"I'm going to make some coffee. Interested?"

"Have we got anything to eat? I really need to get something in my stomach before coffee."

Joey glanced at the counter top. There was an assortment of empty boxes; empty donut box, empty coffee cake box, empty pizza box which had served as the prior evening's meal.

"I'm afraid the cupboard is bare. How about I go into town and get us some real breakfast? Maybe a couple of bacon-egg-and cheese on a roll?" He too was hungry and didn't want to start a long drive home on nothing but coffee. "I can be back in half an hour."

"Sounds great," she replied as she pulled the sheet up over her head.

Joey threw on a pair of shorts while the water boiled for his instant coffee. He took a cup of the black magic with him for the ride into Sharon, the nearest town. On the way, he passed the same beautiful scenery he'd taken for granted on so many drives before. But this morning was different. On this morning, the deep green forest seemed even greener, the pink morning sky never seemed so bright and the lake itself seemed bluer than ever. Everything seemed more beautiful, like it had just bloomed, just for his eyes. He saw it as a good omen. Maybe it meant, he was about to embark on a new beginning in some way; something that would lend purpose and excitement to his life, perhaps.

It took a little longer than he'd expected for the one and only deli in Sharon to come up with two egg sandwiches and by the time he was pulling up to the cabin again it was nearly seven-thirty. As he closed the car door, he noticed another car approaching from the north. It was a large black SUV and it turned into his driveway and came to a stop just behind his Camry.

At first, he thought the driver must be lost. No one would come down this long driveway unless they were visiting or lost. He was even more confused when the driver got out and called him by name.

"Mr. Martinez?" A large black man in a dark suit and sunglasses called out the question.

"I'm Joey Martinez," he said as if he wasn't quite sure.

"Senator Minnick is on a call but would like to talk to you as soon as he's finished." He motioned with his huge head toward the back seat of the SUV. The windows were so tinted Joey couldn't make out who or what was inside.

For a moment, the name meant nothing to Joey. Then he recalled the policewoman saying that the little girl was a senator's daughter. Megan Minnick. The events of yesterday already seemed like a long way off. Joey wasn't sure if the chauffer's intention was for him to stand there and wait for the senator to emerge from the blacked-out car while his egg sandwiches got colder and colder or to go in the cabin and wait in there. He decided to be proactive.

"Okay, just knock when he's ready. I've got my…wife's breakfast here and she'll be cranky if it gets any colder."

Once inside, Joey roused the still sleeping Lonnie from under the sheets. "Hey, get up. The kid's father is here in some kind of limo SUV. He'll be in here in a minute."

It took a moment for Lonnie to put the pieces together; kid-father- SUV. "Oh, the girl's father, the senator guy. He probably wants to say thanks." Lonnie struggled to her feet with the wine-stained sheet wrapped around her and staggered to the bathroom.

Joey unwrapped the egg sandwiches as he heard the toilet flush then the shower flow. He agreed with Lonnie's assessment; the senator must be here to thank them, hopefully, also to offer some good news about the little girl's progress. The last thing he remembered was seeing her vomit, then the sight of the ambulance driving off. He never witnessed the paramedic working on her or loading her into the ambulance. He hoped she was okay and that her father had good news. He also hoped Lonnie would stay in the bathroom.

He put the kettle back on the stove for more coffee and sat at the kitchen table. No point in letting his sandwich get any colder. But just as he was about to dig into the juicy sandwich there was a sharp knock on the door which Joey had left ajar. A tall handsome man with movie-star quality features poked his head through the opening. He had a hint of grey in his closely cropped hair and his shirt, silk tie and suit matched perfectly. Joey guessed he was about forty. This guy was born for politics or Hollywood Joey thought.

"Morning!" He said with too much enthusiasm for 7:35 A.M. "I'm Andy Minnick. We never really met yesterday." He offered his hand and Joey shook it without getting up from the table.

"I'm Joey Martinez. Nice to meet you. How's Megan doing?" He asked then held his breath hoping the news was good and motioning for his guest to have a seat at the table.

"I hope I'm not here too early, am I?" He could hear the shower running in the next room.

"No, I was already in town. Is she okay?"

"Thanks completely to you…, yes. They ran a bunch of tests on her yesterday at the hospital to make sure she had no brain damage, you know…, from being under water so long. But she seems to be a hundred percent. They kept her overnight just to be sure and my wife stayed with her. Mary, my wife, called me this morning to say they'd be releasing her this afternoon."

"Wow. I'm so glad to hear that. I guess I passed out before you went to the hospital and never…"

"You sure did. You were out cold. But you were breathing heavy so the medic guys figured they'd tend to Megan first. That's why I'm here. I never got to thank you."

"Want some coffee?" Joey offered.

"No thanks. Had three cups already today and I need to be in Hartford for a meeting at nine-thirty," he said as he looked at his watch. "I'm just not sure how to thank someone for saving my daughter's life. Megs means everything to me and for a few minutes yesterday I was sure we'd lost her." His voice cracked just a bit, then he continued. "I felt so useless. As you probably figured out, I'm not much of a canoer and can't swim at all. Fact is, deep water terrifies me. That's why I insisted my kids learn to swim at an early age."

Joey sensed a genuineness in the man, a quality he usually didn't associate with politicians.

"And your son? Is he okay? That had to be pretty upsetting for him."

"Yeah, Sean was really shaken up. I think the ride in the ambulance was the worst part for him. They had Megs hooked up to an I.V. drip, an EKG with wires running everywhere and they had her on oxygen so the sight was pretty scary for him. I'm sure he was worried about her. They're very close."

"Well, I'm glad they're okay now." Joey said as he rose from the table. He was hoping to end the conversation before Lonnie emerged from the bathroom.

"Look Joey, there's no way I can ever repay you for what you did. You risked your life to save my daughter, someone you didn't even know. You're an amazing guy. That was real bravery. You're a hero. You're certainly my family's hero. I need to do something to begin to make it up to you. If you ever need anything…anything… just let me know. Assuming I get reelected in November, you can rest assured you have a friend in Washington. Just let me know if there's anything I can do. I mean it."

The little girl's father was getting emotional again and that made Joey uncomfortable. He decided to try to lighten the mood. "Well, if I decide to finally apply to West Point, I hope I can count on a letter of recommendation."

"Anything." The senator said smiling then glanced toward the bathroom. The sound of running water had stopped. "Listen. I'll be back from Hartford by one. That's when Megs is being released from the hospital. Why don't you and your wife come. My wife wants to thank you herself and you can meet Megan. She'd like that. We can also have some pictures taken of you and Megs. You know… the little girl and her savior. Maybe even one of you wheeling her out of the hospital. Your wife too."

The image of a front-page photo of Joey and Lonnie wheeling the little girl out of the hospital flashed in Joey's mind. The caption: "Heroic husband and wife rescue Senator Minnick's daughter." Except they weren't husband and wife. His wife was on a plane flying back from Myrtle Beach. He had to think quickly and he did.

"I'm sorry senator. That would have been wonderful but we're leaving for home right after breakfast. We both need to get back to work."

It wasn't the answer the senator expected. His disappointment was obvious. But he was running short on time. He glanced again at his watch. "Well, that's a shame. Mary's going to be very disappointed."

The senator made a move toward the door. Joey was grateful he'd be gone before Lonnie came out of the bathroom. But as he reached the cottage door the well-dressed man turned and asked, "Hey, you work in Manhattan, don't you?"

"Yeah. I work down at the Trade Center, for Cambridge Partners. How'd you know that?"

"Oh, I was afraid I wouldn't catch you here at the lake so I asked the medic for your info from his report." The senator scratched his head as if he was trying to piece together a mental puzzle. He mumbled something to himself about a scheduling conflict, then said, "Hey, I've got to make some sort of presentation tomorrow night down at Fraunces Tavern. That's right around the corner from the Trade Center. I'll bring Mary and Megan with me and we can meet you there. At least let me take you and your wife out for a special dinner to say thanks."

Joey was panicked. "Aaah, Tomorrow's Tuesday. I'm not sure that will work for my wife. And aah, I may have something on my calendar at home. Can I check both and call you tomorrow morning? Give me your number." As soon as he said the words he regretted them. Why did he even offer that? He should have just said no. He was angry with himself for being so indecisive, so intimidated.

"That would be great. I'm sure Mary and Megs would really like to meet you. So, call me in the morning and let me know." The senator handed Joey a card that simply read: **Andrew F. Minnick, U.S. Senator from Connecticut**. On the back was his phone number and email address.

"Okay then. I've got to run. I look forward to seeing you tomorrow night in New York." And with that he was out the door and back in his big black SUV. As the huge car disappeared at the end of the driveway, Joey noticed another car. This one, a green Camry, not unlike his own, had been parked at the driveway entrance but was now turning in and coming towards the cottage. Again, Joey stood by the door and watched as the new visitor approached. He hoped this one was really lost and wanted nothing more than directions but he had a bad feeling about it.

CHAPTER FIVE

As the Camry rolled to a stop in front of him and the sound of the crunching gravel subsided, Joey could see the driver was an attractive woman, probably about his age he guessed. She was alone and she didn't appear lost. On the contrary, stepping out of the car, she appeared to be a woman on a mission.

"Mr. Martinez?" She called out as she walked toward Joey. She had a green backpack slung over her shoulder. Her sandy hair was short and pushed to one side.

"I seem to be very popular this morning". Joey replied. "And you are?"

"I'm Sarah Bideaux. I'm a reporter for the Hartford Courant." She extended her hand and Joey took it cautiously. The word reporter sent a chill down his spine.

"Being the junior reporter in my group, I've been assigned the envious job of following Senator Minnick around for the last few weeks and right up to the election." The explanation dripped with sarcasm. "Basically, I cover all his speeches, events, fundraisers, stuff like that." She paused but Joey said nothing.

"Anyway, the Senator asked me to come out and get some background info on you and your wife. I know he was just here. He asked me to wait until he left for Hartford because he's in a hurry as usual."

"Why would he want background info on us... me.?"

"I assume you haven't seen today's Courant. I brought you a copy." As she spoke, she opened her backpack and produced a newspaper. She shuffled through the paper looking for the appropriate page then handed it to Joey.

On the bottom right side of the eighth page there was a picture of Joey and Lonnie leaning over Megan Minnick. Joey was pushing down on the girl's chest and Lonnie, whose breasts were protruding from her bikini top, was about to give Megan a breath in her mouth. The photo was in black and white and carried the caption, "**Senator Minnick's Daughter Rescued by Unknown Good Samaritans**". The short story that followed read:

"Senator Andrew Minnick's nine-year-old daughter Megan was rescued from a near drowning on Sunday. The Senator and his family were spending the day at their Lake Senoa cottage when the accident occurred. The little girl fell from a raft near where the Senator and his son were canoeing and was trapped beneath the raft. A neighbor and his wife came to the girl's rescue and delivered lifesaving CPR until Sharon EMS workers arrived and transported the girl to Dutchess County Medical Center. The girl was listed as stable and kept overnight for observation. Senator Minnick who is running for reelection in November, had no comment but a spokesman for the Senator said that the family was very grateful to the yet-to-be-identified good Samaritan and his wife."

"You're lucky that someone standing around had a digital camera and snapped that shot. It's a great picture, isn't it? They really captured the action of the moment. I wish I'd been there and normally I might have been but yesterday was my day off and since the Senator was just hanging out with his family the paper didn't assign anyone else to tail him."

Joey was still staring at the newspaper and trying to calculate the damage it could cause him. If it had really been his wife at his side, this was the kind of once-in-a-lifetime event that makes a person a hero. This was the sort of thing, captured in such a photo, that gets you on the evening news or the Today Show. But, when the woman is not your wife- is someone you're not supposed to be with at your wife's father's cabin- well then, it's a whole different story.

Fortunately, he and Lonnie weren't mentioned by name. Fortunately, the story was buried on page eight. And fortunately, he didn't know anyone from the Hartford area who might happen to see the picture. But, oh shit, what if someone did?

"Right? So, great story? But the Senator isn't happy with page eight and wants me to do a follow up with you and your wife with more of the details about you and what happened. He did say I should leave out the fact that he's a klutz in a canoe though." She winked at Joey. "So, can I come in now and get some basic info from you and your wife?"

Joey handed the paper back to her. He tried to think of a plausible reason a person in his position wouldn't want to talk to the press and the only one he could think of was the truth- and he wasn't about to tell her he was cheating on his wife, in her father's cabin, with his high school sweetheart.

"Look, Miss Biddle…"

"Bideaux. It's French. My grandfather came from France in the thirties to get away from Hitler."

"Sorry…, Miss Bideaux. My wife and I are very private people. My wife is especially shy and would never want to…"

She cut him off in mid-sentence. She'd been given a job to do and knew the Senator would be pissed if he didn't get a week's worth of favorable PR out of this near tragedy.

"Look Mister Martinez, Senator Minnick is only one percentage point ahead in the polls as of this morning. He really needs some good family-values kind of press. His opponent has been hammering him for all that's gone wrong in Washington since Clinton left office. He could really use this story. It highlights that he's got a human side- vacationing with the family and all that. And who doesn't like a story about a cute little girl who gets rescued by a handsome, young, Good Samaritan?"

Just then, Lonnie emerged from the front door in a bathrobe, her hair in a towel. She looked confused.

"What's up Joey? I thought I heard you talking to a man a minute ago." She looked suspiciously at the reporter.

Joey tried to get his body between Lonnie and Sarah Bideaux in hope of herding Lonnie back in the house before she opened her mouth but the reporter was too quick.

"My name's Sarah Bideaux. I'm a reporter for the Hartford Courant. Senator Minnick asked me to do a follow up story on your gallant rescue yesterday." She handed Lonnie the newspaper opened to the appropriate page.

Joey waited for a reaction from Lonnie as she read the story. But she seemed to take her time reading and when she got to the end she spoke the last few words aloud. "...the yet-to-be identified good Samaritan and his wife." She giggled and looked at Joey.

Joey just stared back at her. It took Lonnie several awkward seconds to grasp the gravity of the article. Then she said, "Oh," and smiled impishly at him.

Sarah was too busy pursuing her mission to see the light that had just clicked on over Lonnie's head. "So, the Senator asked me to get your story, what really happened yesterday, and to get some background on the two of you."

Joey interceded, "And I was just telling Sarah that we are really private people. I mean we're not the kind of people who are looking for fame or notoriety or anything like that."

Lonnie understood the anxiety in Joey's voice and realized this could get out of control quickly if they allowed it. She knew he couldn't afford to have his wife find out about their weekend, so she took over when Joey seemed at a loss for what to do.

"Joey," she yelled. "I don't give a shit about this senator guy. All I know is I've got to be back in New York by ten o'clock and we're already late. You know I can't afford to miss this meeting with my boss. I'm already on thin ice for taking Friday off. I have to be at that meeting." She was yelling and whining at the same time and so convincing that, at first, Joey didn't understand the feigned tirade.

"I promise I only need a few minutes of your time Mrs. Martinez." Sarah offered.

Lonnie shouted back, "I can't do it. I need to be in that car on the way to my office in five minutes. Do I look like I'm ready to go? Does this look like Wall Street attire to you?" She pointed at her robe and toweled hair. Then she looked back at Joey and shouted, "Damn it Joey. I told you not to go to town for that fucking coffee. We don't have time."

Lonnie turned and marched into the cabin. As she did she called out, "Joey! Get your ass in here and pack this shit up. I swear to god I'll leave without you in five minutes if you're not ready." It was all very convincing and Sarah Bideaux was at a loss for what to say. Actually, she felt a little sorry for Joey who looked like a deer in the headlights.

"I…I… I have to go. I'm sorry. I can't do this right now." He pretended to be terrified of what his pretend wife would do if he didn't comply.

This was hardly the reception Sarah expected when the Senator handed her this assignment. She assumed the hero and his wife would be delighted to give their story and have a few pictures snapped. Who wouldn't want recognition for doing something as wonderful as saving a little girl's life?

Joey was already halfway through the doorway. Sarah pleaded, "Mr. Martinez, Minnick will have my head if I don't get him his story. He's dying for the press. I need to get this done."

"I'm sorry Sarah. I really am. I have to go. I have work to get to also." Joey was about to close the cabin door behind him when he heard the reporter ask, "Can I do my interview tomorrow?"

"What?"

"I can come to the city tomorrow. I have to be there anyway. Minnick has a thing at Fraunces Tavern I need to cover. I can come to your office at Cambridge first thing in the morning if that's good."

"How the hell do you where I work?" Joey was incredulous.

"I'm a reporter. I do research. But in this case Minnick told me. Please… I promise it'll only take five minutes." She was pleading.

Joey guessed he wasn't going to get rid of the reporter unless he agreed to something. She was too tenacious. He thought he could limit the damage a newspaper story could do if he had some time to think. And meeting at his office tomorrow took Lonnie Rossetti out of the picture.

"Okay. Five minutes tomorrow at my office. Nine o'clock." He slammed the door.

CHAPTER SIX

After the convincing act Lonnie put on for the reporter's benefit, Joey didn't want to take any chances. He asked Lonnie
how soon she could really be ready to leave in hopes of avoiding
any more contact with anyone from Lake Senoa.

"I just have to dry my hair. Give me fifteen minutes and I'm
good to go." Lonnie said as she toweled her curly mane.

Joey was ready in five. He went through the usual routine to
close up the house which included turning off the water at the
main and locking all the windows. He'd already scheduled the local property manager to come in to clean, change the thoroughly
used linens, and remove anything left in the fridge. Basically, the
property manager would leave the place exactly as Joey had found
it. In this case, that meant removing any trace of Lonnie Rossetti
and any clues accidently left behind pointing at Joey's weekend indiscretion. The next time he came up with Claire the place would
appear just as it had when she last left. That is, as long as Cliff, the
property manager did his job well.

And any disappointment he might have felt about not having time to soil the sheets with Lonnie one more time, was

overshadowed by his desire to get out quickly. He just wanted to put some distance between him and the cabin. The abrupt departure meant he'd need to have his kiss-off conversation with Lonnie sooner than he'd planned. He wanted a little more time to think through the words that wouldn't be hurtful but would leave no doubt of his conviction. He'd work on it in his head sometime in the first hour of the drive, deliver the bad news in the second and be pulling up in front of Lonnie's apartment by noon.

And that was a good thing too. He needed a few hours in the afternoon to figure out how he was going to deal with the reporter tomorrow and blow off the Senator's invitation to meet at Frances. And then he had to pick up Claire at Newark Airport at six.

"Oh shit," he said out loud. He remembered he was supposed to call Claire this morning. Why didn't he do it while he was driving to town?

He called out to the bathroom door, "Lonnie. I'll be outside. I have to make a phone call." He hoped he still had enough battery left on his Nokia for the call to Myrtle Beach. As he dialed he looked out the cabin door to make sure the Camry was gone. It was.

"Hey babe. Sorry I didn't call you sooner. I went for a walk to get coffee." He surprised himself with his calm. He wasn't accustomed to lying to his wife. He'd never cheated on her before. He thought this would be harder. He thought the deception would take more imagination. But he found that if he imagined himself walking beneath the Sycamore's on Bloomfield Avenue in front of his house, he had no trouble telling Claire that's where he actually was. As far as she knew he was home all weekend working on that big project for Cambridge that kept him from going to Myrtle Beach. Luckily, they'd agreed to abandon their house phone last year in favor of their increasingly reliable cell phones.

"I miss you Joey." The sincerity in her voice reminded him why he'd fallen in love with her.

"I miss you too." Was all he could come up with. Then, "How are your mom and dad? Jim still trying to break par?"

"Yeah. He plays every day with his pals from the club then with mom in the afternoon on Mondays and Wednesdays. I don't know how he does it. But it keeps him in shape. You should see him. Since they moved down here, he's lost twenty pounds. He looks great. Mom too. She's so tanned."

They chatted for a few minutes about Claire's Sunday at the local fair, then Joey said, "Hey, are you still on the Spirit flight that gets in at six?"

"Yeah. No change. Sounds like you're trying to get rid of me." She said playfully, although he wasn't quite sure.

"No. Not at all."

"Yeah yeah. Alright, I'll see you at Newark at six. Don't be late. I love you."

"Love you too. I'll see you then."

If he hadn't been convinced before the call, he was now. He loved Claire. He wanted things to work with her. She deserved his best shot at it. And even though he continued to believe he was somehow living the wrong life, that he was never supposed to be with Claire or live where he lived or work where he worked; he felt an obligation to do the right thing. He felt he needed to protect Claire from his "other" side; the side he didn't understand.

So, Joey was resolved to put his weekend infidelity behind him and try to figure out if he could be happy with Claire and the life she wanted them to have. That life meant a house in the Jersey suburbs and children. It probably also meant moving up the corporate ladder at Cambridge so they could afford Claire's dreams.

Moving forward with that plan meant keeping his infidelity from Claire. She could never find out about Lonnie Rossetti. It's not that he was afraid she'd leave him. He wasn't afraid of the shouting or arguing that would likely follow. He was genuinely afraid of hurting Claire. To be more precise, he didn't want her to be disappointed in him. Up to now, Claire thought the world of Joey and his integrity. Joey was one of her life-footings. She needed to believe in him. If he took that trust away, Claire would be damaged far more than he.

By the time Joey was back in the cabin, Lonnie was just closing her suitcase and ready to roll.

"I've got to tell you. You are some kind of actress. You had me convinced you had a meeting with your boss," Joey said.

"Actually, I do but it's not till Tuesday morning. But don't tell Lois Lane."

"I won't. But I need to figure out how to get her off my tail tomorrow."

"What do you mean? I thought we just blew her off." Lonnie was confused.

"Not exactly. To get her to leave, I had to promise she could interview me tomorrow morning at my office. At least that way, they'll be no more photos of you." As soon as he said it, he regretted how it sounded. But instead of being offended, she offered, "Look, I'm sorry you're in this mess. It's my fault. I mean, if I wasn't here, you'd be a hero. Shit, you'd be on the news tonight all over the country."

Joey put his arms around her. "If you weren't here, I wouldn't be here. I don't regret a thing. This was a wonderful weekend."

She kissed him gently on the lips. "Then don't sweat it. You'll think of a way to blow her off by tomorrow. And I agree. This was a wonderful three days. I'm so glad we ran into each other the other night."

The first half of the ride back to Hoboken was as Joey expected. He spent the first hour mentally rehearsing how he was going to let Lonnie know this adventure was a one-time thing. She listened to a Billy Joel CD while he prepared his "kiss-off" monolog. By the time they got to the state line, he was ready to deliver the bad news. They couldn't do this again. It was wonderful but he had to try to salvage his relationship with his wife. Getting involved with Lonnie would only confuse him. He needed to think clearly. But as they were crossing the Tappan Zee bridge which spans the Hudson River, it was Lonnie who spoke first.

"Listen Joey. It was great being with you this weekend. I really enjoyed myself and you are amazing in the sack." She glanced over to see if he was smiling. "But you need to sort your shit out before you move on. I don't want to be the other woman. I don't want to be the reason your marriage gets fucked up. If I'm out of the picture, you need to focus on the promises you've made and if they still make sense, then stick with them. If not, you know where to find me. But I can't do this again until you sort that out."

Joey hoped his relief wasn't obvious. For a moment, he thought about feigning massive disappointment, pretending that he was crushed by Lonnie's news. But to what end? She was completely right. He needed to figure out if Claire and her dreams were his future. It had nothing to do with Lonnie.

"You're right. And while I'm not sorry we did this, I'm sorry I made you feel like the other woman. You're fantastic." Several miles of silence followed, then. "I need to figure some things out."

She reached across the console and took his hand in hers. "Do your thinking. Follow your heart, not your head. I think that's your biggest problem Joey. You try to do the right thing all the time. What you need to do is do the right thing for Joey. Follow your heart. Your heart's always right."

Forty minutes later he said good bye to Lonnie in front of her apartment. He knew she was right. He needed to listen to his inner voice, the one that kept telling him there was another world out there. The one that kept telling him he needed to be bold. And he realized, she was the only person who had ever told him that.

He drove away thinking he'd never see Lonnie Rossetti again. It made him sad.

CHAPTER SEVEN

B ack in his apartment, Joey showered and carefully made sure there was no evidence of Lonnie Rossetti anywhere on his clothing; not a single long brown hair or a smudge of her lipstick. He was methodically careful about this. It was too important.

It was a cool, sunny September Monday and ordinarily, if he wasn't in the office on such a day, he'd go for a run or at least a walk down by the river. But he hadn't gotten much sleep the past two nights, thanks to Lonnie, so he decided to take a nap before the drive to Newark airport.

He stretched out on the living room couch and tried to think of ways to get the reporter and Senator off his back. He understood from the reporter the Senator wanted to make some political hay from his daughter's near-death experience so it was likely, the Senator wasn't going away easily. And Joey assumed the Senator would be pushing the reporter to ensure a front-page story in the Hartford paper, so the reporter probably wasn't going away easily either.

Therefore, the task wasn't so much avoidance as it was managing the problem. Since they knew where he worked, and by now, probably where he lived as well, he needed to figure out how to mitigate the damage. How could he give the reporter just enough information to make her happy but avoid any more unwanted publicity? And would that satisfy her?

Or, could he convince the reporter that he and his "wife" found the Senator's shameless use of his daughter's misfortune so distasteful that neither of them would cooperate? Or maybe, even better, could he get her to think that he and his wife might actually cause Senator Minnick some sort of embarrassment? He recalled an old Chinese proverb; "When confronted by a sword, raise your sword higher yet." In other words, go on the offensive. Get the Senator to think any association with Joey Martinez was going to cause him more political harm than good.

One thing Joey realized in the past twenty-four hours was that lying came surprisingly easy to him. Perhaps the best course would be to meet with the reporter… What was her name? Sarah Bideaux, that was it. Perhaps the best thing would be to meet with Sarah in the morning and make her understand he wanted no part of the Senator's plan and, if pushed, would go to the press with his own account of the story; perhaps even exaggerating the Senator's incompetence in the canoe. Bluff the politician. Surely the last thing Minnick wanted a few weeks before the election, was a story that made him look incompetent.

The more he thought about it, the more he was convinced he could make it work. Content with his plan, Joey set the clock on the kitchen microwave for two hours. That would allow him a two-hour nap and wake him at five leaving him plenty of time to drive to Newark. A deep sleep came quickly and he had several dreams about the past weekend. Some were about his repeated efforts to dive into the dark weeds searching for Megan Minnick. Those were cold scary dreams. And some were about Lonnie. Those were much warmer thoughts.

<hr />

As he approached the Newark airport entrance Joey thought about Claire and how devoted she was to her parents. He pictured her sitting on the plane, waiting for it to land and digging her fingernails deep into the armrest. Although Claire was ambivalent about flying in general, she dreaded the landings. There was something, in her mind, about tons of steel falling from the sky in a controlled manner that she couldn't get her arms around. How could something as huge as a plane simply float on down to a soft landing going two hundred miles an hour? It made no sense to her and no matter how many times Joey tried to explain the physics behind lift and thrust, she didn't get it.

And so, now that they'd moved to South Carolina, visiting her parents was difficult for Claire because it meant she needed to get on a plane. Joey understood how difficult that was for her and it made him realize how deeply she cared for her mom and dad. But that was Claire. She was just that nice a human being. She could have waited for her folks to come north as they'd planned at Thanksgiving, but when she heard her mom was getting lonely in their new home, she felt a need to be with her.

That was one of the qualities Joey had found so attractive about Claire when they first met; her unselfish approach to just about any relationship. She was always putting herself second to the needs of other people. She did it with her folks, her students at the elementary school where she taught, even people they got to know on their street in Hoboken. She even did it with Joey. He knew she did. He knew, when they made love, Claire's goal was always to make Joey happy with little concern for her own carnal pleasure.

So why was he so painfully bored? This was the question that had been haunting him for months. In the eyes of others, his life was beautifully on track; the wife, the job, the plans for the future. But in his mind, he was living the wrong life, maybe with the wrong person. He couldn't explain the feeling; it was just there. He felt like none of this was supposed to happen to him; that he'd somehow missed the turn-off for his true destiny, whatever that was.

Once, over the summer, while they were lying on the beach, he talked about his feelings with Claire. He told her he felt like he was doing the wrong job for the wrong reasons and for the wrong company. He didn't say anything about feeling he'd married the wrong person or that maybe he wasn't supposed to be married at all. He didn't say it because he wasn't sure if that's the way he really felt; and why hurt Claire if he wasn't sure?

As he expected, Claire had trouble understanding his confused feelings. His wife, ever the optimist, suggested he give his job more time. Maybe he just needed to get to the next level to feel like he was doing the work he was meant to do. Maybe the next promotion would make it all right. She even suggested that maybe he'd feel differently when they had a family to take care of; the implication being that he might feel better when he had someone else to focus on. And that brought up the whole baby thing, which led to an argument that ended an otherwise delightful day at the shore.

He was convinced that these same doubts were the reason he spent the weekend with Lonnie. He needed to do something that wasn't scripted for him. He needed to do something that was far from boring. He needed to follow a passion for the sake of passion even if he wasn't sure where it would lead. And most of all, he knew that pursuit of that passion was a worthwhile goal in itself. He needed to be passionate about something because that's what was missing in his life; passion for something or maybe someone.

Claire's flight was right on time and, despite her reservations, her plane landed without incident. She gave Joey a big kiss as he greeted her at the terminal exit. "You been behaving yourself while I was in South Carolina?" She said playfully.

"I missed you," he lied. "I don't like it when you're not here."

"I missed you too. Dad and mom look great. I can't wait till you see them in November. You won't believe how great they both look."

"Good, I guess the salt air and sunshine are as good as Jim said they would be. He's been talking about the benefits of salt air as long as I've known you."

The small talk continued for most of the drive back to Hoboken. Joey had planned a quick dinner at Pedro's, their favorite Mexican restaurant, then home for the Monday night football game. He suspected Claire would be in the mood for some "I just got home" love-making but he didn't feel right about it. Not tonight; not so soon after Lonnie. The football game would be his excuse to come to bed late and by then he knew Claire would be unconscious.

Over dinner they chatted about her parent's new house and the neighbors they'd met so far. Joey was half listening. He was distracted by his guilt. Now that he was sitting face to face with Claire, the guilt he hadn't felt all day came rushing at him. He kept seeing Lonnie's naked legs lying next to him as Claire droned on about the color of her parent's living room. He kept feeling Lonnie's teeth biting playfully on his ear. How was he supposed to be interested in wall paint?

After dinner, they walked the few blocks back to their apartment. It was a beautiful evening and Claire wanted to linger on their front steps and enjoy the night air. They sat on the steps leading to their front door for several minutes before Claire asked, "Joey, how do you know you love me?"

"What?"

"I was thinking on the plane ride back from mom's that we never talk about why we love each other. We say it a lot but we never define what that means. You know?"

"Where's this coming from?"

"Well, to be honest, I read an article on the plane in that magazine in the seat pocket. It talked about the fact that married people don't communicate. They talk about stuff but they stop talking about feelings when they get married."

Joey wasn't sure this was the right night to be having such a discussion but he offered, "I guess that's true. I can see that happening to people."

Claire looked up at the starry sky and breathed in deeply. "I hope that never happens to us."

Joey looked down at the cracks in the sidewalk and thought, "That's exactly what's happened to us."

A few hours later, long after Claire had fallen asleep, Joey sat watching the football game and thinking about the events of the last three days. He felt contrite about his affair with Lonnie. He knew that was a huge mistake. Yet he didn't regret it. It seemed like something he had to do to draw a line in the sand; a line that measured the point at which he stopped conforming and began thinking of the "what ifs".

He also reflected on Megan Minnick, the girl whose life he saved. He hadn't really had time to think about it before other than to worry about its consequences. He hadn't had time to reflect on the fact that he'd done something good, something special. He'd saved someone's life; a young girl's life. A half smile crossed his face as he thought about it. Up until that day on the dock, he'd never really been tested. Nothing of real consequence had ever been put before him. This was significant. He'd gone beyond what most people might have been able to do. He dove deep into the dark cold waters, pushing aside strangling wisps of weeds to search for someone he'd never even met. He dove numerous times. He hadn't given up. And finally, he found her and rescued her from certain death.

For the first time since it happened, he felt good about himself.

Then he thought about his plan for tomorrow. He felt he could fend off the reporter and Senator by feigning indignation at their shameless use of this near-tragedy. He'd confront the reporter and

be clear that he wanted nothing to do with her story. If she persisted, which he expected she would, he'd be clear about his willingness to embarrass the Senator. No one would want to think their
elected official is so incompetent that he couldn't paddle a canoe
a few feet to rescue his only daughter.

Confident he'd figured a way out of his dilemma, Joey fell
asleep on the couch before the game was over. He didn't know
he'd passed up a chance to sleep with his wife for the last time.

CHAPTER EIGHT

Sarah Bideaux listened to WINS, an all-news station, on her car radio. She wasn't crazy about driving into Manhattan in rush hour traffic. And the roads were particularly congested today because it was a mayoral primary election day in New York.

As she crossed the 59th Street Bridge and merged onto the FDR Drive, her thoughts were on Senator Minnick. He'd personally chosen her to follow his candidacy and track his campaign for the Herald. His relationship with Andy Mosher, the owner of the paper, had assured that. At first, Sarah wasn't thrilled with the task. Following a U.S. Senator around the state to report on how many shopping malls he did a ribbon-cutting for or the number of semi-attractive babies he kissed wasn't what she had in mind when she graduated from Boston University with her journalism degree.

And yet, having complete access to such a powerful person was, in a way, intoxicating. Most of her peers at the Herald were still doing research work for other reporters. She was sitting at the side of a U.S. Senator. At times, he even asked her opinion on some things, especially if those things pertained to her demographic profile; twenty-something female voters with college degrees.

And besides, she'd already proven her worth at the paper. Her research skills were valued by everyone she'd been assigned to support since joining the Herald. She no longer had to prove herself to anyone. She could do this job in her sleep and was already focused on her next step, maybe a local TV station. She'd decided she was most interested in financial reporting. The collapse of the dot com bubble had intrigued her and she did several supporting stories on the subject so far.

But this morning the fruits of her research skills would be directed at Joey Martinez.

Across the Hudson River Joey was just preparing to leave for the office. Claire had the day off because of the elections. Her school was used for voting so the students and teachers were happy to vacate for the day to make room for the balloting machines. Claire planned on spending the day running a few errands and taking a test of her own. She was in the shower.

Joey was looking in the bedroom mirror and had just finished knotting his red and white striped tie when he heard his cell phone ring. It was only 7:16 A.M., a little early for a call from the office. He glanced at the number on the phone's display but didn't recognize the digits.

"Martinez here." His usual greeting when he didn't know who was calling.

The voice on the other end was that of a female. "Mr. Martinez, I hope it's not too early to call. This is Sarah Bideaux from the Hartford Herald."

Joey froze. "How the hell did she get my phone number?" He wondered. For a moment, he considered hanging up.

"How did you find… how did you get my cell number?" He stammered.

"Mr. Martinez, it's my job to do research. Phone numbers are easy." Her voice was lite and friendly.

"Well, what can I do for you?" He had no idea where this would go.

"I'm on the FDR Drive stuck in traffic and just wanted to let you know I might be a little late for our appointment. I'll probably be downtown by nine. I hope that's still okay."

Joey didn't remember what time she'd said she'd be there so he responded, "That's fine."

Claire's shower was still running so he felt confident she couldn't hear his phone conversation, but just to be sure he walked out to the living room. Maybe it would be better if he could blow off the reporter on the phone rather than having to deal with her at his office, especially since he didn't have a private office and would need to usurp one of the few conference rooms at Cambridge. That would lead to questions he'd rather not answer.

"Actually, it's good that you called."

"Is it? Why's that?" She asked playfully.

"Well, I've got a really busy morning today. It would probably be better if we did this on the phone anyway. The fact is, I don't want my name associated with the Senator's. It's not a political thing. Shit, I don't even know if he's a Democrat or a Republican. It's about the story itself."

"I don't understand. What do you mean about the story?" Her voice was a bit less playful.

"I just don't think it's right for him to politicize his daughter's drowning. It doesn't seem right and I don't want to be a part of it. You can write whatever story you want about him but leave me out of it." He said the words with authority.

"Near drowning, you mean."

"What?"

"Megan didn't drown, thanks to you. It was a near-drowning. That's what the paramedic called it. He also said it was nearly miraculous you were able to save her and bring her back. She'd been under water for a long time. The paramedic said it was nearly six minutes."

Joey knew he needed to get the conversation back on the track he wanted and he needed to do it before hearing the shower stop running. He decided to use his secret weapon. This would surely end the discussion.

"Look Sarah, I don't want to embarrass the Senator." There, he said it.

There was a moment of uncomfortable silence. Then, "How could you embarrass Senator Minnick?"

"Well, you said it yourself. He doesn't want any mention of what he did in the canoe. Or, more accurately, what he failed to do. I mean who wants to read about a father who is so incompetent in a canoe and afraid of the water that he couldn't help his ten-year-old daughter when she needed him most? That sort of PR couldn't possibly be helpful to a guy running for re-election."

He let the words sink in. He was pleased with his delivery and confident his bravado would carry the day. More importantly, the shower had stopped and Joey heard the shower curtain being pulled aside. He knew Claire's routine was to towel off quickly in the bathroom then step into the bedroom to finish drying. He had less than a minute to get off the line.

He said, "So there's no need for you to meet me today. I'm sorry you wasted a trip into the city. I really have to go now."

Again, a prolonged silence; then she said, "That's okay. I need to be in Manhattan today for the Senator's speech at France's Tavern later." The sweetness was back in her voice. Maybe too sweet. "So, I'll meet you at your office at nine for sure."

"No, you won't! I don't want to talk to you about this anymore. The Senator certainly wouldn't like what I have to say." Joey said the words with authority. Didn't she get it the first time?

Joey could hear Claire opening the vanity drawer in search of her hair brush. He had no more than fifteen seconds to end this. He wanted to just hang up. Then a cold voice came on the line. It was the same person he'd been speaking to a moment before but the playful sweetness was gone.

"I'll be at your office at nine and you will give me the interview I want. Do you know how I know that will happen, Joey? I know it because I also know that cutie in the bathrobe at your father-in-law's wasn't your wife. I'll see you at nine. Ninety-fourth floor, right?"

The line went dead.

CHAPTER NINE

"Were you talking to me, honey?" Claire called out as she entered the bedroom.

Joey stood frozen in the center of the living room. The reporter's words still echoed in his brain like a rifle shot. He was paralyzed with shock. How could she possibly have found out about Lonnie? How could she know Lonnie wasn't Claire? It made no sense.

"Honey, did you hear me?" Claire asked. "Who were you talking to?"

Joey pulled himself together for the moment. "Oh, Bobby... um... from the office had a quick question. He went in early today to... um... do something for the London office."

"Which one's Bobby? Is he the big guy with the crew cut?"

"Yeah, that's the guy." Joey realized he was hot, much hotter than he should have been on such a beautiful cool morning. He felt like the world was closing in on him from all sides. How was he going to deal with the reporter now? Holy shit, she's going to come to my office in less than ninety minutes. What the hell am I going to do? His pulse pounded in his veins.

Claire walked over to him and brushed back his hair. "Are you feeling okay? You look flushed."

But she didn't wait for an answer. In her right hand was an envelope. She extended it toward Joey. "This is the money we owe Michael and TJ for the ski trip."

His mind was across the river trying to think of ways to handle Sarah Bideaux. "What?"

"This is the sixteen hundred dollars we owe them for our half of the ski trip at Christmas. They laid out the money for the airfare and hotel. I told them we'd have the cash this week. Michael said he will come to your office at noon to get it. Don't you remember?"

"What? Oh, yeah. I remember. I just forgot it was today." Then he began to focus on the present. "When did you go to the bank for the cash?"

"I went last Wednesday after work, before I left or Myrtle. There are sixteen hundred-dollar bills in here. Don't lose it." She said the words as a mother might admonish a five-year-old boy.

Joey did remember. They'd planned a ski trip to Utah for the week between Christmas and New Year, while Claire was off from school. They were traveling with three other couples and their close friends, the Chattertons, had put the deposit on their credit card. Joey and Claire owed them sixteen hundred dollars. Claire was right. He'd just forgotten he was supposed to meet Michael today for lunch.

"Okay. I got it." He took the envelope and shoved it in his jacket pocket.

"That's a lot of cash to walk around with in your pocket. Make sure you don't get your pocket picked on the train. That happened to my friend Ginny. They took it right out of her coat. She'd just cashed her paycheck."

Joey's mind was already back in Manhattan. He had a vision of Sarah Bideaux standing at the Cambridge Partners reception desk asking for him. He needed to do some quick thinking. Then he had a vision of Claire reading a newspaper with his and Lonnie's picture on the front cover. The headline could have been *"Hero and busty girlfriend save Senator's daughter"*. A cold chill went through him. He needed to get away and think.

"Okay, okay. I got it Claire. I'm not an idiot." But he thought the opposite.

He walked to the front door in a haze. Somehow, he knew that things would never be the same with Claire. When he got home from work tonight, everything would be different. It would be horrible. He felt as though he was leaving the warm comfort of his home for the last time. The next time he came through the door, everything would be somehow different, colder. It was a terrible premonition.

Claire walked out onto the front stoop with him as she usually did each morning. She put her arms around his neck and pulled him in for a kiss. "Hey handsome, get your shit together. You look like you're going to walk into a wall."

She gave him a quick kiss on the lips and watched him walk down the steps toward Bloomfield Avenue.

Perhaps, if she'd known it was the last time she'd ever see him, she might have made it a better kiss.

7:34 A.M.

As usual, Joey did not get a seat on the Path train for the sixteen-minute ride to lower Manhattan. On any weekday morning, the train, which travels under the Hudson River at sixty miles per hour, is packed. Today it was more crowded than usual and Joey had to push his way on at the Hoboken station. He held on to the stainless-steel pole while a Hispanic couple argued about whose mother made better French toast directly in front of him. As much as he didn't care about their breakfast, Joey always enjoyed listening to

New York-dialect Spanish. It reminded him of the conversations his parents would have in the kitchen before they'd catch themselves and switch to un-accented English, the language they insisted was spoken at home.

Although he hadn't thought about them in the last few days, he missed his parents. They would have been horrified by what Joey had done- his infidelity to Claire. For the first time since they died, Joey was glad they weren't around. He couldn't have faced them with this. He'd be too ashamed. They'd barely gotten to know Claire before the accident, but they both really liked her and would have been happy to know she'd joined the family and was looking after their only son so well.

As Joey clung to the pole, he studied his reflection in the darkness of the train window. He looked terrible. His curly brown hair was a little longer than he usually kept it. He remembered he had an appointment for a haircut later in the week. But that wasn't what bothered him about the image staring back from outside the train. It was his eyes. Somehow, they looked different. Sure, they were the same light-green irises he was born with but today they refused to look directly at him. It was as if they too were ashamed of what he'd done.

The Spanish clatter continued all the way to the World Trade Center where Joey and hundreds of others exited and climbed the escalators to the lobby. Cambridge Partners had taken parts of four floors in One World Trade Center right after the 1993 bombing and had added two more whole floors a few years later as the company expanded. Today they monopolized the floors from 94 to 96 and had internal staircases between their floors so avoid dependence on the elevators for intra-office movement.

8:12 A.M.
As Joey walked past the news stand and candy store he passed every morning he realized how little changed since he started

working for Cambridge. Every day he walked the same route over the purple carpet that was ubiquitous in the Trade Center buildings. He passed through the same revolving glass door, the one on the south side of the building, even though he had his choice of four others. Every day he flashed his I.D., a necessary procedure since the bombing, to the same guard, and took the same elevator to the sky lobby on the 78th floor where he changed elevators, then rode up to the Cambridge floors.

The bright morning sun charged through the tall lobby windows making the expansive space seem like a cathedral. Thousands of tenants would pass through the same entrance this morning as they did every morning before the powerful elevators would hurdle them to one of the one hundred and ten possible levels on which to work. Today, Joey was joined in his express elevator by several people he knew by facial recognition only; some of the many faces he saw every morning but to whom he never spoke.

It took less than a minute for the express elevator to whisk its way to the 78th floor sky lobby where everyone would scatter like travelers at an airport, in all directions, seeking their next ride. In Joey's case that meant the elevator bank marked 91 to 99. This morning there were only two other people in the car with him, Andy from accounting and Beth DaRin from the HR department. She was the person who'd originally interviewed him for the job three years ago.

"Morning Joey," she offered. "Beautiful day, huh?"

But Joey was lost in thought. He nodded but said nothing. His mind was on other things. He needed to come up with a plan "B" because Sarah Bideaux had blown his plan "A" out of the water. When the elevator reached the 94th floor Joey and the other two Cambridge employees walked through the glass doors, past the receptionist desk, which was still unmanned, and to their appointed offices. In Joey's case that wasn't an office at all. He, like most other associates, worked on the 'floor' which meant he had little more than a cubical to call his own amongst a sea of identical cubicles. The 'floor', short for the trading floor, was the size of a football field, an expanse of wires, desks and computers that extended from one side of the building to the other. The only enclosures on the entire floor were two glass-walled conference rooms, known as the fish bowls.

On his desk sat three screens, each already filled with numbers and graphs. He logged in and all three screens came alive with new colors and figures reflecting the markets Joey followed each morning; New York, which had yet to open, London, which was just finishing lunch and Frankfurt, which was nearing its close. He slumped into his chair and stared ahead without focusing on any of the data.

8:22 A.M.

A message from his counterpart in London appeared on the center screen. Apparently, Nigel Custerman had been waiting for Joey to log on to bring him up to speed on a trade he wanted executed at the New York open. The message read, "*Call me when you arrive. I need to break GE trade into four pieces. Will explain when you call.*" Joey typed back, "*Give me ten minutes.*"

He glanced at the digital clock in the corner of the screen: 08:24. He had just a little over a half hour to come up with a plan to defuse the ambitious reporter. If he didn't help her, Claire would find out about Lonnie. But if he did help her, she'd want to use his name and image in her story. Either way it would be devastating to his marriage. For the first time in his life Joey felt hopeless.

It wasn't just that Sarah Bideaux was about to blow up his marriage. If he was going to be honest with himself, he'd thought about doing that himself before. Although his affection for Claire was sincere, more and more he was feeling trapped. He often felt he was living the wrong life; that somehow fate had switched the role he was supposed to play and he'd ended up in the wrong body.

He could empathize with men who felt they were supposed to be a woman, or vis-versa, although that wasn't his issue. He just felt that somehow, Claire wasn't his destiny.

And yet he did love her and certainly didn't want to hurt her. He knew that his betrayal, if it became known, would devastate Claire. She put all her faith in him. If she were to learn about his weekend with Lonnie, she'd probably never trust another human being again. She was just that kind of person. To Joey, that would be the greatest tragedy; destroying Claire's trusting view of the world. He'd rather die than do that. Losing a husband to death would ultimately be less crippling to Claire than losing a husband to infidelity.

8:30 A.M.

As he sat at his desk he began to feel the walls closing in. The trading floor was filling with people and the din was rising almost to its normal level for the pre-market activity. He told himself to focus, focus on the immediate problem, the reporter. He envisioned her coming through the glass doors and walking slowly toward his cubicle. There was no place to hide. The only place on the entire floor he could speak with her privately was the conference room but even that was entirely glass. Everyone on the floor would see them.

He was beginning to hyperventilate. It became hard for him to breathe even though he was breathing rapidly. There just wasn't enough air getting in. He felt like he was underwater again, his lungs screaming for oxygen.

He had no plan and without a plan, this was going to be a massacre. Joey knew himself well enough to understand that he didn't spar well if he wasn't properly prepared. Sarah Bideaux would take him apart. She would get what she came for, the truth and the truth would be the end of Joey's relationship with his wife. It would be the end of his life as he knew it. And yet, this was ultimately all his fault. He made the fatal decision to have dinner with Lonnie. He made the plans for a weekend at the lake. All his fault.

He felt that if he didn't stand and move he couldn't breathe. So, he got up and walked to the elevator bank and began to pace. He moved back and forth across the carpeted area several times before an elevator door opened and a woman got out. It was someone he recognized from the foreign exchange department, but more importantly, it wasn't Sarah Bideaux. But he knew it was only a matter of time.

The arrow-shaped light above the elevator door now lit and chimed indicating the car was headed back down to the sky lobby. The door hung open for a seductive moment as if offering Joey an escape. He stared into the empty cube for what seemed an eternity, trying to decide to fight or flee. All the "what ifs" flashed in his mind. What if I'd never met Lonnie? What if it had ended at dinner? What if that little girl had not fallen from the raft? What if I hadn't tried to save her? What if I'd never met Claire?

The elevator doors began to slide closed. Joey stood frozen just two feet from the doors. As they were about to seal shut, a hand reached out from next to Joey and pressed the down button.

"Hey, what's up Martinez? You going down or not?" The question came from Billy Myers, one of the other guys covering the London markets. Joey hadn't seen him approaching.

Myers got in the elevator and looked back at Joey. "Hey Martinez, you coming or not?"

Joey silently stepped into the car and watched as the doors closed the world off behind him.

"I got a call from the receptionist on seventy-eight. I've got a package I need to sign for." Billy seemed in a hurry. "Where you off to?"

"Not sure." Joey whispered.

"What the fuck does that mean?" The trader asked.

Joey hesitated long enough for the doors to open on seventy-eight. "I just need some air." The answer seemed to satisfy Billy, who was already moving in the direction of the sky lobby receptionist and his mystery package.

Joey walked across the brightly lit lobby to the express elevators. He still didn't know where he was headed but he knew he was heading away from his desk, the place the reporter would be in a few minutes. The more distance he could put between himself and that spot, the better. It was as if distance could assuage his problem in some way. The elevator sped toward the ground and Joey exited just as Sarah Bideaux was entering the elevator car directly next to his. They missed seeing each other by no more than two seconds.

8:41 A.M.

He decided to get further away. Just as he would normally do at the end of each day, Joey headed for the Path train entrance in the lower level of the ground floor concourse. He boarded the first train that came into the noisy station, one bound for Exchange Place New Jersey. During the twelve-minute ride under the Hudson River he sat numb and silent, staring at his darkened image reflecting back through the window. He still wasn't sure where he was going but he drew comfort knowing he wouldn't be there when the reporter arrived.

At the same time Joey was traveling west under the river, Sarah Bideaux was introducing herself to the receptionist on ninety-four. "I have a nine o'clock appointment with Joe Martinez," she announced without mentioning her purpose.

"I'll have him come out. Who shall I say is waiting?"

"Sarah Bideaux."

"Why don't you have a seat over there and I'll see if he's at his desk," the receptionist said and pointed to the couches on the north side of the vestibule.

Sarah took a seat on a comfortable black leather sofa facing the huge glass windows. The view from the ninety-fourth floor was spectacular. Looking north from the Trade Center she could see the entire midtown Manhattan skyline. To the left, she could see the river and, beyond the George Washington Bridge, the cliffs of the Palisades glistening in the bright morning sun.

8:46 A.M.

She pulled out her notepad and began to review the questions she was planning to ask Joey. She knew she had him and it gave her great pleasure to realize how much her research paid off. It hadn't taken long to find a photo of the real Mrs. Martinez. The paper's archives were amazing. She was about to add an additional note to her pad when she heard someone yell, "It's way too low!"

She looked up to see the nose of American Airlines flight 11 coming directly toward her from the north. Her brain was unable to process what her eyes were seeing. It made no sense. A fraction of a second later the waiting area erupted in an explosion of glass, twisted steel, and a fireball of jet fuel.

Everyone on the north side of the ninety-fourth floor was incinerated in seconds.

CHAPTER TEN

Claire Martinez had just finished taking the most significant test of her young life. The plastic strip had turned the most beautiful shade of blue she'd ever seen and she couldn't wait to call her mother. Her parents were going to be ecstatic at the thought of becoming grandparents.

Claire knew that she really shouldn't share her wonderful news with her mom before telling Joey but she also knew she needed to tell him in person and that wouldn't happen until later that night. The thought of going all day without telling someone was unbearable. And she knew he was totally unprepared for this news. This had to be done in person and at exactly the right time.

Although they'd talked about children many times, it was always Claire who was the more eager to start a family. While not openly opposed to the concept, Joey never seemed to embrace the notion of fatherhood and often said he wasn't ready yet. It was the word "yet" that Claire hoped was pivotal to the matter. Tonight, she just needed him to see that no one is ever really ready and that his fears are normal. She sincerely felt that everything would work out, that a child would bring them together as a family.

Yet she knew she'd have to explain how this happened. More specifically, why she'd stopped taking birth control pills without telling him. That was going to be the more difficult conversation and she didn't want to lie. The truth was she'd read an article back in July about how prolonged use of certain birth control pills had a correlation to higher instances of uterine cancer in some women. That scared her enough to stop the pills but, in reality, she always believed she could convince Joey they, not just she, were ready for a baby.

As she was about to dial her mom, the phone rang. The incoming number on her handset made her smile. "Hey mom, I was just picking up the phone to call you."

"Is he okay? Did you hear from him?" Her mother sounded frantic. Claire wasn't accustomed to hearing her mother anything but calm.

"What? Hear from who? What are you talking about?"

"Oh, my God. I guess you haven't heard. Turn on the news."

"What? Hear what?" As she responded, Claire reached for the TV's remote and switched on her usual morning station, channel four. She muted the sound so she could hear her mother but the Today Show didn't seem to be aware of whatever her mom was taking about either. Matt Lauer was interviewing some guy in a grey suit and everything seemed normal.

"What are you taking about mom? I just turned on the Today Show. Is who okay?"

"Daddy said he heard on the news just a few minutes ago that a small plane hit the World Trade Center in New York. He said it hit the North Tower. Isn't that the building Joey works in?"

Claire quickly switched from channel four to five, then seven, then to CNN. None of them seemed to know what her father knew. How could that be? "I think daddy got some bad information mom. None of the New York channels have anything about it, and that would be big news."

But, just as her mother began to explain to her nearby husband what Claire had said, Claire switched the channel back to four and Matt Lauer was now alone on the screen and appeared unusually sober. An instant later the World Trade Center filled the screen with smoke pouring from the north side of the building, the building she knew Joey worked within.

"Oh, my God. It just came on TV. Wait, let me turn up the volume."

She heard the words "…some sort of explosion, perhaps a small plane." Matt Lauer was explaining.

"Oh Jesus, it's true."

"And you haven't heard from Joey?"

"No. Let me hang up and call him right now. I'll call you back."

"Okay baby, I'm sure he's fine. Daddy says those buildings are fireproof. But call me back."

As Claire dialed Joey's office number and waited for the call to connect, she tried counting the floors on the towering building that seemed to be effected by the smoke. She knew Joey worked on ninety-four but the image on the screen was taken from a distance and it was difficult to be sure what she was seeing. The Empire State Building was in the foreground with both Trade Center Towers in the distance.

Then Matt Lauer and Katie Couric sat side by side and Claire heard the words, "One World Trade Center is being evacuated…"

When the call connected she got a busy signal. She dialed again, and again, a busy signal. That was a bad sign. Someone was always there to answer, "Cambridge Partners. How can I help?"

So, Claire dialed her husband's cell phone number. A moment later she heard it ringing on the kitchen table. In his cloud of anxiety that morning, he'd forgotten to take his phone.

"Shit!" She screamed. "How the hell am I supposed to get in touch with you?"

CHAPTER ELEVEN

Exchange Place is exactly that; a rail station in Jersey City at which commuters taking the Path Train can change trains and either travel north toward Pavonia and Hoboken or west to other commuter hubs. It's the first rail stop for the Path Line in New Jersey after the trains emerge from the long tunnel under the Hudson River and the last stop in New Jersey for commuters traveling into the city.

Ordinarily, if Joey was on his way home from work, he would transfer at Exchange Place for the train to Hoboken. But today, he didn't have a destination. So today, when he disembarked the train, Joey rode the escalator up to the terminal and exited through a large revolving glass door to the street. As soon as he took a breath of the outside air he felt better.

He walked two blocks to a small park he knew along the Riverwalk and found a park bench. The wooden slates creaked as he sat and he was glad to have put distance between himself and the reporter. He needed a place to think and the trading floor at

Cambridge was too frantic an environment for clear thinking. The only plan he had at this point was to spend whatever time it took to come up with one.

He looked back at Manhattan Island glistening in the bright morning sunlight. The skyline of lower Manhattan was impressive from the Jersey side of the river and his park bench was just a few feet from the river's edge. He regretted never taking the time to enjoy this view before. In fact, he could only think of one other time he'd been in this park. It was two years ago when he had a training class at the Goldman Sachs building, now just to his left. He remembered the views of Manhattan from the Goldman office tower were incredible.

The air was about as clear as he could imagine it gets around a major city. There didn't seem to be any of the usual pollution lingering at the horizon. Just clear crisp September air as far as he could see. It would be a good place to sit and think for a while. The only person within sight was an elderly woman sitting on a similar bench about fifty feet to his left. She was listening to a radio. She certainly wouldn't bother him even though her radio was on a little louder than it needed to be.

But as his gaze shifted from the Bowery, north to the Trade Center, he noticed dark clouds, maybe smoke, drifting east from the towers. Because the clouds were moving away from him rather than in his direction, Joey couldn't tell just how thick the clouds were or where they were coming from. The massive gash Flight 11 tore into the north side of Tower One wasn't visible from Joey's vantage so he had no way to know the smoke was coming from what was left of his office. To him, if it was smoke, it might mean there was a minor fire on one of the upper floors of one of the buildings. It was a curiosity but not cause for alarm. He went back to focusing on what he thought was the immediate problem, the reporter.

Because she seemed so determined to satisfy the Senator's lust for publicity, avoiding her forever didn't look like a viable way out.

He needed to somehow give her what she wanted while protecting his anonymity. That seemed the only way to shield Claire from his infidelity. Perhaps if he could appeal to her as a man who was at her mercy she might sympathize with his plight and agree to conceal his identity but still give the Senator the story he craved. Maybe if he agreed to allow her to embellish the Senator's role in the rescue, in exchange, she would protect Joey.

9:03 A.M.

"That could work," he found himself saying aloud. That is, if she wasn't so pissed off already. He glanced at his watch and realized she was supposed to be at his office by now and probably quite annoyed he wasn't there. He decided to call her, apologize, and offer to meet her to explain his predicament. It seemed like his only real option.

But when he reached into his jacket pocket to find his cell phone all he felt was the envelop Claire had given him as he left the house. It was then he realized he'd left his phone on the table at home. He couldn't reach the reporter. And if he wasn't at his desk when she got to Cambridge, she might try to call him again only this time his phone would ring at home and Claire would answer!

"God damn it!" he yelled, loud enough for the old lady nearby to hear. "How the hell did I get into this?"

He leaned back and raised his hands to his head. Then he heard it; the roar of jet engines straining as United flight 175 banked steeply to its left over the river. Joey could tell the huge plane was flying low, lower than he'd ever seen before this close to the city. It's abrupt turn now aimed it northward, back toward the Manhattan skyline. It looked so low that he assumed it was going to follow the East River north, back toward LaGuardia Airport in Queens. It must be preparing to land there, he thought.

Then, he saw it. A tremendous fire ball exploded about half way up the south tower. Two seconds later he heard the thunderous noise echo across the river.

"Holy shit!"

A black mushroom cloud of smoke billowed skyward. This time Joey had the perfect vantage to see the damage on the south face of Tower Two, a massive black hole. He couldn't believe what he was seeing. A plane had just run into the World Trade Center! It was the sort of thing people thought about occasionally simply because the towers were so high and sometimes invisible in thick cloud cover, but you never really thought it could happen. Not with radar and all the technology available in 2001. Not on a clear day.

"Oh, my goodness." The woman on the other bench gasped. She turned toward Joey. "I think we're being attacked again."

The phrase, "…being attacked again" was lost on Joey. He had no way to understand she was recalling the emotions of a fifteen-year-old high school girl learning of the Pearl Harbor attack. Only this time, the attack wasn't six thousand miles away. It was across the river.

As the thick grey and black smoke drifted eastward, it curled and twisted in tumultuous currents. Joey's first thought was that hundreds of people must have just been killed. He pictured his own office and how many people were crammed onto each floor. Then he thought about all the fire drills he'd been through, usually one every six months, while working at the World Trade Center. They always focused on escaping to a floor below the fire in one of the several fireproof stairways. The guy running the drill would always say you only need to get two floors below the fire floor. There was no need to leave the building.

"Do you think it's the Russians?" The woman asked.

"What?" Joey responded.

"I mean, do you think it's the Russians doing this?"

"Doing what?"

"Hitting our buildings with planes. It could be the Russians."

"Planes? I only saw one plane. What makes you think there was more than one?"

"The other one hit the other tower about fifteen minutes ago? Where have you been? I thought that's what you were watching."

He was angered by his own stupidity. The smoke from Tower One, another plane?

"Are you saying a plane hit Tower One as well?" He got up and moved toward her bench so they would no longer have to yell at each other.

"I'm not saying it. They are." She motioned with her hand to the radio she was holding in the other.

Joey could now hear the radio. It wasn't music she'd been listening to. It was the news. And the distinctive sound of WINS 1010, New York's all-news station crackled from the tiny transistor radio she clutched.

"What did you hear?" He asked.

"They said a plane hit the World Trade Center and they were evacuating the building. It happened about fifteen minutes ago. What a terrible thing."

"Did they say what kind of plane it was?"

"No, I don't think so." She moved a bit to her left on the bench to make room for Joey.

He sat next to her but his eyes were transfixed on the skyline across the river.

"Did they say what floor the plane hit?"

"No, there's been very few details. Just that they're evacuating the building. That's a lot of people to get out of there all at once. I hope the stairways weren't damaged."

Without taking his eyes from the smoking towers, Joey asked, "Did you see the first plane crash?"

"Oh, no. I was reading my book." She raised a copy of a paperback she held in her right hand. "I thought I heard something but I didn't look up. Then when the radio said something had happened at the Trade Center, I looked up and saw the smoke. I used to work in Building Five, you know, the short black building in the front. It was several years ago. I retired right after the bombing in '93. No need to keep doing the commute after James, my late husband, passed." Her voice trailed off in somber reflection.

"When the bombing happened back then, we were all evacuated; at least, my building was. There was thick smoke coming in through the air conditioning ducts. We couldn't stay in the building. Fortunately, I worked on the seventh floor so I didn't have far to walk. Imagine those poor people up there…" She pointed at the towers with her book. "Imagine if you had to walk down all those stairs."

Joey could sense the elderly woman was upset. He offered, "My name is Joey."

"Hello Joey. I'm Rita. Rita Kelleher." She offered her hand but Joey never saw it. He was still staring at the unbelievable sight across the river, less than a half mile from where they sat.

Rita's transistor radio was now sitting on the bench between them. The sounds from the tiny speaker seemed surreal. "We now have an unconfirmed report that a second plane has struck the south tower and the New York City Police Department has issued a statement that several airliners may have been hijacked this morning."

There was some static on the radio that prevented them from hearing the beginning of the next sentence but Joey could make out the words "Flight 77 was on its way from…" Then he heard, "Flight 77 which had taken off from…" Static. "….and bound for…" More static.

"May I?" He asked as he lifted the radio to try to position it in a better line with its transmitter. But it didn't help. In fact, it made the clarity a bit worse. He adjusted the volume so the static wasn't so loud.

"My god." He said. "There are so many people in there. What about the people above the crash? How are they supposed to get out?" His thoughts went back to the fire drills and the instructions to go below the fire floor but not leave the building entirely. He now wondered if that was really good advice.

9:13 A.M.
Joey and Rita sat on the green park bench mesmerized by what they were seeing. An odd silence hung over the river. It made what they were seeing seem inconsistent with the calm clear morning they were feeling in New Jersey. There were no more sounds coming from Manhattan, just the horrible visual; two one hundred and ten story skyscrapers on fire, smoking like two birthday candles just blown out with the rivulets of smoke drifting gently and silently to the east. What they could see wasn't consistent with what they were hearing on the radio or the silence in the air. It made no sense. It defied what the senses were perceiving.

They sat in silence for nearly ten minutes listening to what little information was being repeated on the radio. There was no one else anywhere near them in the park. Finally, it was Joey who spoke.

"I work there." He found himself pointing toward the towers. "I work on the ninety-fourth floor of Building One. I work for Cambridge Partners. We must have two hundred people there." As he said the words, he tried to count the floors from where the smoke appeared to be coming to the top of the building. He wanted to estimate where the plane hit the building. "Eleven, twelve, thirteen fourteen..." He stopped.

"Holy shit!" He whispered.

He knew from this distance his estimate was only that, an estimate, but by his crude reckoning, the smoke was coming from around the ninety-seventh floor, just three floors from where he worked. His mind raced. Who had he seen in the office that morning? Who was at their desks when he left? How would they get down from there?

He pictured the grey concrete emergency stairways they used to practice evacuations during the fire drills. They were narrow and steep with cold metal handrails that turned at each floor in a relentless cascade downward. He couldn't imagine his entire office having to exit at once, especially not if the stairways were already filled with those from floors above trying to get down to the sky lobby.

He needed to call the office to see if his floor had been effected. He had to know if his friends were alright. But when he instinctively reached for his cell phone, he was reminded it was sitting on the table at home. "Damn!"

He turned to his bench mate. "Rita, you don't have a phone, do you?"

The grey-haired woman looked confused. "Of course, I do." Then she realized he meant a cell phone, a tool she had never seen a need for. "Oh, you mean a portable phone. No, I'm afraid I don't have one of those. Did you want to call your family?"

It was the first moment Joey realized he hadn't yet thought about Claire. "I wonder if she's even aware." He mumbled aloud. His eyes went back to the towers. "My wife almost never watches TV in the morning. She's probably out running now anyway." Then he added, "No. I was going to call my office to make sure everyone is okay."

"I bet you're glad you didn't have work today."

The chilling confluence of guilt and relief washed over him. He did a quick calculation of the time he'd left the office. He couldn't have missed the crash by more than two minutes. He guessed he was just getting on the Path train as the first plane stuck. A cold chill ran through him.

"No. I was there less than an hour ago. I was on the ninety-fourth floor, at my desk." He conjured a visual image of the trading floor and the people milling about. He thought about the receptionist he passed in the foyer and about Bill Myers on the elevator.

"I was supposed to meet someone at nine o'clock for a meeting. She was…" The image of the young reporter flashed in his mind's eye. "Oh Jesus, I hope she wasn't early for …" His thought drifted off. It was too horrible to think about. For some reason, he suddenly felt responsible for Sarah Bideaux's safety. She was so young; too young. He thought that odd, considering she was about to ruin his life.

"Well, you're probably very lucky to be here and not there right now." Rita offered, sensing the young man's discomfort.

"I don't feel very lucky. I feel terrible."

9:30 A.M.

"Well you should be grateful you…" Joey cut her off. He pointed at the radio. A faint voice had just mentioned the President's name.

"Listen. They just said something about President Bush." Joey said.

WINS reported the President was about to address the nation from Sarasota Florida. A moment later, the unmistakable voice of George Bush squeaked from the tiny box. "Today we've had a national tragedy. Two airplanes have crashed into the World Trade Center in an apparent terrorist attack on our country…" The message succumbed to static.

Joey felt a need to do something, to somehow help his fellow employees at Cambridge. They were his brothers and sisters for the last few years. He spent more time with them than he did at home. They shared birthdays and celebrations of promotions. He was learning the names of many of his co-worker's children, at least the ones who sat closest to him on the floor. He had to do something to help.

The radio crackled. "We've just been informed that all bridges and tunnels into and out of Manhattan Island have been closed by the Port Authority. This action being taken in response to what we now know to be an obvious act of terrorism. The Long Island Railroad and the Metro North systems have suspended service into Manhattan. Path service between 34th Street and the World

Trade Center and Hoboken has also been suspended. To repeat, all bridges and tunnels into and out of Manhattan are closed to vehicular traffic. Apparently, pedestrians are being permitted on the bridges. We have a report that the Brooklyn Bridge is ...." Static overtook the message.

Any hope Joey might have held, of going back to Manhattan to aid his friends vanished. He now felt like he was safely on the mainland watching something terrible happen to those on the island just across the river. It was a terrible feeling. He was reminded of how he felt two days ago, as he stood on the dock and watched the young boy screaming for his father. The raft was Manhattan and the dock was Hoboken but it was all the same. Something horrible was happening just out of his sight but he felt he needed to do something.

At the Lake, that meant jumping in the water and swimming out to rescue Megan Minnick. Today, he was trapped. Swimming to Manhattan was impossible. And even if he could, what good could he possibly do? It was a horrible feeling of helplessness.

9:44 A.M.

The radio crackled again. "... an explosion of some sort at the Pentagon. There are unconfirmed reports of a major explosion either within the Pentagon Building or in one of the adjacent buildings. At this time, we have nothing to ..." The voice disappeared behind a wall of static and high-pitched noises.

"Oh my." Rita muttered. "It sounds like the Russians to me."

"Whoever's doing it, it seems like it's very well coordinated." Joey responded.

"It does, doesn't it? It's all happening so fast. But that's exactly what happened in '41 when the Japs hit Pearl Harbor. It all happened in a few minutes. I guess that's why they call it a sneak attack."

For some inexplicable reason, Joey thought about his parents. Perhaps it was because he recalled his father telling him about his own recollections of Pearl Harbor when Joey was a child. He remembered being at a park with his father pushing him on a swing. He recalled it was a very hot day. The unforgiving July sun was in his face as he pushed his way higher and higher. To this day, whenever he hears the words Pearl Harbor, his mind is drawn to that warm day at the park and swinging as high as he could while his father told him about the day Roosevelt said would live in infamy.

Phil Martinez was a stern man. Even as a child, Joey could re-member his dad as a strict disciplinarian, a man who insisted his son be respectful of others and particularly of the law. *"I never want to hear that you sassed one of your teachers,"* he'd said more than once. Joey respected him for his adherence to the rules, rules that weren't always fair to a dark-skinned man with a heavy Latino accent.

He also respected the man everyone called Phil for his devotion to Joey's mother. Phil and Maria Martinez were always together. If Phil wasn't at work, he was home. He had no social relationships. He belonged to no clubs, sports teams or church groups. There was work and there was family, nothing else. And right up to the af-ternoon of their accident, he and his wife did everything together.

Thinking about them always made Joey sorry he hadn't taken one more opportunity to tell them he loved them. Saying "I love you momma," was something he did instinctively every time he left the house. But on the day of the accident, he was in a hurry to get to his office and…, well, he knew he'd missed his chance. By the time he got back from lunch that day, his parents, his entire fam-ily, had been erased from his life by a drunk driver as they crossed 125th Street.

"Do you think it's over?"

Joey was drawn back from his daydream about his parents. "What?"

"Do you think the worst is over? Do you think there are more planes up there ready to attack?"

Before he could answer, the radio announcer confirmed that it was in fact, a plane that caused the explosion at the Pentagon. "*...sustained substantial damage to the south side of the building. A total evacuation has been ordered for the Pentagon and for several other...*" Static again.

9:59 A.M.

Joey turned away from his gaze at the twin towers to ask Rita, "Do you think we should go into that building over there to see if there's a TV or something so we can get better information?" He motioned toward the Goldman Sachs building. "They might have a TV at the reception desk."

"I feel like I'm watching history here. I don't want to watch it on TV when I can see it right in front of me." Rita said. She was looking directly into Joey's eyes and he knew she was right. "But if you need to find a phone to call your family to let them know you're all right, go right ahead. I'm fine here with my Sony." She held up her radio.

"I suppose you're right. We don't often get to see history. We either watch it on TV later than evening or read about in the papers the next morning. You're right Rita. I guess I'll have something to tell my children about."

But as he turned back to view the history he'd just referenced, a terrifying chill ran through him. Only one tower stood where there had been two a moment before.

"Why can't I see the other tower?" Rita asked innocently.

Joey's mouth hung open in disbelief.

"Joey, where's the other tower?"

CHAPTER TWELVE

10:59 A.M.

Two miles to the north of where Joey sat, Claire stared at her television screen. The voices of Katie Couric and Matt Lauer continued to fill the room with information about the tragic events across the river, but the image on the screen was live video of the World Trade Center with both towers billowing dark smoke. The camera feeding the image must have been on a rooftop in Brooklyn. It was frighteningly clear, almost too real.

Claire still held the phone in her hand. She'd tried to dial Joey's office number over and over. Each time, she got a recording saying the call could not be completed. She was growing increasingly concerned. Matt Lauer had estimated the first plane hit the north tower somewhere around the ninety-fifth floor! One floor above Joey's trading floor!

She was about to dial the office number again when the phone rang in her hand. Her heart leapt with hope that it was her husband on the other end. "Joey?"

"No, it's mom again. You haven't heard from him yet?"

"No. I'm getting really worried mom. He should have called me by now."

"I bet he's walking down the stairs and there's no reception in those stairways you know. They're solid concrete. He'll call you when he gets to the bottom."

"I hope you're right. If I can't…" But her words were gone. She gasped as she watched the television. The image changed. Something was happening. The top of the south tower tilted a bit to the left, then disappear in a cloud of smoke and ash. The camera broadcasting the event, panned out to reveal the horrifying cascading collapse. The south tower was disappearing.

CHAPTER THIRTEEN

"**O**h my god! It's gone. The south tower isn't there!" Joey was nearly hysterical. "It's fucking gone. It must have collapsed!"

"Those poor people." Rita began to sob.

The radio crackled to life again. "*... as yet. Repeating, both towers of the World Trade Center are being evacuated. The Port Authority has issued a mandatory evacuation and is being assisted in the effort by...*" Several seconds of silence followed. *Then, "I've just received an Associated Press report that the south tower of the trade center has collapsed. An enormous cloud of dust has enveloped downtown Manhattan as a result. We're going live to John Montone who is reporting from the corner of Vesey Street and ..."* The signal faded away once more.

Joey tried to imagine what the area surrounding his building must be like. On a normal day, when large numbers of people were exiting the buildings at the same time, lunch hour for example, the walkways and streets around the World Trade Center buildings are clogged with a sea of humanity. Tens of thousands of people worked in those skyscrapers. When they were stacked within the two towers, in an orderly fashion, doing their jobs, going about their ordinary routines, the outside streets were navigable. But when they all needed to get to the street at the same time, like today, chaos would rule.

Add to the chaos caused by the mass number of people milling about, the collapse of one of the towers, raining down on those people; stone, glass, twisted steel, office furniture, and the poor souls who hadn't yet escaped. The image made Joey drop his head into his hands and shutter. He thought about the innocent people who had evacuated the building and were waiting outside for instructions about when they could return, only to have their building collapse onto them. From the billowing clouds of grey dust, he could see across the river, Joey estimated the dust must have been fifteen to twenty stories high and extended several blocks. In fact, most of lower Manhattan was shrouded in the pulverized remains of the South Tower and the plume of dust could be seen from outer space as it drifted in a southeasterly direction.

Rita was still staring directly at the single tower now protruding ominously through the dust cloud. She hadn't noticed Joey's distress. She was focused on an historical image of the World Trade Center plaza she recalled from her own time there. Her mind conjured the fountain in the center of the plaza with its unusual bronze orb rotating within the flowing water. "The Sphere", as it was called was placed in the fountain in 1971 by its creator, the German sculptor, Fritz Koenig. Usually, dozens of people would be sitting on the fountain's side wall eating their lunch. On a day like today, there might even be a few out there just trying to catch some last rays of September's warming sun. To her, this was a peaceful place. This was a familiar place she could see from her office window. She couldn't imagine it any other way. And yet, the reality before her was undeniable. The massive clouds of dust flowing from the area in all directions told her the bucolic plaza was gone.

She looked over at Joey's slumped body. "This is terrible. This is much worse than the bombing in '93." She put her hand on Joey's back in an attempt to console him. "You really should get to a phone and let your wife know you're okay. She's got to be worried to death."

10:24 A.M.

As Rita gently rubbed Joey's back, the radio crackled yet again. *"… and those orders apparently come directly from the President. U.S. Secret Service agents have secured the area around the White House and are establishing armed patrols of the area. This, in response to the report that a United Airline flight has been listed as missing somewhere over Pennsylvania. Evacuations have been ordered for all federal buildings not just in Washington but across the country. It appears obvious that some…"* Static interrupted the message. Then, *"… can only be described as a disaster. People have been reported walking from lower Manhattan in any direction possible. Many have been coming up Broadway covered in ash, presumably from the smoke cloud in lower Manhattan. The question now is why can't the authorities…"* Again, the radio succumbed to static.

Joey finally looked up from the ground. He hoped against hope that he'd imagined the image that burned in his mind; that he'd look up and see two towers standing side by side as they were intended. But, even through the tears, he could see the horrible singularity of the North Tower protruding above the dust.

"Those poor people." He said.

"I know. So many innocent people." Rita's voice was cracking.

Oddly, even though he was witness to two terrorist acts and listened to radio reports of other missing planes, Joey's thoughts never turned to fear. It never occurred to him that there might be other planes circling that would soon come crashing down on the spot where he sat or into a nearby building. He never thought of his own safety. He worried for his coworkers. He even worried for the young reporter who was on her way to ruin his life.

And now, that all seemed so trivial. The scandal of his infidelity meant so little now. He felt foolish and a bit selfish for devoting so much energy to it. After all, he'd brought that on himself. He deserved whatever came. But the innocent people working at their desks in the World Trade Center didn't deserve what just happened. Their children and families didn't deserve to lose their fathers and mothers.

"Who the fuck would do such a thing?" He bellowed in frustration.

10:28 A.M.

Silence followed for several moments. Rita knew it wasn't a real question. She understood the young man's feeling of helplessness. Then she offered, "I hope we find out. I hope whoever did this pays deeply. But, for now…, I still think you should call your wife."

"What about you? Don't you have someone you need to call? Isn't someone going to be worried about you?"

"My son and grandchildren live in Hawaii. They're not even awake yet. They don't know about any of this yet."

Joey pictured Rita's family asleep, thousands of miles away, completely unaware of the horror. Their sleep was peaceful and innocent. They didn't have to erase these terrible images from their minds yet. He envied their peaceful dreams.

If he could turn back the hands of time, even just forty-eight hours, everything would be different. He would have warned the little girl not to tumble from the raft. He never would have met Senator Minnick or Sarah Bideaux. He could be like Rita's family, still untouched by the harsh reality of this terrible Tuesday morning.

Joey was peering at the lone tower and the smoke when he said, "Rita, I think you should go home. There's probably more information on TV and someone, maybe a neighbor may be looking for you. You shouldn't…"

That's when he saw it. The enormous metal antenna protruding from atop the remaining World Trade Center building began to tilt to the right. Then it appeared to shorten. A second later, the antenna disappeared. Joey stared as the upper floors of Two World Trade Center collapsed onto the floors below, and those onto the floors below them. It seemed to be happening in slow motion, yet it was happening so quickly.

"Oh, my god!" He whispered.

The enormous monolith continued to disappear into the cloud of dust. From Joey's vantage, it seemed to be going straight down into the earth below, somehow collapsing into itself. Now the dust cloud was overwhelming lower Manhattan. In less than ten seconds, the second of the two great towers was gone. Where a moment before, thousands of people sat at their desks, now there was just air. In just under thirty minutes, the two buildings, two-hundred and twenty floors containing, people, machines, computers, steel, glass and concrete, vanished.

A plume of grey dust, two-hundred feet high began to push out into the river. It pushed in all directions and rolled through the canyons of lower Manhattan like floodwaters from a burst dam. For a moment, it seemed like it would extend all the way across the Hudson to where Joey sat.

But it didn't. The air on the New Jersey side of the Hudson remained as clear and clean as it was on any other crisp September morning.

CHAPTER FOURTEEN

The empty space left in Manhattan's skyline after the second tower fell, created an eerie image. For thirty years, the two towers defined lower New York. It would be impossible for a tourist to take a picture of the area without the ubiquitous buildings towering over all else.

Joey found himself unable to look eastward. The vista was too macabre. He'd been a first-hand witness to a historic disaster but had viewed the entire event in near total silence. What his eyes had seen, his mind still couldn't believe. He needed more information and the old lady's radio wasn't giving him enough.

Without saying a word, almost as if in a trance, he got up from the bench and began to walk north. He needed to find a television; a connection to the world of people who knew what the hell was going on.

After walking three blocks he came upon a corner luncheonette. He could see several people at the counter looking up at a television mounted on the wall over the cash register. Like someone from a zombie movie, he entered the store and sat alone at one end of the counter. No one paid him any attention. Their eyes were fixed on the TV.

A grey-haired announcer from CNN was speaking on the left side of a split screen. On the right was the catastrophic image Joey had just witnessed, being replayed over and over; the north tower collapsing onto itself in a cascading fury of dust. The announcer was saying something about the emergency response of the New York firefighters.

A moment later the image changed to Seven World Trade Center, a forty-seven-story building just north of the twin towers. Fire was raging from its rooftop. The reporter was saying that the building was being evacuated. Debris falling from the collapse of One WTC had badly damaged this building as well. Joey wondered if there had been a third plane he hadn't heard about.

Then the TV screen filled with a single picture of lower Manhattan, probably taken from the building directly behind where Joey had been seated a few minutes ago. The image was nearly exactly what he'd seen from the park bench, only taken from a higher vantage point. It showed the enormous plume of grey dust that was still billowing in all directions. It looked like all of New York had been bombed.

Joey had to look away. He stared down at the counter-top and thought about all the people at Cambridge Partners. He conjured the nightmarish image of his friends descending the fire stairs as the building collapsed on them. How could anyone survive? Did they suffer? Did the floor fall away beneath their feet or did the floors above crush them? Was it painful or did death come quickly?

He began to sob. He couldn't remember the last time he'd cried; probably at his parents' funeral. That was sad. This was overwhelming. This was catastrophic. His tears flowed freely and he lowered his head onto the counter. He was embarrassed.

"Hey kid. You okay?" The soft voice came from the waitress behind the counter. She wore a name tag that introduced her as

Leslie and she could have been a double for Aunt Bea from the Andy Griffith show.

Joey wiped his eyes with his jacket sleeve and looked back at the TV screen. He nodded to indicate he'd heard the question and was okay.

"You want a cup of coffee? Might make you feel better. This is rough fucking shit." Leslie was no Aunt Bea.

He nodded a couple of times without saying a word.

"I'll get you some toast too."

"Thanks," he was finally able to say through the heavy sobs. He looked out the luncheonette window and was relieved to see only the cars parked on the street. The luncheonette didn't face the river so he was spared any more first-hand images of the calamity. He turned back to the TV.

The gruesome scene hadn't changed but now a woman's voice was over the footage. "… *have an eye witness on Wall Street, just outside the New York Stock Exchange who says he saw people falling from the north tower just before it began to collapse. Apparently, in desperation, some people who were trapped on the floors above the impact, who couldn't escape, leaped to their deaths. It's hard to imagine any circumstance that would…*"

"Here's your coffee. You want milk sweetie?" Leslie had returned with a smoking cup of coffee and two pieces of heavily buttered rye toast.

"What are they saying? What happened?" Joey asked.

"They're saying terrorists have hijacked a bunch of planes today and are crashing them into buildings. The cocksuckers must be really pissed about something because they're killing a shit load of people. They hit the Pentagon too."

"But who?"

"They're not saying yet, but I bet it's the fucking Arabs again. They're the ones that blew up the Trade Center in 1993, you know. It's got to be them. They came back to finish the job the first jerk-offs fucked up. Remember? They rented those trucks and used their own credit cards. Assholes."

A deep voice came from farther down the counter. "You don't know that, Leslie. You don't know shit." It was a black man, about the same age as Joey, dressed in a U.S. Postal Service uniform. He was eating some kind of sandwich with lettuce falling from the bread as he spoke.

"You watch, Sam. It's going to turn out to be the Arabs. You'll see." Leslie seemed convinced.

"Maybe. Well, somebody's gonna pay big time. Bush ain't gonna let this go."

Joey finished the coffee, then two more. He devoured the toast which seemed to fill a void in his gut. He wasn't sure if it was because he hadn't eaten all day or if he was just so upset. Whatever it was, he felt empty.

He, Leslie, Sam the postal worker, and three more older gentlemen at the far end of the counter, stared up at the TV for the next ninety minutes. They said very little other than to respond to the TV occasionally. A fox-hole camaraderie began to form, each drawing some comfort simply because they weren't alone. They were watching this with other people and just knowing that others were as frightened as they were made it a little more bearable.

The CNN announcers were getting most of their information directly from reporters on the ground in lower Manhattan and from the Associated Press, which somehow seemed to be scooping the more advanced technologies. By noon United Airlines had confirmed that flight 175 crashed in New York and that flight 93 had crashed in a field in Pennsylvania. A few minutes later America Airlines confirmed only that flights 11 and 17 were missing.

12:16 P.M.

CNN reported that all U.S. airspace had been closed. The reporter explained what he thought that meant; "…Almost 4,500 flights that were in the air over U.S. soil earlier this morning have either landed at their intended destination or were rerouted to other airports and forced to land. According to an unnamed spokesperson for the White House, this means the immediate threat of another terrorist strike from the air has been negated. FBI agents are on their way to the three known locations. That is, lower Manhattan, Washington, DC, and an area outside Shanksville, Pennsylvania. The last location, the site of the crash of United flight 93, being only a twenty-minute flight from our nation's Capitol."

One of the men from the end of the counter chimed in, "You have to think those bastards were on their way to the White House."

"Or the Capitol building." Leslie said as she nervously rewashed an otherwise clean spot on the counter top.

"Sounds like they got lost." Sam said. Then, as he rose from his stool, he added, "I need to get back to my dispatcher. He's going to be wondering where the hell I am. Not that any mail's gonna get delivered the rest of the day." He gave Leslie a familiar wave and ambled through the glass doors.

"He's good people." Leslie said. "Sam lost his brother in Iraq about ten years ago. He's never been the same since. The poor kid was blown up by some sort of land mine. He lost both legs and when he got back to the states he got some kind of infection and wound up dying. I'm not sure if Sam's more pissed at the towel heads who put the mine there or the U.S. government for the way they treated his brother afterwards. They didn't take very good care of him."

While Leslie was speaking the CNN reporter had offered an estimate of the number of people who worked in the World Trade Center. Joey hadn't heard the number but could tell from the reaction of the men at the other end of the counter, it had been astounding. For the first time since walking into the tiny luncheonette, he felt the need to say something.

"There might have been two hundred people at my company alone. And we were just a couple of floors." The words were directed at no one in particular, though he was looking at Leslie. He just felt the need to recognize that they were real people; people who had families and parents and other people who depended on them. They weren't just numbers for the sake of counting fatalities. To Joey, the announcer seemed only concerned with the numbers.

"Where did you work sweetie?" Leslie asked.

"A small company called Cambridge Partners. We were…" Joey thought about how to explain the complex world of Investment Banking to Leslie. "We traded stocks. Stuff like that." He decided that was all the explanation he had patience for today.

It was at that point he realized Cambridge Partners was gone. Even if some of the people got out alive, the company's infrastructure was gone. It's computers and systems were what gave it life. He knew there was very little remote backup for their systems; maybe none at all. The partners never wanted to spend money on such things. And without the systems and twenty to thirty critical people, there was no company.

For the first time since arriving in New Jersey and looking back on what had occurred in New York, Joey thought about himself. What if Cambridge really was gone? He'd have no place to go tomorrow. No job. No career. He hadn't been without a job since sophomore year in high school. He suddenly felt disconnected.

It wasn't that he defined himself by what he did, he never really felt comfortable on Wall Street anyway, it was just that he'd always worked at something. Tomorrow would bring an emptiness that he wouldn't know how to deal with. Nothing in his past had prepared him for unemployment. What would he do? Where would he spend his day? At home? Searching the internet for another research job?

Now this was personal. The realization that he'd lost his own job was setting in. No source of income after tomorrow! How long could he and Claire keep their apartment in Hoboken if she was the only bread winner? And then he considered the job market that would exist after today. What would Manhattan even look like? How long before it was business as usual on Wall Street? Would he ever be able to find work?

"So, you're a stock broker?" Leslie inquired.

"Yeah. Sort of."

"How long you been doing that? You look like a kid."

"I'm twenty-seven. I got this job right out of college. It's the only real job I've ever had." As he said the words, he realized how much of himself was invested in Cambridge. He may not have liked the work nor seen himself as a financial wiz but it was all he knew. He'd been so focused the last four years, he'd allowed time for little else. He had few other interests. His focus had been on making a living and doing what others expected of him. He'd become good at both but enjoyed neither.

"Well, you look like a kid." She followed up with, "You married?"

Again, Joey realized he hadn't thought about Claire. "Yeah, about four years now. She's a teacher."

"You should call her and let her know you're okay. If she's been watching TV, she probably thinks you're at the bottom of that pile of dust over there." Leslie motioned toward the door and what lay beyond. "The poor thing must be frantic."

Joey turned and looked out the large glass window. Bright rays of afternoon sun beamed through. There was nothing to indicate anything was wrong just a few miles to the east, across the Hudson. Then he looked back up at the TV screen. The image was of lower Manhattan shrouded in dark billowing dust. The ominous cloud was beginning to drift east and as it did, clearer air was filling in behind, offering the first vivid images of the destruction.

The television image was being taken from a camera some-where on the New Jersey side of the river. As the dust began to settle and the air began to clear on the western-most side of lower Manhattan, an enormous pile of debris was coming into focus. Seven World Trade Center was still ablaze but to its right, lay nothing but rubble piled several stories high. It was all that was left of the twin towers. A small section of the buildings' familiar façade lay at the bottom of the pile, eerily standing in defiance of what had occurred.

For some inexplicable reason, Joey felt an obligation to see the ruins first hand. The images from the television seemed surreal. They didn't encompass the thousands of people who'd just perished. He needed to bear witness to them in person.

He put a ten-dollar bill on the counter and said, "I need to go." As he exited the dimly lit luncheonette, the brightness of the day startled him. He shielded his eyes from the glaring sun which had now settled lower in the western sky.

Leslie's words about calling Claire were still in his mind. But first he needed to see for himself if what the media was transmitting was completely accurate, as terrible as they made it appear. How could it be?

He quickly walked the few blocks back to where he and Rita had been sitting in the riverside park. The old lady was gone. There was no one on the bench. Joey ran to the bench and stepped on to it to give him an elevated view of the city. Everything the TV had been showing was terribly real. He felt as if he'd been punched in the chest. For a moment, he couldn't catch his breath. They really were gone.

CHAPTER FIFTEEN

Joey Martinez staggered to a seated position on the wooden bench. He was beginning to hyperventilate and, for a moment, felt dizzy. He cradled his head in his hands and muttered aloud, "How could this happen?"

He was overwhelmed with grief; grief he didn't understand. There was grief for the people he worked with; many of them must have been killed by the collision of the plane. It seemed to have happened in direct line with Cambridge's floors. Many more were probably crushed as they descended the stairs and the building succumbed to its own weight. The few who did make it to the streets before the collapse were probably standing around on the plaza and crushed by the falling building they'd just escaped.

He also grieved for all the strangers; the people he'd seen in the elevators, lobbies, shops, and restaurants, as he came and went every day. Hundreds of people he'd know in an instant if he saw them in any other context, now buried under millions of tons of debris.

He grieved for the young reporter who, he suspected had made her way into his building just before the attack began and who may not have been able to get out. And there was Ginny, the receptionist, and Ray, the guy who ran the news stand in the lobby, and Manuel, the kid who brought around the coffee wagon. None of them deserved to die this way, this horrible way.

He wondered if they'd ever be able to even find their bodies. With a hundred and ten floors of concrete and steel falling on them, how could there be anything left of what had, moments before, been a person? Their poor families would have nothing to bury. Nothing to mourn. He pictured funerals with empty coffins being lowered into the ground just to satisfy foolish and morbid traditions.

A frigid chill ran through him as he realized how close he too had come to such a fate. If he hadn't left the office when he did, surely, his would have been among the thousands of pulverized bodies lying at the bottom of that horrible pile. Dead at twenty-seven. Nothing left for his widow to bury. He formed a vision of Claire in St. Matthew's church standing next to his empty casket, weeping for her husband who vanished beneath the rubble he used to work within.

Or, worse yet, what if they only found parts of him? What if, after falling ninety-four floors and having One World Trade Center rain down on his body, they were only able to piece together a couple of parts; a finger, an ear, maybe a foot. Would it be even worse for Claire to bury a few small parts of her dead husband and have the image of those dismembered parts burned into her memory? Every time she thought about him, she'd visualize those pieces lying in the casket. She wouldn't see his face, just the horrible image of body parts.

"Hey kid, you okay?" The question came from a tall black man standing next to the bench. He was holding a leash that led to a small spaniel of some sort. The man's face was worn by time but kind. He was wearing a blue New York Giants jersey.

Joey looked up from his hands and realized he'd been crying, probably out loud.

"Yeah man, I'm okay. Thanks."

"This is some kinda shit huh?" The old man pointed eastward.

Joey sighed deeply. "Yep. Some kind of shit is right."

"I was just watching the Price is Right on the TV and this shit come on. I couldn't believe what I was seeing. I had to come down here and see for myself. Bennie needed walking anyway." The man took a seat next to Joey on the bench.

"I was just thinking about the people in my office who must be..." Joey couldn't say the words.

"You work in the big buildings?"

"I used to."

"How the hell you get here?"

"I left my office about a quarter to nine and must have just missed it all. I took the Path here."

"You one lucky boy."

"Seems that way, doesn't it?"

"Seems that way? Boy if you were there, you'd be dead. Those poor souls is gone. They ain't never gonna find no one. It's like an atomic bomb went off over there."

"You might be right."

"What's your name boy?"

"Joey. Joey Martinez."

"Well, Joey Martinez, if you don't think you're one lucky bastard, you's an idiot. You dodged a bullet today kid, and I know something about dodging bullets. I was Newark PD for twenty-four years. I been shot at six times, hit three. Believe me kid, you got a whole new life handed to you today. What's that they say?" The old man seemed to be searching for something, then came up with, "Today's the first day of the rest of your life. That's what they say, ain't it?"

"I guess so."

"You guess so! Boy, you a fool. Thousands of people got killed today and you should have been one of them. Instead, you sitting here, talking to old Kenny. How do you not see that?"

He didn't give Joey a chance to respond. Instead, he rose from the bench and looked the young man in the eye. "Let me tell you something kid. A lot of terrible shit happened this morning. Maybe it ain't over even yet. Shit, they even blew up the Pentagon. But you, you got handed a gift today. You get to start a new life. It'd be a shame if you didn't see that."

Then he spoke to his dog. "Come on Benny. This kid's a fool. We'll go see what's happening by the tunnel."

Joey leaned back on the bench and ran his hands through his curly hair. The old man was right. And Joey wanted to tell him that, but by the time he focused, Kenny and his dog were too far away.

"You get to start a new life." The old man's words echoed in Joey's head. *"You get to start a new life."*

But in Joey's mind, what would begin tomorrow wasn't a new life. It would be a continuation of the old life, the one he wanted so desperately to change. It would mean starting the process of finding a new job, which would mean dealing with headhunters and countless interviews with second-tier companies. Joey didn't have the academic credentials for the top firms. He wasn't Ivy league.

And who knows what the market will be like? A terrorist attack would cause uncertainty in the markets and the markets hated uncertainty. That could mean Wall Street layoffs which would push thousands of talented and well-credentialed young people on to the street. With that kind of competition, he may never find a job.

Then there was Claire. If he really had a theoretical new life beginning today, would he choose to begin it again with Claire? So much of what seemed to make him feel out-of-place, had to do with Claire; her need for a family and the white picket fence. He loved her but did he love her enough to go along with her dreams and abandon his own?

And could he even define those dreams? All he knew for certain was that he wasn't happy with what he had or who he had or what he was doing. He didn't really know much more than that. He just assumed, no, he felt, that he was supposed to be doing something else. But what, and with whom and where?

He wondered how much of this thinking was because of Lonnie. She'd awoken a passion in him that had been asleep for several years; a passion for passion itself. Maybe she was the electricity he needed to jump start his life in a new direction. But what direction was that? And would Lonnie be a part of it?

He had so many more questions than answers. Yet he felt, sitting on that bench in Jersey City, that he was at a crossroad. Through this horrible twist of fate and the good fortune that had miraculously spared him, he had the opportunity few ever get; the opportunity to start anew. He could begin again. He could go back to school, study something new, be something new. But what? And what would Claire say and how would they pay for it?

He knew the moment he found a phone and called Claire, the inevitable gears of life would begin to turn again in the same wrong direction. Of course, Claire would be relieved to hear his voice. She'd want to know about his escape and where he'd been and why he wasn't at his desk with all the others. He couldn't tell her he truth- that he was running from a reporter who wanted to write a story about his infidelity. A reporter who was now probably dead because of him.

And he knew the moment he called Claire, he'd have chosen one of the crossroads, the one that led back to the life he'd come from. Yes, Kenny was right. He was a very lucky man. Most men who dodged a bullet would be thrilled to get a second chance at the life they had before. Most men would see that as a gift directly from God. Any of the men lying beneath the rubble in lower Manhattan would trade their souls for a second chance at the life they had before, for the chance to go home to their families one more night.

But, as he visualized his fork in the road, with the left path leading back home, he kept thinking about what the right path might lead to. He could imagine a bend in the path about a hundred yards ahead beyond which was the unknown. And with the unknown came possibilities; a clean canvas on which he could paint the story of the rest of his life.

He rose from the bench determined to do the right thing. He walked south, back toward the entrance to the Path train. He knew there were public pay phones there at the top of the stairs. He remembered seeing them when he passed earlier.

Three men and a woman were waiting at the phones, each calling a loved one to indicate their safety or inquire about the others'. The man at the phone closest to Joey was sobbing, "I'll be home soon, I promise. Yes, I'm fine. I'm fine."

When the man finished, he turned and wiped his eyes with the back of his shirt. "It's all yours brother."

Joey stepped toward the phone and pulled two quarters from his left pocket. He lifted the receiver and stared at the buttons for several seconds. Then he looked back at the smoke-filled skyline. Then back at the phone. He dropped the two coins into the slot and held the receiver against his chest. He glanced south beyond the terminal and could see a battered green sign that read, "TURNPIKE 2 MILES".

Without dialing her number, he spoke into the receiver, "I'm so sorry Claire".

Then, he began walking.

CHAPTER SIXTEEN

10:08 A.M. September 11, 2006

Claire Martinez stood in somber silence as the names of the nearly three thousand victims were being read by family and friends. The cool September morning blew against her face. Tears rolled down her cheeks as she heard the name William Connelly, one of Joey's friends from Cambridge read aloud by his son. It would be almost another hour before Joey's name would be read alphabetically. When the name Sarah Bideaux was read, it meant nothing to her.

Beside her stood her daughter. Amanda was only four and didn't understand the significance of the morning but she knew her mother cried every time someone mentioned the name Joey, the father she'd never met. She wore a yellow dress with white lace at the collar, just like the one mom had on. Amanda understood that there were a lot of people standing around, seemingly doing nothing, many of them crying. She knew this must be a very sad place and so maintained the silence Claire had asked for in the car.

For the fifth year in a row, the families of the victims gathered at what had become known as ground zero. They listened to speeches by local politicians, prayers from the bishop, and the ringing of the bell which commemorated the moments each of the towers fell. Today was no different but took on added significance because it was the fifth anniversary. Some thought after five years there would be closure. They were wrong.

As anonymous young people read names starting with "D", then "E", Claire drifted back to that horrible day. She remembered watching television all day, something she'd never done before. There were no commercials. It was all too serious for interruptions about laundry detergent or beer. She sat on a small ottoman in front of the television as the towers fell. Her mother called her several times throughout the day to inquire about Joey.

As she watched the second tower fall from the sky, she knew she'd lost her husband. Something told her he'd just vanished, along with thousands of others. She felt it in her heart. Yet, she held on to the hope that perhaps he'd been able to climb down the ninety-four flights of stairs. Perhaps he was safe but just stranded in Manhattan like so many others marooned on the island. She knew he'd forgotten his phone that day so maybe it would take him a few hours to find a working pay phone. There'd been reports on the news that the phone system in New York was corrupted by the collapse of Tower One. Something about the antenna.

But by three in the afternoon, she hadn't heard from him and was beginning to get calls from other Cambridge wives sharing stories of the horror. Julia Connelly had called to say her husband Bill had called her from the ninety-seventh floor saying they were trapped there and couldn't get down. They said their tearful goodbyes on the phone and then at 10:28, the line went dead. He'd not mentioned Joey.

And she got a call from Carol Manning whose son worked just a few desks from Joey. She hadn't heard from Jeff, her only son, all day. She was hysterical on the phone and Claire could offer no comfort.

There was also a call from the mother of Ginny, the receptionist on Joey's floor. She'd been speaking with her daughter on the phone just moments before the first plane hit the tower. Ginny was supposed to call her back in a few minutes with the address of a coffee shop they'd planned to meet at later that day. When she didn't call after fifteen minutes, her mother, who at this point was still unaware of the attack, dialed her office only to get a recording stating the call could not be connected as dialed.

Claire recalled the emptiness of not having a body to bury. No one ever called to say, "Your husband is dead". No one ever confirmed Joey was even there. Only a small handful of Cambridge employees survived; those who were still in the lobby on their way to work or in the elevators. Claire learned later that everyone on Joey's floor must have been killed instantly when the plane struck with thousands of gallons of jet fuel. The catastrophic explosion meant spontaneous incineration of those on the ninety-fourth floor. She drew little comfort knowing he probably didn't suffer.

For days, she waited for someone to come to the door with confirmation of Joey's death. No one ever did. Her mom and dad drove up from Myrtle beach to be with her so she didn't have to wait alone. They stayed several weeks. Finally, on September 30th, she relented and agreed to hold a memorial service for Joey. There was no casket, no body, not even a few ashes to mourn.

The medical examiner's office had contacted her a few times. First, to obtain a DNA sample which Claire obliged by removing several dark hairs from Joey's brush. Then later, thinking they had a match with a portion of a fingernail found at the cite. But it turned out not to be Joey's. The same thing happened again the following January. Claire got a call from the ME's office that they'd made a positive DNA match to a bone fragment the size of a period at the end of a sentence. But when they ran the test a second time, the results were not conclusive.

So, there was never any closure; never a funeral or graveside prayer. She always wondered what had become of Joey's wedding ring. She would have liked to have had that.

This morning, the speeches by the mayor and others were hollow reminders of the emptiness she felt. When the young people finally started reading names that began with "M" Claire bent down to let her daughter know they could go home soon.

"Almost there, honey. Listen for daddy's name. Then we'll go have lunch."

Amanda looked up at her and said, "Is it going to make you cry again, mommy?"

"I think so, honey. Maybe one more time, okay?"

On the other side of the cavernous hole that was now ground zero, Lonnie Rossetti stood alone.

That evening, back in their Hoboken apartment, Claire and Amanda tried to forget about the morning's event by playing Amanda's favorite game- "What's missing?" Claire would lay out six of Amanda's favorite books. Usually they did this on the floor. Then she would tell Amanda to close her eyes and remove one or more of the books.

"Okay, you can open your eyes."

Amanda studied the remaining books for several seconds, then announced, "The Pokey Puppy" and "Elmo Goes Shopping". "That was an easy one mommy."

Claire was glad she could take her mind off the memorial service. It was so draining to go through this every year, especially when she felt she did it every day anyway. Why did she need to do it with thousands of strangers around? She was determined that this was the last time she'd go. There was still talk of a formal memorial and museum at the site but both were still just in the planning phases. If it ever happens, I'll go to that, she thought.

After putting Amanda to bed, Claire made herself a cup of tea and sat at the kitchen table sipping the warm brew. This was the time of day she was most alone. She missed Joey. She missed sharing her life with another adult. As wonderful as motherhood was, it was lonely raising Amanda by herself. Her parents came up a few times a year and she would bring Amanda down to them, but it was the quiet nights like this that were most isolating; the times you wanted an adult to share your thoughts with but were left with only the stuffed animals that needed to be put away.

It was just past nine when the phone rang. Claire didn't recognize the caller ID and considered not answering, but her loneliness got the better of her.

"Claire Martinez?" The voice was masculine and strong.

"This is Claire. Who's this?"

"Claire, my name is Brad Muller. We met at a dinner party several years ago hosted by Cambridge Partners. I don't expect you to remember me. My wife was Cindy Muller. She worked with your husband."

"Actually, I do think I remember you." Claire recalled. "You were into horses, right?"

"Wow, good memory. Yes, we were both riders. I'm surprised you remembered. I don't think we spoke more than a moment or two at that party."

Claire did remember. She recalled Cindy was one of the associates hired around the same time as Joey. There had been a few events to which the associates were permitted to invite spouses, and Claire got to know Cindy casually. She only remembered meeting Brad once. He was very tall and very good looking. Perhaps that's why she remembered. She also recalled he was some sort of international banker and apparently, very successful. He and Cindy had no children and took enviable vacations to Europe. That's about all she remembered.

"Were you there today?" She asked.

"Yes. I saw you there but didn't want to push my way through the crowd to say hello. But that's why I'm calling."

"I hate to sound cruel and uncaring, but those things are starting to wear me out. I'm not sure I'll go next year. Maybe when the memorial opens someday."

"I feel the same way. It's not that I want to forget, but I need to… I don't know, move ahead. I feel like those things somehow drag me back to the way I felt when Cindy died."

"I understand." Claire said honestly. "So, what can I do for you Brad?"

"Well…, I was hoping you'd consider having dinner with me next Saturday?"

"You mean, like a date?"

"Yes, like a date."

CHAPTER SEVENTEEN

The helicopter banked to the right over the flat Florida landscape. As far as one could see, there was little more than swamp. The pilot used his right hand to indicate a spot on the ground he was going to land. It appeared to be little more than a postage stamp of solid soil but as the Heliwing-II descended the two passengers could see why the pilot had chosen this spot. In an otherwise flat world, this spit of dry land, only about ten feet above sea level, would provide the best viewing area.

"I don't think this is it, Jimmy, but we might as well take a look." Micah Wells said to his long-time pilot and friend.

"Okay, but wait till the rotors stop completely before you get out."

The aircraft settled gently to the ground and the skids dug into the soft soil. The cacophony of wind and rotors and engine noise immediately ended, followed by complete silence. There was nothing around for many miles, nothing as far as anyone could see in any direction. Micah jumped out and surveyed the scene. A moment later, the other passenger, a man with olive skin, and dark hair pulled back in a pony-tail, stepped from the copter. He took in a deep breath and held it.

Ordinarily, Micah would not have been in Florida in September. The winter circuit didn't start for another four months. But he was here today for two reasons; to scout for a viable site on which to build his dream, and to meet his future in-laws.

"I don't think this is it either, Micah. There's just too much bog and water to get rid of." He said with a slight Spanish accent.

Now the pilot exited the cockpit to have a look too. He knew his boss and Jose were looking for land for their new project, but he had no idea what would qualify as satisfactory. All he knew was that Micah had asked him to fly them about fifteen miles to the west of Wellington so they could look at land no one else had ever considered. "Virgin land", he called it.

"I think you're right, Jose. It would take years for this area to be dry enough, even if we could pump the water to the west."

"And the EPA will never let us do that. There's too much sugar cane west of here. That's big business to central Florida. They don't want brackish water seeping into their fields and killing off the cane."

"All right. So, I guess we need to look a little closer to town then. Jimmy, let's go up again but try to fly low enough so we can get a sense of where the soil might be solid enough. There's got to be a point at which it switches from this shit to drier land."

"You got it boss. I just need to take a leak first."

As Jimmy relieved himself near the front of the sleek aircraft, Jose and Micah continued to look to the east. "The closer we get to Wellington, the more it's going to cost. You know that Micah." Jose wasn't telling his friend anything he didn't already know.

"I know, but maybe we can find the place where the change happens. We can always do the same kind of canal system they've got now. Shit, you know how much waterfront property they manufactured when they set up those canals? We can do the same thing.

I'm thinking 20% of the project is for the showgrounds and the other 80% gets sold off to developers for homes."

"I didn't realize you were thinking that big. If you use two hundred acres for the showgrounds, you're talking about eight hundred acres for homes? Really?"

Micah was unfazed by the skepticism. "Yep. You need to remember, some of those homes are going to be farms, some maybe twenty acres each. Maybe more." Then he added, "Think big my friend."

"So, you're looking for over a thousand acres then?"

"Why not. If we're going to build a world class equestrian center, let's do it right." Micah turned to the pilot, "You ready Jimmy? Let's see if we can make one more stop on the way back."

"Hop in." The pilot offered as he held the heavy plastic door open for his guests. "I'm just flying it. It's your helicopter."

As the rotors began to whirl again, Jose glanced at his watch to see how much more daylight they could depend on. As he did, he noticed the date, 9-11-06. He hadn't thought about it all day though he was aware of the anniversary. It was not only the anniversary of the catastrophe in New York that ended so many lives, it was the anniversary of the beginning of his; the day he went from being Joey Martinez to Jose of Wellington. The day he was reborn.

CHAPTER EIGHTEEN

As the sleek aircraft whirled its way back toward Wellington, Jose peered down at the ground whizzing by. Just as the land was flying past, so too had the last five years. It was almost a blur.

Once Joey left the pay phone in Jersey City, he started to walk west, toward the New Jersey Turnpike. He knew once he started, there'd be no turning back, no way to undo what he was about to do. He was leaving it all behind; his life, his wife, his career and his identity. He wanted a clean start, a chance to remake his life. And he knew he could never explain this to Claire. It was better that she thought he'd been killed with all the others. It would hurt less.

He hadn't walked ten minutes when a red pick-up truck pulled up next to him and the driver offered him a ride. It seemed the events of 9-11 were bringing out the best in people and Marty, the driver was on his way back to Philadelphia anyway and was happy to have the company.

"Where you headed?" He asked through the window.

Joey thought it sad that he did not have an answer for the question. Where was he headed? He had no idea. He just knew he needed to get far away from where he stood.

"South?"

"Good for you. I'm getting on the pike headed to Philly. I can take you that far. Hop in."

They rode in complete silence for several minutes, then the driver introduced himself. "I'm Marty. Marty Bruscia. I was in Boston this morning delivering some parts when I heard about this shit on the radio. I hear one of the planes took off from Boston, from Logan. You hear that?"

Joey had to admit he knew very little of the facts. All he knew was firsthand; he watched it firsthand and he barely escaped it firsthand. But he chose not to share his real-life experiences of the morning with Marty. Instead he asked, "What was it you delivered in Boston?"

"Our company makes parts for mufflers. There's a big assembly plant just outside Boston. They're a big customer. Today it was aluminum bolts for the upper chamber."

Joey feigned interest and looked out at the New Jersey countryside whisking by. There were very few cars on the road. More than once, he peered into a passing car and saw the driver crying. He assumed they were listening to their radios.

They hit the Philly exit around 4:30 P.M. Marty let Joey off at the first truck stop after the exit. He said it would be the best place to pick up another ride south and he was right. Within fifteen minutes, Joey had a ride in the cab of an eighteen-wheeler headed to Savannah, Georgia. The rig was empty, on its return trip from New York where it had unloaded several hundred wooden chairs. The driver was a woman named Sally.

"So…, what's your deal?" Sally wanted to know before they even crossed into Delaware.

Understanding he'd be in the cab with this woman for over twelve hours, Joey debated with himself about how much information he should share with Sally. It's not as if anyone would be looking for him. That was the beauty of disappearing in the midst of a disaster; no one would be looking for him because everyone would assume he was dead, pulverized beneath a million tons of debris. He assumed there would be lots of similar situations, people who were in the Trade Center this morning who would never be found.

Still, he decided it best if he kept as quiet as possible. He made up a story about being stranded in New York because the airports were closed. According to his story, he needed to get back to Jacksonville Florida by Friday for his dad's seventieth birthday party, so he really appreciated the ride. Instead of talking about himself, he asked questions of Sally and learned she'd been driving big rigs for about ten years and used to be a nurse.

"I went to four years of college to be a nurse. I always wanted to be a nurse, since I was a kid. And as soon as I got out of college and landed my first job at a hospital, I realized I hated it. I couldn't stand dealing with other people's misery all day long. It was so depressing. It just wasn't for me."

"So, you gave it up right away?" Joey inquired.

"No, sweetie. After my parents shelled out eighty grand for college I couldn't just walk away. I stuck it out for three years, three of the longest years of my life. It's not an exaggeration to say I hated every minute." Sally checked her side mirror and changed lanes to pass a car towing a U-Haul.

"When you finally quit, did you know what you wanted to do?"

She thought about that for a while as she drove down interstate 95. Joey noticed she wasn't a particularly pretty woman. She had a face with hard features, almost masculine, but not one you'd call ugly. Joey guessed she probably packed on an extra twenty pounds since she started driving but her forearms weren't fat, in fact they seemed quite muscular as they gripped the large steering wheel. Joey decided if she were dressed properly, people might say she was a "handsome" woman.

"I had no idea. That was the scary part for me. I knew I hated being a nurse, but I didn't know what I really wanted. It's funny though, I always felt like I was supposed to be doing something else, something not at all like nursing. I bounced around from one part-time job to another for about a year. Shit, I even became a bank teller for a few months. Hated that too, but not as much as nursing."

The parallels to his own life weren't lost on Joey. He knew exactly how she felt and he wanted her to know he felt the same way. He wanted to tell her he thought what she'd done was brave.

"So how did you wind up driving an eighteen-wheeler? That's a long way from banking."

"Well, after I left the bank, I got a night job as a delivery person for this drug store in Alpharetta, where I'm from. Turns out I really liked working on my own. I also liked spending long hours in the car driving around a pretty big county. So, a friend of mine, who drove short runs of food deliveries, just from Atlanta to Charlotte and back, he told me to get my CDL and try driving for a living. He said the money was good. He was right about that. I make more than I did nursing and I don't have to deal with nobody's bedpans."

As they rolled down Interstate 95 and the sun set on the Virginia countryside, Joey wrestled with his thoughts. He'd told Sally he thought what she'd done to change her life was brave, yet when he thought about it for himself, he couldn't come up with the same word. He felt what he was doing was anything but brave. He couldn't help feeling like he was running away from all his responsibilities. But aside from Claire, what was he really responsible for? As of this morning, he probably didn't have a job. He and Claire had no debts, no mortgage, no car loan. It's not as if he was running from creditors or the law.

So why then did he feel like his life-changing transformation was any less noble than Sally's? It was Claire. He knew he was causing her pain. But if he'd stayed and they couldn't improve their relationship, would he wind up leaving at some point anyway. And would that have been any easier on Claire? Would she feel better as a tragic widow or as someone whose husband grew bored with their marriage and abandoned her?

As the darkness outside the truck grew deeper, inside the cab the air began to get cold. Joey braced himself against his jacket to stay warm. As he did he felt something uncomfortable; something jabbing him in the left side. It was something hard in his jacket pocket. He reached in and felt the envelope, the one filled with cash that Claire handed him as he left the apartment this morning. He pulled it half way out of his jacket and discretely glanced inside. The sixteen one-hundred dollar bills were supposed to be payment of the only debt Joey was leaving behind, the one his friends the Chattertons had laid out for their ski trip; the one he'd never go on.

He slid the envelope back into his pocket and silently thanked Claire for her unintended gift. That cash plus the sixty dollars in his wallet would be his lifeline for a while. He'd have to make it last. He certainly couldn't use his credit cards. He was supposed to be dead. Dead men don't charge their hotel rooms in other states. He made a mental note to destroy the four credit cards he carried in his wallet as soon as he had the chance.

The credit cards made him wonder, for the first time, about the logistics of his serendipitous decision. How would he develop a new identity? What name would he chose? What prior life would he invent to tell others? How would he get a new Social Security number? How does someone who didn't exist before today get credit? There was much to consider. Fortunately, he had many hours of silent reflection ahead of him on his journey. Sally wasn't much of a conversationalist.

Thinking about money made him think of Claire again. Would she be okay financially? She certainly knew how to handle money. She was, after all, the one who paid all their bills and ran their savings accounts. But would she have enough to stay in their apartment? If Cambridge Partners was gone, would she get anything from his company life insurance plan? He cursed himself for not paying closer attention to what that benefit would be when the lady from personnel explained it all to him.

"Okay with you if we stop for twenty minutes so I can get a bite and take a leak? There's a place about ten miles further, outside Richmond." Sally was clearly used to her routine and probably stopped at the same places on every trip up and down the Interstate.

"That sounds good to me."

"I recommend the apple turnovers. And stay away from the chili. He makes it on Saturday and makes it last the whole week." Sally knew her roadside stops.

After the pit stop and a refueling, Sally and Joey drove through the lower half of Virginia and most of North Carolina without saying much. The darkness became Sally's companion as it had so many trips before. She handed Joey a pouch of CDs, mostly Country Western, and offered to have him chose the music for this leg of the journey. Knowing very little about Country Western music, he picked Johnny Cash's Greatest Hits followed by a Reba McIntyre, basically, the only two artists he recognized. Sally seemed pleased with his choices and Johnny and Reba's melodies filled the cab for nearly four hours as the black pavement rolled by beneath them.

Around midnight, Joey suggested they listen to the radio to see what, if any, developments there were in New York. President Bush had spoken to the nation on television at 8:30 EST and assured a worried populous that America's enemies and those who help them would be treated alike and destroyed. "*The search is under way for those who are behind these evil acts. I've directed the full resources of our intelligence and law enforcement communities to find those responsible and bring them to justice. We will make no distinction between the terrorists who committed these acts and those who harbor them.*" The local Charlotte radio station replayed the speech several times.

The radio announcer also reported that rescue workers had begun to pull survivors from the wreckage. The first survivor found was a Port Authority policeman who was trapped under twenty feet of debris.

"Hard to believe that anyone could survive that." Sally said as she made a lane change.

"Wow. I would have thought there'd be nothing left of the victims. I mean after that much concrete and steel comes down, how could anyone survive?" Joey was beginning to question the wisdom of his prior assumptions. He believed his ploy was nearly fool proof based on the assumption that hundreds, if not thousands, of people would be lost and completely crushed by the weight of the two skyscrapers. With that much force and mass, he thought bodies would be completely disintegrated and never found. Or at least he believed not enough human tissue would remain for positive identification.

But here was a case of a person surviving. The policemen didn't just avoid pulverization, he survived. Joey wondered how many more would be found. Maybe it wasn't at all the way he'd imagined. What if his was the only body never found? What would the authorities assume had happened to him? What would Claire think?

What Joey didn't know, what the world didn't know, was that Officer William Jimeno would be one of only eighteen people found alive. The last survivor, another Port Authority employee Genelle Guzman, would be pulled from the rubble the following afternoon. After that, only the dead were taken from the pile, as it came to be called.

Joey found he couldn't sleep. Even with the gentle rocking of the moving vehicle, something that usually relaxed him easily, he couldn't relax his racing mind. Too much had happened today. There was too much to think about. He considered the events of the last twenty-four hours in which the world's paradigm had changed. Everything was different, not just for him but for everyone. His country was suddenly at war, but with who?

And he thought about all the issues he'd have to deal with in the next twenty-four hours; a place to sleep, a name, an identity, a destination. It was overwhelming and kept sleep away the entire night.

Fortunately, Sally thrived on the adrenaline being pumped from the dashboard radio and had no trouble staying focused on the road. Occasionally, she'd glance over at her passenger and wonder why he wasn't asleep. But she was used to having guests in her cab and she didn't really care if they slept or not, as long as they didn't gab incessantly. In the morning, they'd be gone anyway.

As the sun began to rise on the South Carolina landscape, she suggested another pit stop. This time she and Joey ate a hearty breakfast together in a booth near the window of the truck stop. Joey hadn't realized just how hungry he was until after finishing a four-stack of pancakes. With a full belly, he felt better, better able to think through the next few hours of his new life.

When they got back in the truck Sally explained that she would drop him off at the interstate exit for Savannah rather than taking him all the way to town. If he needed to get to Jacksonville, he'd have a better chance with his thumb out at the exit ramp. Or, she explained, "You can probably get a bus from Savannah, but I have no idea what sort of schedule they run on."

"I'll take my chances on the exit ramp, thanks." Joey was already thinking about rationing the little money he had. No point in wasting any on a bus ride to a made-up destination.

They rode the last two hours through the lowlands of South Carolina listening to the radio. They learned details about the plane crash in Shanksville, but at this point, no one was aware of the heroism that occurred on flight 93 over Pennsylvania.

There were few new details about the tragedy in New York. The stories focused on the rescue effort and the fact that over three-hundred New York firefighters were feared lost. According to the reporter, many of the firefighters were in the stairwells helping the tenants down or carrying fifty-foot lengths of hose up the stairs. Most of the firefighters in the north tower were unaware the south tower had collapsed and continued to do their perilous jobs while everyone else was fleeing the doomed building.

"Your exit's coming up honey. County road 404 cuts across here all the way to Savannah but you don't want that. Stay on the interstate. You'll do better." Sally advised as they approached a large sign that beckoned tourists to enjoy the beaches of Georgia. She slowed the huge rig down and stopped on the graveled shoulder so Joey could safely exit. "Good luck kid. Tell your dad Happy Birthday for me."

CHAPTER NINETEEN

It took only fifteen minutes for Joey to get picked up again. This time it was by an elderly couple on their way to Boca Raton, their winter retreat.

"We're just a couple of early snow birds," Marion, the more talkative of the two, explained. "We live on Long Beach in the summer. We have an apartment there but we're only there from May to Labor Day. Then we head back to Boca. Marv can't stand the fall. He said he finds the falling leaves too depressing. Reminds him that death is coming."

"It is!" The driver said. "At my age, that's about all you think about."

Joey was happy to take a back seat both in the Camry and to the conversation that continued through Georgia and across the Florida border. Marion was right. Her husband of fifty-two years was obsessed with death, mostly his own. And the events of the prior day weren't helping. He was eager to offer his view on the terrorists, "A bunch of Arab bastards," he was sure. "They probably killed five thousand innocent people and Bush probably won't do a damn thing. He doesn't want to upset the god damn Arabs because we need their oil. Maybe he'll have the Israelis do something about it. You know he's done that before."

"Oh, shut up Marvin. This young man doesn't want to listen to your rantings about America conspiring with the Arabs. It's too nice a morning."

Marion was right. It was a beautiful morning in northern Florida. And if it weren't for their chronic bickering, he might have been happy to recline in the back seat, with the sun shining on his left and the orange groves whizzing by on the right. But they argued about almost everything. If the radio commentator reported the local weather would be sunny all day, Marv would take the position that the Florida weathermen are all in the pockets of the Florida department of tourism. "They always say it's going to be beautiful down here. That's just so they can attract more tourists."

And Marion would respond with her own view, which was always exactly the opposite of his. And so, at the rest area near Daytona Beach Joey announced he would not be continuing on with them. "I think I'll spend a few days visiting an old college buddy in Daytona", he lied. "But thanks for the lift. I really appreciate it. You guys have a nice winter."

As Marion and Marvin Slotnick drove off, Joey spotted the ubiquitous golden arches of McDonalds about a quarter mile from the highway. He decided to treat himself to his favorite lunch, a quarter-pounder with cheese and a vanilla shake. He slung his jacket over one shoulder and walked to the combination McDonalds and convenience store.

He used the restaurant's bathroom to wash his face and hands. The mirror over the small sink was made of some sort of reflective metal, not glass and his image appeared cloudy. Still, it was the face of a very tired man, a man who hadn't slept soundly since he woke up in the arms of another woman two days ago. Since then, life had been turned upside down and inside out. Nothing was as it had been.

After enjoying his cheeseburger and shake, Joey wandered into the adjoining store and purchased a tee shirt, sun glasses and a Florida Gators baseball cap. He also bought a backpack into which the put his sport jacket and oxford shirt. He still had on the khakis and loafers he'd started the previous day with but at least now he felt like a Florida tourist, not a New York Investment Banker. As he pushed open the store door he dropped the sunglasses into place, donned the cap and began the half mile walk back to the interstate.

Even before he reached the highway, a yellow Nissan pulled up beside him and an attractive thirty-something blonde with a pony tail and a Miami Dolphins shirt stuck her head out the passenger's window. "Need a ride?"

"I'm heading south on 95."

"Cool, so are we." She said. "Hop in."

Joey tossed his new backpack into the back seat and climbed in. "Thanks so much. I'm Joey."

"I'm Wendy and this is Tony," she said pointing to the driver with her thumb. "We're going all the way to Key West. How about you?"

"Miami would be great." Joey had given some thought to a destination while having lunch. It occurred to him that, absent any other immediate plans, he would take a few weeks to hang out on the beach and think about the future. Maybe he could pick up a part-time job and grab a cheap motel room while he planned the rest of his life, or at least the next phase of it. He assumed the sixteen hundred dollars he had in his pack would hold him for a few weeks even if he couldn't find work. Also, Miami would be a place he could blend in. With his fluent Spanish and olive complexion, he'd look like a million other Latinos in southeast Florida, even if he'd never thought of himself as one before.

"Okay. Miami, it is. That's probably only three more hours. Where you from Joey?"

He thought about the question. At some point, he would need to script a completely different past for himself. He'd need to have answers to questions like this and others. Ever been married? Where'd you go to school? Got any kids? Parents still alive? What do you do?

But for today, he'd be Joey one more time, at least until he got to Miami. "New York area, mostly Jersey lately."

"Were you there yesterday when those fuckers hit the Trade Center?" The driver wanted to know.

"Yep, but I was off yesterday so I watched the whole thing from a park bench on the Jersey side."

"No shit? Did you see the planes hit the building?"

Joey wasn't in the mood to relive yesterday's tragic events or share any more information about himself so he just said, "No, just later, after they collapsed."

Tony wasn't satisfied. "So, what do you mean you watched from a park?"

"I was sitting, reading a book, on a park bench on the Jersey side of the river." It occurred to Joey these two might never have been to New York and wouldn't be familiar with the landscape. Based on their accents, they didn't get out of the trailer park often. They had deep south tongues but with a hint of Appalachian back country to distinguish them from properly educated southerners. He guessed they were both about thirty and would have been surprised to learn if either had finished high school. He wondered if he was just being a judgmental elitist. They seemed like nice enough people.

"Have you ever been to New York?"

Wendy was the first to chime in. "I once was at JFK airport on my way to Pittsburg. We had to change planes there but I never got to see nothin.'"

Tony explained the farthest north he'd ever been was Washington, D.C. "I ain't mixed much with you Yankees."

So, Joey explained the geography surrounding Manhattan as they rolled down the interstate. "The Hudson River sort of divides New Jersey and New York before it empties out in the harbor where the Statue of Liberty is. The Trade Center is at the bottom of Manhattan, which is an Island."

"You mean was." Tony added.

"Pardon me?"

"The Trade Center ain't there no more. Just a big pile of shit now. I saw it on the news this morning at the diner."

Joey was surprised that he was offended by this hick's referral to what used to be his home as a pile of shit. Until yesterday it was two majestic skyscrapers that housed thousands of people by day and glistened by night. And today it was a pile of dead bodies, many of whom were Joey's workmates. It was a graveyard, not a pile of shit.

To avoid an uncomfortable confrontation with his host he decided to drop it and remain quiet for the next two hours. Based on the conversation he overheard between Tony and Wendy, he assumed Tony had a temper. He also had several prominent tattoos on his arm and neck, although Joey had no idea what they were. Wendy too had spent time in a tattoo parlor. On the underside of her left arm, running from elbow to wrist, was a swirling serpent.

Joey spent the next two hours thinking about what sort of work he'd like to try once he got to Miami and settled into a motel. If he was truly going to remake his life, why not try something totally new? Nothing related to finance or Wall Street in any way. Something completely different, but what? Having a totally blank canvas was liberating but also frightening for its lack of direction. Maybe carpentry, he'd always enjoyed those sorts of projects he'd done with his dad. Or maybe something related to music, or animals, or the environment.

Or maybe he could register with some sort of temp agency and get sent on a different assignment almost every day. That might be best as a start. He could sample many different fields and see what interested him most. It would be exciting to do something different every day. In his other life, he was tied to the same desk and routine day after painful day.

For the first time in the last twenty-four hours, he felt encouraged. He wasn't rushed. There was no timeline for him to make a decision. If he chose to do one thing for a month, then something else for a day, he was completely free to do just that. There was no one to answer to, no expectations of him. He wasn't working to achieve someone else's dream. He could have his own dream. And he was free to pursue it or not.

It then occurred to him that he'd have to come up with a new identity and, more importantly, documentation supporting that identity. Surely, employers would want a social security number and maybe even work history. He had no idea how one could obtain a bogus I.D. or driver's license or social security card. The last time he needed fake I.D. was when he was seventeen and wanted to be able to buy beer.

Even if he worked at a temp agency, they'd want some I.D. to put him on a payroll. He decided he'd have to do some research, maybe at a library, to determine what employers will be looking for. So, maybe his first few days in Miami, his new home, would be spent in a library researching how he could re-enter the human race, or at least the documented human race.

He decided to begin his research while still in the Nissan. "Tony, I'm going to be looking for a job after I settle down in Miami. But, I lost my social security card a long time ago. Do you think I'll need to get a new one?"

"How the fuck would I know?"

"No, I just thought you'd remember from when you started your last job."

"It's been a long time since I worked for anyone who'd ask for a social security card." He looked over at Wendy and gave her an impish grin.

Joey picked up on the clue that Tony wasn't part of corporate America, and pressed the matter into an area Tony might have more expertise. "Well, what if I just wanted to get a new one, maybe even a fake one?"

"Why would you want a fake one if you have a real one?"

"Well, maybe I don't want Uncle Sam taking a big slice of what I earn." Joey watched Tony's eyes in the rearview mirror for a reaction. But before Tony responded, Wendy asked, "Hey, can we stop at the next rest area? I've really gotta pee."

"Sure, honey lips. There's one coming up in two miles. How bout you, Yankee? You gotta pee?"

The roadside rest area was just that; a place to rest and use a toilet. There were no other services, no vending machines, no gas, and no staff. It was one of those places the state of Florida lays out every fifty miles or so for the relief of its drivers, usually truckers, who just need to rest their eyes a few minutes and maybe take a leak.

Tony pulled the Nissan into a spot about a hundred feet from the only building, the one with two restrooms clearly marked men and women. Wendy hurried from the car and disappeared behind the appropriate door. Joey wasn't sure how long it would be till he had another opportunity so he decided to use the facilities as well. As he stepped from the car he remembered his backpack and considered leaving it in the car for the few minutes it would take to accomplish his mission. "Are you going to lock the car, Tony?"

But Tony was already out and on his way to the restrooms. He hadn't locked the car so Joey grabbed the pack and slung it over his back.

The restroom was surprisingly clean and well maintained. The men's room had three urinals and one stall. Tony was already standing at one of the urinals. Joey chose the one next to Tony. He was glad he decided to pee. He needed to more than he thought. He looked straight ahead at the ceramic tiles and felt relief. Then he felt a hand on the back of his neck!

Tony had stepped away from his urinal and grabbed Joey's neck. As Joey struggled to understand, he was pulled away from the wall, then violently pushed at it. The last thing he felt was the pain of his forehead crashing into the ceramic. Then he felt nothing.

Tony let the lifeless body drop to the floor then relieved Joey of his backpack and wallet. He was back in the car fifteen seconds later. Wendy was waiting in the passenger seat. He tossed her the wallet and pack as he started the car and drove back to the highway. She opened the pack and unfolded the sports jacket. An envelope fell out.

"Holy shit Tony! We hit the jackpot on this one!"

CHAPTER TWENTY

The first thing he saw was color; reds, whites and blues, all flashing somewhere off to his left. He was lying on something very hard and uncomfortable. His head throbbed.

"Can you hear me sir?" The voice was deep and authoritative.

Joey tried to focus but his eyes weren't doing what his brain asked. He saw something bright and shiny directly in front of his face. It came into focus a moment later, a silver badge.

"Sir, can you hear me?" The Florida State Trooper was kneeling beside him, holding his head off the cold restroom floor.

Joey moaned, "Where am I?"

"You're on the floor of a rest area on Interstate 95. Do you know how you got here?"

Joey just groaned, "My head is killing me."

"You've got a pretty good bump up there," the officer said referring to Joey's forehead. "I've already called for an ambulance. They should be here soon. "I'm trooper Brashman. What's your name?' He asked with a very sympathetic tone while preparing to write on his pad.

The room began to come into focus now. Joey could see the ceiling light fixture above him and the face of a mature policeman. The trooper must have been in his late fifties and had the worn look of a man who spent a lot of time outdoors. His face was chiseled with wrinkles and his grey hair was cropped close under his wide brimmed hat.

Joey tried to sit up but the officer put his hand firmly on Joey's chest and said, "You'd better stay put until the EMT's get here. They may not want you moving around too much till they're sure you don't have any neck or back injuries. And I need your name for my report, sir."

"Joe Martinez." But the moment he said it, he realized he may have made a mistake.

Joey brought his left hand up to feel the throbbing area on his forehead. He could feel a significant bump over his right eye and it stung to the touch. "Jesus, what the hell happened?"

"That's what I was hoping you would tell me. These nice folks found you on the ground about fifteen minutes ago and I just got here." He motioned to his left where an elderly couple stood a few feet away.

When Joey saw the man and woman standing by the doorway, he began to remember. He recalled standing at the urinal and seeing Tony step away and then go behind him. He remembered feeling the hand on his back then the pain of crashing into the tiled wall.

He instinctively reached for his wallet and found an empty back pocket. Then he sat up, in spite of the policeman's warning, and looked for his backpack.

"I had a backpack. It was brown. It had all my... It had all my stuff in it." To the experienced policeman, he sounded exactly like what he was, a man who had just been robed, perhaps robed of a lot.

"Looks like you might have been attacked from behind and robbed."

The realization hit Joey hard. "Shit!" He yelled.

"Did you see anyone in the restroom when you came in?"

"Those bastards robbed me! I can't believe it."

"Who are you talking about, sir?"

"The people that were giving me a ride. I came into the bathroom with Tony, at least that's what he said his name was. He was standing right next to me. Then I felt him shove me against the wall. I guess I blacked out."

"You said 'they'. Who else was there?"

"His girlfriend. She called herself Wendy."

"What sort of car were they in?"

Joey thought for a moment. "An old yellow Nissan. I don't know what kind of Nissan."

"Can you describe the two people for me?"

As Joey began his recollection of the two tattooed assailants, he heard a siren outside. The ambulance had arrived and two young female EMT's walked into the restroom carrying what looked like a lot of luggage. They laid their equipment down next to him and politely nudged the officer to one side.

"What have we got?" The taller of the two women asked the policeman.

Officer Brashman explained what he'd learned and estimated the time of the accident as best he could. While the EMT's began hooking Joey up to a few of their toys, the officer finished his questions and offered Joey a copy of his report.

"Sir, we'll get out a call for the yellow Nissan which is probably still in Palm Beach county, but I have to be honest with you, if we don't come across them in the next ten minutes or so, they could be anywhere. Can you give me an estimate of the value of what was taken? You may need it for your insurance claim and it would be helpful to have it on the police report.

As the EMT began to fill the blood pressure cuff secured around his right arm, Joey felt for his wallet again. "Oh shit! They got my wallet and my backpack." He thought it better not to mention that his backpack was filled with hundred dollar bills, so he told the cop, "Between what was in my wallet and my backpack, I'd guess about eighteen hundred bucks."

The state trooper made a few written notes then said, "Okay, Mr. Martinez, I just need a date of birth a phone number, and home address, sir."

Even with his forehead pounding, Joey was lucid enough to know he'd better give the cop a bogus address. Since he was the victim, not the criminal, he assumed there'd be little need to check it out and if they ever did find the two pricks that mugged him, he wasn't in a position to testify against them in court anyway. Hopefully, this was the last he'd ever see of anyone in the room with him.

He needed to come up with enough information to satisfy the policeman, but information that would never lead back to him. So, he just made up an identity. "Sure, January fifteenth, nineteen-seventy-four", one day off from is actual birthday. "My home address is 27 Meyer Avenue, Hoboken, New Jersey, and my home number is 203-443-6664", the address and phone number of the pizzeria he and Claire used to order from regularly.

"One forty-four over eighty." One EMT said to the other who was recording Joey's vital signs.

"O2 is ninety-nine percent on room." Meaning their patient's oxygen level was just fine for someone with a head injury.

The trooper stood and said to the tall EMT, "You know where to find me if you need anything Betty." Then he offered, "Mr. Martinez, you're in good hands. Betty and Mary Jane are the best in the county. They'll take good care of you." He leaned down and handed Joey a card. "If you have any more questions about your case, here's where you can reach me." Then he turned to the elderly couple still standing in the corner. Can I ask you folks a few questions outside please?"

The EMT who was removing the blood pressure cuff began asking Joey a series of routine questions concerning his prior health, allergies, medications, and symptoms. Joey was now leaning on his elbows and asked if he could sit up to a more comfortable position.

Mary Jane obliged and helped him steady himself against the wall. "Don't try to stand just yet, sir. We'll help you get up in a moment. Just a few more questions first."

It seemed like it took forever but the two medics were finally done checking him out and treating his head injury, a treatment that amounted to nothing more than an ice pack.

Then the taller one, Betty, spoke into the radio pinned to her lapel. "Wellington ambulance to Wellington Medical Center."

A moment later, the crackled response came, "Go ahead Wellington."

"We're inbound with a twenty-seven-year-old male with head trauma and sustained LOC. We're twelve minutes out."

Hearing that he was being taken to a hospital, Joey sprang to his feet. "I don't need a hospital. I'm fine. The ice pack was just what I needed."

Betty quickly responded, "Sorry sir. We have to take you to the hospital. You lost consciousness. And we don't know for how long. You really should have an MRI."

"I appreciate your concern and the fact that you came in the first place, but really, I'm okay." Joey was standing but still a little wobbly on his feet. He steadied himself against the wall.

"Sorry Mr. Martinez but in the state of Florida, if you sustain a head injury and lose consciousness, even just for a moment, we must take you to the hospital. It's the law."

Joey couldn't believe he could be forced to accept medical treatment if he didn't want it. In as nice a tone as possible, he asked, "And what if I refuse?"

"Well then I have to get trooper Brashman back again and he will take you into custody in our ambulance and accompany us to the hospital."

"You're kidding, right?"

'No sir. I am not kidding. And you really should have that MRI, although that's really up to the doctor." She gave him a smile and added, "It's for your own good."

And so, resolved not to get the police involved again, Joey walked to the ambulance, got on the stretcher and rode the seven miles to the hospital where, because he was brought in by ambulance, he went to the head of the line of waiting patients. In the end, he was grateful for the EMT's persistence because while waiting for the MRI, he felt nauseous, a symptom he learned of a concussion. Although he didn't vomit, he was glad to be in the hands of professionals.

It took two hours to get the results of the MRI interpreted by the radiologist. All his blood work had come back negative, which the doctor assured him was good news. And, since it was his first time in a hospital, he learned he had type AB negative blood, which, according to the same doctor, was the rarest type of human blood.

During that time Joey was on a gurney in the hallway of the busy emergency room, listening to each new case come through the door. A twelve-year-old girl was on the gurney next to his. She'd been thrown from a horse and broke her right arm.

While the girl's father filled out the admitting paperwork, Joey asked her, "What were you doing on a horse?" He was just trying to make the time pass.

"I was showing. There was a juniors show before the Grand Prix." She said as if he was supposed to immediately understand what that meant.

Before he could ask, he heard a female voice calling his name. "Joe Martinez?"

To his surprise, the radiologist was a very attractive woman who looked a little like Lonnie Rossetti. He sheepishly raised his hand to indicate his presence in the crowded hallway and the doctor walked over. "How are you feeling Mr. Martinez?"

It felt odd to have someone about his age call him Mr. Martinez. "I was a little nauseous before but I feel pretty good now."

Without looking at him, she offered, "Well, it's not uncommon to have a little nausea when you have a concussion and that's what you have." Now she looked him in the eye. "Do you have someone to drive you home? You shouldn't drive for twenty-four hours." She went back to writing on her chart.

Relieved that he was being released from the hospital, Joey lied. "Oh, yeah. I have a friend who said he'd pick me up."

"Okay, good. I'd keep some ice on that bump", she used her pen to point at his head, "For at least a few more hours."

"I will, thanks.

"The admitting nurse needs to get some insurance info from you, then you'll be on your way. But if you feel dizzy tonight, call your doctor. And definitely no alcohol for a couple of days."

The beautiful young doctor in the crisp white coat then handed her chart to another woman, not nearly as pleasing to the eye, and hurried down the long hall.

"Hi Mr. Martinez. My name's Jeanne. I just need to get some information from you. I got most of it from the ambulance report but I need your insurance card and social security number."

Even with a pounding head, Joey was able to think quickly. "Well, the reason I'm here is because I was mugged and they stole my wallet. So, I don't have my insurance card. But I know my insurance is from Oxford. It's a New York plan. I work in New York."

"Do you know your group number?"

"I'm afraid I don't." He said apologetically.

Jeanne made a few notes on her clipboard. "Okay. We can figure it out based on your social security number."

He realized that was his cue to spout out the nine digits but he needed a moment to think. He certainly couldn't give her his real number, so he said, "124-42-7655", a number just a few digits from his own.

"And the name of your personal physician?"

"I don't have one. I'm never sick." That was the truth.

CHAPTER TWENTY-ONE

For the first time in his life, Joey felt truly alone. As the sliding doors closed behind him and he exited the hospital, he had no idea what he was going to do. He'd been told he was in a place called Wellington, about ten minutes west of Palm Beach. The Wellington Regional Medical Center faced an eight-lane road that ran north and south, but the door he'd just passed through emptied onto a lesser road, four lanes that ran east to west.

He had sixty-two dollars and forty cents in his pocket, the only money not taken from him by Tony and Wendy. He had no plan, no place to spend the night, no idea what was around him, and he knew no one in the area. He didn't know which direction to travel and didn't know what to expect at the end of the journey even if he did.

The only good news was that the throbbing in his head had subsided and it wasn't raining. Either of those would have made this frightening situation even more unbearable.

"Okay kid. You need to pull it together." He spoke to himself aloud as he descended the hospital steps. "This is the freedom you wanted. You're just going to be starting from rock bottom, that's all."

He took a seat near the bottom of the steps and assessed what he had going for him. "Focus on the positives." He told himself. He recounted the cash in his left pocket and did a quick calculation to determine that sixty-two dollars could last him several days if he ate nothing but fast food, used their bathrooms, and found a safe place to sleep outdoors. The weather was clear and balmy so shelter from the elements wasn't an immediate concern.

He had shoes and socks, a relatively clean pair of khakis, his new tee shirt and his Casio watch. Everything else had been taken from him. What he found most frightening wasn't his lack of resources, but the fact that there was no going back. He couldn't possibly call Claire and ask her to come rescue him.

Or could he? It had only been thirty-two hours since the towers collapsed. He could make up a story about escaping the collapse but have no memory of how he got to Florida. Surely, considering the magnitude of what had happened, it was possible that he'd been so traumatized by the events that he went into some sort of shock and wandered around for a day in a fog. Just being able to say, "I don't remember," would be a completely understandable excuse under the circumstances. Why else would he possibly be in Florida without any money?

Claire would be so happy he was alive she would do anything to get him back to New York.

So, there was a way back, a way out of the mess he found himself in. He could find a phone in the hospital and call Claire. He could go back to the life he had.

Or he could figure out how to deal with the first few days of his new one. From the hospital steps, he envisioned a giant fork in the road requiring him to make a life-altering choice. But the choice had to be made now. In a few days, it would be too late. There would be no going back after this. This was a one-time opportunity to escape the path he thought he'd chosen before it was too late.

He stood and looked ahead at the road before him, Forest Hills Blvd., a fitting name for the metaphor of his fork in the road. On the corner were two signs, placed there for the benefit of drivers traveling southbound on the larger road, route 441. One sign pointed to the east and read 'Palm Beach International Airport'. The other pointed to the west and read 'Wellington'. One represented a way home, the other, the unknown.

He took a deep breath and turned to the right. He began the walk toward Wellington, a town he'd never heard of before that day.

CHAPTER TWENTY-TWO

He hadn't walked two miles when he realized he needed a more comfortable pair of shoes. His Johnston & Murphy loafers were perfect for sitting at a desk but a bit stiff for long hikes into the unknown. He resolved to buy a pair of good sneakers as soon as he could afford them. Joey smiled to himself at the thought of having to save up to buy a pair of sneakers. My, what a difference a day makes.

Forest Hills Blvd. ran directly west into the setting sun. Somewhere along the way, he'd lost his sunglasses. Maybe Tony had taken those too. Either way, he squinted and cupped his hands above his eyes at each intersection. Along the way he passed several upscale housing developments surrounded by impressive walls and with names like Olympia, Palm Crossings, Wellington Trace, and Palmetto Gardens. The further west he walked the nicer the developments seemed to get.

By seven P.M. the sun had settled behind the horizon's palm trees. Joey knew he needed to find a place to spend his first night on the road, his first night as a homeless man. He hoped the next major intersection would provide a few commercial buildings; maybe a 7-Eleven or Dunkin Donuts. He was very thirsty. But the next three intersections all yielded nothing but entrances to more housing developments, most with well-guarded gatehouses.

By eight o'clock it was completely dark and Joey was no longer comfortable walking on the side of the road. Cars were coming by fast and his clothing offered little reflective value to oncoming headlights. He smiled at the irony of surviving the Trade Center disaster only to be killed by a hit-and-run octogenarian in rural Florida. He decided to get off the main road for the night and looked for a wall he could scale to gain entrance into one of the communities. The walls were designed more for privacy than security so finding one low enough to climb wasn't a problem. Perhaps he could find a home that wasn't occupied and spend the night sprawled on one of their patio lounge chairs.

He shimmied over an attractive brick wall on the south side of the road and found himself on a golf course. There was enough moonlight for him to walk across the spacious fairway and observe the backs of several homes that lined the course. One of them was completely dark, not even the usual security lights on the perimeter. It was a Spanish style ranch with red tile roof and a huge pool that backed up to the sixteenth hole of the Palm Beach Polo Club, the private community Joey had invaded. He approached the house cautiously but it was clear, no one was inside. The patio furniture surrounding the kidney shaped pool had been stacked to one side, giving him the impression that the owners were away for an extended time. It seemed perfect.

Joey pulled one of the cushioned lounge chairs from the stack and positioned it near the pool. He then observed a cabinet next to the house and found a pile of towels, pool chemicals and plastic cups. He helped himself to a cup and a towel, both contained the logo of the Palm Beach Polo Club.

He walked the perimeter of the house looking for a hose spigot. He was grateful the owners hadn't turned off the water and assumed it was necessary for the pool maintenance people to top off the pool every so often. Tonight, it was his water fountain and he drank three cups of the cool water before returning to the pool.

He stripped naked and quietly slid into the pool. The water which had been heating in the summer sun for months was warmer than he expected but still refreshing and would serve as his personal bath tub this evening. Joey floated on his back for several minutes, staring up at the moon. For the first time in a few days, his muscles began to relax. He thought about Claire and wondered if she was looking up at the same moon in Hoboken. The common focal point created the illusion of a connection with his wife that he hadn't felt in some time.

Then he thought about Lonnie. He wondered if she tried to contact him to see if he'd been killed the previous day along with so many others. If she'd tried to call, did Claire answer his phone? Did they speak?

In the stillness of the warm water he reflected on how much had changed in the last four days. On Saturday night, he and Lonnie had sat on the dock, sipping red wine and looking up at the same moon. They made love for hours and when he arose on Sunday morning, he had no idea his life was about to hit a wall in a few hours. But maybe his life needed to hit that wall. Maybe a full speed collision with the wall was the only catalyst that could rescue him from the life he didn't want to lead.

When he got out of the pool he toweled dry then lay on the lounge chair thinking. He resolved to think only about the future. Nostalgic memories of Lonnie or Claire would only drag him back to the past. He needed to focus on the future, the immediate future. Where would he go in the morning? How would he earn a living, or at least enough so he could survive the next few weeks? Who would he be?

The last question was the one that concerned him most. He had no doubt he'd be able to survive. He had faith in his resourcefulness. But he needed to craft an identity. Who would he be? What imaginary background would he come from?

And so it was, as he lay naked on the moonlit lounge chair, that he crafted his new self, the one he would use from that day forward. The one he would embellish so deeply that, after some time, even he would believe it true. He laid down as Joey Martinez, the investment banker from Hoboken, New Jersey, but he would arise a new man.

He decided to keep his last name, for to do otherwise would dishonor his father, but his first name would become Jose. The identity he chose for himself was that of an immigrant. Jose, he determined, had migrated to the U.S. from Ecuador, a country Joey currently knew almost nothing about but one he thought so obscure that no one else would either. He came to this country in 1994, when he was nineteen with his brother, who traveled to California and hadn't been heard from since. Jose himself had lived in New York, doing many different odd jobs, working under the radar so as not to alert the Immigration officials of his illegal status.

He decided Jose had gone to City College part-time and it was there he refined his command of the English language. He majored in business but never graduated. He'd spent some time working as a gardener for a wealthy woman in Summit, but when she passed away her children sold the house and that's when he decided to move south.

Jose just arrived in the area. From that point on, Joey's and Jose's lives intersect. Like Joey, Jose had been mugged Tuesday morning, spent time in the local hospital and was now in need of work and a home. He'd been robbed of all his money, had no place to live and was walking around with just the clothes on his back.

Joey felt good about the new character and went over the story several times in his mind, each time adding another layer of detail to the fabrication. He fell asleep thinking of Jose's hometown in Ecuador and could see the modest house in which he'd grown up.

In the morning, Jose was careful to replace the towel he'd used and left the lounge chairs just as he'd found them. He climbed the wall again and continued walking along Forest Hill with the early sun already hot on his back. It took almost an hour but he finally came to a commercial area, a shopping mall called Wellington Green. It was a strip mall like thousands of others scattered across the country; a supermarket flanked by Barnes and Noble, Gap, CVS, and two dozen other ubiquitous names. One of them was Subway, and even though it was only nine-thirty, the smell of baking bread charmed him.

He feasted then used the toilet in the back of the store. When he came out, the store was empty except for the young man who'd just made his sandwich. The teenager appeared to be preparing some of the meats for display and Jose allowed him to finish his task before asking, "Where would you suggest I go if I'm looking for day-laborers? I'm new to the area."

The young man whose name tag indicated he was Karl, responded, "I know my dad goes to the Home Depot when he needs help. He runs a landscaping company and is always picking up extra guys when things are busy. But don't get your hopes up. This time of the year all the day-laborers have gone back to Mexico. Not much here to do over the summer. Not much going on until January."

"Why's that?" Jose was curious.

"Cause the show doesn't start until January. All the people come back right after Christmas. Until then…" He motioned with his hand at the empty store. "This is pretty much the way it will be for a few more months. Things pick up around Christmas, then get crazy until May. Then they all go back up north."

"Who's they?"

"The people with the horses, the show people and the polo people. They're only here four months out of the year. The rest of the time, Wellington is a ghost town."

Since Karl didn't seem in a hurry to get back to work, Jose decided to probe a bit more. "What show are you talking about?"

"The horse show over at the Equestrian Center. That and polo is what keeps this area alive. Me, I can't stand horses, but the people who have them sure love them. Some of the horses have nicer barns than some of the people who work in them. That's the truth. I seen some of them."

"So, what's the show you're referring to?"

"I don't know exactly what it's called but the people with the horses compete just about every day. They always have something going on over there. They get big crowds to come and watch, especially on Sunday afternoon when they have the Grand Prix."

Jose recalled the little girl in the hospital mentioning the Grand Prix. That's where she broke her arm. But he still didn't know what it was.

Jose ordered another Diet Coke and asked, "So, what's a Grand Prix?"

"Didn't you ever see those people on TV. They ride horses and jump over shit. You know, like fences and bushes. That's how Superman got paralyzed. He was jumping over a bush and fell off his horse. Not Superman, the guy who played him in the movies."

Jose was beginning to understand. Karl was describing the sport of Show Jumping. He knew very little about it but had seen clips of it from the 2000 Olympics. He had no idea he was standing in the American epicenter of the sport, at least the winter epicenter. For four months a year, most notable riders converged on the town of Wellington, Florida for the sport's winter circuit, where they competed for millions of dollars in prize money.

"Anyway, not much going on here till after Christmas. You can ask my dad. He should be here any minute."

"Thanks. Maybe I'll stick around and chat with him a bit." Jose thought an adult's perspective may offer more clarity.

"My name's Karl," the store clerk offered.

"I'm Jose. Jose Martinez."

"Nice to meet you." Karl said, then, "I got some more work to do in the back. You can hang out as long as you like. I don't expect much business till lunch time."

Karl returned to his duties laying out the shiny lunch meat and condiments while Jose sat at a table in front of the store and paged through a magazine. Based on the free reading material available on the rack in front of the store, Karl was absolutely correct- this town was all about horses. Most of the ads in the magazine had something to do with horses, or equipment for horses, or stable supplies, or clothing for riders. He was astounded to learn a pair of riding boots could cost nine hundred dollars or that a used saddle would fetch two thousand. He'd never seen such focus on a sport before. Even the advertisements for pool cleaning services had an equestrian theme; either a horse-like logo or a cleaver use of terminology such as 'pony for your thoughts' as a bikini clad woman relaxed on an inflatable raft in her pool. It truly was a town devoted to one animal.

The second magazine he picked up confirmed his belief further. It was a real estate brochure in which most of the homes listed had barns, stables, paddocks and show rings as part of the property. They were beautifully manicured properties with aerial photos highlighting how close they were to the Equestrian Center, the center of the Wellington universe, on Pierson Road. Many of the advertised properties had no price listed, but instead requested interested parties to inquire with the broker. But others did have prices that seemed crazy to Jose. In fact, he had to look deep into the brochure before he came to a single home that cost under a million dollars, and that was only because, in the back of the glossy magazine, there were also condominiums listed.

He tossed the magazine on the table and searched for something else to read. Someone had left today's edition of USA Today on a nearby table. The cover was full of color photos of the remains of the World Trade Center and the large pieces of the façade that somehow survived the collapse. The accompanying stories spoke of the recovery effort and that no one had been found alive after the first twenty-four hours. Hope was fading that anyone else would be found. Another story on page two quoted New York's mayor, Rudy Giuliani, as saying the New York Fire Department had lost three hundred forty-three members in one day, including the fire department's chaplain, Father Mychal Judge, who was killed by debris when the first tower collapsed. There was a color photo of several firefighters carrying the lifeless body of Father Judge from the wreckage.

The next eight pages were all photos, most in color as was the trademark of USA Today. The most shocking photo for Jose was a large black and white picture of a cloud of debris rolling up Broadway with pedestrians running for their lives. Jose recognized the precise spot from which the photo was taken. It showed a deli he would often frequent for lunch. It already seemed like a lifetime ago.

Looking at the paper became too painful. He kept thinking about all the people he worked with and all the people he would see each day as he went to work; people like the guy at the news stand, the lady who sold buttered bagels in the lobby, or the security guard who would always say good morning as he held the elevator for him. He wondered if any of them got out alive.

Then he thought about Sarah Bideaux, the young reporter who was scheduled to meet him at nine that morning. He felt enormous guilt about her. Even though she was pursuing him and insisted they meet, he never would have met her if it hadn't been for his weekend with the lovely Lonnie. Because of his infidelity, a young girl was probably dead. Who said adultery is a victimless crime?

He made a mental note to find out if the reporter had been killed. Someday soon he would call the newspaper she worked for. What did she say that morning? The Hartford something? He'd figure it out when he had time and know for certain. He hoped she was late that morning. A few minutes could have meant the difference between life and death.

The rest of the newspaper was filled with related stories about victims, those who narrowly escaped, the history of the buildings themselves, and the threat of a seawall collapsing and flooding all lower Manhattan. There were no advertisements, no comics and no crossword puzzles. The entire forty-two pages were devoted to the disaster.

Jose noticed his left leg was getting very warm. He realized his leg was in the sun and adjusted his chair, making another mental note to come up with a pair of shorts. His New York khakis were far too heavy for the Florida sun, even in September. A change of underwear would probably be a good idea too.

The glass door swung open and a heavy-set man wearing camo shorts and a grey tee shirt walked in. As he passed Jose's table he could see lettering on the broad back of the man's shirt- 'Wellington Home Maintenance'.

"Hey pop," Karl called out from behind the counter. "What can I get you today?"

"Light day kid. Just give me three Italians and a meatball. They're only five of us today. I'll take my usual."

"Okay. Give me ten minutes." Then Karl remembered Jose sitting at one of the front tables. "Hey Pop, this guy was asking about day laborers. I told him to talk to you when you got here." He motioned toward Jose who put down his paper and rose to greet the older man.

"Alex McCurry," he said extending his hand. "Nice to meet you."

"Jose." He shook the man's hand firmly. "Your son makes a great sandwich."

"Where you from, Jose?"

"Originally from Ecuador, but for the last ten years or so, around New York."

"That's some kinda shit going on up there now, huh?"

Jose held up the newspaper as if to imply, "Yes, I was just reading about it."

"Bush is gonna bomb the shit out of those assholes. They're never gonna know what hit em. He's got to do it or they'll think we're soft. The whole world is watching to see what we do."

"I think you're right." Jose decided not to get into it.

"Damn right." The elder McCurry took a seat across from Jose. "What's this Karl tells me about you needing day laborers? Not many around here this time of year. Those that are, usually have regular gigs."

"I wasn't looking to hire one. I was asking about myself. I need work."

Alex studied Jose. He was surprised someone in khakis and fancy loafers would be asking about day work. Jose didn't seem to fit the part. Most of the day laborers Alex employed barely spoke five words of English and were a lot shorter than Jose. They certainly didn't wear loafers.

Most of the migrant workers who traveled to southern Florida searching for work had experience as farm workers or landscapers. One fellow, who came every year, had a thriving gardening business of his own in Mexico in the spring, summer and fall, but traveled to Wellington to work as a day laborer for Alex because he could make so much more money in the U.S. in just those three months.

His experience with day workers from Mexico, Columbia, and Guatemala, the three areas that seemed to have discovered southern Florida's potential, was that these were very honest, hard-working men who mostly had families in their homelands that depended on the money they sent back each month. To them, the United States was a place to earn incredible money in a just few months, money that allowed their families to live better lives back home. Alex had tremendous respect for the workers he hired because he could see how much most missed their families and their homes.

"What exactly are you looking to do?" He asked Jose with a note of skepticism.

"I'll do pretty much anything. I just really need a job. You see, I traveled down here intending to get away for a bit, and I got mugged yesterday. Lost everything but the clothes I'm wearing. I spent most of yesterday in the hospital and I don't want to call home for help, not that anyone would be in a hurry to send me money." He realized he was starting to ramble.

Alex held up his hand, "Okay, okay. I get it. You need work. Ever do any landscaping work?"

"Sure, I was the property manager for a lady up in New Jersey for a couple of years. I took care of the grounds, the pool, and the house whenever she wasn't there."

Alex rubbed his chin and thought for a moment. "Okay. I'll tell you what. I got most of my summer guys slotted already for tomorrow but I need to do some clean-up work at a farm in town. Important client. Might take three days. Can you start tomorrow at seven? I'll pick you up here at seven." He pointed to some tables outside the Subway that serviced the adjacent bagel store. "A hundred bucks a day plus lunch. I get to choose the lunch."

"Sounds perfect, thanks. I'll be here."

CHAPTER TWENTY-THREE

Jose returned to the vacant house in the Polo Club for his second night without a home. The covered patio provided welcomed protection from the rain that passed through just after midnight. He set the alarm on his watch for five A.M. and slept soundly on the lounge chair until then. The walk to the strip mall didn't seem as long the second time.

As promised, Alex drove up in his red Dodge pickup, stopping only long enough to grab a coffee at the bagel store and to tell Jose, "Hop in."

On the way to the job, Alex explained the project before them. "Basically, this is our monthly maintenance. This guy, Micah Wells is a big shot rider and has a ten-acre farm on Appaloosa Trail. He's only here from Christmas to May and I take care of the property the rest of the year. I check on the house and the stables every week but once a month we go in and prune back the palms and clean up any fronds that have fallen off the trees. We rake out the rings and the driveway and check the sprinkler system."

"Doesn't sound like three days of work." Jose said.

"Yeah, well you haven't seen the farm yet. It's pretty big and has a five-hundred-foot wall of Indian palms that borders the road. Believe me, there's plenty to do. But we should be done on Sunday. You can work all three days, right?"

"Yeah, no problem."

"Great." Then Alex added, "You don't seem to have much of an accent Jose. How long did you say you've been here?"

"I got here in 1994 but I went to an American school in Quito for three years. My English got pretty good there. I also went to college in New York for two years. I studied business."

"What's Quito?" Alex asked as he turned a corner with one hand on the wheel.

"That's where my family was from. We lived in the city most of the time. Quito's the capital and biggest city in Ecuador. There was an American school there because of the American embassy I guess."

Alex McCurry seemed satisfied with his passenger's answer. Actually, he was happy to have an employee who spoke any English at all. Usually, he needed to stick around on a job site to interpret the customer's directions for the workers. When he occasionally came across someone like Jose, who could not only understand but then communicate the instructions to other workers, he would usually pay them a premium for the day. Since he'd already told Jose he'd pay one hundred dollars, and Jose had agreed, he saw no reason to tinker with things just yet.

He made another turn onto an unpaved road. Jose was surprised to see mansion-like homes lining the dirt road, each with expansive fields, barns and well-groomed paddocks. Most had meticulously maintained white three-board fences bordering the properties. What made the beautiful farms seem so out-of-place was that they were adorned with palm trees and other Florida-style fauna.

The pick-up pulled up to a massive iron gate and Alex leaned out to punch a code into a well-disguised keypad. At first nothing happened, but then slowly, the huge gate began to slide to the right, revealing a long driveway. Both sides of the cobblestoned driveway were lined with colorful flowers, plants that looked like they required a lot of water. Jose wondered why anyone, who wasn't here most of the year, would go through the trouble of keeping such high-maintenance flowers.

At the end of the driveway was a large courtyard, surrounded by an impressive home, a barn and another home, probably a guest cottage Jose supposed. In fact, the second home was for the staff of ten that were required to keep the farm running over the winter.

Alex pulled the truck to a stop in front of the larger home and announced, "Okay kid, time to go to work."

Both men stepped out of the truck and as Jose slammed the door closed, he noticed the immense silence that surrounded them. There was no noise from the road, no drone of air conditioners as is so prevalent in Florida, and no sounds from the barns, all of which were empty. It was a most unusual quiet.

"First the easy stuff," Alex said as he motioned for Jose to follow him toward the house. He untangled a ring of keys from his pocket and searched for the proper one. "We'll do a walk- through of the main house. I want you to look for any signs of mice."

"What am I looking for, exactly?"

"Mouse droppings, tiny little black tic-tacs. That's the best way to describe them. Look on the floor along the walls. Mice usually stay close to a wall. Let me know if you spot any."

As Jose followed the walls around the first floor he noticed they were all adorned with pictures of horses. Some were just pictures of horses; others were smartly framed action shots of a horse jumping over a fence or an imposing wall of white wooden rails. In all those shots, the rider on the horse was a slender young man with dirty blond hair. Often, next to the photo would be hanging a large ribbon with the words Champion Grand Prix. The pictures always showed the place they were taken; Aachen, Rome, Calgary, Ocala, Wellington.

Jose marveled at the photos for two reasons; first, the photographer had captured the precise moment for maximum action, the moment the horse and rider were air-borne flying over an obstacle. The other aspect that astounded Jose was the height the horse achieved in doing so. It appeared the horse and rider were jumping over six feet in the air.

"Wow, do horses really jump this high?" Jose said pointing to one of the larger photos.

"The good ones do. At least they do in the big events. I think some of the Grand Prix have jumps of sixty-six inches. That's almost as tall as me. But I'm no expert."

"Hard to believe something so big can jump so high, and with a rider on his back."

After assuring themselves there were no signs of mice on the main floor, Alex led Jose up the rounded staircase to check the rooms on the second floor. There Jose found no mice but many more of the oversized photos of horses jumping. In fact, the entire focus of the house seemed to be on that singular subject.

"Who lives here?" He asked as they began to descend the stairs.

"A young fellow named Micah Wells. He's one of the best riders in the world, especially for such a young guy. He's hoping to get to the Olympics in 2004. More important, he and his dad are two of my best customers. He's referred a lot of business my way."

"I didn't know this was even an Olympic event." Jose said staring at one of the pictures.

"Yep, for over a hundred years now. In fact, it's the only Olympic event where men and women compete against each other as equals."

Alex checked the bathrooms for leaks, the filters on the air conditioning system, and the hoses leading to the washing machine. He took his job very seriously and the last thing he wanted to have to report to Mr. Wells was that something leaked on his watch. The whole point of good property management, he felt, was to avoid problems, not just report them after the fact.

The rest of the day Jose spent picking up palm fronds after Alex cut them from the thousands of trees along the property's perimeter. He loaded three small dump trucks with the heavy leaves before lunch and three more after lunch. Alex was so pleased with the pace of Jose's work, he offered to drive him 'home' when they were done.

When Jose politely refused the offer, Alex said, "Hey kid, it doesn't take a genius to figure out you got no place to go. I mean, you're wearing the same shoes, pants and shirt you had on yesterday." He looked at him as they stood next to the red truck, "You been sleeping in the park?"

Jose had never been more ashamed. Admitting he was homeless was the easy part. The hard part was that he couldn't tell Alex why. He couldn't tell Alex he had a wife at home who was mourning his death. He couldn't tell him that before Tuesday, Jose didn't exist.

"No. I've been sleeping in the back yard of an empty house. There's a lounge chair. It's not so bad. It's just till I get back on my feet. The muggers took everything I had."

Alex had a sense about the kid standing before him. For some reason, he liked him. Maybe it was because his son had recommended him or maybe it was his naïve way. He didn't know what it was but he sensed he had found a diamond in the rough; someone who, with the proper tutelage, could become more than he seemed to be. He decided to take a chance on the young man.

"Well, I can't have you showing up for work every day wearing the same smelly cloths."

Jose was afraid he was about to be fired after just one day.

"So, here's what we'll do. Can you commit to working for me for the next three weeks? I can use another guy."

"Without hesitation Jose responded, "Absolutely, that would be great."

"Okay then. Here's what we'll do. I'll front you the three hundred dollars for today, tomorrow and Sunday. You get yourself some proper work cloths over at Target. And some decent work shoes too. Then you come back and stay in my bunk house till we can work out some other arrangement for you. It ain't fancy but it was built for eight guys and there's only four in there now."

Jose was overwhelmed. "That would be wonderful. Thank you so much Mr. McCurry. You will not regret this. I promise."

"All right then. Get in." He motioned for Jose to get into the truck. "I'll give you a ride to Target. You pick up what you need." He took out his wallet and counted out fifteen twenties and extended the cash to Jose. "This should get you started. I got to go check on my guys at another job before I head home so I can swing back and pick you up about an hour after I drop you off. If you ain't there…, well then I guess I'm not the judge of character I thought I was."

CHAPTER TWENTY-FOUR

Jose worked for Alex McCurry for the next three months; six days a week with Sundays off. He quickly became Alex's right-hand man. Jose's command of both English and Spanish made him invaluable to his boss and his knowledge of business practices in general allowed him to stand in for Alex at a few meetings with prospective new customers. The relationship worked well for both men.

At Thanksgiving, Jose was invited to dinner at Alex's home along with the other four regular laborers, Jose's roommates, two Mannies, a Jorge and a Jimmy. All four men were from the same small town in Mexico, about forty miles south of the Texas border. They all crossed the Rio Grande at night a little over two years ago. Their English was limited to what they'd learned from American TV so Jose worked with them at night to share some landscaping basics.

After a generous dinner, prepared completely by Alex's wife, Erica, Jose returned to his room in the bunkhouse and thought about Claire. He assumed she was at her parents for the holiday. Was she still grieving? He wondered if she ever had a memorial service for Joey and if so, who showed up. He'd read stories in USA Today about many families that were forced to hold services for their lost loved ones after 9-11, the term by which the Trade Center tragedy had come to be known, without a body because so many were never accounted for. He hoped she wasn't still sad. He hoped she'd begun to move on.

Christmas was a tough time. Jose's sense of guilt about the pain he'd caused Claire was beginning to weigh heavily. Although the Christmas season is southern Florida doesn't have all the same magic as the crisp winter days in the northeast, there were enough reminders of the season, especially in all the stores. Every time he heard a Christmas carol Jose's heart would sink with sadness. He wasn't sure if his longing was for Claire or for days gone by with his parents. Either way, his memories of Christmas were all pleasant, no matter who he was with.

The thing Jose used to enjoy most about the Christmas season was the shopping, particularly surprising Claire with a special gift, one she didn't expect. He recalled shopping each year at Lord & Taylor, the city's hustle and winter bustle always put him in the mood. He liked waiting until the week just before Christmas, when the frenzy was at its peak and the shops began having last minute sales. This year he had planned to get Claire a diamond bracelet. He begun saving for it right after the fourth of July.

The other reason Christmas was a difficult time for Jose was that Alex's business got very busy in mid-December in preparation for all the people who'd be returning to Wellington just after Christmas. The core of his business was landscaping but the property management side had grown significantly the past few years creating a lot of work in December. Winter plantings needed to be done so that flowers would be in bloom when the owners returned. Most palm trees required pruning this time of year and most of his clients had hundreds of them adorning their homes. And there was the cleaning. After eight months of neglect, even the homes Alex arranged to be cleaned monthly, needed freshening. The worst thing that could happen to his reputation would be if an owner returned to Wellington to find their house smelling musty. No matter how hard he worked all summer, their impression would be that he'd neglected their home while they were away. They would look for another property manager.

This year, Jose was a huge asset to Alex. He was able to round up a crew of laborers, most of whom had just returned from Mexico, and broke them into teams according to their abilities.

He had become an extension of Alex which allowed Alex to focus on building the business and take on a few commercial accounts. Effectively, Jose was now a supervisor of men and manager of work. It was clear to Alex that something in Jose's past had prepared him for this. But every time he probed into Jose's past, Jose would chalk up his experience to the two years he'd spent at City College. Alex sensed there was more but respected the man's right to keep a few secrets.

They worked right up to Christmas Eve and although Jose was exhausted, he went to midnight mass with Alex, Erica, and Karl. The theme of the pastor's sermon was rebirth, one Jose thought fitting for both the season and his situation. After mass, Erica insisted he go back to their home for a nightcap. "It's a Christmas tradition for us.' She said. "We always have a drink after church to start the holiday off right." Erica liked her cocktails.

She opened a bottle of Chianti and poured generous servings for the three men. For herself, she mixed a potent gin and tonic. "Cheers," Alex offered. "To a good year."

Karl excused himself after the first drink but Erica poured a second for herself, Jose and Alex. Since the bunk house was only a hundred yards away, Jose wasn't concerned about getting home and accepted the third round when it was offered.

"So Jose, there's someone I want you to meet next week." Alex said.

"Come on honey. No work talk tonight. It's Christmas." Erica's speech wasn't as crisp as it had been before the cocktails.

"Okay," he said, raising his hands in surrender. "But on Wednesday, you and I are going to pick up the Wells at the airport. That's who I want you to meet."

"Oh, you'll like them. They are such nice people." Erica added. "We've known Micah and his dad for years."

Jose rose to leave but Erica stood and blocked him. "You're coming for dinner tomorrow, right? I think Santa brought you something for under the tree."

"I'll be here Erica. I wouldn't miss one of your holiday dinners."

As he walked back to the bunk house under a starry December sky, Jose reflected on the last three months. The McCurry's had become like family. They'd treated him almost like a second son. He knew Alex appreciated his work, that was clear by the raise he got after the first few weeks. But Erica and Karl had accepted him too. Maybe it was because he made Alex's life a little easier, maybe because he'd been something of a good luck charm for the family. Alex was convinced that everything had gotten better since Jose arrived; the business, his nagging back pain, even the weather.

Although he wouldn't take credit for the improved weather, Jose did feel like he was making a difference in the McCurry's lives. Alex didn't have to work as hard with Jose around. Karl seemed to be back on track, eager to restart community college in January. Even Erica seemed to have a bounce in her step. She was sixty-two but still liked watching Jose work in the barn with his shirt off and sweat rolling down his back. More than once, she'd made a special trip out to bring him a glass of water.

Whatever the reasons, Jose enjoyed being a part of their lives. It felt good to belong and helped him feel less lonely.

Christmas morning 2001 began with a massive headache. Jose knew it was the red wine but couldn't resist when the McCurry's insisted he have one more for the road back to the bunk house. Usually, a couple of Aleve took care of his head and today was no exception. After a casual walk around the neighborhood, he felt almost normal and by noon he was fine. It still didn't feel like Christmas but he knew Erica and Alex were doing their best to help him feel at home. Even the twinkling lights in the palm trees didn't bother him as much as at first.

Christmas dinner with the McCurry's was as nice as he could have hoped. Erica made a lasagna that was better than any he'd ever had in New York, and completed the meal with a home-made chocolate cake. It was all perfect and helped Jose forget about Claire, although he wondered where she was spending the holiday.

True to her word, Erica had a gift for Jose, "Santa left this for you. He said he noticed how well you sketch diagrams of the projects you work on with Alex so we…, he thought you could use these."

Inside the colorfully wrapped box was a 11 by 14 sketch pad and professional drawing pencils. "I hope you like it." Erica said with enthusiasm. "You draw so well, you should have better tools."

Jose had never thought of his diagrams as anything more than just that, diagrams; certainly not art. But he was moved by her thoughtfulness and reached across the sofa to give her a kiss. "Thanks so much. You have no idea how much this means to me." He meant it. The McCurry's meant so much to him. They had thrown him a life jacket precisely when he needed it most. They might have saved his life. When he thought back on the first few days after 9-11, he wasn't sure how he would have survived had Alex not come into the sandwich shop that day and offered him a job. He resolved to make it up to them with his loyalty and hard work.

"My first drawing will be for you, Erica. What would you like me to try to draw?"

"Draw what you see, Jose. That's what artists do. You should draw what you see and what you feel."

The next day, Alex took Jose with him to the Palm Beach International airport to pick up Micah Wells and his father, Bert. Alex knew they'd be arriving with a lot of luggage in tow and needed Jose along for the heavy lifting. Although most of the equipment the Wells would need for the winter circuit would be shipped down on trucks with their horses, the two men usually traveled with several heavy trunks filled with personal items. Alex was happy to spend the morning helping them from the airport to their farm.

As the Wells men appeared in the baggage claim area, Jose was struck by the differences between them. Micah Wells was in his early thirties, fit but physically slight. He had light sandy-brown hair he wore a bit shorter than was currently fashionable. He had soft features and a gentile way of movement; some might say graceful. He was impeccably attired in well fitted jeans, a Brooks Brothers shirt and penny loafers that even Jose could tell were expensive.

Bert Wells, on the other hand was all horseman. He was barrel chested and stocky but very fit. His face was lined with years of sun and hard outdoor work. He was very tanned and wore a white tee shirt that was intended to display his bulging biceps. He was sixty-four, but strutted with an arrogance that befit his appearance.

On the drive to the airport Alex had explained that Bert Wells had been a capable rider when he was young but lately had focused on the buying and selling of horses and leveraging his reputation to provide riding lessons for children of the well-healed enthusiasts. He'd built the Wells farm pretty much with his own hands over the past twenty-five years and had expanded it whenever the opportunity presented itself. He was one of the founding members of the Winter Equestrian Festival back in the early seventies but had sold his share to others years ago. He had two sons, Micah and Jake, each with different mothers. Although Alex had never met Jake, he'd been told the boy and his father had a falling out some time ago and hadn't spoken since he moved to California right after college. He was a successful banker somewhere in San Diego.

Micah, on the other hand, was mostly home schooled to allow him to travel with the circuit and participate in as many events as possible. He never thought about college but had developed his father's sense for business and, as he put it, "Learned from the best." While his peers were spending winter breaks binge drinking in Cancun or Panama City Beach, Micah was traveling all over Europe with adults twice his age and competing in Grand Prix events where seventy thousand people would pack the stadium and cheer as he and his mount would clear increasingly difficult jumps.

Micah Wells attributed his early successes to his parents. His mother, also an able rider had been seriously injured in a fall from a horse in 1997 and died from complications from that injury two years later. Micah, who was very close to his mother, was devastated by her death. He gave up riding and, for a while, considered a career in real estate. But his father would have none of it and pulled him aside one day after working several hours in the barn. "Listen kid," he started, "Life isn't determined by what happens to you. Shit's going to happen. That's inevitable. It's how you react to it that will determine your life. So, basically, you determine how your life will go. You can choose to sit around and feel sorry for yourself, or you can get off your ass and decide to be happy. It's your choice that will determine your life." He stressed the words "your" emphatically.

Micah told that story to many people and thanked his father's direct approach for getting him back on a horse and for all his later successes. The two men worked together every day since that talk in the barn. Micah, who was achieving financial success on his own, partnered with Bert on several investments, all related to horses in one way or another.

Today, Bert and Micah were coming from Woodfield, a small town just north of New York. Bert had purchased eighty acres of farmland there in the sixties and had turned in into one of the premiere horse farms in Putnam County. The sprawling complex contained two huge barns and stables, a massive indoor riding ring, several outdoor rings, and four houses. Micah lived alone in the house they called the cottage. Bert and his second wife, Fiona lived in the main house on the highest hill. One house was for the farm hands, mostly Irish kids who had visas to work in the U.S. for a couple of years. And the last house was exclusively for guests; clients who would visit the farm to consider the purchase of one of Bert's horses.

The complex was called Wells Hill and had been their home since Micah was born. In the equestrian world, it was a well-known destination. Bert would hold events there every year, most to raise money for local charities, and the parties that followed the riding were rumored to be some of the most lavish and wild affairs west of the Hamptons. On more than one occasion, the sheriff was summoned to ask the revelers to keep the noise down only to find the state's governor playing the sax on stage with a small contingent of Count Basie's orchestra.

The elder Wells greeted Alex with a bear hug. "Good to see you Alex. You look great." Then Micah gave Alex a high five followed by a quick man-hug. "You keep getting younger old man. How does that happen?"

"Hard work is what keeps you young. Hard work, every day." Alex responded cheerfully.

"How are Erica and Karl?" Micah asked.

'Good. Everybody's good." Then Alex turned to Jose and said, "Jose, meet Micah and Bert Wells."

Jose extended his hand and was surprised at the powerful grip of the older man. When Bert shook hands with someone new, he liked to let them know he spent three hours a day in the gym. "Nice to meet you kid." He barked while squeezing the blood from Jose's hand.

Micah's greeting was one he obviously used many times before. He patted Jose on the arm and said, "I hate to shake someone's hand after my father's crushed it. It always makes me seem like a wimp. If you need to go to the hospital, it's on our way." He offered a big and sincere smile.

"Nice to meet you both. Alex has told me a lot about you."

"Jose's been working for me the past few months. He's even learned a thing or two about horses." Alex offered as an explanation for Jose's presence.

"Well anything you learn about horses from this guy, you can forget. He doesn't know shit about horses." Bert said playfully.

Alex and Jose retrieved four large trunks from the baggage carousel. Each was labeled "Micah Wells Inc." They were extraordinarily heavy and Jose understood why Alex had brought him along. They each put two on a redcap wagon and wheeled them out to the truck. Lifting each on to the truck bed took both men.

"You bring your rock collection back to Florida Bert?" Alex joked.

Bert saw his chance to show off a bit and quickly grabbed one of the remaining trunks by the large brass handles and heaved it on to the truck without help. "You guys need to get to the gym more."

"I bet that's the one full of socks and breeches." Alex returned. They all laughed.

On the thirty-minute ride back to Wellington, Alex filled the Wells in on the local gossip and recent real estate transactions. Jose was surprised to learn that many of the beautiful farms in the area changed hands regularly. Apparently, there were two forces at work. The first was the constant need of the well-healed to continually own bigger and better homes; bigger than yours and better than the one before. The other reason for the farms changing ownership often was that many of the owners were not as liquid as they would have the world think. As fortunes were made and lost on Wall Street, the "new money" as they were called, would need to mortgage and remortgage their properties, sometimes overextending themselves.

Bert was particularly interested in one high-flying corporate lawyer who had to sell out since they were last in town. "I knew that asshole was full of shit." He said. "Bullshit artist from the get-go. I knew it."

And sometimes the farms would change hands just because it suited the needs of the owners. If one owner was expecting a larger than normal number of horses that season, they'd need additional stable space. If they could find an owner whose numbers were down for the year, they might arrange a swap of some sort or just agree to lease stable space at the other's farm.

Micah filled Alex in on some projects he had in mind for the farm; new rails for one of the fences, some additional plantings near the south barn and a fresh coat of paint on the inside of the main house. Micah viewed both family properties; the one in Wellington and the farm back in Woodfield, as home. And it was his intention to live on these farms for the rest of his life. He was an insightful young man and could see his future well down the road. His future was at these farms; Wellington in the winter and Woodfield the rest of the year. When he married, he and his wife would raise their children on these farms and they would likely be riders too.

That's why he took such pleasure in constantly improving the appearance of each property. He was planning on generations of Wells living there.

"I've got the colors picked out for the house. I'll show you the color samples when we get to the farm."

"You got it. When are Fiona and the rest of the staff coming down?" Alex asked as he drove.

"The horses and the staff are leaving Woodfield on Friday. They should be here on Saturday night. Fiona's flying down with the Bronsons and should be here New Year's Eve." Micah said.

The Bronsons he was referring to were some of the junior members of the family that ran the biggest trucking company in the east. They were long-time friends of Bert and serious about their horses. Bert had trained two of the Bronson children. Both had become capable riders. They'd also bought a few horses from Bert over the years.

As they rounded the corner onto Appaloosa Trail, Micah admired the farm's entrance, one he'd designed himself. A thick hedge of Eureka Palms led to the gate then arced over it and continued along the road. In front of the palms was a well-manicured row of colorful begonias. It was a simple yet striking entrance. Micah felt it was appropriate; not too much fanfare for a ten-acre farm. Many more were considerably larger and grander with far more grandiose entry ways.

As they passed through the iron gates Micah saw the surprise Alex had planned for them. It was a large blue banner flying from the flagpole, just below the American flag. On the banner were bold white letters that spelled out "Athens or bust!"

"I like it." Micah clapped his hands in approval. The reference was to Micah's focus on the upcoming summer Olympic games in Athens in 2004. He'd missed the U.S. team's trip to Sydney in 2000 by one time fault. It was a devastating second place and cost him a place on the team. His next chance would be Athens and he was determined to make the U.S. team.

Jose had helped Alex raise the banner earlier that morning and understood its significance. He asked, "What do you have to do to make it to the Olympic team Mr. Wells?"

"First of all, that old fart is Mr. Wells," Micah said pointing to his father. "You can call me Micah. And, to answer your question, the Olympic team is chosen by a series of four qualifying events a few months prior to the Olympic games. Four team members are chosen and one alternate. You don't want to be the alternate because they have to travel to the Olympic site with the team but if all four team members and their horses are sound a few hours before the games begin, the alternate gets sent home with little more than a tee shirt for his effort. It used to be done differently. In my father's time, it was very subjective. Riders would be chosen based on their popularity, not necessarily their ability or that of their horse. It's a lot more fair now. With the right horse, I think I've got a pretty good chance this time."

A few days later, while Jose was painting a door he'd removed from Micah's house, he heard the roar of large trucks down-shifting out on the main road. A moment later six large tractor trailers pulled into the compound. From the first two trucks, crates of equipment began to emerge carried by able-bodied young men. These were the Irish kids Alex had referred to that worked for the Wells. From the other four trucks, sixteen magnificent horses were unloaded and taken to the stalls.

Jose was intrigued and put down his paint brush to get a better look. He knew nearly nothing about horses but he could tell these were beautiful animals. Each horse had a blanket on its back bearing the emblem Micah Wells Inc. Each stall in the barn contained a brass plaque showcasing the resident horse's name. And they were majestic names like, Ruby, Donatella, Nightingale, and Prato's Pride.

He'd never been so close to so many large animals at once and it was a little intimidating at first. But the young Irish grooms seemed so at ease in their handling of the horses, he quickly realized these were very gentle creatures. Still, he couldn't get over the size of the horses and kept thinking back about the pictures he'd seen in Micah's house of the horses jumping high into the air to clear an obstacle with riders on their backs. Standing next to these magnificent creatures, it seemed impossible something so large could jump so high.

The next day, Jose was again working at the Wells compound when another significant arrival occurred. Bert's second wife, Fiona had arrived. Jose watched from the front porch where he was scraping a piece of handrail, as she emerged from the shiny black SUV for the first time. She was, by most men's assessment, a gorgeous woman. Fiona Wells had striking auburn hair surrounding an angelic face. She wore a white linen pants suit that accentuated the sculptured curves of her long body. But what surprised Jose most was her age. She was thirty-three; about half the age of her husband.

Two of the grooms came running over to take her luggage from the back of the SUV as Fiona walked toward the front of the house, the place Jose was working. As he moved his drop cloth aside so she wouldn't trip, she noticed the consideration and said, "Thanks. I'm okay." Then she stopped at the front door and turned to Jose to add, "My name's Fiona," and extended her hand. Jose wasn't sure if he should shake it or genuflect and kiss it as one would do when meeting royalty. Before he could decide, Bert Wells came bounding out the front door to greet his wife. "Hey beautiful. How was your ride down?" He gave her a swift kiss then realized Jose was standing next to them.

"Hey, did you meet Jose? He works for Alex."

"Welcome back to Florida." Jose offered in the most flawless diction he could muster.

"Nice to meet you, Jose." She said in the sexiest voice he'd ever heard. Then she walked into the house with Bert on her arm.

Jose spent most of the next few weeks working with Alex on projects at the Wells' farm. He was an able painter, a skill he'd picked up as a child helping his dad around the house, and so, he was given responsibility for the interior painting. He got to spend a little time with Micah because Micah insisted on reassessing his color selection after each room was completed. He had an eye for color and wanted to be sure each room complemented the other. Along the way, the two young men talked about their backgrounds. Jose was fascinated by Micah's life. He'd been to so my interesting places and met so many famous people, none of which seemed to have jaded the man. Jose found Micah to be extraordinarily grounded considering the success he'd already achieved. He liked him from the start.

And Micah listened eagerly to the fabricated history Jose weaved about his life growing up in Quito and moving to the U.S. as a kid. He was careful not to add to much detail to the stories for fear of tripping himself up in the web of increasingly complex lies. But he found it hard not to answer Micah's questions, so sometimes he'd add tangential lies to the stories. Then he'd have to remember those stories in case he was questioned again. He became quite good at the lies, but felt bad about doing it to Micah.

Bert and Fiona weren't around much those first few weeks of January. They'd planned a trip to the Bahamas and from there went to Belgium where Bert had some horses to inspect. But Micah was working at the farm every day, usually riding horses or giving riding lessons to others. The winter events at the showgrounds were about to begin and there was much Micah needed to do to prepare.

On one occasion, as the painting project was nearing completion, Alex stopped by to talk to Micah. They took a long walk out by the center ring and the two men leaned on the fence talking for nearly an hour while a rider on a grey mare cantered around the ring. Jose was finishing some window trim painting and could see them from the house. At the conclusion of their talk, the two men shook hands and started back toward the house.

Jose was washing a paint brush in the laundry room slop sink when they came in. It was late afternoon and he was looking forward to finishing up his work and getting back to the bunk house for a shower. He hoped the two hadn't come up with another project for the day.

"I'm heading back to the farm," Alex announced. "Jose, leave all the drop cloths with Jimmy. He'll wash them tomorrow. I'll see you back there later."

When Alex had left the room, Micah said, "You almost done?"

"Yep. That was my last brush."

"Good. Let's have a beer out on the porch." It was the first time Jose had been asked to stay beyond his work.

"Si, amigo." Jose like to sprinkle in some Spanish to keep up the façade. "A beer sounds great."

"Micah grabbed two Red Stripes, his favorite, from the kitchen fridge and led Jose out to the porch. They sat in white wicker rocking chairs and looked out onto the center ring.

"My mom bought these chairs for us at a garage sale up in Woodfield. They're kind of falling apart but for me, they have sentimental value."

Jose couldn't see any sign of wear on the chairs but nodded. He tipped the neck of his bottle in Micah's direction and offered, "Cheers. Thanks for the suds."

"I really love this place, Jose." Micah said as he leaned back on his rocker and studied the farm. "I was pretty much born here, and I'll probably die either here or in Woodfield." He looked at his beer then added, "That's another place you should see. It's beautiful and about eight times as large as this place. I'd like you to see it someday."

"Maybe someday I will."

"Well, that's what I wanted to talk about." Micah began.

Jose suspected Micah wanted to talk about another project for the farm. "What's up?"

"I spoke to Alex already so he's okay with this. I'd like you to come and work for us."

"You mean directly for you? Not through Alex?"

"Yeah. Actually, you'd be employed by our corporation but you'd be working here at the farm until May, then up in Woodfield. You could travel with us sometimes when we have shows in Europe. You'd like that, wouldn't you?"

Jose's reaction was pure panic. Three things about Micah's proposal terrified him; going back to New York, being employed by a corporation where he would need a social security number to be on a payroll, and Europe, for which he would need a passport. Because he'd been so busy working for Alex, he hadn't looked into what he'd need to do to get a new social security number, real or otherwise. Alex paid him in cash and asked no questions.

"What would I be doing? I mean I know nothing about horses."

"You're right about that." Micah said with a smile. Then he explained. "Look Jose. I'm a guy who has to have a plan. I plan out everything. My plan right now is to make the Olympic team and win a medal in Athens in two years. To make that plan work, I have plans for my horses, so that they're ready. I have plans for the farm and I have plans for all the people that support me. It's all got to come together for me to get to Athens and win."

"Sounds good, but what's that got to do with me?"

"You haven't met Bret yet. He's the guy who runs our organization, or at least the horse side. His wife Terry, runs all our finances and the business. Without the two of them I'd be completely lost. They'll be coming down next week. Bret's dad passed away in Ireland and they needed to go over and take care of things for his mom."

Jose gave him a quizzical look.

"So, Bret and Terry Kennedy currently run everything and that allows me to focus on riding and sales. That's the way I like it. I need to be focused. But I've been thinking that there's too much for Bret to do. He's responsible for both the horses and the facilities, the farms themselves. That's a lot. I'd rather if he could focus on just the welfare of the horses and get somebody else to deal with the farms. That's where you come in. In time, I think you could be that person. You'd need to learn a lot about the farms and how they support the business but you seem like a really bright guy."

"I'm flattered that you think so. And I appreciate the offer." Jose said.

"Hold on. I'm not offering you that job yet. Like I said, you'd need to learn a lot before Bret would entrust you with the farms, but I think in a year or so, you could get there. For now, let's say I'm offering you the position of..." Micah thought for a moment, then came up with, "Let's call it facilities assistant. If things work out, I'd like to have a facilities manager and an equestrian manager. I think that gives me what I need to focus on a medal in Athens; that and a whole lot of luck. I've spoken to Bret about this already and he agrees with the concept. Of course, he hasn't met you yet but he will."

Jose searched his mind for any excuse he could use to deflect the conversation. "Alex has been so good to me. He relies on me a lot now. I'm sort of his bridge between the customers and our day-laborers. The language thing."

"I've already talked to Alex. You're right. He doesn't want to lose you. But I'm a customer too and the customer is always right, right?" Micah smiled. "Listen, think about it a few days. By then Bret will be here and you guys can meet. Come up with whatever questions you have and the three of us will talk."

Jose couldn't argue with Micah's logic. The man had a master plan to win an Olympic medal and a hundred sub-plans to help him achieve that goal. He had to admire Micah's battlefield strategy. He was like a general, moving troops and supplies and equipment to the proper place all to be ready for the decisive battle at the time of his choosing.

Maybe this was the completely different life Joey Martinez envisioned when he created Jose. Maybe this was what he was supposed to be doing. Or maybe it was too soon to know. In any event, even if he wanted to help Micah Wells get to Athens, he still had the issue of an identity to deal with. His fabricated life needed documentation.

CHAPTER TWENTY-FIVE

Working for Micah

For two days, Jose wrestled with the problem of his lack of credentials. He first considered using his actual social security number. That would be easiest and allow him to obtain a passport. He was unaware of any use Claire would have for his social security number until he did a little phone research with the Social Security Office in Palm Beach. He learned she was entitled to a small death benefit as a spouse. He assumed, at some point she would claim the benefit, no matter how small and that would lead to problems for him.

What he didn't know at that time was that the federal government planned to pay surviving families of 9-11 victims millions of dollars to protect American and United Airlines from a crippling assault of lawsuits. That too would be driven by the social security numbers of the victims.

In the end, he decided he couldn't use his own number. He used his Spanish to ask some of the day laborers employed by Alex to determine if they knew how to come up with a social security number. But what he learned confirmed his belief that they had no use for fraudulent documentation since they had no intention of ever paying taxes, obtaining a driver's license or availing themselves of any of America's social service programs. They were truly off the grid and saw themselves as temporarily displaced Mexicans just earning a living a little north of the border. *Visitantes* was their term for their status.

He knew of no other way to document his ability to work in his own country, a reality he found painfully ironic. But, then again, Jose Martinez didn't actually exist, and he had no idea how to create him with a paper trail. He resolved to turn down Micah's offer. He saw no other way.

Now what he needed was an explanation that would seem plausible. He didn't want to insult Micah or jeopardize his job with Alex. He needed to explain why he couldn't work for Micah even though he'd been able to attend City College for two years. Surely that would require a social security number. He spent the whole night, lying on his bunk thinking about the story that would satisfy both Micah and Alex.

On the day Bret and Terry Kennedy were due to arrive, he asked to speak to Alex before they headed to work. He wanted to make sure Alex understood his problem and the reason, real or not, for his decision. Later that day he would talk to Micah. He was supposed to meet Micah and Bret for a beer at the Wells farm after work, presumably so Bret could get to know him. Now, it didn't seem to matter.

As he and Alex leaned against Alex's pick-up, he explained to his boss that he was flattered by Micah's offer and appreciated that Alex would let him go. He understood Alex would need to replace him and, in the meantime, have to work harder himself. "But I can't take the job," he explained.

"When I enrolled at City College, I used a fake Social Security number. They use your social security number for pretty much everything so I had to have one. The fake one worked fine for almost two years. Then I got called in to the dean of admissions office one day because they said they must have recorded my number incorrectly since it got bounced back as belonging to a woman in Idaho who was eighty-seven years old. The school assumed it was their mistake but I needed to come up with a correct number, so I told them they had just transposed one digit. That got me out of her office but I knew I was done at school as soon as they realized that number was bogus too. That's why I never finished college."

Alex nodded and said, "That's a shame, kid."

Jose continued his story. "So, ever since then, I've only taken jobs that were off the books. I worked for the lady in New Jersey and she always paid me in cash. I send some to my mom each month. She has no one else."

Jose paused to assess Alex's facial expression. He'd hoped his story of woe would resonate with him. Instead, Alex turned to him and said, "That's it? That's why you can't take the job?"

"Yes! Micah wants to put me on their payroll and mentioned maybe going to Europe next year with them for the shows over there. I can't do either. I have no social security number and no passport. I'm been in this country illegally for almost nine years. If I try to leave, I'll never get back."

"Why can't you get an Ecuadorian passport?"

Jose wasn't prepared for that question and had to think fast. "Don't you think I've tried? There's no record of my birth there. All the paper records of births between 1950 and 1988 were destroyed by the big earthquake that hit Quito in 1989." A fact he fabricated in the moment. "The building that was Quito's *ayuntamiento*, what you call town hall was leveled by the quake then flooded by the rains that came a few days later. They have nothing. I've tried everything. They just throw up their hands and say "*Me doy por vencido*", in other words, can't be done." Jose made it sound quite believable.

Alex leaned back on his truck and said, "Well, I think you should talk to Micah about it. Tell him the truth. Somehow, they get work papers for all those Irish kids to work here. He might have a way to help. One thing I've learned working around here is that rich folks usually get what they want and have a way to get things done that you and I can't."

"You think?"

"Yeah, talk to him. Worse that can happen is he can't do nothin and you keep working for me."

That afternoon, Jose and the two Mannies planted fifty-five azaleas at the winter home of a popular rock star whose daughter was a rider. Each plant weighed about a hundred pounds. By the time they were finished, Jose's back ached so badly he laid down in the back of the pick-up truck and rode back to the farm letting the bouncing road massage out the knots. It helped a bit but he marveled at how the other laborers were able to work so hard and never seem to tire. They were at least ten years older than Jose, or seemed to be. It was hard for him to tell, their Mexican features disguised a lot of wrinkles and replaced them with deep crevasses that could have been from age or just many days in the hot sun. Either way, their stamina was amazing.

It was after six when he finally got back to the bunk house. He stood under a hot shower longer than usual to assuage his back pain. It helped. Then he put on a clean pair of jeans and tee shirt and biked the four miles to the Wells farm. Karl McCurry was happy to offer Jose his old ten-speed since he now drove his father's old Dodge and since Jose didn't have a driver's license, or at least, so everyone had been told.

The last half mile of the trip was on Appaloosa Trail, a dusty dirt road pocked with horse manure. By the time Jose arrived, a thin film of light grey dusk covered his clothes. He brushed himself as he walked to the front porch where he could already see Micah and, the man he assumed was Bret Kennedy. Alex had described Bret correctly; he was a stocky man with short military-style brown hair, probably about thirty-five and already considered one of the best trainers in the world. If he and Terry hadn't worked for Micah's father so many years, he might have succumbed to the generous offers of employment he received from so many other farms. And like Micah's dad, Bret Kennedy was very fit. He looked a bit like a beat-up rugby player.

"This is the guy I was telling you about." Micah stood to introduce Bret to Jose. "Bret Kennedy, this is Jose."

Bret stood and extended his well-tanned arm. "Got a last name?" He said in a heavy Irish accent as he gripped Jose's hand.

"Martinez. Nice to meet you sir."

"Sir? Are we in the fucking army? The name's Bret."

"Bret it is."

Micah offered both men a beer from a green metal cooler next to his rocker. They all sat.

"Where you from, Jose?" Bret asked.

"Originally, from Ecuador, then about eight years up north, around New York and New Jersey."

"I filled Bret in on your background a bit and what you've been doing for Alex around here." Micah offered. "He was impressed by your cutting-in on the living room ceiling. And this guy's hard to impress."

"You did all that free-hand, no tape, huh?" Bret asked.

"Yeah, my dad and I did a lot of painting when I was young. I guess I have a pretty steady hand with a brush." Jose recalled his real-life experiences with his father, painting for their landlord.

The three men spent a few minutes talking about the projects Jose had been assigned since working for Alex McCurry. Bret was attracted to the young man's willingness to do just about anything and his ability to learn quickly. But he was concerned that Jose had so little knowledge of horses. Although his responsibilities would be focused on the facilities, not the animals, everything they did had to take the welfare of the horses into consideration. To stress the point, he offered the following examples to Jose.

"Suppose you're weed-whacking the grass around the fence posts. You gotta know if there are any animals around. The sound of that weed-whacker starting up could spook a horse, make him take off on a rider. People and animals could get hurt. Or, when you're choosing a varnish to use on the timbers in the barn, you need to consider the horses. Some have allergies to certain chemicals, some may chew on the wood if they smell something in there they think is food. Everything you do to or for the property has to be done with the horses in mind."

Jose nodded his understanding.

Bret continued, "Micah tells me you don't know shit from Shinola about the animals. We can solve that. You'll learn, but you need to always keep in mind, the horses come first. You're out cutting fields on a tractor and a summer thunderstorm comes up out of nowhere; fuck the tractor. You need to help us get the horses in the barn and tied down. They hate thunder. You're out hammering fence posts and a groom rides by on a horse, you stop hammering till he's out of sight. Get it?"

Jose liked Bret's aggressive, in-your-face approach to learning. There was no grey area left for uncertainty. "Yep. Horses come first."

Bret turned to Micah after taking a long swig from his beer bottle, "I think I can teach him what he needs to know. But keep him away from my animals until I say he's ready."

Micah knew his friend long enough to know he was playing the bad cop to Micah's good cop and smiled a bit. "I think it will work."

Micah stretched on the rocker and gazed out on the expansive lawn surrounding the compound. He had a good feeling about Jose. He sensed the man had potential that either he didn't know about himself or he wanted to keep secret for some reason. Either way, Micah was intrigued by the young Ecuadorian and respected how "Americanized" he'd become in just eight years.

"We haven't talked about money yet and as my father always says, 'You ain't done nothing till you figured out a price for it'. So, let's get to it." He leaned forward. "I know Alex is paying you a hundred a day off the books. That's…"

Jose cut him off. "Wait. There's something else we need to talk about first. Don't get me wrong. I'd love to come and work for you. That would be fantastic. But I've got a problem."

Jose explained his problem along with the entire fable about City College and the earthquake in Ecuador. Along the way he used a few Spanish terms just for story authenticity. He was beginning to feel comfortable with the lies. He practiced them so many times in his head, he might have begun believing them himself. When he was through, he clasped his hands and leaned forward. "I don't know what to do."

The reaction he got from Micah and Bret was not what he expected. They looked at each other and began to smile broadly. "That's your big problem?" Micah said.

"Yeah. How could I possibly travel to other countries without a passport. I don't even have a driver's license."

Bret leaned forward and put his hand on Jose's knee. "I think we can find a work-around for this." Then he looked at Micah and said, "Sounds like a job for Bert, huh?"

Micah realized Jose was confused by their reaction and tried to clarify what he and Bret knew but Jose didn't. "Jose, this happens to us all the time with the kids from Ireland. Don't worry. My dad knows a guy who knows a guy who can get you a passport that's as good as mine. It usually takes a few weeks and we'll need to get a passport photo of you, then he takes care of the rest. He can deal with the social security thing too. He's very resourceful." He looked over at Bret and gave him an impish grin.

And so it came to pass, that Jose Martinez came into existence on paper and in the eyes of the U.S. government, the social security office and the Florida department of motor vehicles. By the end of February, 2002, on paper, he was a legitimate U.S. citizen with a clean driver's license.

CHAPTER TWENTY-SIX

The helicopter banked hard to the right. Micah and Jose had checked out two more potential sites but neither were deemed to be workable. The equestrian center Micah hoped to build required at least one thousand acres of property if it were to be financially attractive to the developers. Micah wanted a two-hundred acre showground, leaving the rest for real estate development, mostly private homes and farms. To accomplish that, he needed to find a plot that was far enough from the ocean that it would be affordable and dry enough so it could be drained and turned into a series of canals and farms.

He'd been lining up potential developers for two years but coming up with a viable site was the challenge. Most of what they looked at today was just too wet and would have produced more lakes and canals than dry buildable land.

"Let's take a run over the coast before the sun goes down," he said to his pilot. "We'll see if we can spot some hot bikinis on the beach. Maybe find Jose a date for Saturday's Grand Prix." Micah liked to joke with Jose about not having a girlfriend, especially now that he himself, was engaged.

As the copter came down low over the coast of Palm Beach, Jose marveled at the spectacle. Miles and miles of pristine white beaches lined with some of the most expensive real estate in the world. Most of the homes were sheltered from those traveling by road by dense rows of hedges. But from the air, Jose could see the elaborate pools and gardens that surrounded the costly mansions. Many had tiled roofs and stucco walls, usually in a Spanish style of architecture. Some we very modern with expansive use of glass. And others were traditional Florida mansions with high arches and formidable pillars protecting the entrances.

It was late in the afternoon so most of the beachgoers had abandoned the sand but a few lingered at the water's edge hoping to observe a spectacular sunset. Jose could see from the altimeter they were only ninety feet in the air. At that altitude, it seemed they were racing along the shoreline.

"What exactly are we looking for over here? I mean besides a date for me?" Jose asked.

Micah shouted back, "Nothing. I just wanted to see the ocean. We live a few miles from it and we never see it because we're so wrapped up in the horses. We should just come to the beach next Monday and do some body surfing."

Monday's were the only days there were no events at the equestrian center. In fact, it had become an unofficial custom that everyone associated with the horses had Mondays off. After the Sunday afternoon Grand Prix, everything shut down until Tuesday morning. Everything except the nightclubs and bars which held their best events on Sunday night, allowing the riders, grooms and polo players to blow off some steam. The local police were busiest on Sunday nights.

"Okay, Jimmy. Let's head back to the farm. I'm meeting Lauren's parents tonight. I've got to shower before we drive into town."

"You know, for someone who has ice water in their veins when they're on a horse, you seem to really be sweating this parent thing. How bad could they be?" Jose asked.

In fact, Micah was meeting his fiancé's parents for the first time and was uncharacteristically nervous. All he knew about them was that they were from New York and had done a great job raising Lauren. But they weren't horse-people and he wasn't sure if they were comfortable handing their only daughter to someone who made a living in such a nonconventional fashion.

"I'm not nervous," he lied. "I just want to make a good first impression."

"Hey, this is 2006. You don't have to post a dowry or anything. You just have to be you."

Jimmy, the pilot chimed in, "Maybe that's what he's afraid of."

As the sleek helicopter headed back to the farm, Jose thought about what he'd just said. It was 2006. So much had happened to him in the last five years, since that horrible day in New York. It all seemed like a lifetime ago. In fact, it was a lifetime ago because it was a completely different lifetime. Back then, he was Joey Martinez, the unhappy, unsatisfied research analyst. He was married to a woman with whom he shared no dreams and trapped in a life he felt wasn't meant for him.

Today, he was Jose, the trusted facilities manager for one of the greatest horsemen in the world. People respected and admired the properties he managed and he had the confidence of his friends Micah and Bret. That was important to him.

He'd traveled to places he'd never dreamed he'd see; Dubai, Aachen, Barcelona, and Calgary. Although he wasn't part of the contingent Micah took to Athens for the 2004 Olympic games, he watched it all on television and roared as Micah and the U.S. team stood on the podium for gold medals. In some small way, he felt he had contributed to the effort. He knew he'd helped his friend achieve his life-long goal and he felt good about that. His friendship with Micah Wells meant a lot to him.

Jose had also discovered a hidden talent; something he always sensed was there but had never practiced. The Christmas gift from Erica McCurry, a set of drawing pencils and a sketch pad, had opened a door for him. He became passionate about drawing and his small apartment at the Wells compound was covered with his art, mostly drawings of the farm, the horses and even the people in his life.

And the person he sketched the most was Fiona Wells. He was fascinated by the beautiful woman. He watched her from a distance as she rode her grey mare around the center ring at the farm. He maneuvered to sit next to her when he was invited to family meals and enjoyed the sound of her faint voice. And he always volunteered to drive her and Bert to the airport whenever they left for one of their frequent trips to Europe, then anxiously awaited her return.

Jose was aware of his unhealthy attraction to Fiona. He knew nothing would ever come of it but he sensed, or maybe wanted to believe that she flirted with him from time to time. She was married to the patriarch of the estate and, for that reason alone, was completely off limits. Nonetheless, he fantasized about the two of them living on an island in the Mediterranean, growing grapes from which they made white wine and making love in the afternoon on one of the many cushioned lounge chairs surrounding their oversized pool.

The other face he sketched a lot was Lonnie's. This surprised him because, at the time, he'd considered their weekend at the lake house to be a one-time indiscretion. He never intended it to be more and, from the tone of Lonnie's send-off, neither did she. Yet, he kept thinking about her over the years. He wondered if she'd married. He asked himself, if she suddenly appeared, would he want to see her again. And if so, how would he explain his disappearance.

Oddly, he felt she would be the one person who might understand, and maybe forgive him.

So, he drew her. He had several sketches of her hanging in his apartment and several of the more intimate drawings in his portfolio, where he secretly kept the drawings of Fiona. His favor-ite pose for Lonnie was a view of her smiling face while she held her arms stretched over her head. It was etched in his memory from their last morning at the lake. It was a wonderful time, before all the trouble started.

CHAPTER TWENTY-SEVEN

Micah had arranged a two-bedroom suite for Lauren and her parents at the Chesterfield in the heart of Palm beach. Ordinarily, he would have invited them all to stay at his home, but this was September, a time of year he wasn't usually in Wellington, and the house wasn't ready for guests. The Chesterfield was a boutique hotel where he and Lauren had spent their first night together. He knew the irony wouldn't be lost on her.

Tina and Stan Barone had flown down from Long Island just to meet him. Unofficially, Lauren Barone was his fiancé, but Micah wanted to wait till he'd met her parents, and formally asked for her hand, before giving her the two-carat engagement ring he'd selected weeks ago in New York. He felt it would be disrespectful to her father to do it any other way.

Because Micah was in Wellington for just a few days, the usual contingent of farm vehicles, a Land Rover and a couple of SUVs, were not at his disposal. Instead, he was driving a silver Lexus that he'd taken in lieu of payment for a group lesson he'd done earlier that year. He didn't even like the car but when the cash-strapped client offered it as the final payment, Micah felt obligated to take it to maintain the relationship. The Range Rover was his transportation of choice.

As he headed east on Southern Boulevard, he thought about the commitment he was making. Marriage was something he always assumed was part of his future, he just didn't think it would happen so soon. He was thirty-two, Lauren was twenty-three; yet he knew he'd found the right woman. From the first time he saw her, sitting on the rail at a warm-up ring at the show, he was smitten. Lauren had been working as a groom for another family and spent the winter season with them in Wellington in 2006. Being a capable rider herself, she was well aware of who Micah was and his in position in the equestrian world, but she declined his first two requests for a date. She assumed his lofty status had gone to his head. When she finally agreed to go out with him, she was surprised that someone so successful and famous in his field could be so humble and grounded. They fell deeply in love and saw each other constantly while they were in Wellington.

In the spring of 2006, when they both returned to New York, Micah to Woodfield and Lauren to her job as a groom in East Hampton, they were a three-hour drive apart and only saw each other every other weekend. But in late August, when Micah was in Bridgehampton for the annual Hampton Classic, they spent every spare moment together and it was there they decided to spend the rest of their lives together. Anne Kursinski, a three-time Olympic veteran, won the Classic but Micah won Lauren Barone's heart.

And still, Micah was nervous about this evening. He understood that Lauren's parents knew little about his chosen field. In fact, they'd never been to an equestrian event. He wasn't even sure how much Lauren had told them about him. All he knew for sure was that for a long time, she hadn't told them about him at all. She was worried they would not approve of the significant difference in age.

He deliberately parked the Lexus two blocks from the restaurant so as not to appear ostentatious in his arrival. He knew he was a few minutes late and that they'd be sitting at the outside table he'd reserved at Bice, his favorite place on Worth Avenue. He walked the two blocks, throwing on his sport jacket just as he arrived at the restaurant.

Lauren rose to greet him with a kiss appropriate for the occasion, but not one reflecting the two-week absence they'd endured. She wore a white sun dress that reminded Micah how much she looked like Steve Martin's daughter in the movie "Father of the Bride", although he never knew the actress' name. Lauren made all the introductions and everyone sat.

At first, Micah asked a lot of questions of the Barones. How'd they meet? What did Stan do for a living? He knew Tina was involved in real estate so he asked her views on the market.

It was during the appetizers that the evening got interesting. That's when Lauren's father decided he needed to know a lot more than he did about the man his daughter was in love with.

"Is your family from Florida, Micah?"

He explained he was actually from Woodfield and only spent the winter in Florida and that his mom had passed away. He didn't mention the riding accident.

Stan asked some follow-up questions about Woodfield and did Micah know so-and-so who Tina thought lived there but neither were really sure.

"Your dad still around?"

This one was easy for Micah. "Oh yeah. My father and I do a lot of business together. I live on his farm and we work together almost every day. He's sort of my hero."

Getting to the question he most wanted an answer to, Stan Barone asked, "So, what exactly do you do?"

Micah could tell the question was really, "How are you going to support my daughter?", a very reasonable question for the father of the prospective bride.

"I ride horses." He said as he twirled a bit of spaghetti.

"Yes, Lauren's told us that. But what do you do for a living?" Stan asked politely.

Micah took a sip of water and responded, "I ride horses. I get paid to do that, especially if I win." He was, unfortunately, unaware of Stan's naivete on the subject and failed to satisfy him.

At this point, Stan Barone was doing calculations in his head about how much longer he'd have to work before retiring so he could support his daughter and her cowboy of a husband. He considered diplomacy but decided to cut to the chase.

"So, let me understand. You ride horses in competition. And when you win, you get paid? Is that right?"

Without looking up from his pasta, Micah innocently said, "Yes, sometimes the prize money is significant."

The elder Barone continued his inquiry. "So, let's say you are wildly successful at this. Could you someday do this, say, at the Olympics?"

Again, without looking up from his pasta, Micah casually, and as humbly as he could, responded, "Yes. I won a gold medal in Athens two years ago."

Micah and Lauren were married the following November at Oheka Castle on Long Island.

CHAPTER TWENTY-EIGHT

Marco Brunelli climbed out of the lavish pool and glanced around. The warm Mediterranean sun filled the hillside surrounding his villa. From where he stood he could see the Amalfi coastline for miles until the mountains plunged into the blue sea at the horizon. His home in Ravello clung to the side of the mountain between Marmorata and Castiglione.

Marco toweled himself dry. His longtime valet, Paulo, handed him a cell phone with the words "*Questa e la chiamata che stavi aspettando*", this is the call you've been waiting for. As the automobile magnate donned his sunglasses, he studied his surroundings. His pool and patio hung precariously on the edge of a mountain six hundred feet above the sea. His eleven-bedroom villa, terraced carefully into the mountainside, had been featured years before on "Lifestyles of the Rich and Famous" and Robin Leach and his camera crew had been Marco's guests for nearly a week.

"*Ciao, questo e Brunelli*," the well-tanned Italian said into the phone.

"Marco, it's Micah. Bon giorno. I have good news." The voice from America reported.

"Ciao, Micah. Tell me."

"I found Gabriella's horse."

"Quanta?" The Italian wanted to know what his daughter's latest amusement was about to cost him.

"Well within your budget, my friend. I picked her up a few weeks ago in Canada and have been working with her every day since. She's a talented horse and very gentle. Gabriella will love her."

"Quanta?" The skeptic repeated.

"Six hundred thousand U.S."

"Bene." Marco was happy to hear his friend had underspent his budget by four hundred thousand dollars. "When can we see her?"

"Come to Florida and have your daughter ride her. If she's not thrilled with the mare, I will keep her myself. Like I said, she's a beautiful mare. You'll stay with Lauren and me. I'll cook."

"Do you want us to come or not?" he joked.

"Alright, we'll go out. But plan to stay a few days. We can play golf and you can stay for the Grand Prix on Sunday.

"Sounds wonderful, my friend. Stella, Gabriella and I will see you Friday. Ciao." He turned to Paulo and instructed him to have his plane scheduled to fly to Wellington in two days. One of the many perks of being CEO of a race car company was the Gulfstream 280 he convinced the board to put at his disposal.

And Marco always enjoyed the company of Micah and his wife, Lauren. Besides being a seventy-five percent owner of Micah's top horse, Ruby, the horse he took to the Olympics in Athens, he and Micah had become close friends. Usually, he didn't like doing business with friends but Micah Wells was an exception. He trusted Micah to do the right thing all the time. His most recent purchase was an example of that trustworthiness. Marco had authorized Micah to spend up to one million U.S. dollars in pursuit of an exceptional horse for his daughter and Micah stood to receive a twenty-five percent commission on the sale. Yet he negotiated the sale down to six-hundred thousand on Marco's behalf, costing himself one hundred thousand of potential commission. "*Ho fidu-cia che l'uomo con la mia vita,*" he said to Paulo. I trust that man with my life.

And Micah enjoyed his relationship with Marco and Stella Brunelli and their twenty-year-old daughter, Gabriella. He'd started training Gabby when she was fourteen and watched her blossom into a very capable rider, not one likely to ever compete at his level, but a rider who enjoyed the thrill of show jumping almost as much as Micah himself. And with Marco's money providing her increasingly better mounts every few years, she was beginning to win young-rider events all over Europe.

While Gabriella was the initial focus of their business relationship, Marco and Micah worked together on several projects. Although he'd never been on a horse himself, Marco, like many other aristocrats, enjoyed owning horses that others could showcase. He enjoyed going to the events and watching Micah jump. He loved the people that surrounded the sport; not just the super-rich, but famous athletes, rock stars and people from Hollywood to whom he might not otherwise have access.

Once, after a huge victory in Germany, Micah asked Marco, "What pleasure do you get from spending so much money on an animal you don't want to ride? I mean, when I win on Ruby, I get all the credit. I get all the accolades and I get most of the prize money. What do you get out of it?"

Marco responded, "*Vorrei arrivare a dire che il mio cavallo!*" I get to say, that's my horse!

To show his good friend and valued sponsor the proper respect, when the Brunellis' Jet arrived on Friday afternoon, Micah himself drove to the airport to pick them up. Gestures like that were not lost on Marco. Marco had once done the same when Micah and his father arrived for the FEI World Cup in Verona, Italy's biggest equestrian event, and Micah always remembered how important that made him feel.

Micah had been riding that morning and went to the airport in his breeches. When he greeted Marco, who was wearing a four thousand dollar Brioni suit and Hermes tie, he said, "Why do you crazy Italians feel you have to dress for a plane ride like it was the 1950's?" Then he added, "And it's your own plane!" They embraced and laughed.

On the drive back to the farm Stella asked in broken English, "Why no children yet Micah? She such a nice girl." It was a question others had asked too. And Micah offered Stella the same answer he gave everyone else, including his father, "After Beijing." The reference was to the upcoming Olympic games in Beijing later that summer. Although he had not yet officially qualified for the U.S. team, everyone in the sport expected he would. That expectation put great pressure on Micah and he needed to focus all his attention on that goal. A pregnancy would be a major distraction. To make the Olympic team again, he needed to score well on four upcoming events. He needed to stay focused.

When they arrived at the farm, Jose and Bret were there to greet them. Micah knew Jose and Marco would hit it off even though they had almost nothing in common. Marco knew Bret for many years.

"Ciao Marco," Bret said with the strongest Irish accent he could muster. "Wait till you meet her. She's a magnificent animal." His excitement for the mare they hoped to sell Marco could not be contained.

Marco looked to Micah as he stepped from the SUV, "You never told me the horse's name. Quai e suo nome?"

"Green Runner", Bret announced with pride. He'd looked up the Italian translation the night before. "Guida Verde." This time he said the words with proper Italian inflection.

Jose had begun to take luggage from the trunk when Stella and Gabriella emerged from the far side of the SUV. He'd seen photos of Stella Brunelli in Micah's home and she appeared very much as he expected; a slightly overweight but attractive woman in her late forties who dressed stylishly. And Gabriella looked like so many other female riders; young, tall, slender, privileged and pretty. With a riding helmet on and attired in the usual breeches and tight-fitting shirt, they all looked alike to Jose.

Bret was already leading Marco, Gabriella and Micah to the barn to view the new horse. Lauren came from the house and greeted Stella with a warm hug. She glanced at Jose as if to say, "I see they've left you. Would you mind bringing the bags inside?" He was happy to oblige.

"Guest bedrooms upstairs?" Jose inquired from experience.

"Yeah. That would be great. Thanks so much, Jose." Then she added, "Stella, this is our good friend Jose. Jose's been working for Micah for about… six years now." She glanced at Jose to confirm her guestimate. "Jose is the facilities manager here and in Woodfield. He keeps both farms looking beautiful. Wait till you see the flowers in the back."

Stella Brunelli offered Jose her hand. "Nice to meet you Jose."

He was reminded of the moment, years before, when he first met Fiona Wells. Both aristocratic women had offered their hand and he wasn't sure if he should shake it, kiss it or genuflect. Although the women couldn't have been more sincere, Jose felt they were somehow making a clear distinction between their place and his. Even though, over the years he had gained everyone's respect for the outstanding job he did managing the farms, he always felt beneath them. He was a manager of stuff; buildings, flowers, supplies, equipment and logistics. All important to the operation. But he wasn't one of the "horse people". In this world, it was the "horse people" who were royalty.

After dropping the luggage in the bedrooms, Jose joined the others touring the barn. He caught up to them just as Gabriella was meeting her new horse for the first time. Bret had led Guida Verde from her stall, which already had a brass plaque with her name on it, out to the central ring. Gabriella wasn't dressed for riding so Bret mounted the mare and cantered around the ring to display the majestic animal's style.

"She's beautiful," Gabriella gushed. "Un bel cavallo".

"I can see why you think this is a special animal Micah. She seems aware. She seems to know we are watching her and that she is being evaluated." Marco said. "It's amazing."

As Bret and Guida Verde continued to circle the ring, Micah, Marco, Gabriella and some of the grooms leaned on the white rail fence watching. When Jose approached, he hung back a few feet, not wanting to interrupt their moment. These were the times he felt most isolated. Leaning on the rail were people of all ages and backgrounds but they had one thing in common, a love of horses. It wasn't something you learned. You either loved the beasts or you didn't. He needed to let them have their moment before he interrupted.

Micah spotted him out of the corner of his eye. "Jose, I want you to meet Marco and his lovely daughter Gabriella. They just arrived from Italy and will be staying with us a few days."

Jose extended his hand and Gabriella took it first. "Hello," she said with no discernable accent.

"So, you are the special lady who is going to take Guida Verde from us?" Jose said. Then he looked to Marco and offered his hand. "Mr. Brunelli, I've heard a lot about you from Micah and Bert. It's a pleasure."

"The pleasure is mine," returned Marco with a solid handshake. Then they all turned their attention back to the ring.

"Poppa, posso ride adesso?" Gabriella asked. "Poppa, can I ride her now?"

He knew his daughter had mustered all the self-restraint within her to have waited this long to ask. It was all she spoke of on the plane.

"Si." Then he looked to Micah to be sure it was okay with him.

"By the time you have your boots and breeches on, Bret will have her all warmed up for you. Go." Micah said and gave her the shooing motion pointing toward the house.

After she was gone, Micah turned to Marco and said, "You're going to have your hands full with that one. She's turned into a beautiful woman."

"Si, my friend. My daughter is a passionate young thing. Fortunately, so far, her passion seems to be focused on her riding and her schooling. She's very serious about both and, to the best of my knowledge, hasn't had a serious boyfriend yet. But, she's only twenty."

"And how are the lessons going in Verona? Is she happy with Frankie?" Micah was referring to the woman he'd recommended for riding lessons in Italy, Francesca Santi, herself a very accomplished Grand Prix rider.

"Si. It's very good. And her university work is ahead of schedule. She could graduate this June if she wanted. But, I think she wants to...how do you say...milk it out a bit longer."

Micah remembered that Marco's daughter was studying art history at the University of Verona. That's one of the qualities that made him so good at horse-trading. He made a point of remembering things about his clients and their families. "Art is a complex thing," he said. "I can see that it would take some time to master it." He winked at Marco to indicate his friend was being manipulated by his beautiful daughter.

Acknowledging the sarcasm, Marco said, "Si, I have a weakness for my daughter. She knows I can't say no. That weakness has cost me many Euros."

The two men were laughing as Gabriella emerged from the house in her riding attire. From what Jose had learned over the years, the petite young thing was probably wearing close to three thousand dollars of boots, skin-tight breeches, tailored shirt and helmet; all to ride a horse that couldn't care less about her wardrobe. He'd also learned there was much formality to the sport. For example, gentlemen riders in an event were expected to wear a tie and jacket of a certain color and cut. To do otherwise, while not a formal violation of the rules, would be unthinkable.

Jose studied the beautiful young Italian. Her shapely figure was now accented by the tight-fitting riding gear. Her dark brown hair was pulled back in a bun to accommodate her helmet. As she approached the men, he couldn't help thinking of a photo he'd seen years ago of a young Jackie Kennedy, also a capable rider. Then again, most of the young girls in the sport looked pretty much the same once they donned a helmet.

Bret spotted Gabriella and walked Guida Verde over to where they stood. Dismounting, he said to her, "She likes to pull to the right a bit just before a jump. Other than that, she's perfect. Try to land softly." He knew the only jumps in the ring were set at two feet-three inches, a very modest jump for an experienced rider, but it would give Gabriella a sense of what the mare could do. "Take her around a few times before you try a fence. Get to know each other."

Bret then offered to give her a leg up but instead, Gabriella took the reins and walked to the front of the horse and gently stroked her head. She was looking the animal directly in the eyes and softly whispering something in Italian to her new friend. Only after two minutes of the intimate greeting did she accept Bret's offer and took a leg-up into the saddle. Bret adjusted the stirrups and told the horse to behave. Then he gave her a pat on the hind quarter and said, "You two get to know each other out there."

Gabriella leaned forward and stroked the mare's long muscular neck. "Facciamo questo insieme," she whispered. Let's do this together.

What Jose remembered most about that afternoon was the grace with which Gabriella Brunelli rode. He'd seen hundreds of other women riding, some world-class riders, but none rode as gently as Gabriella. It was as if she was riding on a cloud, barely touching the earth, each hoof landing silently on the sandy ring floor. The rider and animal seemed to be one; each trying to circle the ring as quietly as possible and each trying to disturb as little of the sand as possible.

On their second canter around the ring, Jose took out his phone to take a picture. As Gabriella and Guida Verde approached the spectators, he zoomed in close and captured a great shot of the two faces. They already seemed to be old friends. They already seemed to understand the cadence of the other.

On their third pass, Gabriella easily took the mare over a jump, it's hind legs clearing the top rail by nearly a foot. Then she did a double and two more singles, all with the same easy stride.

"I told you this was a special animal," Micah said to Marco.

"Si, I see what you mean." Marco was almost teary. It gave him great pleasure to see his daughter so happy. He was a very emotional man.

That night was "dinner night", the one night each week that Micah and Lauren treated the entire farm staff to dinner at a local restaurant. There were events at the showgrounds later that night so it had to be an early dinner at their favorite Mexican restaurant. Marco, Stella and Gabriella joined them but Jose stayed behind. Bert and Fiona weren't due back from Ocala until Sunday so the hostess was surprised when Lauren only asked for a table for twelve.

The next morning, when Gabriella came out to the barn to rub down Guida Verde, Jose was waiting for her. "I have a gift for you," he told her.

"For me, a gift?"

He proudly handed her a portfolio jacket. Inside was a letter-size drawing he'd worked on the previous night and well into the morning. As Gabriella turned the drawing over to study it, she gasped, "Come e bello!" How beautiful!

It was a drawing in charcoal, Jose's favorite medium, of the photograph he'd taken of Gabriella riding her new horse. The focus of the drawing was their two faces perfectly aligned and in harmony. What made this picture different from most of his others was that after drawing the faces in charcoal, Jose added color to capture the motion of the scene. In this case, he used a mixed shade of green oil, recognizing the horse's name. While the oil was still wet, he then used the palm of his hand to smear it in a way that told the story of the gentle motion he'd witnessed. The effect was unique and dramatic.

"You did this? You painted this for me?" She was close to tears with joy.

"Yes." He showed her the photo he'd taken on his phone. "I took this yesterday while you were riding and used it as my model for the drawing. I'm glad you like it."

"It's…how you say…amazing!" She leaned forward and gave him a soft kiss on the cheek. "I go show my mother."

CHAPTER TWENTY-NINE

That winter Jose painted several more versions of what he came to call the Gabriella shot. He tried different uses of oils and water colors and experimented with different cloths to smear the paint before it dried. In all cases, he was striving for the illusion of motion.

Being completely self-taught in the craft, he labored under no preconceptions of what could or could not be done. He tried whatever he liked, no matter how unconventional it seemed. He even used small blocks of wood, leftovers from the barn construction, rubbing the paintings to obtain the motion effect. Nothing was off limits. And he was becoming quite prolific.

His small apartment, on the top floor of the Wells' bunk house, was beginning to become overrun with his art. Piled against every wall leaned stacks of canvas. His bedroom walls were covered with paintings and drawings of horses, each with the horse's name handwritten beneath. Sometimes, when he wasn't busy with work around the compound, he'd walk the paddocks over at the equestrian center and take photos of the elegant animals. He liked to do so in the afternoon for the best light.

In the evenings, he'd go to the shows, even if no one from the Wells farm was riding, to photograph other riders and their horses. Bert Wells gave him his old camera so he'd have a powerful zoom lens to take close-ups as the riders jumped or maneuvered their way around the complex courses. Jose became a fixture at the show grounds.

It was Fiona who suggested he rent a booth at the show to display his work. Surrounding the International arena, the center ring reserved for the biggest events, were dozens of small booths selling everything from cotton candy to expensive saddles. There were displays of home-made crafts, usually with an equestrian theme, over-priced accessories for dogs, jewelry, fine riding boots, even a local chiropractor who, for fifty dollars, promised to miraculously relieve your neck pain in fifteen minutes.

Fiona and Bert Wells became Jose's champions. Bert used his considerable position in the equestrian community to convince the Center's board to allow one additional booth for Jose's display and Fiona used her persuasive charms to get him a prime location, right next to the ice cream vendor, the show's most popular attraction. By the end of February, 2008, Jose was sitting in his booth four nights a week, displaying his work.

He had no idea what price to ask for his work. He considered pricing the pieces at one hundred dollars, which, if he sold five paintings a month, would cover the cost of the booth rental. When Bert learned of his plan, he stormed into his apartment. Jose was in the process of selecting the pieces he wanted to show that night.

"Fiona tells me you start your booth tonight. That's great kid. But she also tells me you don't know shit from Shinola about selling something." Bert was trying to be helpful. "You're crazy if you give these things away for a hundred bucks." He pointed to the many canvases blanketing the apartment.

"Listen to me kid." He put his arm around Jose. "These people paid hundreds of thousands if not millions for their horses. I think they'd be insulted if you thought a painting of their pride and joy was only worth a hundred bucks. I say you charge five grand. If the pricks want to jew you down a little, don't let them. Make them think you don't give a shit about the money. That's the only attitude they respect. These are horse people. They don't give a fuck about money. They boast about paying too much for something."

Jose was flabbergasted but didn't want to insult the wisdom of his mentor. He was embarrassed to do so but put tiny yellow stickers on the bottom of his canvases that said $5K. The very first night, he sold two paintings, both to the owners of horses he'd admired and painted. Both were in the same style he used for Gabriella's drawing; a charcoal backdrop with colorful highlights of vivid oils.

The next night he sold two more. Fiona and Bert made a point of stopping by his booth several times during the show, just to be seen. It wasn't lost on Jose that their stamp of approval was contributing to his success.

On the third night, an admirer walked by and commented that Jose's work reminded him of a "Painful blend of Monet and Leroy Neiman", the American artist known for his brilliantly colored expressionist paintings, usually of athletes. Not knowing if he was being mocked, insulted or complimented, Jose simply said, "I've heard that before."

CHAPTER THIRTY

Any other year, Memorial Day would be a day of rest for everyone in the equestrian world. But with the Beijing Olympics just a few months away, for anyone whose rider was still in the running for one of the four places on the American team, there were no days off. Not until after Beijing. And, as of Memorial Day 2008, all four spots were still up for grabs.

Two of the four qualifying events were held earlier in the month. All the favorites, and several underdogs, did well enough to still be in the running. There were still twelve potential Olympic riders vying for the coveted spots with two more qualifiers later in June. Micah Wells was expected to be one of them.

But tonight, he was a host, or co-host to be precise. He and his father were hosting their annual charity ball at Wells Hill to benefit St. Jude Children's Hospital. The celebration was considered the kickoff event of the summer season in the world of show jumping and this year, Bert Wells had promised his guests a special surprise. He'd called in a favor and booked the Beach Boys as the surprise musical entertainment.

Everyone who was anyone in the equestrian world would be there; not just the premier riders, sponsors, owners, trainers and vets, but basically, anyone who had invested in a serious horse. That included invitees with surnames of Mellon, Gates, Bloomberg, Springsteen, Spielberg, and Hoffman. Those who were invited and unable to attend would send significant checks in their place. It all made St. Jude very happy.

This year, Jose was especially excited for the ball; not because of the Beach Boys but because Bert had insisted he donate a few paintings to be live-auctioned to the highest bidder. Jose wouldn't benefit directly from the auction but Bert promised the bidding would set a new floor for his work in the future. He had three of his favorite works framed professionally and displayed on easels scattered around the massive courtyard.

The other reason Jose had been looking forward to the event was that Gabriella Brunelli and her parents would be there. They'd flown in to JFK that morning and were staying in the city. Gabriella had called him from the airport to say they'd arrived and would be staying the entire week. She asked if he could get any time off during the week to show her around the city. He felt a personal debt to her for kick-starting his commercial enterprise and after all, spending a day with a beautiful young billionaire-heiress sounded like a delightful divergence from work at the farm. He knew Micah would encourage him to go anyway, if, for no other reason, to keep an important client happy.

Four hundred guests had been invited. Three hundred seventy were expected to attend. The courtyard was decorated with extra flowers and even a few palm trees Bert brought in for the Wellington effect. There were forty-eight round tables with white linens and colossal centerpieces of yellow roses and hydrangea. A twelve hundred square foot dance floor had been erected in the center of the yard, each panel illuminated from below.

Bert, Fiona, Micah and Lauren Wells stood at the entrance and personally greeted and thanked every guest. Jose stood near the bar watching for the arrival of the Brunelli family. Oddly, Gabriella was the first woman Jose took an interest in since 9-11. For nearly seven years he felt numb about women. He couldn't get past the profound guilt he harbored for hurting Claire and for causing Sarah Bideaux's death. He felt unworthy of a woman's trust. Those two ghosts lingered nearby whenever Lauren had tried to fix him up with someone. After a while, she gave up. It's not that he didn't want a relationship. He just couldn't get past the guilt. Every time he'd been introduced to a single woman, the saw the ghosts.

But his limited time with Gabriella had been different. He didn't understand why, but he was grateful for the composure he felt when around her. Maybe it was the language barrier. The Italian beauty spoke fluent English but had trouble with the finer nuances of our complex language. He was happy to help her understand the difference between "ticked off" and "full of ticks". It made her approachable.

So, his objective tonight was to monopolize Gabriella and share with her the itinerary he'd planned for later in the week. She'd said she'd already seen the big tourist attractions; the Empire State Building, Statue of Liberty, Museum of Modern Art. So, he planned to show her some of his favorites; Central Park at night, Little Italy, walking over the Brooklyn Bridge and Coney Island.

A few years ago, he would have declined an invitation to walk around Manhattan, even with Gabriella. But he was no longer concerned about being spotted by someone from his past life. His appearance had changed dramatically since 9-11. He now had a goatee and his long dark hair was pulled back in a ponytail. His skin was darker than it had ever been due to all the time he spent outdoors rather than behind a trading desk. He looked very much like the persona he created- an Ecuadorian immigrant.

At eight o'clock, Bert Wells took the stage and welcomed his guests. He spoke for a few minutes about the good work being done by St. Jude in Memphis and the research break-throughs they'd achieved since the last gala. He introduced the auction of

Jose's three paintings, gave a quick background of the artist and instructions on how to generously bid. Then, with fitting fanfare, he introduced the surprise entertainment and two of the original Beach Boys ran onto the stage. They started their first set with Sloop John B and the dancefloor filled.

Jose spotted Gabriella near the stage and edged his way toward her. The music was loud so when he got near her he needed to shout his well-rehearsed greeting. "Benvenuto al nostro festa pazza," Welcome to our crazy party.

She responded with a kiss and hug, then said, "I need a drink."

They spent the first hour dancing and talking during the breaks. "I want to show you something," he told her. "Come with me."

He took her to see one of the three paintings displayed. It was a more complex version of the original drawing he'd given her. Unlike the original, this one was alive with multiple colors. Guida Verde's face was ablaze with several shades of green and Gabriella's was resplendent in a brilliant reds and blends of red and white. She immediately recognized the colors of the Italian flag. "Ce bella." She was very touched.

Meanwhile, Bert Wells was working the crowd and making a point of letting his guests know the girl in the red, white and green painting was Marco Brunelli's daughter and that the artist lived right here at Wells Hill. He didn't mention Jose was their facilities manager. He was determined to drive up the value of Jose's work and letting the crowd know the artist was among them seemed to be helping. Bert was a skillful tactician. He knew all he needed to do was convince two or three patrons they had to have one of Jose's pieces. That would start a bidding war at the auction and hopefully create a frenzy of bidding activity.

And he was right. When the auction began, the opening bid on the first piece was twenty thousand dollars. When the bidding got to fifty-five thousand, one of the finalist asked if the artist would sign the work. When Bert assured her he would, the bidding went to seventy-five thousand.

The second piece also went for seventy-five thousand, again, with Bert's assurance the artist would sign the work. By the time Gabriella's piece was displayed, Bert had everyone's attention, precisely the crescendo he'd planned. With much fanfare, he found Gabriella in the crowd and introduced her as the subject and Guida Verde as her gifted horse. She was embarrassed but enjoyed being the subject of so much attention for the moment.

"To be fair," Bert told the crowd, "I must exclude Gabriella's father, Marco, from the bidding. Besides, he already has an earlier version hanging in his villa in Ravello." He knew that would be like throwing blood in the water for the sharks. Many in the crowd would like to say they had the same artwork as Marco Brunelli.

The bidding started at thirty thousand and quickly went to one hundred thousand in ten thousand dollar jumps. Jose was astounded. A hedge fund manager from Greenwich, who looked to curry favor with the Italian auto magnate, took the work home for two hundred forty thousand. In a little over twenty minutes, Jose's works, fueled by Bert's skillful showmanship, had raised almost four hundred thousand dollars for the worthy charity. He was bursting with pride.

He was being congratulated by several guests when Gabriella found him and handed him a champagne flute. "Salute," she said softly. It was clear to Jose, this was not her first glass of champagne. Her body was swaying with the music.

Jose was about to ask her to dance when Bert grabbed his arm and maneuvered him toward one of the barns. He wanted to showcase Jose to the three winners and, as promised, have him dedicate each work personally with a black flair he produced from his jacket pocket. It was clear, Bert had choreographed the auction long before it began.

Jose was happy to oblige and equally glad to learn the picture of Gabriella and Guida Verde had been purchased for the hedge fund manager's daughter, herself, an avid rider. He signed the back of the oil painting, "From Jose to Mandy. Always ride softly." Then he signed the front of the work with the only name he ever used on his artwork, "Jose".

By the time he returned to look for Gabriella, she was dancing in the midst of several young people. He watched her from a distance. She seemed to be enjoying everything about the evening and was a much better dancer than was he. As "Good Vibrations" was ending the group of dancers began to disperse. But then the first few chords of "God Only Knows" echoed through the courtyard and he noticed Gabriella was now standing with just one person. The pace of the evening slowed and couples embraced for the slow dance under the stars. Gabriella and the tall, dark boy were already in each other's arms and moving to the rhythm of the music.

Lauren Wells noticed Jose standing alone near the bar and walked over to him. "Want to dance sailor?"

"I'm not much of a dancer," he replied sheepishly.

"I guarantee you're better than Micah. He hates to dance. Come on." She motioned for him to join her on the dance floor.

They drifted around in circles for the rest of the song, then gyrated to "I Get Around". Jose wasn't exaggerating, he wasn't a dancer. When the song ended, Lauren pulled him by the hand toward the bar. "His name is Christiano Berra."

"Who?"

"The guy dancing with Gabriella. The guy you were looking at the entire time we were out there."

"I don't know what…"

"Oh, bullshit! Anyone can see from a mile away, you've got the big-time hots for her. Why not? She's fabulous."

"Okay," he confessed. "I was hoping to get to know her a little better tonight." She heard the huge disappointment in his voice.

"Well, don't worry about him. He's bad news. Her parents would never allow her to go with him. Hell, I wouldn't let her date him!" She emphasized the word "I".

"You know him?" he inquired.

"I know everyone here, duh."

"Why don't you like him?"

"He's a polo player from Brazil. He spends most of the winter in Wellington with his parents. They're here too. Them, I like. They rent a farm just down the road. But he drinks way too much and I think he's into some drugs too. Just generally bad news."

"Sounds like there's some personal history here?" he asked impishly.

"Yep. We had one date when I was eighteen. He was probably twenty. I spent the whole night trying to keep his hands out of my Jackson Brown tee shirt. He's a pig." Lauren left no doubt about her feelings for the man.

None of this information was making Jose feel any better as he watched Gabriella and the pig talking near the bar.

"You should go over and rescue her." Lauren advised. "Bring her a glass of champagne."

"Does she know him? I mean, before tonight. Did she know him?"

"Probably just by reputation. The Brunellis don't spend much time in the states. Gabby does most of her riding in Europe."

Lauren spied Micah waving her over. "I've got to go kiss some ass. You're on your own. I say, go for it." She gave him a sisterly kiss on the cheek for encouragement and wandered over to her husband who was talking to the Lieutenant Governor.

Jose decided to take Lauren's advice but wanted a shot of courage before doing so. He asked the bartender for three flutes of champagne; one for at the bar and two to bring over to Gabriella. Still, he thought the idea of him upending a rich international polo player was ludicrous. Gabriella was the daughter of a billionaire. What could she see in him?

Unfortunately for all concerned, he waited too long to gather his courage. By the time he made his move with the champagne flutes, Gabriella and Christiano were walking from the dance floor toward the front gate. The crowd was thick but he decided to follow them, keeping a safe distance. When he got close to the front gate, he could see that the valet was already on his way to retrieve Christiano's car while Christiano and Gabriella held hands waiting at the valet table.

Jose leaned against a stone wall contemplating his next move. Maybe Lauren was judging him too harshly. Maybe Gabriella knew what she was doing. Maybe an heiress could only see him as the nobody he was. Or maybe she just had too much to drink, in which case, should he stop her from driving off with Christiano? Or, would that just appear desperate?

When the Porsche convertible arrived at the valet area and the polo player helped her get in, he knew there was nothing he could do. The car rolled down the driveway and disappeared behind a bend of thick privet hedge.

Jose felt like a heartbroken teenager. Still leaning against the wall, he drank both glasses of champagne, then rejoined the party.

CHAPTER THIRTY-ONE

U sually at 6:13 A.M. Bert Wells was talking a brisk walk around the farm. He liked to be the first one to see everything. If a tree fell during the night, he wanted to be first to notice it. If one of the horses was sick, he wanted to be the one to report his suspicion to Bret. He liked being first.

On the morning after his fundraiser, his pace was particularly brisk. It had been a great night. They didn't have a final count yet but it looked like they'd raised a little over two million dollars for the St. Jude Children's Research Hospital. He felt satisfied. Bert and Fiona knew they led a very privileged life, so doing something for others just made sense. The phrase he liked to use on his friends when trying to pry a donation from them was, "Your kids already fly first class or private, so what the fuck are you saving it for. Do some good with your fucking money!" His in-your-face approach to philanthropy usually worked.

As his walk took him around the back of the main stable and into the courtyard, he was impressed that Jose had everything back to normal already. The stage, the tables, the chairs were all gone.

All that remained of the previous evening were the three palm trees which sat in large pots at the front gate as if they were waiting for a bus. That's what he admired most about Jose; the kid was a doer. He was probably up till near dawn supervising the crews from the rental company so that, in the morning, all signs of the party would be gone and Wells Hill could get back to the business at hand. And the current focus of that business was Beijing.

If Micah made the U.S. Equestrian team, it would mean millions of dollars in endorsements, additional sales, and bonuses from his sponsors. While any compensation from the Olympic organizers would be de minimus, the ancillary benefits were considerable.

And so, Beijing was everyone's focus and everyone on the farm had a role to play. The third qualifier was in two weeks in Lexington, and Micah needed to finish in the top three to keep his Olympic hopes alive. Jose's role was probably the most indirect. He wasn't directly involved with the horses or with Micah's training. But Bert wanted to make sure Jose understood the importance of the status quo. In other words, if the farm operated smoothly, as it usually did, everyone else's job would be easier. If a shipment of feed was delivered on the day it was expected, everyone could stay focused on their objectives. If something needed repainting or if a road needed to be repaved, don't even think about starting that project until after Beijing. Horses don't like the smell of most paint or the roar of tractors.

Bert wanted to stop by Jose's apartment to give him a hearty pat on the back both for the successful auction and for the efficient clean-up, but it was way too early. He'd find him later. He decided to take one extra lap of the property before heading to the gym, but first he needed to stretch out a stiff leg muscle. He pushed against a fencepost to extend his calf muscle.

That's when his cell phone rang.

⇒⊣ ⊢⇐

Jose's day usually started around 6:45, but he'd been up with the catering and equipment rental people until nearly five A.M. so, this morning, he treated himself to two extra hours. He showered, dressed in his usual jeans and Wells Hill tee shirt and headed to the barn to see if there was any coffee left.

He was surprised to find the barn empty. The horses were all in their stalls but the grooms were absent. Normally, they'd be in the wash stall bathing horses. Today, the wash stall was dry. It was nearly nine and none of the usual chores seemed to be getting done.

He walked back to the bunk house but no one was there either so he headed for the main house. As he approached the front porch, Lauren descended the creaky wooden steps to greet him. She looked terrible, as if she'd just be awakened from an incomplete night's sleep. She was still in her pajamas. Something was very wrong with the cadence of the farm. No one was doing what they'd normally be doing on a Tuesday morning.

"Where is everyone today?" He shouted as he approached.

Lauren waited for him to draw near. When they were face to face at the foot of the porch steps, she took both his hands in hers. He could tell she'd been crying.

"Jose, I have some terrible news." Her lips were trembling.

His first thought was that Micah had heard from the Olympic committee and that he was out of the running for some reason. At Wells Hill, that would be terrible news.

"What's wrong?" He asked.

"Gabriella Brunelli was in a car accident last night on her way home from the party. She was killed." Her voice broke. "We got a call from Marco early this morning. Jose, I'm so sorry. I know you…"

He cut her off. "Wait… What…, what happened? No."

Lauren cleared her throat, then explained. "It seems she left the party around midnight with Christiano Berra, in his car. The police say he must have been speeding and the car went through a curve too fast. The car flipped over several times and both Gabriella and Christiano were thrown from the car. They're both dead."

"I saw them leave." He whispered. "They were in a convertible."

She put her arms around him and pulled him close. He wasn't sure if that was for his benefit or hers, but it felt like the right thing to do.

Until that moment, he had no appreciation for what Claire felt when the Towers came down. The shocking pain was unbearable. He was overcome with emotion and began sobbing uncontrollably.

But he didn't know if he was crying for Gabriella or Claire.

CHAPTER THIRTY-TWO

The days following Gabriella's death were a blur for Jose. Her parents took her mangled body back to Italy for a funeral and burial near their villa in Ravello. Everyone on the farm traveled to the funeral except Jose and the grooms. Micah chartered a plane so they could be back in time for the weekend events at the North Salem show grounds. They returned late Friday night after saying their good-byes to the sweet young rider earlier that morning.

Bert and Micah felt particularly pained by the loss since their party was the catalyst for the tragedy, leaving them with a feeling of personal responsibility. Ironically, Lauren and Micah had debated inviting Christiano to the party in the first place. It was Micah who suggested, "We need to do it for business reasons. I can't stand the guy either but his parents buy two or three horses a year from us." Lauren deferred to her husband's judgement and was now torturing herself over it.

A pall hung over the entire farm for weeks and Micah made a point of dedicating his next two events to Gabriella's memory. He won both Grand Prix.

But, in a speech he made to the farm staff after returning from Italy, he reminded everyone that, as hard as it was, their focus had to get back to Beijing. They understood that even the best riders only have so many Olympic opportunities in their lifetimes. If they lost focus now, they'd have to wait four more years, until the London Olympic games. And 2012 seemed like a lifetime away. Everyone understood.

But for Jose, the loss was different. Although he told no one, he blamed himself for Gabriella's death. If he hadn't stopped to drink that glass of champagne, he might have gotten to her before she agreed to leave with Christiano. He replayed those few moments over and over in his mind. Did he really need the alcohol to summon the bravery to speak to a twenty-year-old girl? Because of his childish insecurity about approaching a woman, that woman was dead. Two or three seconds might have made the difference. He hated himself for his cowardly behavior. He could never look Marco Brunelli in the eye again.

What he didn't completely understand was that much of his self-loathing was in response, not to Gabriella's death, but his own. By killing Joey Martinez on 9-11, he'd caused Claire a pain he previously could not understand. And now, nearly seven years later, he was disgusted with himself. For the first time, he felt the shocking grief Claire must have felt and it sickened him to think he'd done that to another human being; one he loved. He sobbed every time he pictured her standing over an empty grave.

Although they didn't grasp the underlying cause, Lauren and Micah could see their friend was hurting, hurting more than seemed appropriate for the casual and brief relationship they knew Jose enjoyed with Gabriella. At first Lauren thought it might have been Jose's first experience with death. But Micah reminded her of the night Jose told them about his parents' accident. So maybe that was it. Maybe Gabriella's death resurrected ghosts from Jose's past because hers was also an auto accident. Whatever the reason for his malaise, they were genuinely concerned and Micah spoke to Jose about it one morning after his first ride.

It was a cool June morning and the two men were putting away new rails that had been delivered the previous afternoon. When the short task was done, Micah suggested they grab a diet Coke from the stable fridge.

"Jose, I want to talk to you about something that's worrying me."

Jose used an open hand motion to indicate, "Sure, what's up?"

"We're all worried about you." He waited a moment to see if Jose would respond. When he didn't, Micah continued. "Ever since the accident, you've been real quiet. It's not like you."

Jose thought for a moment, then said, "It hit me a lot harder than I expected. I'll be okay. Don't worry."

"Well, we are worried. If you've learned anything in the seven years we've known each other, you know that we're a family on this farm. We worry about each other. So, what's eating you, man? Why is this so hard for you?"

Micah was right. Everyone on the farm had treated him like he was part of their family and he wanted to tell him everything. But that wasn't possible. He knew that. He knew his despicable secret would have to remain his, even if it haunted him every day of his life, as he feared it might. He couldn't tell Micah. He could never tell anyone. He'd be a pariah.

So instead, he said, "It's probably about my folks. The accident just brought up a lot of grief I thought I'd left behind in New York. I'll be okay, really."

"Don't get me wrong, Jose. I'm not saying you've neglected your work. On the contrary. Everything's great with the farm. We're concerned about…, well about your mood. Have you painted at all since the accident?"

At first, Jose thought it an odd question. But then it occurred to him that he hadn't. He hadn't even thought about painting since the accident. He'd been so focused on his postponed grief that joyful things like painting hadn't even entered his mind.

"No, I guess I just didn't think it was right."

"What do you mean, right?"

"I don't know. I guess, for me, painting is a joy, a pleasure. I love painting. It makes me feel wonderful. It feels like that's what I was always meant to be doing. I'm so happy when I paint, especially when I finish a good one."

"I get it. That's exactly how I feel after a clear round. I'm passionate about riding and it makes me feel great when I do it well."

"I know. I've seen you after a good ride. It's almost like a high…, like something…orgasmic."

Micah smiled. "What do you mean almost?"

It was the first smile he'd seen cross Jose's face in three weeks. "So, why did you stop painting?"

Again, Jose thought for a long moment. "I guess I just didn't feel like I deserve to be happy. I mean… I could have stopped them and I didn't."

"What?"

"At the party. I wanted to spend more time with her, with Gabriella, but I was too timid. I hesitated a few seconds, and that's when he must have convinced her to leave with him. If I'd just walked over and acted like a man, maybe she wouldn't have gotten in the car. Maybe. I don't know."

"That's what you're beating yourself up over? Come on. Hey, if I hadn't sold her old man a horse, she wouldn't have even been in America that night. Should I feel like I killed her too?"

Jose hoped that by sharing half of his guilt, the half about Gabriella, he might have deflected the inquisition enough to satisfy Micah. "No, of course not."

"Then neither should you, man. Hey, Christiano Berra was an asshole. He probably had enough coke in him that night to kill a horse. She was a big girl. She made a bad choice. Not your fault. It's a shame, but it's not your fault."

Jose nodded.

"Okay, so here's what we're going to do. Lexington is this weekend. I need to be in the top ten to stay alive and I plan to do it. I want you there with us. Come to Kentucky, it will take your mind off things. It's beautiful countryside. You can paint again. You can be happy again."

"Sounds good. I've never been to Kentucky."

Micah walked back to the house. He didn't see Jose sobbing. And even if he had, he wouldn't have understood why. Jose was overcome with emotion by the enormous contradiction in his life. He now realized what a terrible thing he'd done to Claire. He hated himself for causing her so much pain. He was a monster and deserved to be shunned by decent people. And yet, the most decent people he'd ever met were embracing him. They were worried about him. They loved him.

He felt their love and knew he didn't deserve it. It made no sense to him.

CHAPTER THIRTY-THREE

Micah was right; Kentucky was beautiful. The show grounds were fifteen miles from the city, out beyond rolling hills of the greenest grass Jose had ever seen. Everywhere he looked there were expansive paddocks lined with fastidiously maintained white fences following the sloping contours of the landscape. For a while, Jose was able to put Gabriella and Claire behind him.

The Lexington was a two-day event, concluding on Sunday. Micah, Lauren and Jose arrived on Thursday afternoon. Bret, the horses and two grooms had been there since Wednesday morning. Micah's first competition was Saturday morning. He was scheduled to ride thirty-second in a field of forty. It was common practice to group riders according to their world ranking. Generally, if there were forty riders competing, the best ten in the field would be the last ten to ride. The first thirty riders might be organized randomly, and the positions for the last ten spots would also be determined randomly. But everyone knew the last ten spots had been reserved for the elite riders.

This arrangement suited Micah just fine. He liked to watch as many riders as possible jump the course before he had to compete.

He watched for their mistakes; too many strides between the second and third jumps, too few between the ninth and tenth. Too wide a turn or too slow a pace. It all helped him with his game plan. He was a strategist. Nothing was left to chance.

Before each event, when the course had been laid out and the grandstands were still only a quarter full, he and the other riders were given an opportunity to see the course for the first time and to "walk" the course. This meant literally walking, without a horse, the path of the course, from one jump to the next. This was where Micah's planning excelled. He would walk the course, carefully counting the number of steps from one jump to the next. He did this for each of the sixteen jumps. Then he would pace off the width of the turns he needed to make at each end of the course, again counting his steps. When he was through, he converted his steps into his horse's strides and committed the whole formula for a successful ride, to memory. Hours later, when his horse would be seeing the course for the very first time, Micah had already flawlessly ridden it in his head a hundred times.

Jose always enjoyed watching the course walk. While other riders, even the elite, would walk the course in groups, sometimes chatting among themselves as they did, Micah always walked alone. Jose could see his lips move as Micah counted the steps and did the conversion to strides. He was truly a general preparing for battle. And he was usually the most well-prepared general on the field.

On the Friday night before he was scheduled to ride, Micah took Lauren, Jose and Bret out for a steak dinner. According to the seat-back magazine on the plane, it was the finest steakhouse in Lexington. He'd been there many times before and the owner came to the table to say hello and wish him luck. But while the others were feasting on a thick cut of Angus beef and washing it down with red wine, Micah had a grilled chicken breast and a small salad along with his usual diet Coke. Nothing was left to chance for the general. There was a battle to be won tomorrow and he would be at his best. If there was feasting to do, it would have to wait until Sunday night.

"I'd like to ride Ruby at eight o'clock," he said to Bret while they were in a cab heading back to the hotel.

"You're the boss. She'll be ready by seven-forty-five. Your course walk is at nine-thirty. The event starts at ten so you'll probably go around eleven-twenty."

"Good. I want to watch the first ten or twelve riders from the stands. I'll sit with Jose and Lauren."

On Saturday morning, the skies over Lexington were bright. The air smelled of all the sweet blossoms that burst in the spring. Micah and Ruby cantered around the warm-up ring until the rider was sure the horse was steady. If asked to explain how he knew when Ruby was ready to jump, he couldn't tell you. He just knew.

As planned, Micah watched the first ten riders from the grandstands with Lauren and Jose. He and Lauren spoke a language Jose didn't understand; a language about the subtle nuances that meant the difference of millimeters, the difference between clearing a jump or knocking the top rail off its perilous perch. Jose heard Lauren point out a woman in a bright silver jacket sitting at the opposite end of the arena. She thought it might be a visual distraction for Ruby as they neared the fourth jump. Micah agreed.

Over the years, Jose had learned only the basics about the sport of Show Jumping. He learned it was a rich man's game, the price of entry was considerable. He knew that, unlike other sports, men and women competed equally and that the prize money for victory was significant, even for the already-rich. In its simplest form, the objective was to get your horse to jump over a series of hurdles without knocking anything down and within a specified amount time. If you knocked down a rail, you got four faults, two rails-eight faults, etc. If it took you eighty-three seconds to complete the event in which the maximum allowed was eighty, you got one fault.

Typically, the rider with the fewest faults and the fastest time at the end of the event was the winner.

Often, several riders would complete the course with no faults, called a clear round. All those riders would then compete in a jump-off, a sort of sudden death overtime. In the jump-off, the course was rearranged and shortened. There would be fewer jumps, but in the jump-off, speed mattered. So, at the end of the jump-off, if there were still more than one rider with no faults, the clear rider who completed the course in the least time was the winner. It was here that milliseconds mattered.

"All right. I need to get down to the warm-up ring." Micah said to Lauren and he gave her a kiss.

"Good luck, baby." She said. Then added, "Don't forget the silver lady on the fourth jump."

Micah gave her the thumbs up sign and disappeared down a set of stairs.

"He seems very calm." Jose offered

"This isn't the day to get nervous. He's a worry-wart every other day, every day leading up to an event, but not on the day of the show. He knows he's done everything he possibly could to get here. Now, he just has to execute. No point in being nervous today."

"That makes sense. What about you? Are you nervous?" he asked.

"I know how much making the U.S. team means to him. It's all he's talked about since he got back from Athens. Yes, I'm a wreck."

"Well, you certainly don't show it."

They watched another eighteen riders negotiate the course. So far, there were only three clear rounds. Everyone else had at least one rail down which meant they were going home. The final jump seemed to be giving most riders trouble. It was an oxer, which meant the horse and rider had to clear a greater horizontal distance. Even the horses that cleared it were hitting the back rail.

For some it stayed in place. For others, it fell. Such was the difference between success and complete failure.

When Micah's name was announced, there was a modest applause from the crowd. The stands were still only half full. At a qualifying event like this, most fans didn't show up until the second half. Then the stadium would be filled to capacity.

He and Ruby cantered into the ring. Micah glanced over at Lauren and gave her a nod, then cantered through the start timers. They cleared the first jump with room to spare. The silver lady turned out to be no trouble. Micah and Ruby looked a little slow and Lauren worried that even if he went clear on the jumps, he may suffer a time fault. But on the last four jumps he was able to make up some time and as he approached the final double, Lauren reached back and grabbed Jose's hand.

"Come on Ruby. One more big jump!" She shouted.

But Micah knew most of the other riders were having trouble with the final jump because they hadn't allowed enough strides in the approach. Most others were taking six full strides leading up to the fence. Micah had counted seven, and as he and Ruby left the ground he knew he'd gotten it right. The horse's hind hoofs cleared the top rail by four inches and they were in the jump-off. That alone assured him a ride in Sunday's Grand Prix but if he placed in the top three in today's jump-off he also got points that counted toward his qualifying for the Olympic team.

As Ruby landed, and the perilous rail stayed atop the fence, the crowd cheered and Lauren turned to Jose and hugged him. "We did it!"

There were still seven riders to go and the first four failed to go clear, keeping them out of the jump-off. Jose found himself silently rooting for the long wooden rails to drop. Each fault meant one less competitor in the jump-off. One less person for Micah to beat.

But each of the last three riders went clear, leaving seven in the jump-off. The ring was raked and rearranged and twenty minutes later the order for the jump-off was announced. Micah would ride fourth.

Because some of the jumps had been relocated, he and the other six riders got to walk the shortened course again. Micah did his usual calculation of steps and strides. But in the jump-off, he needed to run Ruby much faster than he had in the first round. The jump-off would likely be won by a matter of fractions of a second. He needed to shave strides in order to save those precious fractions.

Lauren turned to Jose. "This is why he's one of the best. He knows where to find time. Just watch. You'll see."

When the competition began the first two riders each had a rail down. The third rider went clear in 43.22 seconds. The fourth rider, a young woman from Canada, also went clear but in 41.44 seconds. She was now in first place. The fifth rider, another Canadian, followed suit but in 42.12 seconds, moving him into second place.

Micah rode next and from the start the crowd could tell he was running the course faster than the others. After each jump, he would turn Ruby on a dime and sprint for the next fence, then do it again. As they approached the final jump, Lauren knew he had the best time so far. He just needed to clear the last jump. He squeezed his thighs against the powerful mare's midsection and they leapt as one. The top rail held. His time was 39.07!

The fickle crowd, which was now at capacity, roared its approval. Micah gave an uncharacteristic fist pump and waved at Lauren as he returned to the warm-up ring. But there was still one more rider, a German with two Olympic medals. Everyone knew it wasn't over yet. But Lauren and Micah understood that the worst Micah could do is come in second. That got him into Sunday's Grand prix and the points he desperately coveted.

"Looks like we're going to China." Lauren beamed.

"Doesn't he have to win?" Jose asked.

"It would help, but I think he's got enough points with this showing to make the team."

The experienced German rider cantered into the ring. To Jose's untrained eye, his horse seemed larger than all the others. The horse's name was True Loch which Jose thought a bad omen, but it was no larger than the others. It was the horse that won the silver individual medal in Athens and for which the German rider had been offered three million Euros. The combination seemed like formidable opponents.

Knowing it was the last combination, the crowd cheered at every jump. One clear, two clear, three clear. The frenzy rose. Four, five and six all clear. On the seventh fence, True Loch's front hoof touched the rail and it shook but held its position. He cleared the final jump and Lauren looked up at the scoreboard.

40.02 glistened in bright red light.

Micah was on his way to China.

CHAPTER THIRTY-FOUR

While most of the 2008 Summer Olympic games were held in Beijing, the equestrian competitions were held in Hong Kong, which had established a huge horse racing industry dating back to its British colonial days. As a result, strict quarantine measures for horses had been well established in the region, and were likely to result in fewer problems with equine disease than other cities in mainland China. Additionally, there were already some stabling sites for horses within Hong Kong, hence less construction was needed to accommodate the influx of foreign animals.

But Hong Kong was also known for its hot and humid weather with typhoons common in August. The afternoon temperatures typically reached 85 degrees with 85-90% humidity. Therefore, all jumping competition was held in the evening. Even so, some competitors believed it would be unfair to work their horses in such weather. Swiss dressage rider Sylvia Ikle was one such rider, and the Swiss decided not to send a dressage team.

To combat the heat, the horses were transported from the airport in Hong Kong to the stabling facilities in air-conditioned vans. The stables were air-conditioned as well. For the first time in history, there was also an indoor arena for training that was completely air-conditioned. Misting fans were placed under the tents at both venue to cool off horses that worked outside. There were also vast quantities of ice water available. There was a veterinary clinic on site, which tested the horses' urine several times to ensure they were all properly hydrated. Even Bret was satisfied the Chinese had taken the necessary precautions. As a result, he and his grooms were happy to spend so much time with the horses.

But because the equestrian events were held twelve hundred miles from Beijing, Micah and his three teammates would miss the opening ceremonies. Instead, they all gathered for dinner in Kowloon the night before the first day of competition, and from a bar, high atop the Peninsula Hotel, watched the lavish ceremonies on television.

"Did you see the fences and standards at the racetrack?" Micah asked his teammates. "They're incredibly ornate. I guess the Chinese are trying to showcase their culture, but the ring is full of dragons and giant red fans." The riders had begun to call the jumping venue the "racetrack" because the 18,000-seat stadium was next to the Hong Kong Racetrack.

Bezier Madden, one of the two females on the American team, asked, "Where's Lauren tonight? She's not wandering around Kowloon on her own, is she?"

"Noooo. Lauren and her parents are staying here at the peninsula. I think they're having dinner downstairs. My father, Fiona, and my friend Jose are staying across the harbor on the house boat of an old friend."

The first day of the individual competition was Friday. As the traditional trumpet sounded to begin the event, the temperature in the ring was 87 degrees, and that was at 7:15 P.M. Ironically, the organizers had gone to great lengths and considerable expense to recreate the Olympic cauldron, the eternal torch, at the venue.

But because a commuter train line ran next to the stadium, they weren't able to hoist the cauldron as high as they would have liked. So, the heat from the raging torch only made the spectators and riders even more uncomfortable.

Micah rode sixteenth, had a clear round and was pleased with the way Ruby jumped. Jose and Lauren watched the event from a standing position near the gate. Her parents, Bert, and Fiona got the four-person box allocated to each rider. After the event, they all went out for a late dinner along the harbor. Millions of twinkling lights glistened across the water and Jose couldn't help thinking about how much the skyline of Hong Kong reminded him of Manhattan. It made him reflect on how far he was from home, in so many ways.

Saturday was a down day for the riders and they all took tours of Hong Kong. Sunday was the start of the team competition. It rained briefly a few hours prior to the event but that only seemed to make the humidity more unbearable at show time. Officially, Jose wasn't working on the trip, but he constantly asked Lauren, Micah and Bret if there was anything he could do for them. He didn't want to just be a spectator. He wanted desperately to help in some way; to feel part of the Wells Hill effort.

In the first round of the team event on Sunday evening, the U.S. team did well. Beezie had the only rail down so the Americans only carried four faults into the second round. Micah and Ruby went clear but by the time he dismounted after the event, his red show coat was soaked through with sweat and he could tell Ruby was feeling the effects of the oppressive humidity. Bret was concerned enough to add Vetrolin to the bathwater he used on the mare that night. He kept a careful eye on the horse all night.

Monday night began the final rounds of the team jumping and the U.S. team was in the lead with only four faults. But the Canadian team, led by veteran Eric Lamaze and the Swiss team featuring the World Cup champion Christina Liebherr riding a horse named No Mercy were close behind. At the end of the second round, the Americans were tied with Canada at 20 faults. The Swiss had locked up the Bronze medal with 30 faults and it was a two-country race to determine who would take home the gold. Canada and the U.S. would compete head on in a jump-off.

The master of ceremonies let the crowd know there'd be a forty-minute break while the course was raked and reconfigured for the jump-off. Princess Haya, the president of the FEI, went to the warm-up ring to wish both teams good luck. Micah and two of the Canadian riders, Ian Miller and Eric Lamaze, were chatting about how familiar this all seemed. The three men had been in head-to-head competition so many times before. They were all fierce competitors but when they weren't sitting atop a horse, they shared a professional friendship.

"Do you think they'll put a triple in the jump-off?" the younger Canadian asked.

"We'll find out soon enough." Miller responded, then added, "Hey Micah, how about a side bet?"

"I can't imagine stakes that would satisfy you Ian."

Micah then caught Lauren and Jose out of the corner of his eye, standing next to the entry gate. He checked his watch to be sure he had time, then quickly walked over to them. Lauren was the first to speak.

"Silver or gold, I don't care. I just want this to be over. The tension is killing me. How can you be so calm?" She said.

Micah looked at Jose and replied, "You see why I love this woman? She does the worrying for both of us." Then he kissed Lauren on the forehead and said, "Only the gold will do."

Bret was calling for him and Micah returned to the warm-up ring. He could hear the PA system from the main arena announcing the start of the jump-off in fifteen minutes. That didn't leave much time for the riders to walk the course. He handed Ruby back over to Bret and, with the other American riders, joined the Canadians in the arena.

Jose and Lauren watched from a distance as each rider paced off the new configuration. It was a much shorter course, with only eight jumps, the last of which was a wall of heavy cardboard blocks, colored red and white to look like bricks. Although this type of solid obstruction was common in Grand Prix events, it created difficulty for some horses because they couldn't see what lay beyond the blind jump. Horses like to see what they were jumping onto. Uncertainty frightens them.

When Micah got to the last jump, he stopped and seemed to be doing some calculation in his head. Then he turned and walked back to the prior jump and walked off the distance to the last jump once more. Again, he stopped and seemed to be lost in thought. By now, all the other riders had completed their walks and were heading back to the warm-up area and Micah was alone in the arena. Finally, he walked back to the previous jump one more time and paced the distance again, but this time taking longer strides. He nodded and turned toward Lauren, giving her the thumbs up signal. He was ready to jump.

The format for the medal-round jump-off differed from the norm. Each team would ride all four of their riders in alternating succession. Faults and time would be recorded and aggregated by team. Each team got to drop off one rider's ride, effectively leaving the team's best three rides on the board. If, at the end of all eight rides, the teams were tied on faults, then the team with the lowest accumulated time would be the winner.

The first rider for Canada had one rail down early in his ride. The first American went clear. The next Canadian, Ian Miller, also went clear, but the second American had a rail down on the sixth jump. The third Canadian had a clear round going into the final jump, the wall of cardboard bricks, but his horse refused the jump, stopping abruptly at the foot of the imposing wall. The rider tried again but again the horse refused to jump. As a result, the rider was disqualified and the Canadians were forced to use that as their dropped round, meaning that they carried four faults.

Micah rode next for the American team and rode clear. The excitement in the arena was electric and Eric Lamaze took the field for the final Canadian ride. A clear round was necessary for the Canadians to have a realistic chance, as it was unlikely the final rider for the U.S team, the experienced Beezie Madden, would falter. Even if she did, the cumulative U.S. time was three seconds lower than the Canadians. Lamaze needed to ride the ride of his life and to do it fast.

The roaring crowd became silent as the Canadian began his ride. He cleared the first and second jumps without incident and at the fastest pace yet. He coasted through the middle of the course and was well ahead of the clock as he approached the final jump. As he and his horse left the ground the crowd erupted into a frenzy of applause and cheers. He landed on the far side of the wall, all bricks intact. His time was 37.25, the fastest yet.

The scoreboard read 4-0, indicating the Canadians had four faults and the Americans, none. But the Americans had one more rider to go. The U.S. team could win the gold if Beezie had a clear round or had one rail down but took the course in under 36.60 seconds. If she had two rails down, the Canadians would take the gold.

Everyone in the stadium was on their feet. The oppressively humid air didn't keep anyone from cheering, but as she began her ride a hush came over the audience. Beezie's strategy was to ride clear and not worry about the time. Her horse was strong but not known for its speed so she was determined to clear the course.

At each of the first seven jumps, the crowd roared its approval as she and her twelve-year-old gelding Authentic, leap effortlessly toward the next. With each jump, the cheers got louder. The intensity in the arena gave her the adrenaline to push for the final jump, the wall of cardboard bricks. On the sixth stride, she and her horse leap with all they had and cleared the wall!

Jose and Lauren embraced then began jumping up and down. American flags were waving throughout the jubilant crowd. The U.S. team had once again taken the gold medal and the rest of the team streamed out into the arena to congratulate its final rider.

A few minutes later, the four Americans stood atop the podium as the Star-Spangled Banner was played.

The plane ride home from Hong Kong was bitter-sweet. Micah, Lauren and Jose occupied the first three seats in the first-class cabin. They'd been upgraded from business-class when the airline found out Micah was an Olympic athlete. The large gold medal hanging around his neck probably helped.

Bert and Fiona decided to stay in Asia a few more days and do some sightseeing in China. Stan and Tina Barone were on a different plane headed for Honolulu and their second honeymoon. Bret and the grooms would travel back with the horses and land in Newburgh, New York for the mandatory equine quarantine.

For Micah, the ride home was bitter-sweet because although he'd fulfilled his goal of making the U.S. team and winning a medal, he'd fallen one rung short of his dream. He'd now won team gold medals in back to back Olympics, an amazing accomplishment for anyone. And he was still only thirty-four, much of his riding was still ahead of him. But they were team medals. He hadn't yet won an individual medal. He'd failed to do so in Athens and failed again in Hong Kong when his teammate, Beezie Madden edged him out for the Bronze.

Normally, he would have spent much of the long ride home strategizing about his quest for an individual medal at the next summer Olympics in London. Normally, he would have agonized about what he needed to do better next time and lay out a four-year plan for accomplishing that.

But this time, Micah relaxed, had two beers and fell asleep holding Lauren's hand while she watched a movie. His next goal wasn't about medals. He'd promised Lauren their next adventure would be starting a family.

CHAPTER THIRTY-FIVE

2014

She already looked through all the magazines in the waiting room. Her appointment was for nine A.M. and it was now almost ten. Dr. Gueyer, Claire's ophthalmologist, had been held up in surgery and was due back in his office soon. Claire had a million errands to run that day and debated cancelling her appointment and rescheduling for the following week, but it was difficult to see Dr. Gueyer and his assistant promised she would be his first patient when he arrived.

Amanda's third-grade school play started at eleven and she and Brad had both promised to be there. She hoped the doctor, the most respected eye doctor in New York, had already reviewed the results of her tests and would be ready for her as soon as he arrived. And she hoped the results were better than he'd hinted they could be the last time she saw him. A week ago, she went through a series of tests including a lengthy field-of-vision test, to determine how rapidly her macular degeneration was progressing. Although he said the disease, which is caused by a deterioration of the central portion of the retina, was rare in someone as young as Claire, he had seen cases of it before and in those cases, where the patient was young, the disease had progressed rapidly. So today, she was to find out if the latest treatment of drops had helped. If not, the prognosis wasn't good.

"Claire Muller", someone called out. "Is Claire Muller here?" The receptionist wanted to know.

Claire stood and went to the window. "I'm Claire Muller."

"You forgot to fill out your health insurance information on page three."

"Sorry, I've been here eleven times in the last three months. I assumed you already had it. It hasn't changed."

The young girl behind the reception window, snapped her gum and said, "We still need it." And handed the clipboard to Claire.

Rather than argue with the nose-ringed juvenile, Claire took the board and returned to her chair. She filled in the missing info and realized she'd also forgotten to sign the form. As she signed her name, she reflected on how much she liked the sound of it. "Claire Muller", she almost said aloud. She and Amanda both took Brad's name after they were married. It seemed like the right thing to do. Brad would be the only father Amanda would ever know so why have a different last name than mom and dad? It certainly made things simpler at school.

And Amanda loved Brad. Right from the start, she was comfortable with him. And why not? He went out of his way to learn about the things important in her life. He pretended to be extraordinarily interested in butterflies, her favorite things, and he introduced her to horseback riding, her current passion. The two of them rode almost every weekend, even in the winter when riding in Central Park was even more beautiful, especially when covered in snow.

Claire and Brad married after a short and intense courtship. Both were aware of the danger they were each trying to replace what had been lost on 9-11. Claire's grief counselor warned her about that danger, but after five years, both were ready to move on. They'd separately done their grieving before they met so the fact they'd both lost their spouses in the same horrible way, was almost an incidental coincidence. It didn't define their relationship.

And they were very much in love. Brad insisted Amanda accompany them on their honeymoon in 2007 and the three were inseparable since. That was nearly four years ago and since then, life had been blissful. Claire and Amanda moved into Brad's New York apartment during the week and they bought a small farm in Connecticut, about an hour north of the city for the weekends. It was there he introduced Amanda to riding.

But the bliss was interrupted a few months ago when Claire began to have trouble seeing the numbers in their elevator. At first, her doctor suspected she'd suffered a mild stroke, something he called a transmural myocardial infarction, or TMI. But a series of tests ruled that out and, when the only symptom continued to be her loss of sight clarity, he recommended she see Dr. Gueyer. He diagnosed the macular degeneration immediately and seemed hopeful it could be treated and retarded with medication. When the first two drugs didn't help, he recommended an experimental treatment, the one Claire had just completed. But that treatment wasn't yet approved by the FDA and Claire had to travel to Switzerland for he expensive medication.

That was three weeks ago and the treatment center in Zurich released Claire back to the care of Dr. Gueyer so that follow-up tests could be done to determine what, if any, improvement had been obtained. The goal was to slow down the degeneration by fifty percent, which would have afforded her a few more years of viable day vision and maybe a decade of night vision. The treatment in Zurich was her last chance. The best ophthalmologists in the world had reviewed Claire's case. Brad made sure he left no stone unturned and used his considerable wealth to find the best doctors. They all pointed the Mullers to Dr. Gueyer.

"Mrs. Muller, the doctor can see you now." Claire felt a chill run through her. This was it.

When she entered Dr. Gueyer's office she expected to be led to the examination room as she had been so many times before. Instead, the assistant led her to what looked like a well-appointed conference room. Dr. Gueyer was seated at one end of a long mahogany table behind a pile of folders. He rose to greet her and asked her to sit next to him. He was dressed, as usual, in a bespoke suit and crisp white shirt with French cuffs. He did not look like he had good news.

"Good morning, Claire. Let's get right to it." He said as he closed one of the files and placed it on top of the others. "I'm afraid the results show no improvement. It looks like Stargardt disease. The carotenoids are still very low and there appears to be no additional vascular stimulation where we hoped to stimulate the nerves. We can continue to try the Visudyne, but I don't want to mislead you. The Visudyne itself has not been shown to retard the decline."

He paused to let the words sink in. He'd never seen a case where the victim of macular degeneration was so young, certainly not someone in their early thirties. He didn't have suitable answers for her. He couldn't tell her why this was happening or if she'd done anything to cause it. Most likely, it was a genetic defect she inherited. That much he'd explained when she first came to him. Most cases of advanced macular degeneration were handed down from one generation to another with no genetic testing for it available yet.

Claire was determined not to cry. "How long before…," she hesitated. "How long before I am…, blind?" She could hardly say the word.

The rest of the consultation with Dr. Gueyer was a blur of technical terms and messages of hope, the only ointment he could offer. She came away understanding that this wasn't going to kill her. That was the good news. And, the doctor felt it was unlikely that she would ever be completely blind. Instead, he predicted she would gradually lose most of her sight over the next year but that she'd still be able to distinguish shades of light so that if someone walked directly on front of her, she'd know it but have no chance of knowing who it was. He'd used the term ninety-eight percent to quantify the loss of sight.

The last thing he'd said to her was the most troubling. When she asked if she had likely given the trait to her daughter, he said there was a fifty-fifty chance.

CHAPTER THIRTY-SIX

The July sun beat down on the fields behind Jose's home, just a half mile from Wells Hill. He'd decided to build his house near the farm so he'd still feel like part of the team. And being close to the farm, he'd take a walk over almost every morning to see Micah, Lauren and their two children.

As he crossed the dry field and looked up at his home, sitting atop a small hill, he realized how much he loved this place. The modest house had been his paradise for three years. Now that he no longer worked directly for the Wells family, he could spend more time here and in the spacious studio next to the house.

Since the auction at Bert's charity event six years ago, his celebrity had taken a meteoric path. His paintings were on display at almost every equestrian gathering across the U.S. and Europe. His style of work, which had become known as color-motion, was being emulated and studied in universities wherever art was taught. He'd been interviewed on the Today Show twice, once in New York and once during the 2012 Summer Olympics in London. He was, at least in the world of equestrian art, quite famous.

And with that fame had come fortune. No longer did he need to sit in booths next to Grand Prix events. He had three galleries in Woodfield, Manhattan and Wellington. They were filled with his work, some of which sold for two hundred thousand dollars. Bert Wells had been right. People with the means to own horses were people who wanted to boast they'd paid a fortune for one of his paintings. Especially lucrative was the commissioned work where wealthy parents would have him paint their teenage daughter atop her very expensive horse. Everyone wanted the "Gabriella" pose where the young girl was leaning way over her horse's head in the midst of a jump.

So it was, that the second worst day of his life gave birth to his fame and fortune. Gabriella's tragic accident had created a demand for his work that he was barely able to meet. By the winter of 2009 he had so much commissioned work he had to tell Micah he could no longer oversee the farms.

"I knew this day was coming as soon as you started to draw." Micah said. "You've got way too much artistic talent to manage a farm. You wasted thirty years of your life doing things that kept you from your destiny. So, you're going to be busy playing catch up, my friend."

Jose helped Micah find two junior people to manage the farms under Bret's direction. The new arrangement worked but Micah missed working with his friend and the sage business advice that often came from their collaboration. He also missed having Jose around the farms. They'd become more than friends. As Lauren once put it, "Now you have two brothers."

The pinnacle of Jose's rise to the top of "equine-pop art", as one writer had put it, was the day Leroy Neiman came to see him in Wellington. It was the winter of 2012, just a few months before the prolific artist died. He was ninety and frail but traveled to Florida to meet Jose while attending a charitable event in Palm Beach. He was interested in hearing how Jose blurred his color to create the illusion of motion. When Jose informed him, he started by using his palm to smear the paint, the world-famous painter replied, "Son of a bitch! I knew it."

And Bert Wells, now seventy-seven and still quite fit, took great pride in his role launching Jose's career. He was a magnanimous advocate of his work and often traveled with Jose to open a showing or temporary gallery. He liked to refer to himself as Jose's sponsor drawing on the metaphor of Michelangelo and the Medici family. And, in some ways he was. Bert gave Jose the two acres of land adjacent to the Wells Farm in Woodfield on which to build his house. "What the hell. We're not using it," he told Micah. "And besides, it will be nice to have him close by."

Micah couldn't have agreed more. Now that they had two daughters, Lauren traveled with him less and less. Micah would frequently call on Jose to accompany him to events, especially when there was also an opportunity to promote his artwork. Their alignment was symbiotic. Jose benefited from his proximity to the two-time Olympic gold medalist, and Micah appreciated having someone to accompany him to all the social obligations that came with Show Jumping events. Lauren usually found them tedious anyway and now that Lizzy and Kate had commandeered so much of her time, everyone benefited from their "bro-mance" as Lauren called it.

Lauren had embraced motherhood. She spent every minute she could with her daughters, and when she couldn't be with them, there were only two women she would entrust them to; Bret's wife, Terry, and Erica McCurry. Even the girl's step-grandmother, Fiona Wells, had never been asked to babysit. Lauren was very protective of her girls.

Ironically, neither of the girls who were now five and three years old, had shown any interest in riding. Bert had given them each a pony for their second birthdays, but so far, they seemed more interested in other childhood adventures like Playdough and

Sesame Street characters. They were completely at ease around horses, they just had no interest in riding them.

This morning, Jose was lost in thought. His publicist had arranged a two-minute segment for him on the CBS show, Sunday Morning which was scheduled to be shot at his home the following week, then aired as "filler" whenever CBS needed a short human interest piece. But he was uncomfortable with television.

Back in 2012, when NBC interviewed him as a color piece for their London Olympic programming, he wrestled with the same dilemma. Although it had been eleven years since 9-11, with millions of people watching television, he feared someone might recognize him. His appearance was vastly different but someone that knew him well, like Claire, might... Well, why take the chance? Back then, NBC agreed to only show him in sunglasses and an oversized fedora. With his darkened skin and long black ponytailed locks, the image fit the persona of the eccentric artist known only as Jose. Most of their video focused on his paintings and the subjects of his work.

But this time, CBS was looking for more. According to his publicist, they planned on filming him at his home, doing the things he did every day; painting, walking the grounds, spending time in the stables. It all sounded like a lot of facial close-ups and that made him very uncomfortable. While he'd been able to enjoy his notoriety within the equestrian world, where no one knew him before 9-11, he was never able to get comfortable with broader fame and resisted it at every turn; a behavior no one close to him could understand.

He decided to talk to Bert about it tonight. He was scheduled to have dinner with Bert and Fiona at their home that evening. He'd picked up two good bottles of red wine, Fiona's favorite, and was looking forward to seeing his friends. They'd been away in Spain for three weeks and had just gotten home the previous night.

As he was preparing to leave for the short walk to their house, he heard a car coming up his gravel driveway. It was Fiona's white

Infiniti. Thinking that Bert had driven up the hill to save him the walk, he was surprised when Fiona stepped out of the car. She had on a spaghetti-strap yellow sun dress and matching sandals.

"Give me a hand, will you? I have dinner."

Fiona explained that Bert hadn't fully recovered from the jet-lag and just wanted to go to sleep early. But he insisted she bring the dinner she'd prepared to Jose. "Have dinner with the kid. I'm too tired. I'm just going to take a pill and sleep until morning. That'll catch me up. You have a nice dinner with Jose." Were his exact words.

"There's a big pot in the trunk with the stew. Don't tip it. It's very full." She admonished. Fiona had a long loaf of French bread under her arm and a bowl of salad balanced in her left hand. "I just need to warm this up a few minutes."

"Why don't we have a glass of wine out here on the porch while your stew heats up? We can eat out here too if the bugs don't get too bad." Jose suggested.

Over the years, Jose and Fiona had spent much time together. Since Bert played the fatherly role for Jose, Fiona, who was only a few years older than Jose was more like a sister than the arm-candy wife of his former employer, sponsor and friend. He and Fiona had often talked about how it felt being outsiders. They were the only two people associated with the Wells farm, that didn't eat, drink and sleep horses. United by this common thread, the two of them often found themselves left out, when conversations around the farm turned horse-technical.

She put the pot over a low flame on the stove and joined Jose on the over-sized porch. He was already in one of the wicker rockers prying the cork out of the Pinot Noir. They each took a glass and sat back admiring the view from the hilltop. They could see most of the Wells farm and, in the distance, the reservoir than hugged the Taconic parkway. The air was still and the cicadas were beginning to do their noisy dance. It was the quintessential July evening in the lower Hudson Valley. If Jose painted landscapes, this would be the perfect scene.

"Cheers." Fiona offered as she extended her glass.

"Yes, cheers." Jose countered, then added, "I'm glad you're here, Fiona. There's something I want to ask your opinion on."

"What's that?" She said, settling into her rocker.

"A television crew is supposed to come up next week to do an interview for a morning show on CBS. It could be a great way to cross-promote the galleries."

"That's great. Congratulations."

"Yes, it could be wonderful but I don't want to do it and I don't know how to turn them down without seeming…"

She cut him off. "Wait. Why wouldn't you want that sort of favorable publicity? Isn't that exactly what you pay your publicist to do for you?"

He took a long sip from his glass before beginning the story he'd rehearsed earlier for Bert. "There are people from my former life I don't want to find me. Before I left New Jersey, I owed some money, not a lot, but enough to get me in trouble. I owed it to a loan shark named Oscar." He looked down at the glass he held in both his hands and feigned contrition. "I had been betting too much on football games and wound up owing this guy about four thousand bucks. That's part of the reason I left New Jersey. Oscar and his goons were about to break a few of my fingers so I decided to disappear." The word sent a chill down his spine.

"Wow. But that was thirteen years ago." Fiona refilled her glass and his.

"Well, these guys don't like to get stiffed. They would make a point of coming after me just to let others know they never forget a debt."

"So, even if they found you, which is highly unlikely, but even if they did, pay them and be done with it. You can certainly afford to make this go away. Why keep hiding?"

"First of all, it's not that simple. These goons have to maintain their reputation. If their clients don't fear them, they're done. It's not just the money. It's the fact that someone skipped out on them. That makes them look really bad. I'm sure they're really pissed about that. But the bigger issue is the vig, the interest. When I ran up my tab, I was being charged twenty percent a week interest. Over thirteen years, that's, well, I can't even imagine how much that would be. That's why they can never find me."

"I see. And it probably wouldn't do your reputation any good either. I mean if a bunch of goons show up at one of your galleries. Probably not the sort of press your publicist is looking for."

Fiona stood and put her hand on his shoulder. "So, don't do it. You're a big boy." Then she went into the kitchen to finish the stew.

She returned a few minutes later carrying two bowls of steaming lamb stew. "And besides, you go to great lengths to maintain this mysterious image of the eccentric, reclusive artist. Why would you want to do a Sunday morning show lifting that veil? I say tell Stacey you're not interested in revealing yourself to the world. You want to remain mysterious."

"Thanks. That makes perfect sense."

"Besides, your mysterious side is the side I like best." She winked and took a sip of wine. "I hope you like the stew. It's one of Bert's favorites and one of the few things I can make to his satisfaction."

Over dinner on the porch they talked about Micah and Lauren's girls, the extension being planned for the big barn and Fiona's upcoming trip to Ireland to visit her parents. Conversation flowed easily for them. They'd spent a lot of time together waiting around at horse shows while the horse people did their thing. There was an unspoken comfort between them.

They spoke about Fiona's parents and growing up in a small Irish town and what it was like having four brothers. Jose spoke of how much he would have liked four brothers, which was the truth.

He craved the moments he could be truthful without revealing himself. That was one of them.

"I really missed the whole brother thing. I think it would have been nice to have a peer to share your childhood with." He said.

"Don't you have a brother that moved to California?" Fiona asked, recalling the lie Jose had not.

"Umm… yes… but it's been so long since I saw him and we were never close as kids." Jose recovered.

"That's a shame. And you haven't seen him in how many years?"

"Close to twenty now. He may have gone back to Ecuador for all I know." He said. Then, "Let's talk about something else."

They finished dinner, Jose cleared the table and joined Fiona on the porch rockers with two fresh wine glasses and a new bottle. She'd taken her shoes off, her feet up on the wooden railing surrounding the spacious porch. Her soft cotton dress hung from her outstretched legs.

"One more glass?" he offered.

"Sure. I have nowhere to be."

A silence lingered between them for a few moments. It was Jose who broke it with a question that he wondered about often. The first bottle of wine had freed it from his lips.

"Can I ask you something, Fiona? Something a little personal?"

"Of course. What is it?"

"I've thought about this question a lot and if I'm out of line, just say so."

"Now I'm intrigued. What is it?"

He looked her directly in the eyes. "You're a beautiful and intelligent woman. Why marry someone so much older?"

"I get asked that question all the time. The funny thing is, the answer has changed over time." She sipped her glass. "When we first married, I told people Bert was the first real grown up I'd ever met. Up until Bert, the men I knew were boys, first the teenagers in Ireland, then the assholes in their twenties here in the states, who all thought they would change the world with their dotcoms or the merger they were working on. I went to Vassar and studied French literature. These clowns were trying to impress me with the size of their bonuses. And sometimes, their boners!" She laughed and coughed on her wine.

"And when I got a little older, and Bert and I had been married a while, I told people it was because I loved him so much. That too, was true. Our age difference made no difference when I was thirty and he was sixty." She held her wine goblet in both hands as if she needed to warm herself with the red liquid. "But, now, now that I'm forty-seven and he's seventy-seven, things are very different. Now, when I look back on my life, I'm really not sure why I was attracted to him in the first place. As you can see, as most people see, we are very different people. His passion is and has always been his son, his farm and his horses. I'm not in the top three and never will be. It's a very lonely feeling being married to someone and not being in the top three."

Jose was awed by her honesty. He wanted to say something to tell her she was wrong, that surely, she was important to Bert as something more than a trophy wife. But he didn't want to lie to her, so he asked another question.

"What about a family? Did you ever want to have a family of your own?"

Fiona wiped a tear from her face and took a deep breath. "Yes, in the worst way. But I can't have children and Bert was opposed to adopting. He said we could just be part of Micah's family. There was no discussing it. He didn't want to start over with babies, not as his age. It's a shame because I think he would have been an excellent father. He certainly has the energy. I mean, look at him. He's in better shape than some of the grooms." She paused, then, "I guess it just wasn't meant to be."

Jose felt terrible that he'd asked her to turn over such a painful stone. Her sincerity and honesty were touching. In contrast, he'd been nothing but dishonest, insincere and disingenuous with her about his life, the one before 9-11. Her vulnerability made his callous shell of lies seem cruel and he hated himself for it. He regretted starting the conversation at all.

"I'm so sorry," he said. But he didn't understand exactly what he was sorry for. He just felt sorry for her and for his deceit.

It was an emotional moment for both of them. Fiona had revealed her loneliness. It felt wonderful to finally tell someone. And his reaction was obviously compassion and understanding. He seemed to be expressing real empathy. He was visibly upset by her pain. She wanted to touch him; to let him know she appreciated his empathy. She reached across to his rocker and put her hand on his arm.

"Thank you, Jose. You are the best listener in the world. I could talk to you all night."

That misguided trust only shamed Jose even more. He wanted desperately to offer her some truth about himself, something that would make her understand what he really was. But what was he, really? He'd been Jose for so long he didn't even know Joey Martinez any more. And wasn't that what this odyssey was all about, to find his true self, the person he was supposed to be? He'd done that. He was the talented painter, Jose. That was the person who was buried under all the conventional bullshit for his first twenty-seven years. That was the person he freed on 9-11. That person wasn't a lie. That person was real. So, what would he tell her that would make him feel less unworthy?

In the end, he said nothing. To break the uncomfortable stillness, he poured them both another glass of wine, finishing the second bottle. Then he asked, "Would you like some ice cream? I have vanilla and Cherry Garcia."

"Maybe a tiny bit. Thanks."

When he rose to head for the kitchen, he staggered and realized he'd had too much wine. "I think I've had enough wine." He said lightly.

"I'm going to use your bathroom." Fiona said, heading for the house. "Not too much ice cream for me. And just vanilla, please." She walked down the hall, swaying a bit from side to side, but Joe didn't notice.

When he returned with two small glass bowls of ice cream, Fiona wasn't on the porch. He found her standing in the hallway looking at the drawings on the wall. Some of the drawings were of gallant horses leaping fences, some were of riders and their horses, and three were portraits of Fiona. All were done in charcoal and were some of his earliest work.

"I never saw these before." She was staring at the portraits. "Why me?"

He'd had enough wine to gather the courage for the truth, at least about this. "When I first met you, I…, umm…, had something of a crush on you." He admitted sheepishly.

Her eyes never left the pictures. "Wow, I never knew. I'm…, I'm flattered."

"I remember the first time I met you. You were stepping out of the car coming from the airport. You had on a white linen pants suit. I was struck by your beauty and the graceful way you moved."

She leaned against the opposite wall, her eyes still fixed on the drawings hanging three feet away. She was incredibly touched. "So why didn't you ever tell me? Why wait twelve years? Why now?"

There was a minute of complete silence. Then Jose said, "Alcohol."

They both started to laugh, the kind of laughter that only gets more intense when you try to stop it. Within seconds, their laughter was uncontrollable and she put her hands on his shoulders to steady herself. As the laughter began to subside and they each caught their breath, their foreheads came together, more as a place of mutual rest than anything else. Time seemed to stand still. They held that position, both looking down at the floor as their heads rested on one another, like two spent prizefighters at the end of the fifteenth round.

Jose cleared his throated and said, "Our ice cream is melting out on the porch."

Fiona breathed in deeply and exhaled softly, "I don't want ice cream."

She tilted her head and kissed him on the lips, gently at first, then passionately, losing herself in him. Jose was shocked but, embolden by the wine, he kissed her back. He put his arms around her and pulled her in close. She responded with her arms around his back and thrust her tongue into his open mouth.

Then the kiss suddenly stopped. Fiona pulled away first and stood before him. No one spoke. The silence seemed to last for hours. They looked deeply into the other's eyes. Then, without taking her eyes off his, she took three steps backward into his bedroom and stood in the near darkness. Again, a long moment of blissful silence.

Then Fiona reached behind her and unzipped her sun dress with one slow motion. She let her dress fall to the ground and extended her hand toward Jose. "Come here."

CHAPTER THIRTY-SEVEN

They awoke around midnight, entangled warmly in each other's bodies. They'd made love three times, in three different ways, then fallen asleep. But now the euphoria of the alcohol was being replaced by headache and dehydration.

Fiona was the first to get up and retrieve her dress and panties from the floor before heading for the bathroom. Jose sat up in bed and bit his lip. He had no idea whatsoever, how the next five minutes of his life were going to go. Fiona was the first woman he'd been with in over twelve years. Up to now, he hadn't understood the lack of desire. He just assumed it was all about his constant guilt. But, for him, the last few hours hadn't been about sex at all. For him, they were about being close to someone who'd shown vulnerability and wanted the comfort of another human being.

Fiona emerged from the bathroom fully dressed. She walked to the side of the bed and sat next to him.

"I'm so glad I came here tonight. But, I have to go. You know I do."

He nodded his head without saying a word. She kissed him on the forehead and added, "You're amazing." She stood and walked a few steps toward the bedroom door, then added, "I think our ice cream melted."

⛌

The next morning Jose was awakened by the sound of a siren in the distance. He looked out from under the sheets and saw his clock said 7:47 A.M. The sheets still smelled of Fiona's perfume. His head was pounding so, rolling over, he pulled the sheets over his eyes hoping to find sleep again. He didn't want to face reality just yet. There were too many hard things to deal with now that the sun had washed away the dreamlike happiness of the evening.

And how could he face Fiona? He felt he'd taken advantage of her vulnerability. It wasn't right. And she was married to Bert Wells, a man who'd been nothing but generous to Jose since they met. He was his sponsor, his mentor, and his friend. Bert had welcomed Jose into their family and graciously shared his good fortune with him. How could he do this to Bert? How could he ever look him in the eye again?

He just wanted to go back to sleep and postpone the difficult reality ahead of him. But the sounds of sirens persisted and were getting louder. It sounded like there were more than one. So, Jose threw off the covers and headed for the bathroom. He tossed three Tylenol back with a glass of water and got into the shower. The steamy water helped clear his eyes but the pounding in his head continued. He lingered under the hot shower for several minutes, just leaning on the tiled wall allowing the warmth to cascade over his shoulders.

When he stepped out of the shower he noticed a red light flashing in his steamy mirror. At first, he thought it came from something in the bathroom, maybe his electric toothbrush charger. But as he toweled off he realized it was the reflection of something outside the room, something outside his house.

He wrapped the towel around his waist and walked into the living room. The red flashing light was reflecting off the ceiling. Its origin was outside, down the hill in the direction of the Wells farm. As he stepped toward the window he could see two police cars parked in the Wells' driveway, their emergency lights still flashing. Then he saw an ambulance and a white SUV with a medical symbol on the roof and door. Both were in the courtyard.

He raced back to his bedroom to throw on some clothes and a pair of moccasins, then dashed down the steep hill toward the commotion below. As he ran through the tall dry grass, his wet ponytail bouncing against his neck, he realized he'd put on the same clothes he'd worn last night. The same blue tee shirt Fiona had gently lifted over his head and the same jeans he struggled to extricate himself from when they'd fallen onto his bed.

Why were all these emergency vehicles at the farm? Something must be terribly wrong. He worried that something happened to Lizzy or Katie. They were always falling. Or maybe someone had taken a bad fall from a horse while out on a morning ride.

As he approached the clearing that led to the stone wall separating his property from theirs, he could see three of the grooms standing with Lauren outside Bert and Fiona's house. A policeman was talking to them. The other policeman was standing by the front door, writing something. The epicenter of attention was definitely Bert and Fiona's home.

His run slowed to a walk, and then to a dead stop. What he saw paralyzed him. Two men were carrying something out the front door. They had on reflective jackets with medical emblems on the back. They were at opposite ends of a long black bag. Jose recognized the scene from so many crime dramas on TV. It was a body bag. They were carrying a body from the house toward the ambulance.

Jose froze just a few feet behind Lauren and the grooms. They hadn't noticed his approach and were fixed on the macabre scene before them. Jose said nothing. He couldn't. He just watched as the body bag was placed on a gurney then lifted into the ambulance.

Micah wells came through the front door of his father's house. He was visibly upset and shaking his head. He stopped a few feet from the door and turned back, as if waiting for someone else to join him. Time seemed to stand still. Then Fiona walked through the door and Micah put his arm around her.

Lauren now noticed Jose standing behind them. She turned and embraced him tightly. "Oh, Jose. I'm so sad." She was sobbing.

"What is it, Lauren? What's happened?"

"It's Bert. He's gone. He must have had a massive heart attack in his sleep last night. He never woke up this morning. Poor Fiona tried giving him CPR but she realized he was gone. She called Micah. She was hysterical. The poor thing. Micah called 911 and went over but he could tell right away. Bert must have died late last night." Her sobbing made it hard to speak. "The medic said it looked like he died last night. Fiona said he'd gone to bed very early because he was tired. He might have already been dead when she went to bed later. Oh, the poor thing."

Jose thought about Fiona. She might have gotten into bed last night, after leaving his, and slept next to her dead husband the entire night. While she lay there, did she think about Jose? Was she filled with regret or contrition? Was she considering telling her husband what she'd done? The images horrified him and he felt such sorrow both for Fiona and for the loss of his friend. The friend he was betraying around the time Bert was dying at home, alone. How could he do such a terrible thing? How could he ever atone for this?

⇒⊢ ⊣⇐

259

The weeks after Bert's death were some of the worst in Jose's life. He was tortured by the memory of his selfish betrayal of his good friend; another secret he couldn't share with anyone. Another demon haunting his sleep.

It had been Bert's wishes to be cremated and to have his ashes spread around the fields of Wells Hill. Micah made sure his father's wishes were carried out to the letter. A week after his death, Bert Wells was scattered in the tall grass behind the main sables by his two granddaughters who didn't really understand what they were doing but enjoyed running through the grass tossing handfuls of ash into the wind. Micah had invited two dozen close friends but almost a hundred people showed up to pay respect both to Micah and to Bert.

Marco Brunelli and his wife Stella were there. It was the first time they'd been back to the farm since Gabriella was killed six years earlier. Even though his business relationship with Mica had continued, it was too painful for the Italian to ever come to America for an event. He'd buried himself in his work in Europe. Stella was an empty shell of the gregarious woman she'd been. She looked twenty years older.

An elaborate luncheon in the courtyard, followed the service. Micah and Bret each said a few words about the man they'd lost. Bret told funny stories about some of the mischievous antics he and Bert had engaged in over the years; stories that gave life to the man. Micah got choked up when he spoke which brought tears to many in the crowd. Who doesn't feel pain for a grieving man eulogizing his father?

"My dad had his faults. Anyone who really knew him, knew that." He said. "But he loved things passionately. He loved his wife, Fiona. He loved his son and the woman he treated like a daughter." He motioned toward Lauren. "He loved his grandchildren and he loved his horses. But most of all, I think he loved his farm. Sometimes I find it hard to understand how a man can love a piece of land. I mean, it's just fields and trees, and barns and paddocks.

It can't love you back. But to him, it was alive. Wells Hill wasn't just home. It wasn't just his business. It was a part of him. And now, he's a part of the farm, forever." He brushed back a tear, then finished, looking out at the rolling fields, "I love you dad, so much."

After the last guests had departed, late in the afternoon, the family and grooms gathered at Micah's house to reminisce and look at old pictures from Bert's office. It was cathartic for everyone. Bret and Terry had known Bert most their adult lives. They told touching stories of how he'd helped them financially when they were first married and trying to get their first mortgage.

Each of the grooms had nice things to say about Bert. He'd helped all of them get to this country, sometimes legally, sometimes using the same backroom approach he'd employed for Jose. They were all grateful to the man who'd taught them so much about horses.

They all sat around Micah's spacious living room for hours, drinking toasts to the deceased and telling stories. It helped Micah feel less of an orphan to have people around. And it helped Fiona feel less alone. And less terrified about her future. Living on a horse farm, when your life isn't focused on horses just doesn't make sense. She didn't belong here, yet this had been her family.

When the time came for everyone to leave, to recognize that life goes on and they must go back to their lives, the grooms were the first to excuse themselves, each kissing Fiona and embracing Micah. Bret and Terry walked back to their house promising to host dinner the next night.

"I'm supposed to ride in the Rolex this weekend but I think I'm going to skip it. Ruby could use the rest anyway." Micah said. Bret didn't argue. He knew Micah was hurting and needed time to heal.

"I'm going to be on my way too." Jose said as he rose to leave. "Anything I can do, you let me know." He said to Micah as they hugged.

When he turned to say goodbye to Fiona she was already standing with outstretched arms, waiting for his embrace. When they did, she said, "I'll walk out with you. Will you walk me back to the cottage? There's something I know Bert would have wanted you to have."

"Of course."

It was the first time Jose had been alone with Fiona since the night of Bert's death. The sun skimmed the horizon as they walked from the main house to Bert's cottage. No one spoke. They just looked down at the graveled path in silence. When they arrived, it was Jose who spoke first.

"I wish you could begin to understand how terrible I feel. I wish I could take away some of your pain. You just look so sad. And I'm so sorry for everything."

She looked at him quizzically. "I'm not."

"You're not what?"

"I'm not sorry for everything. Weren't those your words? I'm not sorry my seventy-seven-year-old husband died peacefully in his sleep. What a wonderful way to die; at home, in your own bed, on the farm you loved so much. And I'm not sorry we spent the night together. There, I said it. Does that make me a terrible person?"

"No, of course not."

"Your mouth says no but your eyes say yes."

"I'm sorry. I just feel so guilty."

Fiona took his hands in hers and tried to lighten the mood. "Hey Benjamin, you were seduced by a beautiful older woman." She winked.

"Benjamin?"

"Don't tell me you never saw The Graduate!" She said playfully. "One of the best movies ever. Dustin Hoffman played Benjamin and Anne Bancroft was the seductress."

He gave her a totally blank look.

"Wow, one night we should watch it. On second thought, no. He winds up running off with Anne Bancroft's daughter."

Then her mood changed back to the sober widow. "Seriously, Jose. There is nothing to feel sorry about. I loved our time together the other night. I don't regret it at all. Yes, I will miss Bert terribly. But I'm not going to be morose about it. We loved each other, but..." She paused as if not sure she wanted to continue. Then, "But we both knew Bert would probably die while I was still relatively young. I knew it and he knew it. We talked about it a lot. He wanted to make sure I was prepared. And I was. I am."

Jose leaned against the front railing but couldn't come up with something to say.

"So, please stop saying you're sorry. Okay?" She touched his chin with the side of her hand.

"Okay. I will." He said. "So, what was it you said Bert wanted me to have?"

"Well, actually, Bert wanted me to have it but I'm not comfortable with it. Remember I said Bert had prepared me for many years without him. He was very conscientious about making sure I'd be okay after he was gone. He's taken care of me financially. He prepared me for this emotionally. He really looked out for me in many ways. Come with me." She took him by the hand and led him inside her home.

Jose had no idea where this was going. When they were inside the room that had been Bert's office, Fiona went behind the desk and opened the top drawer. She removed a handsome box made of heavy brown plastic.

"He gave me this three years ago, when we were in Florida. He never felt totally safe in Florida." She opened the box revealing a Colt hand gun and a cartridge of bullets. It was a Rock Island Armory, 45 caliber pistol, something of a collector's piece, although at the time, Jose was completely unaware.

"I want you to have it. To be honest, I just want to get it out of the house. Guns terrify me and I don't want it here. And I don't want to give it to Micah because he has young children in the house." She slid the box across the desk in Jose's direction. "He taught me how to load it but I really don't remember. The bullets are in this thing." She pointed to the cartridge.

"I don't think I've ever held a gun in my life." Jose was being very honest. Guns scared him too.

"Well, please take it just to get it out of here. You can sell it if you like. I don't care." She closed the box and handed it to Jose. "Please, you're doing me a favor."

Under the circumstances, the only appropriate response seemed to be, "Thank you."

CHAPTER THIRTY-EIGHT

In June 2014, the long awaited National September 11 Memorial and Museum finally opened to the public. The Memorial itself, the two square fountains located on the exact sites of the twin towers, had opened three years earlier, but construction of the museum was complicated by several factors. At the same time the museum was being planned, multiple skyscrapers were being built on the site, including the hemisphere's tallest building, as well as two major transit centers with railroads running through them. All the while, the entire site had to be refortified against the Hudson River.

The greatest challenge facing the museum's planners had been combining the historical nature of the construction with a memorial. This was, after all, hallowed ground. The remains of 1,080 of the nearly 3,000 people killed that day had never been identified. The office of the Chief Medical Examiner for the City of New York faced an unusual situation. The OCME had recovered nearly 22,000 human remains from the site but most were either so minuscule in size or so degraded that forensic technology was of no help. Over 1,000 families had received no physical remains of their loved ones.

Without remains, families like Claire Martinez-Muller, had no place of rest for their deceased. Many families therefore, advocated for an area within the museum to serve this purpose. But the unidentified remains couldn't be placed in a mausoleum within the museum. The OCME still needed to periodically remove remains to conduct increasingly sophisticated analysis in hopes of making future positive identifications. Therefore, a special OCME repository for the 1,080 unidentified remains, a working laboratory, was constructed within the museum, behind a bedrock wall and adjacent to the public space.

This was all of great interest to Fiona Wells because she'd lost a close friend on 9-11 and the remains of Judy Mc Sass were among those yet to be identified. When Fiona learned the unidentified human remains were to be placed within the museum, she decided she needed to visit the sacred site as a final memorial to her childhood friend. But she couldn't bear the thought of going alone and everyone on the farm was busy with the summer event schedule. So, she turned to Jose.

"Please come with me, Jose. I don't want to do this alone. Judy's parents are in Ireland and there's probably no one here who will go to say a prayer for her. I feel like I must go. She was my friend since we were six years old. Please don't make me go alone."

There was probably no one else in the world from whom Jose would consider such a request. Going back to Ground Zero was something he'd hoped he'd never have to do. It was a life he'd tried to forget, especially now that he'd found a new one. The thought of even seeing the place he used to work, the place where so many of his colleagues died, was unbearable.

But, for some inexplicable reason, he agreed to go with her. Maybe it was curiosity. Maybe he needed to do penance in order to finally close that door. Or maybe, he just wanted to help a friend. Whatever the motivation, they agreed to visit the Memorial and Museum on a Wednesday in mid-August. Fiona had read Wednesdays were the least crowded days.

It had been only a month since Bert Wells' granddaughters scattered him around the farm, so when Lauren heard Jose was going to the city with Fiona, she pulled him aside for a talk.

"Jose, you need to keep in mind that Fiona just lost her husband. I'm not sure opening old wounds like the death of her friend Judy, is a great idea. Look, I know you like Fiona. That's obvious to everyone. You've always thought of her as some sort of big sister, I get it. But if you've got other interests, I think you should back off for a while. She needs space and time. You don't..., we don't want her doing something she'll later regret."

"I know exactly what you're saying. Believe me, I know. And I'm dreading this trip for a bunch of reasons, but she asked me to go with her. How can I refuse?"

When the day arrived, Fiona booked a car to take them into lower Manhattan. They agreed they'd have dinner afterwards, then take a train home from Grand Central Station. Having a car wait for them, since neither had any idea how long they'd spend in the museum, didn't make sense.

As they sat in the back of the black town car, Fiona told Jose her recollections of September 11, 2001. "Bert and I had only been married a few years. We had just gotten back from a trip to France. Bert was looking at horses, of course. I had called my friend Judy to tell her about the trip because she'd never been to France. She was at work. She worked for Aon Insurance. She worked on the thirtieth floor of the Trade Center, I think building number one. I remember it was a Tuesday morning and I called her about 8:30 in the morning. She was having coffee at her desk and eating a blueberry muffin. Don't ask me why I remember that, but I do."

"Anyway, we spoke for about ten minutes, then she had to take another call and said she'd call me back. But she never did. I don't know what happened to her but they never found her body. That's why I need to go there. It's where she's buried." She looked like she was about to cry, but then pulled it together. "I promise not to be a blubbering fool today."

"It's okay. I understand." Was all he could think to say.

For several minutes, she looked out the window and watched the Hutchinson River Parkway fly by. Then she asked Jose, "Where were you that day?"

He knew this question would come up. How could it not? And he decided it might be somehow cathartic for him to tell her part of the truth.

"I think I told you once before, I used to work for this woman in Summit. After she passed away, her kids didn't need a property manager anymore so I was out of a job and on my way to Florida to look for work. I met a friend for breakfast at a diner in Jersey City, then had about an hour before my train left for Washington where I planned to get a bus to Miami. So, I was sitting on a park bench in Jersey City, looking out on the Manhattan skyline." Jose recalled the diner, the woman and the elderly black man he'd encountered on the bench. In some ways it seemed like yesterday, yet it was a lifetime ago.

"The lady next to me on the bench had a radio and we watched as the planes hit the towers and as the towers collapsed. It was horrible. I had a lot of friends there too. Guys I knew from Ecuador were working at the restaurant, Windows on the World. None of them made it out." Then, for reasons he never understood, he added, "And the woman I was seeing at the time, worked in Tower One. She worked for Cambridge Partners. Her name was Sarah Bideaux. She was so young and innocent. It was so unfair."

"Oh my, I didn't know that. Your girlfriend was killed at the Trade Center?"

"We'd only gone out a couple of times, but yes." He stared out the window visualizing Sarah's face. Maybe he did need to make this trip. Maybe it would finally set him free from some of the guilt he harbored, at least the guilt about the young reporter.

"I'm so sorry, Jose. You never told me that."

"It was a long time ago," he lied.

They arrived at the site just after noon. As they stepped from the car, Jose was filled with overwhelming grief. The entire area was completely different. He couldn't get his bearings. They were on Chambers Street but nothing was familiar. He found it very disorienting, almost sickening to be somewhere he knew so well, yet recognized nothing. Thirteen years ago, at this time of day, he would have been walking the same street in search of lunch; a slice at Steve's pizzeria, a sandwich from Ernie's, maybe even a Whopper at the Burger King which should have been right where he was now standing. Everything was different.

He reached for Fiona's hand. "This is all so different, so confusing." He was looking up for a familiar building. There were none. Then he turned and saw the black edifice that had once been the Merrill Lynch Building with a Brooks Brother's store in the lobby. Finally, something to give him a bearing. From this spot, if he turned in the opposite direction, he would have been facing the six main buildings that surrounded the WTC plaza and the Sphere; the four small black buildings and the two towers.

But on this day, when he turned, expecting something to be familiar, everything was new and nothing was the same. It was frightening; far more frightening then if he'd never been here before. It was like putting someone inside a room where the walls are painted with vertical stripes to make the room appear taller at one end and shorter at the other. It was an optical illusion.

They crossed Chambers Street and followed the crowds toward the twin waterfalls; the two acre-sized pools with thirty-foot waterfalls cascading down all four sides. Like eerie shadows, the two pools occupy the vacant spaces left by the now absent twin towers. Surrounding each pool on all sides were the names of the victims engraved in walls of glossy granite. What Jose found most inspiring was the center void into which the water fell a second time, perpetually disappearing from view. It seemed fitting considering all the victims who were never found.

The noon-time sun shined down directly, creating a glistening effect as the water rolled over the granite's edge then rolled over once more into oblivion. Jose scanned the names on the stone nearest him. None were familiar. He wondered how many names of the people at Chambers Partners he'd even remember. Then he scanned the surrounding landscape. There were trees and benches in all directions but no sign of a museum. He hadn't realized the entire museum was built underground. Only the glass atrium of the entrance pavilion was above ground.

When they did find the entrance, standing like sentries were two steel columns, over eighty feet high that used to form part of the exterior façade of the North Tower. The "tridents" as they were called, were so large, they had been set in place before the museum was built. Then the pavilion was built around them. The steel had rusted but the shape was familiar and defined the exterior of the towers, at least as Jose remembered them.

"I'd never been to the World Trade Center," Fiona said as she admired the colossal steel piece. "But I recognize the design. See, up there, where the steel branches into three arms. That's the way the outside looked, right?"

Jose said, "Yeah," but he had to swallow hard as he did. This was going to be an emotional ride for him. Not only was the museum haunted by the ghosts of those he knew, but even the buildings and artifacts themselves he found distressing. He was sorry he'd agreed to come and was no longer sure he could endure too much of it.

They descended the long escalator from the pavilion entrance to the concourse lobby. In the lobby were two disturbing reminders of what had once been. To their left was a miniature version of the Sphere, the orb at the center of the WTC plaza that Jose had seen almost every day. On the wall behind the sculpture hung a large photograph of lower Manhattan, taken from Brooklyn at 8:30 A.M. on September 11, 2001, just sixteen minutes before the first plane struck. The photo showed a pristine blue sky with the two colossal towers glistening in the morning sunlight.

Several large groups of tourists were gathered around the reception desk so Fiona suggested they take the ramp to the lower level exhibits, then work their way back up. The hope was to be moving in the opposite direction as the tours. At the bottom of the ramp, they entered Foundation Hall, a cathedral-like space with soaring ceilings. Dominating the view was a portion of the original slurry wall, the retaining wall built to keep the Hudson River out of the excavation site when the original World Trade Center was being built, a wall that withstood the devastation of 9-11.

They moved on to Memorial Hall with its massive wall of 2,983 individual watercolor paintings in various shades of blue, the shades the artist saw in the 9-11 morning sky. Commemorating the people killed both on 9-11 and in the 1993 attack, every square is a unique shade of blue combining to create a panoramic mosaic of color. Jose read Fiona the inscription on a nearby plaque that explained the words in the center of the mosaic, "*No Day Shall Erase You From The Memory Of Time*", a quote from Virgil, as having been created from pieces of forged steel recovered from Ground Zero.

At each end of the same wall were two identical markers which read, "*Reposed behind this wall are the remains of many people who perished at the World Trade Center on September 11, 2001. The repository is maintained by the Office of Chief Medical Examiner of the City of New York.*" Fiona had found the place she needed to be, the place where she could say a silent prayer for her friend, Judy who rested behind the huge blue wall.

"I just need to sit here a few minutes by myself," she said to Jose. "You go ahead. I'll catch up."

Jose understood her need for solitude. He wondered how many of his co-workers lay behind the same wall. He wondered if the remains of the reporter were there. Then he thought about Claire. Had she sat in this very spot, saying a prayer for him? He didn't want to think about it.

He walked away from the wall and found himself standing in front of a sign that read, "*In Memoriam*" flanking a large glass doorway that led into the most solemn quarters. The exhibition gallery, a square within a square, echoed the geometry of the Memorial pools above. Within the outer square were portrait photos placed floor to ceiling on all four walls, surrounding visitors with the faces and names of all who were killed in the attacks. The "*wall of faces*" as it was called, gave life to the numbers. The 2,983 were an abstraction no longer. The four walls were a true cross section of humanity, people from two and a half to eighty-five, from ninety nations, encompassing a spectrum of ethnicities, faiths and economic classes, arranged in alphabetical order.

Jose was frozen where he stood, the souls of nearly three thousand looking back at him. At the moment, the room was almost empty lending to the solemnity and eeriness. As all the dead stared back, he took two steps toward the wall. The first name and photo he focused on was a fireman named Ronnie E. Gies. Realizing the photos were arranged alphabetically, curiosity drove him to the M's. He found several Martinez's before he spied his own college yearbook picture and the name Joseph P. Martinez. The image looked nothing like the man standing before it.

Then he turned and went to the first wall searching for the name Sarah Bideaux. He quickly found it on the bottom row. Her picture froze her in time as a high school senior. He heard himself whisper, "I'm so sorry." He felt pain and tightness in his chest, pain he'd become familiar with over the years.

He overheard a tour-guide explaining to her group that in the next room, they could, using a touchpad, select the name of a victim and see a short presentation about them prepared by their family. He thought that was a nice touch but couldn't bring himself to do it. He didn't want to hear Claire's voice or know what she'd said about him.

He turned back to the walls and searched for people he worked with at Cambridge; Beth DaRin, the girl from HR, Richard Oh from accounting, William Meyers from the trading floor. They were all there staring back at him. He checked several other names he remembered from his office. They were on the wall as well. It seemed as though no one he could recall from Cambridge had escaped.

He felt a gentle tap on his shoulder and turned to see Fiona Wells. "Did you find your friends? The ones from Windows on the World?"

"Yes. It seems no one made it out." He was on the brink of tears and said, "I need to leave."

"That's okay. I did what I needed to do. I said good bye to Judy. We can go now."

CHAPTER THIRTY-NINE

2016

"More wine?" the attractive stewardess asked.

"No, thank you." Jose replied, then adjusted his position in the seat. They'd been on the plane five hours and had several more ahead of them before reaching Rio de Janeiro. Terry Kennedy and Lauren Wells sat to his left in the two center seats of the first-class cabin. Both were asleep. Jose and the two women were on their way to join Micah, Bret and the horses in Brazil for the summer Olympic games in Rio.

Micah had once again earned a position on the U.S. team. He and Bret had traveled to Rio a week before to allow the horses to go through the mandatory equine quarantine and for Micah to conduct some pre-Olympic interviews with the U.S. media. Because of the ongoing concern about the zika virus in Brazil and its perceived danger to child-bearing age women, Micah insisted Lauren stay behind until just before the opening ceremonies. Lizzy and Katie stayed in Woodfield with their nanny.

For Lauren and Terry, this was their first visit to South America. But Jose had been to Rio three times before to appear at art exhibits and fundraisers for the IOC. His paintings had become synonymous with the Olympics and the equestrian events. The woman who ran the International Olympic Committee had asked, as a personal favor, that Jose attend one of the preliminary meetings, two years earlier, when plans were being drawn for the Olympic site and specifically how the equestrian venues would be decorated. It was an honor he couldn't refuse.

Jose checked the in-flight map and was pleased to see their plane was now over the northern tip of South America, approaching the Venezuela coast. He wanted to get some sleep before they landed. But the stewardess's motion had awakened Lauren and she was pleased to see Jose was not asleep.

"Hey, Jose," she whispered. "Want to watch a movie together?" Lauren had been wonderful to Jose, especially in the weeks and months following Bert's death, a time when her kindness would have been better directed at Micah, who took his dad's passing badly. But she struggled to know how to comfort Micah. His pain was private. Jose, on the other hand, was outwardly shaken by the elder Well's death and Lauren was happy to have someone she could help.

"What do you want to watch?"

"How 'bout a comedy? They have the Amy Schumer movie. It's supposed to be funny."

"Okay, come and sit next to me so we can watch it together."

For the next two hours, Lauren and Jose huddled together under a blue American Airlines blanket and giggled at the bawdy movie. They had become like brother and sister in many ways. They shared meals together all the time at the farm. Jose was often called on to sit for Lauren's daughters and, when Micah was on the road, it was to Jose she turned to open the difficult jar or fix the cable box when she'd screwed it up. In New York, his home was just up the hill and in Wellington, he'd bought a modest ranch style cottage about two blocks from the Wells farm. In many ways, they were family.

And yet, there was never any sexual attraction between them. Lauren was a beautiful woman and Jose, a very handsome guy, but their relationship was platonic, at least on the surface. The only time a line was crossed was about a year ago when Micah was in Calgary and Jose and Lauren had taken the girls to Disney World. They were on their way back to the hotel after a full day at Epcot Center. Lauren had two Martinis at dinner and was a little sleepy as they rode the Monorail. Liz and Katie had fallen asleep in the seat in front of them and Lauren was resting her head on Jose's shoulder. Half asleep, she leaned up and kissed him on the lips, then realized what she'd done and immediately apologized. The next day at breakfast, she explained that she was asleep and must have been dreaming that it was Micah's shoulder. But neither of them ever understood what had actually happened.

When the movie ended, Lauren turned on her side and pulled the blanket over herself. "I'm going to sleep for a bit."

Jose was happy about their relationship. He enjoyed being her friend and watching over her when Micah wasn't around. He liked the role of protector. He liked being the person Lauren turned to when she needed a friend or advice about any subject other than horses. On that subject, she was the expert. He closed his eyes and reflected on the last few years.

Ever since the London Olympics, four years ago, life around the Wells farms had been different. When the U.S. team failed to win a medal and none of the U.S. team members medaled individually, Micah became obsessed. He retired Ruby and searched the world for another championship mount. He swore an oath to himself and to his staff that in 2016 they would once again bring home an Olympic medal and Marco Brunelli was happy to sponsor his quest. He told Micah to spend up to six million Euro to find the right horse in which he would have a sixty percent stake in all prize money.

More for companionship than anything else, Micah and Bret asked Jose to accompany them on their quest and, in the fall of 2012, they traveled all over Europe looking for the right animal. It was in Belgium they finally found Runaway, a six-year-old mare with superb lineage and hind muscles that Bret said, "Looked like she could jump an eighteen-wheeler." Once again, Micah called Marco and asked for his blessing to purchase the mare and once again, he'd underspent his allowance, if only by a little.

"If you think she's a horse that can win us a World Cup and Olympic medal, do it," the Italian said. "*Voglio un vincitore!* I want a winner."

It took nearly two years before Micah deemed Runaway ready for Grand Prix events. He worked with her every day, sometimes for three hours at a time, a training schedule Bret was unhappy with. He preferred shorter rides with ample rest before increasing the jumps to Grand prix heights. But Micah insisted and his methods were tested at the 2015 Longines Classic in Wellington. It was Runaway's introduction to the public and she didn't disappoint. After the event, Micah gave the championship blue ribbon to a delighted nine-year-old girl who was waiting for an autograph. The moment was captured by several photographers.

Jose remembered that night clearly because something else happened that night; something that hurt him badly. He had watched Runaway's debut from the VIP box along with Lauren and Fiona. After the victory and post event celebrations at the showgrounds, Lauren excused herself to go pick up her daughters who had stayed with a friend. Jose and Fiona walked the half mile back to the farm under a spectacular star-lit sky.

It had been nearly six months since Bert's sudden death and Jose and Fiona had spent many hours together reminiscing about Bert. Sometimes they would also talk about the night they'd spent together, the night Bert died, but always in a way that honestly tried to understand the emotions of the night, not the passion.

They'd never slept together again and both seemed to enjoy the separation. They would sometimes attend social events together, not as a couple, although they would arrive and leave together, but as an equestrian socialite and a famous artist who happened to be good friends. The close arrangement suited both.

As they neared the farm's entrance gates Fiona stopped a few yards from the keypad. "Jose, I have something to tell you," she said looking down at the graveled driveway. Then she was silent.

"Is everything okay? Are you alright? He wanted desperately to know.

"Yes, I'm fine." She smiled. "Isn't that just like you, worrying about me."

"Well, what is it then?"

"I've given this a lot of thought. I didn't want to do anything rash right after the funeral so I made myself wait, but I think I'm sure. No…, I am sure. This is the right thing for me. I need a new direction."

He looked at her not understanding where this was going. For a moment, he thought she might be referring to him as the new direction. Perhaps she wanted to rekindle their relationship or at least see if there could be one. He touched her chin gently and raised her head so he could see her face.

"What are you saying Fiona?"

She looked into his eyes, a move that summoned all the bravery she could muster. "I've decided to move back to Ireland to be near my family, my other family."

He was stunned. "When?"

"In a few months. I'll need to work something out with Micah and Lauren about the house, but I'd like to be back by Easter. I think it will be best for me."

"Wow. I didn't expect this. I'm going to really miss you."

"I'll miss you too, very much. That's why I wanted you to be the first one I told."

He held her hands in his. "Are you sure about this?"

"No, I'm never completely sure about anything. But it feels like the right thing to do." Again, she looked directly into his eyes. "To be honest, you were a big part of my decision. I've thought about us a lot lately, or actually, if there could be an us. But I think part of the reason I was drawn to you was because of Bert; always knowing that I'd be without him someday. That I'd be alone."

Six days after they arrived in Rio, Lauren, Terry and Jose sat in the V.I.P. box at the National Equestrian Center in Deodoro cheering on the U.S. team who'd advanced to the final round. The evening air was thick with a moist Atlantic breeze and about as hot as any Jose could remember. At one point in the afternoon the I.O.C. officials were debating postponing the finals until the following morning because it was so oppressively hot. The concern, as always, was for the horses, not the riders.

The French team had already clinched the Gold Medal but four countries were still in contention for the Silver and Bronze: Germany, the Netherlands, Brazil and the U.S. Amazingly, three riders from each team came into the final round with clear scores from the previous day. In the history of the Olympics, that had never happened before.

Lauren was on the phone with Micah and looked concerned. She turned away from Jose and Terry and cupped her ear to make sure she was hearing correctly.

"That's horrible." She said into the iPhone. "Alright. Good luck sweetie."

Now Terry's phone was ringing. "That will be Bret," Lauren said. "I'll fill you in. Tell him to get back to work. We have a medal to win."

"What's going on?" Jose inquired.

"There's something wrong with Beezie's horse.. She's withdrawn."

"Oh, shit." Terry said a bit too loudly for the nearby spectators to ignore.

"So, what happens now?" Jose had no idea how such matters were handled.

"Unfortunately, the way it works is that each team of four riders gets to drop its worst score. But if we only have three riders competing, we have to use all three scores. We're at a huge disadvantage."

Terry added, "And Beezie is usually our anchor rider because she's the most experienced. We were expecting to use her ride and have the luxury of dropping someone else's. She and Cortez are so good together."

"And Micah just told me, he's now the anchor rider." Lauren added.

"So, we need to hope for Germany, the Netherlands and Brazil to really shit the bed, right?" Jose asked.

"Worse than that. We need to hope two riders from each team do poorly. That means at least one rail down each. It's very unlikely. Or maybe a time fault."

"What's that mean?"

The rider has eighty-two seconds to complete the round. If they jump a clear round, no rails down, but use more than eighty-two seconds to do it, they get one penalty point. It's not as bad as the four points you get for knocking down a rail but it could be important if there's a tie."

Terry added, "The U.S. certainly can't afford any time faults, not now."

"It doesn't seem fair."

"Yeah, but it's the only way to handle a withdrawal. You can't make the other teams drop a rider just because one of ours is out."

"I guess not. But, boy, that seems to put us at a huge disadvantage."

"It sure does. Shit, Micah's going to be so disappointed."

Jose felt badly for his friend. He knew how much Micah wanted to redeem himself after the Americans did so poorly in London four years earlier. He had such high hopes for Runaway. Everyone thought the Americans would medal in Rio. To go home empty-handed would be an embarrassment.

But fifty minutes later it was clear the Americans had a fighting chance. Germany had a time fault they couldn't drop and the Netherlands had two riders with rails down so the best they could do was Bronze if the U.S. and Brazil failed to medal.

Brazil's third and fourth riders took rails down on the same jump so they were eliminated from a medal soon after. The American's fate was in their own hands. Clear rounds by all three riders, with no time-faults would win the Silver Medal and hand Germany the Bronze.

The first two Americans did their part, riding flawlessly. It was now up to Micah. As he and Runaway were announced, Lauren clasped Jose's hand for support.

"I hate this!" She said. "I'm so nervous for him."

Terry leaned over. "He's not ranked number one in the world for nothing Lauren. He can do it."

Jose remembered watching Micah walk the course earlier in the evening. He seemed to be unsure about the next to last jump, a wall of foam bricks. He paced it off again and again, shaking his head.

"I'm worried about the last jump." Jose said. "He seemed unsure of something when he walked the course."

"Hey, it took fifteen years but you're finally learning something about our sport. And yes, I noticed that too." Lauren gripped his hand tightly.

The crowd was still as Micah Wells began his canter to the first jump. Eighteen thousand people, who'd been cheering wildly moments before for the Brazilians, were now silent. All you could hear was the sound of Runaway's hoofs hitting the turf and her heavy breathing as she cleared jump after jump.

On the seventh jump, she clipped the top rail. The sound of her hoof striking the wood elicited a loud "oooh" from the spectators. The rail wobbled for several seconds but remained atop the standard. Micah later claimed he never even heard it.

As he made the final turn approaching the last three jumps, he caught sight of the clock: 71.14 seconds. He was two full seconds behind where he'd hoped to be at this point and now needed to press it. Lauren saw it too and closed her eyes. She couldn't bear to watch. She knew Runaway had the strength for the jumps but she wasn't sure she could do the last three that quickly.

Micah guided her over the first jump easily and pushed her hard to get to the second in one less stride than he'd planned. As they approached the wall of foam bricks, Runaway sensed the urgency and cleared the top bricks by nearly a foot. The final jump, an oxer, lay forty feet ahead. Rider and mount seemed determined to get there quickly. Runaway's strides were longer than before and her snorting breath let the crowd know she was giving it all she had. The arena was on their feet, prepared to cheer, regardless of the outcome.

Ten feet from the jump, she lifted Micah off the ground and flew toward the obstacle. She cleared the top by less than two inches in front, but it appeared to Jose that she wasn't going to clear it behind.

Suddenly Runaway's hind legs folded up like the retracting wheels on a 747 lifting from a runway. Her last hoof missed the rail by millimeters and they landed hard on the far side. The crowd went wild. Jose looked up at the clock which was frozen at 81.45.

"He did it!" he screamed.

Lauren opened her eyes. She knew from the sounds of the arena that the U.S. team had won the Silver Medal thanks to the flawless ride of Runaway and her husband. She cried with pride as thousands of spectators waved miniature American flags.

CHAPTER FORTY

The week leading up to the 2016 Hampton Classic was filled with torrential rains. The dirt roads leading into the Bridgehampton show grounds were pocked with muddy ruts, making entrance and egress difficult the first day of the event. Jose made the drive from Woodfield on Wednesday morning, two days after the start of the show. Everyone else from the Wells farm had been there since Sunday.

As he neared the facility, passing farms and vineyards along route 27, he thought about all the summers his parents had driven the same path on their way to Montauk and the annual family vacation. As a teenager, the weeks they'd spent on the easternmost tip of Long Island included some of the happiest days in his memory. He and his father would take long walks along the rocky beach near the lighthouse and watch as surfcasting fishermen reeled in enormous silvery striped bass. His mother would go to the Montauk docks and buy dozens of clams with which she'd make delicious chowder. The tastes and smells of the area filled him with a feeling of warm happiness.

That warm feeling made him think about how proud his parents would have been of his artistic accomplishments. His works had been on display all over the world, or at least, those parts of the world that appreciated equestrian sports. That included places Jose never thought about going before he met the Wells family. Places like Dubai, Aachen, Rome, Calgary, and most recently Rio. A single painting could sell for over a hundred thousand dollars, although none had ever topped the two hundred forty thousand paid for the Gabriella work at Bert's auction.

More importantly, Jose loved what he was doing. The money meant little to him as he had no one else in his life to share it with. He was happy to create works of beauty, donate them to worthy causes and watch the bidding soar. He was always humbled by the process and the accolades that came the artist's way were reward enough.

But then he realized his parents had never known Jose the painter of Wellington. The son they knew was Joey the conformist. The thought of his father knowing what he'd done to Claire filled him with shame. He had been such a devoted husband and father, he could never understand Joey's escape and transformation. All the happiness and success that followed would be meaningless to the elder Martinez. He was grateful he'd never have to explain his life to his father.

As Jose pulled his Jeep into the VIP entrance at the Bridgehampton show grounds, he could see the enormous center ring where the main riding events would be held. In the surrounding rings, preliminary events would be held all week, leading up to the Grand Prix on Sunday afternoon. Micah's success here in Bridgehampton was legendary. He'd won the event more than any other rider. He'd also won it three consecutive years, but he hadn't stood on the winner's podium since 2010 and he'd never won with Runaway, so Jose knew Micah really wanted this one.

The surrounding rings would also be busy all week hosting lesser events and junior events, show-jumping for those under age eighteen. It was here that many aspiring and talented young riders first became noticed. Usually the fortunate offspring of wealthy parents who purchased gifted horses, these teenagers would likely be the world-class riders of the future. And the Hampton Classic was often their coming-out event.

As he'd done the previous year, Jose booked a booth near the center ring to showcase his work. This year, he'd pledged all the profits to the New York Firefighters Burn Center, a foundation he'd learned about from one of Micah's clients who sat on the board of New York Presbyterian Hospital. A Captain from the FDNY agreed to spend the day with Jose in the booth and Jose was afraid the firefighter was already there, looking for him. So, after parking in a field of grassy mud, he made his way through the main entrance and walked the long path to the main ring. He was relieved to find only the security guard he'd hired to keep overnight vigilance over his paintings standing near his booth.

"Good morning Manuel. I trust you had an uneventful evening."

"No offense Mr. Martinez, but if a ring of thieves were to perpetrate the great Hampton Classic heist, they'd probably skip the art and go straight for the horses. I hear some of them are worth ten million bucks."

"No offense taken. And you're probably correct." Jose said.

The security guard made a valid point. The combined value of the animals housed in the nearby stables exceeded one hundred million dollars, a risk not lost on their owners. Armed guards, provided by the show's sponsors, were stationed at each entrance to the area to protect the horses from two perils; theft and tampering, the latter being the greater danger. Grand Prix level horses needed to be under constant surveillance to prevent someone from tampering with their diet. If someone were to sabotage a horse's feed with any of a hundred controlled substances, intended to enhance performance, the rider and horse faced severe sanctions including banishment from the sport for up to three years. Micah had told Jose stories of just such sabotage by a groom trying to eliminate his rider's competition. Protecting the horses was serious business.

Manuel gathered his reading material and cell phone into a backpack and said, "Okay then, I'll be back at eight tonight. Have a good day."

A few minutes later, a tall grey-haired man in a snappy blue uniform approached the booth.

"Mr. Martinez? I'm Captain Mullin, Billy Mullin from the FDNY."

"Nice to meet you," Jose responded with a hearty hand shake.

Billy Mullin was just what you'd expect of a seasoned city firefighter. His face wore the scars of his twenty-seven years on the job, his hands the callouses of much hard work. He was erect and disciplined in his walk and his voice was direct and precise.

"I'm a little unclear on just what you'd like me to do today, sir."

"First of all, it's not sir, it's Jose. Second, you should probably take off that heavy jacket. It gets real hot here by noon. As for what you can do, I think the Burn Center asked for you to be here to answer questions about the Foundation itself. Someone who's thinking about spending twenty or thirty grand on a painting, may want to know more about the charity they're supporting."

"Well, the thing is…, I can only stay a few hours. I've been called in for mandatory overtime this afternoon. Sorry about that but August is a brutal month for vacations and we get short-handed. I can stay till noon, if that's okay."

"No problem, Captain. Noon is good. I have a friend coming to help after lunch anyway."

"Okay. But the name's Billy."

The morning was quiet with only five people wandering through the exhibit area between events. Most of the morning events were younger riders whose adoring families focused their attention on their rider and weren't the types to drift through the booth area looking to drop several mortgage payments on a painting. Still, Billy and Jose enjoyed a few stories about the life of a firefighter and Billy's family. And one woman did want to know more about the work of the Presbyterian Hospital's burn unit and the Cornell University involvement. She didn't buy a painting.

After Billy departed for his OT back in New York, Lauren showed up, as promised, with a bag of sandwiches for lunch. She'd offered to keep Jose company a few hours in the afternoon while Micah was tutoring a client's daughter in one of the practice rings.

"Any bites this morning?" She asked.

"No, it's mostly families today." He said. "What's for lunch?"

"Nothing fancy. Ham and cheese on rolls with lettuce and to-mato. Yours has mayo."

"Excellent. What do you want to drink? I'll go get it."

"Water's fine for me."

Jose made the short trip to the beverage area while Lauren entertained two women who strolled into the booth just as he left. Next to Bert Wells, she was probably Jose's greatest advocate and pitchperson. She made a point of engaging the prospective buy-er in a conversation about their interest in horses, art, the show, the weather, whatever they wanted to talk about. Then she'd tell them about her relationship to the artist and his background as an Ecuadorian immigrant. She always made a point of mention-ing the artist was a very good friend of her husband, Micah Wells. If they were horse people, that would be all the endorsement re-quired. Micah's name was the highest form of brand recognition in equestrian circles.

Her current guests were attractive women in their early for-ties who didn't know much about horses. Like so many others at the show, they were merely tourist, New York urbanites who rented over-priced homes in the Hamptons for the summer and were told the Hampton Classic was something you "had to do". The local gossip magazines were filled with pictures of well-dressed vacation-ers sharing a cocktail and posing with a celebrity at the Classic.

Valarie's friend Lonnie was visiting for the long weekend. They had serious interest in neither the art nor the show. They were just here to see what all the fuss was about that so severely clogged the roads around Bridgehampton. Lauren had tried to strike up a con-versation but the ladies would have none of it.

As Jose returned with the two bottles of Fiji water, Lauren and the two women were facing away from him, admiring a painting of two horses dancing wildly in a coral. It was one of Jose's recent favorites because it was different. There were no riders in the pic-ture, just two wild horses caught in full motion.

Lauren saw him approaching and said, "Ah, here comes the artist now."

The two women turned to face the creator. The woman on the right was a dirty blonde in a blue skirt and Ralph Lauren tee shirt. She looked to be around forty-five. Her friend looked a little younger, wore her long brown hair in a pony-tail and fit nicely into her jeans and white Polo shirt. At first her face was obscured by her baseball cap, but when she looked up Jose knew immediately it was Lonnie Rossetti.

For Jose, the moment was pure panic. It had been almost fif-teen years since he'd last seen her, yet she looked nearly the same as he remembered. Her hair was a little longer, her hips a little fuller but the face was exactly that etched in his memory, the face he thought about so often.

But his instant recognition wasn't reciprocated. Lonnie showed no sign of knowing who was standing in front of her. She extended her hand and said, "Nice to meet you. Your friend has been telling us all about you. I'm Lonnie and this is Valarie."

Jose was frozen in terror. He made no movement to take her hand. Instead, he looked down at the floor, as if searching for something lost. When the obvious lapse in manners became too prolonged to ignore, Lauren interceded, "Jose, are you okay?"

He cleared his throat in exaggerated fashion and returned, "Something in my eye. Excuse me." He turned away from the women and walked a few steps away from the kiosk. "Just a minute."

At a loss for any better ideas, he pretended to be rubbing his eye, trying to free the imaginary object. He used those few precious seconds to think.

His mind raced for a solution. If she had already recognized him, it was certainly too late to escape. What bothered him most was the thought of being outed in front of Lauren Wells, someone who'd put so much faith in him, someone who'd been so kind to him. The shame would be unbearable.

But Lonnie didn't seem to know him. How could that be? Had he meant so little to her? Was his sensual recollection of their weekend so completely one-sided? Or, maybe, it was his appearance. Had he changed that much? He knew his hair was much longer and pulled back in a tail, his beard nearly full, and the tone of his skin had darkened. And he was nearly twenty pounds heavier. But was he unrecognizable? And by someone with whom he'd shared a bed?

"Are you okay?" Lauren asked again.

There was no place to hide. He had no choice but to face the women. He looked up.

"I'm okay," he said. "Just got some dust in my eye." He tried to add just enough diluted Spanish accent so as not to make Lauren suspicious of his intentions but enough to add a bit more to his disguise. It seemed to work.

"I've been telling Valarie and Lonnie about your early works, the charcoals and etchings." She turned to the women, "His early works were so innocent. Now people say his work is filled with passion and color. That's how he conveys the powerful motion."

"I like it. I think this one is beautiful." Lonnie said pointing to the painting of the two thrashing stallions.

"I am honored by your appreciation of my efforts." Jose said still feigning the wisp of an accent. He was beginning to perspire.

Valarie was next to speak. "Is this the price?" She said bending over to read the tiny label attached to the frame. "Twenty-two thousand?"

Lauren jumped in. "Jose has generously donated all the proceeds from today's exhibit to the Firefighter's Burn Center at Presbyterian Hospital. So, you're actually not buying a work of art, you're making a tax-deductible contribution to a very worthwhile cause."

"Ummm, nice but it's not for me, thanks." Valarie was ready to move on to the next booth to torture another craftsman.

But Lonnie seemed intrigued. "Why the Burn Center?" She asked.

Again, Lauren took the initiative. "It's a favorite charity of one of Jose's biggest sponsors. And my father-in-law used to be on their board."

"Oh, I didn't realize this was your wife." Lonnie said, referring to Lauren.

"No no, I meant my father-in-law. My husband's father." She empathized the word husband. "Jose and I are just very close friends. Actually," she shot Jose an impish grin, "Actually, Jose is quite available."

Now Valarie was really ready to move on. She had no intentions of buying a painting nor did she see her friend Lonnie pursuing an Ecuadorian immigrant with paint under his fingernails. "We should get going."

But Lonnie picked up on Lauren's obvious cue. "You go ahead honey. I'll catch up in a minute."

Valarie shot Lonnie a disapproving look but said, "Take your time. I'm going to get something to drink."

Jose wished he could have gotten away too. Yet, there was something pulling him toward Lonnie. The moth flirted dangerously with the flame. And that flame was as beautiful as he remembered. The years had changed Lonnie very little. She looked more mature but in a fashion, that added to, not diminished her beauty.

He took a step toward the flame. "I can tell you have little interest in my art. So, are you here to follow a particular rider, or just crowd watching? I'd guess crowd watching."

Before she could answer, Lauren said, "Jose, could you live without me for about a half hour? I want to give the girls lunch before the afternoon sessions." She was already on the move. "Nice to meet you. Enjoy the show." She shot back to Lonnie as she exited the booth.

An awkward silence lingered between Jose and Lonnie. They studied each other for a moment. Finally, Jose, again employing a hint of an accent, said, "So, which is it?"

Lonnie didn't understand the question. "Pardon me?"

"Are you here to watch a rider or the crowd? Personally, I prefer to watch the crowds. There are so many interesting faces in the crowd."

She seemed distracted. Was she trying to figure out why this man seemed so familiar? Was she digging into her memory of a weekend long ago? Jose was nervous but the moth took the offensive. "You seem distracted. Is something wrong?"

"Sorry. I was just thinking about someone I used to know. You remind me of someone."

The moth made one more dive for the flame. "*Quien es ese?*" He asked.

Lonnie recalled enough high school Spanish to realize he'd asked something like "Who's that?"

"He was someone I knew a long time ago; a young man who was killed at the World Trade Center." She nearly whispered the words.

"*Alguien cercano a usted?*" Someone close to you?

"At one time, yes."

Jose felt the warmth of the flame and was both lured toward it and terrified by it. He was pleased Lonnie remembered Joey fondly, and wanted to know more, but thought better about it.

"That's a shame. I too knew many people killed that day, *ese horrible dia.*"

Jose was relieved that it was Lonnie who changed the subject.

"Your friend told us you're from Ecuador. How long have you lived in the states?"

"I came when I was a teenager, I came *con mi hermano.*" He lives in California and I haven't seen him in twenty years. I don't even know if he's still here or if he went back to Quito. That was our home town."

"That's too bad but I know how you feel. I haven't spoken to my brother in years." She said.

"So, if you have no interest in horses, what are you doing here?"

"You had it right. Just people watching. My friend Val is obsessed with the Hamptons. I'm just visiting for a few days to get some sun and help her prepare for a big party she's having tonight. She rented a house in Southampton for the summer. I'm a guest." Lonnie realized she was rambling and finally cut herself off.

Jose sensed her discomfort and wanted to help. "So, what do you do when you're not vacationing with the rich and famous?"

"I'm a lobbyist. I work for a company that lobbies congress on behalf of the aeronautics industry. I used to work for JetBlue but felt constricted by the corporate bullshit. So, this gives me a chance to live outside the lines a bit."

"Sounds like an interesting job." Jose said.

"It is. I love it, at least for now. Sometimes I'm not sure what I want to do. You know? Like when you're a kid and think about what you want to do when you grow up. I'm still not sure what I want to do when I grow up."

The more Lonnie spoke, the more Jose became confident she would not recognize him. In a way, that was wonderful. In another way, it pained him to think he'd changed so much. Lonnie seemed to be the same person he left on the streets of Hoboken. She was full of life and spontaneous. She was sexy to the point of distraction, yet very polished. And she was still very beautiful. For the first time in fifteen years, he longed for a time gone by.

"I get it." He said. "I understand what it's like to be so unsure about what the future holds. My mother used to call it *el gran desconocido*, the great unknown."

Lonnie knew she needed to catch up to her friend. They were on their way out of the show when they stopped at Jose's booth. There was much to be done at Val's house before their party.

"Listen, I've got to run. We're having a big party tonight at Val's house and she's counting on my help to get ready. It should be a lot of fun. The house is on the beach. Why don't you stop by? I'd love to hear more about your life in South America."

The moth circled the flame again, trying to decide if it's warmth was worth the risks.

"Thanks, but I need to be here until the show closes tonight. People expect to talk to the artist."

"Too bad. What time does the show end?"

"Nine."

"Nine? This is a Hamptons party. We probably won't get started until nine. The band doesn't start playing until ten. You can come when you're done here. Come on. It will be fun."

Jose thought for a moment. Then he asked, "This man I remind you of; was he *tu amante*? Was he your lover?"

Lonnie turned away from him. She stared at one of his paintings for several seconds. Then said, "Yes. He might have been the one. We just didn't have time to find out."

Jose was still thinking about what Lonnie said several hours later. The words, "He might have been the one," haunted him. What did that mean? At the time, she seemed so okay with the way things ended. It seemed she understood that he needed to sort out his own life before even thinking about a relationship with someone else. Fifteen years ago, she seemed fine with just having a weekend of casual sex and moving on. No expectations.

All that seemed inconsistent with her affirmation. If she thought Joey was the one, why not fight for him at the time? Why let him walk out of her life with no expectation of ever seeing him again?

His daydreaming about Lonnie was interrupted by a well-dressed elderly woman who wanted to know more about one of his paintings. "Is this Pedro Marresco?" She wanted to know, pointing to the rider on one of Jose's newer works.

"You know your riders." Jose offered.

"I should. He's riding one of my horses and he just about lives with us now." She leaned on a hickory cane and took a closer look. "But I can't tell what horse it is. There's so much blue. When did you do this painting?"

Jose took the artwork off the tent wall and examined the back of the canvas. He made a point of recording the date he took the photo used to sit for the painting, the horse and rider's names. It helped in just such situations.

"So, Pedro is riding Thunder Blue and I used a photo taken at an Olympic qualifier in Lexington on May sixth earlier this year. For me, the color blue brings to mind speed. That's what I felt when I saw them jumping. That horse was like lightening. Were you there?"

"No, I can't travel much anymore. My god damn legs aren't worth a damn. But I remember the event. He finished third, I think." She looked around for a place to sit.

Jose grabbed the one folding chair he had available in the booth and set it up for her.

"I can't stand still very long anymore either." She said as she gratefully took the seat. "Let me give you some advice kid. Live now. You don't know how long you've got or what kind of shape you're going to be in when you get to my age. Life is very short. Don't waste a minute or an opportunity to have fun. You just don't get enough of them."

"I'll keep that in mind." He said, then, "My name is Jose. And you are…?"

"Nadene Topping. The cemeteries around here are full of my relatives. The name goes back to the sixteen hundreds."

She wasn't exaggerating. Someone from the Topping family had lived on the east end of Long Island since 1675. At one time, the family owned one-third of all the farmland east of Riverhead. Now most of those fields sprouted starter-castles for the Wall Street bankers who had to have a piece of the Hamptons, at least for a few weekends each summer. Some of the land had been converted to vineyards and some to luxurious horse farms of twenty or more acres. Nadene's family dripped of old money.

"Well, it's a pleasure to meet you Nadene." Jose explained that the proceeds from his sales would go entirely to the Burn Center and told her a little about the Center itself.

"That's very nice of you, young man."

"Well, I don't always donate my work. But when the shows are around home, you know, New York, I like to look for worthy causes. The Burn Center happens to be a favorite charity of one of my major sponsors."

"Oh, who's that?"

"The Wells family."

"Oh, sure. I used to know Bert quite well." She looked back at the painting Jose was holding.

"Is that the only one you have of Pedro?" She wanted to know.

"Uh, no. I have another but on a different mount."

"I'll take them both. One for me and one will be a gift for him. He's got a birthday coming up and I never know what to get him."

"That's very generous of you." Jose said as he searched for the other painting.

"Bullshit! I said I'm a Topping. If I don't give away at least a million a year, the society columns crucify me. Besides, my grandchildren don't need my money and there's already enough shit around here with the family name on it, so, we don't need another wing on a hospital or Topping library annex. And, you can't take it with you, you know." She winked.

"I guess not."

"Can I give you a check?" She was reaching deep into her taupe Gucci bag for her checkbook.

"Yes, if you don't mind, you can make it out to the New York Firefighter's Burn Center."

She began writing. "How about I just make it an even fifty?"

As Nadene Topping was scribbling her name on the check, Lauren returned to the booth with a handsome well-dressed man and a teenage girl. Lauren recognized Nadene immediately.

"Mrs. Topping! How are you?" They hugged and exchanged kisses. Lauren noticed the check in the elderly woman trembling hand.

"Did you buy a painting?"

"Two." She turned to Jose, "And if you would have them delivered to the address on my check, I would be very grateful."

"Thank you so much mam. That was very generous." He glanced at the check and saw a Southampton address. "And, I will deliver them myself. Is tomorrow morning okay?"

"That would be fine." She said as she slowly made her way from the booth and back out into the passing crowds. "Good to see you Lauren. Give your husband my regards." Then she added, "And nice to meet you too Jose."

When Nadene had been absorbed by the stream of pedestrians, Lauren turned to Jose. "She's quite a character, but a really nice lady and she has a heart of gold."

"Seems so."

It was only then that Lauren remembered the two people she brought to meet Jose. "Oh, I'm sorry." She said a little embarrassed. "Jose, I wanted you to meet Brad Muller and his daughter Amanda."

Jose extended his hand to the gentleman. "Nice to meet you Brad." Then he turned to the young girl. "And you Amanda."

She was a beautiful teenager. He guessed not more than fifteen, but older in appearance. She had striking jet black hair pulled back in a bun and an olive complexion that caused Jose to think the girl's mother might be of Latin descent. Her father seemed about as white and WASP-like as they come. He could have been a double for Mitt Romney.

"Actually Jose, we've met once before." Said the Romney look-alike. "I was at Bert Wells' charity ball a few years ago up in Woodfield and bid on one of your earlier works, the Gabriella Brunelli piece. You were kind enough to sign it for my daughter Mandy. She still has it hanging in her room. Don't you sweetie?"

"Well it's nice to know my most valuable work hangs in the room of such a beautiful young woman." Jose said, although he didn't really like the idea of his artwork on some spoiled teenager's wall, probably next to a One Dimension poster. He'd pictured artistic success somehow being different. Still, Amanda Muller was something special herself. In a way, she reminded him of Gabriella.

Lauren explained, "Micah's been schooling Amanda for a few months now and today she had her Hampton Classic debut. She rode really well."

The young girl was clutching a blue ribbon so Jose offered, "I see you medaled. Congratulations."

"Thank you. I couldn't have done it without Lauren's advice and Micah's coaching."

"Tribute helped too." Her father interjected. "That's her horse. The one Lauren found for Mandy about a year ago."

"Well, it sounds like there's plenty of credit to go around but you should still be very proud. I'm sure your dad is." Jose said.

Lauren interjected. "Listen Jose, Mr. and Mrs. Muller and Amanda will be staying with us in Bridgehampton tonight so why don't you join us for dinner after the show?"

"Actually Lauren, I've been invited to a party in Southampton by a very interesting woman I met today. Otherwise, that would have been nice. Thank you for the invitation and I'm sorry I won't get to meet your wife." He said looking at Brad.

"Anybody I know?" Lauren asked impishly.

"You know everybody so I wouldn't be surprised."

"Well, another time then. And I want to hear all about this interesting woman. And you'll probably be seeing a lot of the Mullers this winter. They've rented a house in Wellington just a few farms over from us. Amanda's going to do the juniors circuit this winter."

"That's right. Claire and Mandy will be there the whole winter. I'll commute on weekends so I can watch the weekend events." Brad said.

Jose, not knowing the consequences of his statement, said, "I'll look forward to seeing you then, and to meeting Claire."

CHAPTER FORTY-ONE

anuel was a little late returning for the overnight shift, and
by the time Jose navigated the snake of traffic exiting the
show, it was after ten. He stopped at his motel room to quickly
shower and change out of his dusty jeans and tee shirt. But, as the
clock on his dashboard shined 10:47, he was turning on the Cold
Spring Point Road and driving past a string of starter-mansions on
the Peconic Bay.

Before leaving his booth that afternoon, Lonnie had insisted
he come to the party and wrote the address on the back on one of
her business cards. Her body language left little doubt her invitation was sincere. Still, Jose viewed the invitation as a dangerous
temptation. Again, the moth was powerless to resist the pull of the
warm glow. As soon as he'd told Lauren about the invitation, she
began pestering him for a good reason not to attend and clearly,
he couldn't tell her the only good reason.

The road was a narrow paved street with sugar-white sand on
both sides and intruding onto the surface in a way that seemed
very Hamptons-ish. The homes to his right bordered the bay and

the homes on the left the pond. The moonless sky painted a black backdrop to the well-lit homes and even if it wasn't for the dozens of cars lining the street, he would have been able to find the party house by the music.

He parked and sat in silence for a moment while he summoned the fortitude to face Lonnie again. It surely seemed she didn't know him. But she said he reminded her of the man who "might have been the one", as she put it. Jose wondered what good could come of his being there. Worse case- Lonnie recognizes him, gets furious, and shames him with the awful truth. He'd be an outcast, lose the friendship and respect of everyone he knew, and probably go to jail. Could it be any worse? There seemed overwhelming arguments against getting out of the car.

And yet, she'd said he might have been the one. Could a man not explore that possibility? Could any man not want to know for certain if he'd missed his opportunity to find the love of his life? His fists clenched the steering wheel as his mind waged war with the facts, each side using those facts to support its position. He had to find out. He had to know if he'd walked away from the one woman who loved him for what he knew he needed to become.

His hand gripped the car door handle, then paused before opening it as if it somehow knew better. But in the end, the fateful seduction of perhaps being "the one" to someone was overwhelming.

As he neared the front door of the contemporary beach house he could hear the Spenser Davis Group pounding out "Gimme Some Lovin". The people inside the house paid him no attention as they pulsed up and down dancing to the percussive tune, and he wound his way through the house and onto the rear deck. Most of the guests were in their thirties and forties. It was impossible to categorize the group based on their casual beach attire, but he suspected, and rightly so, that they were well-fed Manhattanites who liked to party hard.

One young Tom Wolfe want-to-be, dressed all in white approached Jose holding a bottle of wine by the neck and slurring something about Hilary Clinton. He was clearly drunk and Jose side-stepped him to pursue his hostess.

The deck was massive, extending in multiple levels onto the beach. There had to be a hundred people standing around with another fifty sitting and standing on the sand facing the bay. The DJ was to Jose's right behind one of two portable, but well-equipped bars. He couldn't have been more than eighteen, and reminded Jose of a young Will Smith, but with dreadlocks.

Jose scanned the crowd but saw neither Lonnie nor her friend. He got a glass of Riesling from the bartender and continued his search on the beach. It was there he spotted her talking to a woman and two men. He took a step back to view the scene from an unnoticed distance. She wore a white sun dress and looked incredible. But were these just four individual people engaged in casual cocktail party conversation or were they two couples? He hadn't considered the possibility that Lonnie might be very much involved.

Jose decided to wait in the shadows, observing what he could before deciding to approach Lonnie. But then she turned her head to look back at the deck crowd and spotted him. She immediately hurried toward him.

"Hey, you came! I'm so glad you did."

It sounded perfunctory but she wore a sincere smile.

"Your friend has rented a beautiful house." He laid the accent on heavily.

"Would you like a tour? I need another drink anyway."

"That would be nice." Again, with enough Latin accent to help camouflage his sins.

Lonnie stopped at the bar for another Cosmo, then pulled him by the hand toward the house. They had to muscle their way through the thick crowd of dancers and, for a moment, Jose feared she was going to want to stop and dance. She held her drink out with one hand to guide them through the masses and pulled him with the other.

"Just follow me!" She yelled back through the music.

But when she got to the kitchen door she realized the crowds inside were even thicker than on the deck. Navigating a tour was going to be impossible. She turned to him and said, "There's too many people in there. How about a raincheck on the tour and we take a walk on the beach?"

"Sounds perfect."

"Follow me."

They walked along the side of the house until they got to the beach and the cacophony of music and voices faded in the distance.

"You may want to leave your shoes here," she said. He noticed she wasn't wearing any and slipped out of his Topsiders.

"Just leave them here. We'll come back this way and get them." Her voice was as soft as he remembered.

They walked east along the shore of the bay passing lavish waterfront properties of the rich and famous. The sand beneath their feet was soft but speckled with small white stones and colorful translucent shells she explained were seasonal. At least that's what she'd been told by the oral surgeon from the upper west side who had her ear before Jose appeared.

After several hundred yards the beach was shrouded by steep cliffs on their right that led up to the Sebonack Golf Club and its extraordinary guest cabins that overlooked the bay with vistas of the north fork in the distance. There were huge boulders littering the beach now, remnants of a retreating glacier from the last ice age. This was also information Lonnie had gathered earlier from the well-informed dentist.

"Let's sit on one of these rocks." She suggested.

The air was filled with a warm August breeze and stars filled the sky above the bay. It was a beautiful evening. They were now far from the party which had faded into the silent distance. Lonnie sat on the flat top of a massive boulder that was half in the water and half out. At high tide, it was probably nearly submerged but now it offered a perfect sofa for two.

"So, tell me about Ecuador. Is it always humid? That's how I picture it in my head; this hot, humid jungle. I've never been there but that's how I see it." Jose could tell this wasn't her first Cosmo of the evening. He tried to picture the imaginary city he conjured in his mind so many times for conversations like this.

"It's not always humid but the temperatures are pretty constant. We're on the equator you know." He used just enough accent to sell the notion of him on the streets of Quito as a young boy.

"When I was young, we used to go to the sea, to the Pacific, and jump off cliffs on hot days. We'd see who could make the biggest splash entering the water but it really didn't matter. We just wanted to cool off."

"How long did you say you've lived in America?"

Jose recited his fable about coming to the country with his brother, working in New York and New Jersey, classes at City College and the job with the elderly woman in Summit. He'd told the story so many times before. Each time he retold it, it gathered more detail, more colorful background. Now, he almost believed it himself, it had become so real by repetition.

Then he inquired about her life, pressing for details specifically about the last fifteen years. He learned she'd moved up the corporate ladder at JetBlue and had been the only female senior Vice President at the airline before walking out to escape the overwhelming strangulation of bureaucracy. She loved her current job as a lobbyist. It afforded her the freedom to be creative, although she had to deal with a whole different world of bureaucracy, that of the federal government.

He probed about her past relationships, without appearing too intrusive.

"I was married for a short time a long time ago." She explained, then went on about the virtues of not marrying anyone under thirty. "We're just too stupid when we're young."

She also mentioned two relationships that occurred in the last few years but it didn't sound like either lasted very long or ever got to the point of cohabitation.

But what he really wanted to know about was what she meant when she referred to their relationship back in 2001 and used the words, "He may have been the one." Mustering his most convincing Latin accent, he asked, "You mentioned this afternoon that you had met a man years ago that you thought might have been the one but with whom you didn't have time to find out. Tell me about that, if I'm not being too personal."

She finished the last of her Cosmo and rested the empty glass on the rock. "No, it's okay. I don't mind. It's been a long time and time has helped heal the wound."

"So, it ended badly, this man of yours?" Jose asked.

"He was a boyfriend from high school who I met again years later. In high school, well, we were just kids, but I really liked him. He went off to college and I got involved with another guy, and, well we just drifted apart. We didn't see each other for several years. I got married to Eddie, and divorced; Joey, that's his name, Joey, he got married too. By the time we accidently met years later, Joey and his wife were already talking about having kids. I know that because he and I had an affair. It lasted only one weekend because I didn't want to break up anyone's marriage. But after we parted I made myself a promise that I would keep in touch with him, you know, to make sure he knew I was really interested but only if things didn't work out with his wife. Like I said, I didn't want to break up a marriage. But I figured, if it went bad on its own, I wanted to make sure he knew I was falling in love with him."

"How can you say you loved this man after only one weekend?" Jose wanted to know.

"I'm not sure. I'm not sure I loved him at that point. But I never got a chance to find out. He was killed at the World Trade Center on 9-11. So maybe I'm just romanticizing, you know, about the love I couldn't have. Isn't that what happens? You always want what you can't have?" Her voice trailed off in a whisper. "I never saw him again."

"And this is the man I remind you of?"

Without looking up, she answered, "Yes."

"What was so special about this man?"

She sat quietly for several moments just staring out at the bay. Then, she said, "I think it was his spirit. I could tell he was tortured by our affair. It wasn't like him to cheat. It sounds strange, but that's what I liked most about him, that he was tortured by our relationship. It really bothered him to be unfaithful to his wife." She was silent a few more seconds, then added, "And he was tortured by who he was, or rather what he was becoming. Joey was some kind of trader and made lots of money but he felt he was supposed to be doing something else. Like he had missed his real calling, whatever that was. I could tell that really bothered him."

"That's a tragic story."

"Like I said, maybe I've romanticized it a bit but it feels that way to me. I think I could have fallen in love with him. I think we could have been happy together. And I've never said that about another man."

Jose didn't know what to say. How often does a man hear a woman talk so candidly about the man she's sitting next to? It was as if he was listening to someone speak about him and he wasn't in the room. It was very strange. And yet, it was wonderful to hear her say she might have been falling in love with him. Especially because she felt that way because she understood him. No one ever understood him before; not Claire, and certainly not his parents. They all had a life planned for him, a life that had nothing to do with what he wanted. Although, to be fair, even he didn't know what he really wanted back then. All he knew was that he was sure he didn't want what everyone else expected him to become.

He reached out and took her left hand in his right. "I know it sounds like an odd question but what would you say to that man, what was his name?"

"Joey Martinez"

"What would you say to this Joey if he were alive today? If he miraculously somehow came walking down the beach right now, what would you want to say to him?"

She slouched back on the rock and thought for a moment. As she did, Jose already regretted asking the question, for two reasons; first, he wasn't entirely sure he would know what to do with the answer, and second, because he feared the moth might have flown a bit too close to the flame.

"I guess my first question would be…, what happens after you die?" She pulled her hand from his. "But I don't want to think about that. What's done is done. I hurt for a long time after 9-11 but eventually, I moved on. I'd like to say I convinced myself I needed to move on and get on with life, but I think what really happened is that time just makes the hurt go away. It happens slowly but I think that's what happened."

She turned toward him abruptly and said, "But let's stop talking about the past. I want to know more about you; what it's like to be a famous artist. You must travel all over the world. What's that like?"

Her mood swing startled him but he was relieved the moth had flitted away from the flame for the moment. Or had the flame just flickered?

"I love painting. It's what I always wanted to do." He lied.

"I have to be honest. I tried to Google you when I got back this afternoon. I wanted to know more about you."

"And what did you learn?" He asked.

"Nothing. I didn't even know your last name."

Pure panic gripped him. He hadn't considered this issue. If he had, he probably wouldn't have even considered coming to the party. How could he be so blind, so completely stupid? He sat in silence for a long time, hoping the moment would pass and Lonnie would move on to another question. She didn't.

"So, what's your last name? I may need to check you out tomorrow."

"Why would you need to check me out tomorrow?"

She leaned in to him and kissed his lips. He put his arm around her and returned the kiss. Her mouth was open, her tongue probing the inside of his.

"We're going to fall off this rock." She giggled.

Jose slid off the rock, his feet coming down in the shallow water that was washing up on its seaward side. He offered a hand to help her down the back of the boulder and she slid straight down, landing on her knees in the damp sand where she remained, brushing the sand from her seersucker dress.

"Let me help you," Jose offered, gently brushing the crinkled white fabric.

Lonnie got to her feet and leaned back against the rock. She raised and clasped her hands over her head, her dress rising halfway between her knees and waist provocatively revealing perfectly tanned thighs. It was pure seduction and the moth was helpless in its warmth.

Jose stepped in close running both hands up the back of her smooth legs. She unclasped her hands to pull him in on her and kissed him passionately. His body pressed her against the cold boulder. His hands moved further up the back of her legs and as they reached her butt he realized she was not wearing underwear.

Freeing her mouth from his for just a moment, she gasped, "Touch me." Then returned to his mouth, sucking violently on his tongue.

Jose moved one hand to the front of her leg, then probed gently between her thighs. His thumb felt the moist soft skin it craved and he began to slide it back and forth, the wetness increasing with each stroke.

"Touch me," she said again.

Jose was completely aroused; a sensation Lonnie could easily feel pressing against her. She reached down and slid her hand into his loosely fitted linen trousers. She found her target and began rubbing him with an open palm.

Both of them were panting heavily, their mouths still interlocked in deep kisses. Then suddenly, Lonnie pulled her hand from his trousers. She slammed both her hands behind her against the rock and said, "What are we doing?"

Jose kissed her neck, his thumb still deep inside her. In his most provocative Latin accent he whispered in her ear, "I don't know what you are doing, but I am trying to make a beautiful American woman feel very wonderful."

When she offered no resistance, he began kissing her shoulder, then the fabric covering her breast. Still no resistance. He withdrew his hand from between her thighs and slowly fell to his knees, kissing her body through her dress all the way down. He used his head to tunnel under the front of her dress and began kissing the inside of her thighs, first the left, then the right.

"Oh god." She moaned softly, then adjusted her stance to spread her legs wider. Her feet were now planted firmly in the sand; her back against the rock.

Jose began to pleasure her with his tongue and with gentle kisses. She moaned again several times, acknowledging his motion and directing him to precisely where she hoped he would concentrate his effort. He followed her cues and tears streamed down her face. She had never felt so adored.

"Take me," she said. "I want you…, I want you deep inside me." She twisted and turned completely around. Her face now pressed against the cold rock, her legs spread apart.

Jose let his trousers fall to the sand and pressed against her. He lifted the back of her dress over her waist and she reached around to guide him inside her yearning warmth. His hands cupped her breasts. They moved as one, both pushing their bodies into the other. As he thrust forward, she pushed back creating a sensation neither had ever experienced before.

She climaxed only moments before him then they both fell against the huge rock panting and completely spent.

CHAPTER FORTY-TWO

The rocking chair creaked with each movement back and forth. Jose had been sitting on his porch rocking and thinking for nearly an hour since he rose at 7:15. The previous evening with Lonnie had been haunting his sleep and was now tormenting him. He wanted to see her again.

He'd been waging a formal debate with himself since sitting down. What time was too early to call and is it nearly suicidal to call at all?

On the later, he'd tossed caution to the wind twenty minutes ago after concluding he had a work-around to the "what's your last name?" issue. He'd decided he would tell her his real last name was Santo-Martino but that he'd shortened it to Martinez for purposes of his craft. "Someone advised me Martinez sounded better, more like an artist. But for legal purposes my name is Santo-Martino." That would be his story.

He'd also decided that Lonnie would never recognize him for who he really was. He came to believe his own logic because he was convinced she had a romanticized recollection of their weekend together; one in which she probably recalled him as nearly a perfect man, one with sculpted muscles, flawless facial features and far better grooming than the person she seduced last night on the beach. That man was a forty-three-year-old Ecuadorian immigrant with a serious accent, dark skin, long black hair and a beard that covered much of his face. He was also a long way from sculpted, having gained over twenty pounds since that fateful weekend.

And in so many other ways, he really was a different man. Even Lonnie said it. She mentioned that Joey had been tortured by his infidelity, one of the reasons she was so attracted to him. Jose, on the other hand was a man who had turned his back on the woman who loved him to pursue his yet unknown destiny. Lonnie knew a man she respected for his moral compass. Jose, by his own estimation had none. And Jose was something Joey never was; sure of his place in the world.

No, he was confident he could rekindle the relationship with Lonnie without fear of being discovered. And once again, she had rekindled in him that passion for passion itself. A life with Lonnie Rossetti was possible and the more he thought about it, the more he realized how much he'd thought about her through the years as evidenced by all the paintings of her he'd started and never finished.

He held the worn-out business card in his hand. Her cell number was on the back and now nearly unrecognizable because of his constant spindling as he contemplated his next move. How early is too early to call someone who hosted a party the previous night? Would she be up helping her friend clean up? Or would she still be sleeping off those Cosmos?

She answered on the third ring.

"Hello?" Her voice indicated she'd been sleeping.

"It is Jose. Por favor. I am so sorry I woke you."

"It's okay, Jose." She sounded happy to hear from him. "What time is it?"

"Nearly eight-thirty. How are you feeling? How is your head? You drank a lot last night."

"Not really," she lied. "I can hold my booze."

"That, I am glad to hear." He hesitated a moment, then continued. "I was hoping you were free tonight. I would like to take you to dinner and to the Grand Prix. My friend, Micah is in the finals."

"Sounds like fun but I'm heading back to New York in a few hours and I've got a flight to Washington tonight. I'll be there all week."

He couldn't tell if there was regret in her tone.

"I'm sorry to hear that. I… I really enjoyed our evening. I hope I can see you again." He held his breath and waited for a response. The silence seemed to last an eternity. Then,

"I'd like that too."

"How about next weekend?"

"I get back on Saturday morning. How about you come into Manhattan Saturday night? I'll cook you a proper Italian dinner? Then maybe we can hit a comedy club or something."

"Sounds wonderful. Call me when you return and I will look forward to seeing you Saturday night."

And he did look forward to seeing her all week. He daydreamed about her. He fantasized about their love-making and he painted a new canvas of her. In it she was sitting alone atop a large rock at the shoreline. He even went back to the rock to recall the exact details of the massive stone. The painting took him all week to finish and when he was done he showed it to Lauren and explained that this was the woman he'd met at his kiosk.

But on the following Saturday morning she called to cancel. "I'm sorry, but I've been thinking about this all week." She explained. "I made a mistake last week. The more I thought about it, the more I realized I was attracted to you because you remind me of someone else, that man I told you about."

Jose said nothing.

"It's not right. It's not fair to you and it's not fair to me. I keep seeing my friend Joey. Even now while I'm on the phone with you, I'm picturing his face on the other end. It's crazy, I know, but I don't think it's the way to start a relationship. It's not healthy for me. I mean, I had a really hard time when he died. I was in a lot of pain. I don't want to resurrect those memories and that's what happened with you."

Jose tried to interject, "But, we…"

She cut him off. "Look Jose, you're a really interesting guy and there's a part of me that would like to get to know you, but…, just not now. I'm having a lot of trouble with this. Seeing you would just make the pain start again. I know it's been a long time, but I'm not ready."

Silence again, then, "Please understand."

He wanted to scream into the phone, "Lonnie, it's me!"

But the line went dead. Once again, she was gone.

CHAPTER FORTY-THREE

Brad Muller leaned over to tie his shoes. He and his family had been invited to celebrate New Year's Eve with the Wells family, and, as Lauren had put it, "Only a very few close friends." He was pleased to have somewhere to spend the evening. Since arriving in Wellington on the day after Thanksgiving, his wife had been having a rough time. Even a sighted person would need some time to adjust to the pace of the equestrian village and its nightly social affairs. For anyone living in perpetual darkness, acclimating was a nightmare.

He understood Claire's reluctance to venture out. The entire community was about witnessing events. At the International arena, crowds watched skilled horsemen fly over hurdles in complete silence. At the practice rings, riders went about their work, again, in silence. After the events, people gathered together to watch video replays of the winning rides, the only sounds coming from the crowd at the end of the ride. For a blind woman, it was a very quiet and lonely place to be. Without sight, there was little to do to fit in.

Claire couldn't even enjoy the thrill of watching her daughter Amanda ride. Of course, she attended the events but had to rely on Brad's verbal interpretations of what was happening. Either that, or listen for the subtle nuances of the horse's hoofs as they made contact with the earth or the gasps and sighs of the crowd.

It was for that reason that Claire had seldom ventured out of the six-bedroom house they'd rented for the winter, just a few blocks from the Wells farm. She'd filled her days out by the pool with audio-books and listening to music on ear buds perpetually connecting her to her iPhone. For Claire, the worst thing about being blind was silence, for silence offered none of the sensory clues she needed to interpret the world around her.

Neither was she looking forward to this evening; a room filled with people and furniture she didn't know. But she'd agreed to go for Amanda's sake. She understood that her daughter needed to fit in here. If her promising career was to continue on the trajectory Brad thought it could, she needed to know these people. Back in New York, Amanda had been taking lessons from Micah Wells for almost a year now and Lauren Wells had found her a fantastic horse. Micah and Lauren had been wonderful to her daughter, so for that reason too, she felt an obligation to attend the first social engagement of the new season in Wellington.

Brad looked up from his shoes to spy his wife putting on her make-up. He never understood why she always sat in front of a mirror at her vanity to do so. Perhaps it just made her feel a little more normal or perhaps it was the comfort of doing things the way she always had. Maybe it was her way of striking back at the darkness that was her constant companion.

"Need any help, hun?"

"Are you asking to find out if I need assistance or to find out how much longer I'll be?

"A little of both I guess. But you look great. You know I love that green dress." Brad always made a point of verbally acknowledging what Claire was wearing so she had validation she'd chosen he correct color dress.

"I'll be down in five minutes. Check on Amanda. See if she's even out of the shower yet."

"Will do. Hey, why don't we just walk over to the Wells? This way I can have a few drinks and not have to worry about you driving us home."

"Very funny, asshole. Go check on your daughter."

When she heard the footsteps in the hallway, Claire put down the lipstick and sat still for a moment. Nights like this always worried her. She needed to psych herself up for them. Sighted people had no understanding of the difficulty of entering an unfamiliar room, trying to remember new names without the faces, or dealing with the silent but clearly discernable discomfort others felt around the blind. Then there was the constant fear of embarrassment; the kind that comes from spilling something, tripping, or, the worst kind, talking to someone you thought was still in the area when actually they'd left minutes ago.

Lauren Wells, being the special person she was, had stopped by that afternoon to tell Claire who would be at the party and a little bit of background on each. Lauren knew Claire would feel better knowing she already knew many of the guests. She expected Micah, Lauren and their two daughters, of course. She'd also met Bret and Terry Kennedy and Alex and Erica McCurry at a previous party. They all seemed like nice enough people. Lauren mentioned that some of their grooms would also be there although she wasn't sure which ones because they'd all planned to attend a big New Year's Eve bash at the home of the drummer from Green Day, a party none of the young people in Wellington wanted to miss.

The only people Claire didn't already know were the Frelinghausens, who Lauren said were delightful, Micah's lawyer, whose name Claire had forgotten, and their friend Jose, the local artist. She was familiar with Jose only by reputation and because her daughter had one of his most valuable works hanging in her bedroom thanks to the generosity of her husband. Lauren had gone out of her way to assure Claire she'd love Jose.

"He's so sweet. He minds the girls all the time for me when Micah drags me to some unavoidable social obligation. I wish I could find him someone."

"What do you mean?" Claire asked.

"No, I just mean, find him a girl. He's such a sweet guy. I wish he had a girl in his life."

He's always been single?" She inquired.

"Yes. He came here from Ecuador in the nineties with his brother. As far as I know, he's never had a serious girlfriend. And he's adorable. You're going to love him."

From down the hallway, Claire could hear Brad coaxing Amanda along. Amanda was certainly looking forward to the evening. She loved anything that involved horse-people. She also enjoyed the company of older people, probably because she was far more mature than the average fourteen-year-old.

And she knew Brad was looking forward to it. He'd made the commitment to spend most of the winter in Florida and was the sort of guy who loved meeting new people. Perhaps that's why he was such a successful investment banker.

So maybe the evening wouldn't be so bad after all. And after Lauren's build-up, she was looking forward to meeting this painter, Jose.

CHAPTER FORTY-FOUR

J ose arrived at the Well's house in time for dinner with the family. As he walked through the doorway, Lizzy and Kate rushed at him, hugging his waist.

"Jose's here!" They shouted. "You want to play a game of Sorry before dinner?"

"Girls, leave Jose alone for a minute. He just got here. Besides, dinner will be ready in two minutes." Lauren called out from the kitchen.

"What time are your guests coming?" Jose called back.

"The party folks are coming at nine, but Bret and Terry are joining us for dinner first. I've prepared one of your favorites- take-out from Oli's."

Lauren motioned to the wine siting on the huge center island. "Would you open a bottle of red and a bottle of white, Jose? Micah's still in the shower and I need to dry my hair."

"No problem." Then he said to the adoring girls, "Why don't you set up Sorry in the den? We can play after dinner."

As they ran down the hall he thought about how much they'd grown in just the last couple of years. When Bert passed away they were barely knee high. The image of them standing with Lauren at the service was etched in his memory. Now they were like real people. Lizzy was seven and Katie five and a half. They were both the image of their mother but had Micah's coloring, dirty blonde curls and milky white skin. Oddly, both still had little interest in horses. Lizzy was obsessed with pop music and Katie with dolls, any sort of dolls.

There was a perfunctory knock on the door and Bret and Terry walked in carrying a huge wooden bowl filled with salad. Almost no one waited to be shown in at the Wells' home. The "Come in, we're open" mat was always out.

"I'll take a glass of that red if you're pouring," Bret said. "Red or white, honey?"

Terry paid her husband no attention. She was already walking down the hall to see the girls.

"Make it two reds then barkeep."

As Jose opened the bottle he asked, "Do you know who else is coming tonight?"

Bret's powerful Irish accent had trouble with the Frelinghausen's name but he stumbled through the German tongue twister. "And I think the Mullers, McCurrys and a few of the grooms may stop by later. Jimmy and Patrick might be coming too. I'm not sure."

"Who are the Mullers again?"

"Clients. Mandy Muller is a talented fourteen-year-old that Micah and I have been schooling for a while. Her parents are here for the whole season. Her dad, I forget his name, is some big-shot investment banker. Her mom is sweet but almost completely blind. Poor thing is only about forty. She's been blind for quite a while. Nice enough people though."

"Oh, yeah. I've met the father and daughter. Lauren brought them by the booth in Bridgehampton last summer. I don't remember meeting the mom. And now that I think about it, he's the guy that paid a quarter mil for the Gabriella painting at Bert's charity thing years ago. Right?"

"One and the same."

"Still stands as the high-water mark for my work." Jose said proudly.

"For now." Micah added as he emerged from another wing of the house. "Hey Bret. I see you wasted no time hitting the grape juice. You better pace yourself old man. It's New Year's Eve you know."

Jose held up an empty wine glass and pointed it toward Micah with a questioning look.

"Sure. I'll have one glass of white. What the hell? It's New Years."

Bret pounced on the opportunity to rib his best friend. "Did they run out of Diet Coke at the Publix, Micah?"

"They might have but I never will. We must have ten cases of it in the barn and five more in Lauren's secret pantry. Hey, Popeye had his spinach. I've got Diet Coke. It's what makes me fly. I'd feed it to Runaway if I thought it would make her jump a little higher. Then again, all that phony sugar's probably not good for her."

"But you'll drink it by the gallon!" Bret added with a certain Irish sarcasm.

"Bret, I promise- when I retire, my beverage of choice will go back to Red Stripe. Until then, I can't afford the calories." Micah was very careful to keep his weight under one hundred forty, the maximum he felt a horse should have to jump with.

Jose brought the conversation back to the subject of the evening's guests. "I'm glad Alex and Erica are coming. I haven't seen them since before Rio."

"He had a minor stroke you know?" Bret said.

"Who, Alex?"

"Yeah. He's a lot better now. They said it was a TIA, whatever that is. It wasn't very serious, but I can hear it in his speech. It's a little off."

"How would you know if his speech was off. You barely speak English yourself," Micah joked.

The three men stood around the center island in the kitchen. This is what Jose loved so much about his family in Wellington. Micah and Bret had such deep respect and love for one another they could joke and say just about anything without crossing the line. For Micah, it was always about Bret's Irish lineage. For Bret, it was the iron rod he claimed Micah sat upon as a boy, making him a "wee bit stiff."

Again, Jose tried to return the conversation to an adult keel. "That's really a shame. I'm glad he's okay. Must have been hard on Erica though."

"Yeah, well the two of them don't need any more shit to worry about." Bret said.

"What do you mean?"

Micah stepped in to explain. "Alex took a huge financial loss back in the fall. He'd taken on a big job for a developer; put months of work into this guy's project; probably laid out two hundred grand of his own money for plantings alone. Then the developer, I think his name was Matusak, goes belly up, declares chapter 11, and completely stiffs Alex. It basically wiped Alex and Erica out, that, and not being able to work much after the stroke. They're really hurting. I've been trying to refer work to them but there's not much going on down here right now. I wish I could do more, but you know Alex. He's a very proud guy."

"Wow. That's a shame. I had no idea." This information about the people who'd been so kind to him years ago, made Jose realize he'd been a little self-absorbed lately. Ever since the Hampton Classic and seeing Lonnie, he'd been busy touring with the equestrian schedule of events and promoting his work. Ironically, for him, the fall had been great. He'd sold nearly thirty paintings, each for somewhere between ten and thirty-five thousand dollars. It seems he'd become a big hit in Europe as well as the U.S.

"Well, if you hear of any work for Alex, make sure you let him know about it." Micah added.

Lauren and Terry entered the room, having heard the end of the conversation. "Isn't it awful? I think Erica's taking it even harder than Alex." Lauren said as she took a seat at the counter and poured herself a glass of white wine.

"Well, hopefully, 2017 will be a better year for them." Terry said.

Bret added, "How bout we eat?"

After dinner, as he'd promised, Jose played Sorry with the girls on Lizzy's bedroom floor. Thirty minutes into the game he was trying to figure out how to lose quickly so he could rejoin the adults in the other room. Every so often he could hear another group joining the party. Finally, after Katie had rolled three consecutive sixes, he employed a little-known codicil in the Sorry rulebook which he claimed professes if you roll a six, three-times in a row, you automatically win the game, regardless of your current position on the board. Katie was ecstatic. And he was free to join the adults.

As Jose reentered the living room he spotted Micah speaking with Alex McCurry at the counter. Bret and Terry were chatting it up with Erica while a historical video of one of Micah's winning rides looped endlessly on the eighty-inch flat screen hanging on the far wall and an Elton John song echoed in the background. Several people Jose didn't know were standing near the sliding glass doors leading to the pool.

He recognized Amanda Muller, the young rider, talking with two of the grooms. And Lauren was on the couch engaged in a conversation with a woman whose back was to him.

"Jose, it's nice to see you again." Brad Muller approached Jose from the kitchen, a fresh beer in hand.

"Mr. Muller. Nice to see you too."

"Please, call me Brad."

"Okay, Brad it is. I hear you're with us for the entire season. That's great."

"My wife thinks so too. I'm not sure if I can be away from New York as much as she and Amanda would like me to but I'll give it a try. And with the Aero Club right here, flying back for a day or two is so easy."

Jose reached for a beer, twisted off the cap and asked, "What is it you do in New York, Brad?"

"Mostly M & A work in the technology field. I spend a lot of time out in Silicon Valley talking to twenty-five-year-old, soon-to-be billionaires trying to convince them to use my firm for their offerings. The hardest thing for an old guy like me, I'm pushing fifty, is keeping up with the pace of these kids. They've got way too much energy for me."

"Sounds interesting," Jose lied.

"Hey listen. I'm glad you're here tonight. I wanted to ask a favor. No, actually, I want you to paint a picture for me. I'll pay you of course. I'd like a painting of my daughter and her horse and I'd like it done in the same way you did the Gabriella Brunelli work; you know, a close up of just their heads." He put his arm over Jose's shoulder and continued. "I'd like to surprise her with it for her birthday. Can you do that? I mean, can you paint such a work without the subject knowing about it?"

"Sure. I do it all the time. What I do is work from a photograph I take while they're riding. I have a great zoom lens so she won't even know I'm there."

"That's fantastic. Can you have it done by her birthday? It's the end of April."

"That's not a problem. I'm going to be here in Wellington most of the winter. Once I have a good photo, I can do the painting in a day or two."

"Really? I would have thought it took much longer."

"Nope. Sometimes it takes me longer to capture the right photo than to turn it into a painting. Did you want oil or watercolor?"

"Whatever you think. I know she loves the one of Gabriella. That's an oil, right?"

"Actually, that was a combination of charcoal and oils. It was one of my first of that style."

"That would be great."

"Just get me her riding schedule for the next few weeks and I'll make a point of being over there to get a shot; secretly, of course."

"I will. She rides almost every day but I'll let you know when she's competing in the ring. My wife is going to be very excited. Hey, I want you to meet my wife. I don't think you have, right?"

"No, is she here tonight? I spotted your daughter over there. All the grooms are flirting with her by the way, but I don't know who your wife is."

"Let me introduce you. Claire's talking to Lauren." He motioned for Jose to follow him to the couch.

The two men approached the long leather couch from behind. Jose could see Lauren seated on the couch and speaking with Brad's wife but her back was to the men. Lauren spotted them walking over.

"So, who won the Sorry game? As if I need to ask." She said without getting up from the deep sofa. Then Lauren made a twisting motion with her hand, indicating she wanted them to come around to the front of the couch. She knew Claire would extend her hand to greet someone new.

Brad gave Jose a gentle nudge and as they circled the end of the couch, he said, "There you are. Claire, I have someone I'd like you to meet. Jose, this is my beautiful wife, Claire."

Without rising from the couch, Claire extended her hand forward, anticipating someone would soon shake it. She was wrong.

When Jose saw the woman's face and realized she was his wife, he froze. Like a deer staring at the approaching headlights, he was paralyzed with fear. He couldn't move. His body would have obeyed his brain's commands but it sent none to be obeyed. Much like a website crashes when overloaded with incoming requests, his mind couldn't handle the myriad data being forced in.

How could this be? Claire wasn't blind. She lived in New Jersey as far as he knew. She didn't have a fourteen-year-old daughter. She wasn't married to Brad Muller. How could this person look so much like his wife, the woman he left standing over an empty grave?

The barrage of information trying to assault his mind included some facts; this woman looks like Claire. The names are the same. She seems to be the right age. And so on. But the incoming info also included much that was driven by his enormous guilt; the image of a young Claire weeping at his funeral. Envisioning her sitting silently at the kitchen table in their apartment on the night of 9-11. Gradually losing hope over the next few days and finally, having to bury an empty casket.

Suddenly, he felt light-headed. His body was under attack and the blood rushed from his brain to distal areas to protect itself. His knees buckled and he fainted, falling backward into one of the grooms chatting with Amanda.

"Oh my god!" Lauren shouted. She leaped to her feet and scrambled to the floor next to Jose's pale and limp body. She put her hand on his wrist to feel for a pulse.

"What's happened, Brad?" Claire asked as she retracted her outstretched hand.

"I'm not sure honey. Jose seems to have collapsed. Please just stay where you are for a moment."

"Micah!" Lauren screamed. "Call 911."

CHAPTER FORTY-FIVE

The world began coming into focus. The first image emerging clearly was Lauren's face. It was very close to his. Then he heard his name.

"Jose. Are you alright?" She was shaking him by the shoulders. "You scared the shit out of me."

He had no recollection of why he was on the floor with a dozen people staring down at him.

"You passed out." Lauren said softly. "Are you okay?"

But he couldn't answer. He was too confused. His brain was still under attack. In the distance, he heard a siren.

Micah had gone to the driveway to open the security gate and clear a path for the ambulance. As the EMS workers came through the front door carrying several bright orange bags, Lauren rose from her spot on the floor to give them room to deal with Jose.

"He was just standing there one minute, then fainted dead away." She said to the first EMT.

"How long was he unconscious?" The EMT who introduced himself as Bradley asked.

"Maybe two or three minutes. But he hasn't said anything since he first opened his eyes."

The other EMT, a short woman bearing the name Nina on her name tag, asked the guests to all move away from Jose to give them room to work. They quickly complied and gathered near the T.V. which was still beaming silent images of Micah and Runaway cantering gracefully.

"What's his name?" Bradley asked.

"Jose Martinez." Lauren answered.

The EMT took a knee next to Jose. "Good evening mister Martinez. My name is Bradley. Can you tell me what happened to you?" As he asked the question his hands were busy setting up a bottle of oxygen with a long tube leading from a regulator on its top. He turned on the valve and held the facepiece next to Jose's mouth without covering it.

Jose blinked a few times sucking in some of the sweet oxygen flowing towards him. "I don't know. I guess I fainted because... I'm on the floor." He looked to Lauren's concerned face for validation.

She was immensely relieved to hear him speaking. Her first fear was that he'd suffered a stroke. Hearing his voice was like music.

"Did you hit your head when you fell?"

"I don't think so."

"Does your head or neck hurt?"

"No."

"Does anything hurt right now?"

"No."

"Do you know what day it is, Jose?"

"Um, New Year's Eve. December 31st."

"And do you know where you are?"

"I'm at my friend, Micah's house."

The EMT looked to Lauren to see if that was correct. She nodded.

"One last question, Jose. And this is the tough one. Who is the President?"

"Trump."

"Well, not for a few weeks yet, but close enough. Jose, do you want to try sitting up for me?"

"Okay." Jose rested on his elbows and allowed the EMT to help him to a sitting position.

"How's that?

"Okay." He said tentatively.

"Anything hurt now?"

Jose shook his head.

"Jose, is it okay if I take your blood pressure?" he asked while preparing the BP cuff.

"Yeah, sure. I feel a lot better now."

"Sometimes all it takes is a little O2 to make you right. But let's just check a few more things before you sign up to run any marathons." Bradley began reading off a series of numbers to Nina who recorded them on a tablet.

"BP 142 over 80. O2 is 100 percent. Pulse is 86." He turned his attention back to Jose.

"Jose, are you allergic to anything?"

"I don't think so."

"Did you have anything unusual to eat tonight? How about anything with a lot of MSG?"

"No, nothing unusual. I had dinner here about an hour ago. Really, I think I'm okay now." Jose was trying to get to his feet.

The EMT put his hand on Jose's chest and asked, "Can you just sit for me a few more minutes? Let's make sure all that blood gets back to your head before we try standing."

Then he turned to Lauren. "Are you his wife?"

"No. He's not married. He lives a few doors down."

"Does he live alone?"

"Yes."

He turned back to Jose. "Jose, I think you're going to be just fine. I really do. But our protocols say that if someone loses consciousness from a standing fall, we need to take you to the ER so they can check you out. We're not doctors and even though your head doesn't hurt, you may have hit it in the fall. You don't want to find out you've got a blood clot later tonight. Especially if you live alone."

Jose started to object but the EMT cut him off. "The other thing is, something caused you to lose consciousness. It might have been a simple syncopal episode but it could also be something more sinister and that's for the doctors to determine. So, my suggestion is you let us take you over to WRMC and let them check you out."

Lauren interjected, "Yes, of course he'll go." She gave Jose a stern look as if to say, "Don't dare argue with me. You already scared me to death once tonight."

Jose nodded his consent and the BP cuff and oxygen were removed and stowed. Bradley helped him to his feet and held him under his arm.

"How we doing so far?"

"Yeah, okay. I can walk."

Bradley told Lauren they were taking him to Wellington Regional Medical Center and that if she wanted to ride along she could.

"No, but we'll follow in our own car if that's okay?"

Jose and the two EMT's were making their way toward the front door when Jose caught a glimpse of the cause of his distress. Claire and Brad were standing near the door. She was staring in another direction but listening carefully to all that was going on. She had a perplexed look on her face; as if perhaps trying to figure something out, a familiar voice perhaps?

⇒⊹ ⊹⇐

Later that night, after a very young female doctor assured Jose he didn't have a concussion, and Lauren and Micah had returned home, he stared up at the stark hospital ceiling. He was being kept overnight for observation. The doctor said he was free to leave in the morning if he didn't develop any symptoms overnight.

But being observed meant just that, so he was on a gurney in the hallway next to the nurse's station. There was little chance he'd get any sleep with the routine hospital din in the background and garish lighting directly above.

Lying there, hour after hour, he had time to think about what he'd seen. Now that the shock of seeing her in Lauren's living room had dulled, he was able to think clearly about Claire. He assumed she'd married Brad Muller not long after 9-11. How else could they have a teen age daughter? Or, more likely, Amanda was Brad's daughter from a previous marriage. After all, she didn't re-semble either of them. Amanda's complexion was olive; Brad and Claire, quite Anglo-Saxon. If that were the case, then maybe Claire had married long after 9-11. For some selfish reason that made him feel a little better.

So, Claire had remarried. He was glad she wasn't alone. But why was she blind? He didn't have enough information to put that together. He'd find out from Lauren.

And since she was blind, she hadn't seen him and never would. That was fortuitous, at least for Jose. As soon as he had the thought, he was riddled with guilt. How could he be grateful she was blind?

So, he reviewed in his mind, the facts he had. First, he'd prob-ably fainted merely from the shock of seeing Claire. That made sense to him. Second, Claire was not a threat to him. She couldn't see. And if he didn't have to speak to her, how could she ever sus-pect who he really was? Third, her husband had asked Jose to do a painting of their daughter. He saw no problem there, as long as he didn't have to deal with Claire.

The more he had time to think about it, the more he felt good about things going forward. Perhaps, seeing Claire again, through the one-way glass of her blindness, might even be nice. He was grateful she'd married so well. He hoped she was happy.

And, she had the family she always wanted. She had a beautiful daughter.

CHAPTER FORTY-SIX

J ose and Brad had agreed to meet Thursday morning for breakfast. Jose positioned the meeting as a discussion to flesh out the exact look Brad wanted for the painting of Amanda and her prize horse, Tribute. He said he needed to know more about the light, coloring and motion Brad desired. What he really wanted was an opportunity to interrogate Brad and learn more about Claire's life.

So it was, that on the morning of January 5, 2017, Jose crossed from one dimension to another. Although his interest in Claire was sincere and justified; after all, he wanted to know she was well taken care of, he was to learn more than he'd hoped.

They met at the Welli-Deli, a local breakfast spot a short bike ride from both their homes. Sitting at an outside table, under a trellis of brilliant bougainvillea, Jose spooned his yogurt while Brad had only coffee.

"So, they only kept you overnight?" Brad asked.

"Yeah, I'm fine. I must have just gotten up from the floor too fast. I'd been sitting on the floor playing a game with the kids. They said it happens all the time. Not to worry."

"How's that hospital?"

"Well, I've only been there twice as a patient and twice to visit Lauren when she had her babies, so I can't tell you much but its seems very modern. And the staff is very attentive."

"Good to know. I like to know where the nearest good hospital is. You know, just in case something comes up with my wife's condition. We didn't really consider it when we rented the house."

Jose nodded his understanding. Then asked, "What exactly is Claire's condition? I mean, has she always been blind?"

"No. And she's not completely blind. She can see a certain amount of light. If something's directly in front of her and very close, she can see a shadowy figure, but no detail."

Jose was concerned. "Can she discern facial features?"

"Oh, no. Just the difference between light and dark. Claire has been this way about six years now. She has a very advanced case of macular degeneration, a disease usually reserved for older people."

"That's a shame." He was sincerely sorry for Claire.

"Yes. I can't imagine what it must be like to walk around in a foggy darkness all the time. She's very brave and very determined to be independent. I really admire her will."

"Do they know what brought this on? I mean, is it from an accident, or just something that happens?" Jose wanted to hear Brad say it couldn't be caused by emotional distress.

"No, just a genetic defect. Some stray chromosome got its wires crossed at some point. Just one of those tragic things. But she makes the best of it. Actually, I think I love her even more because of it."

The sun was shining through the flowery trellis and the air was sweet with morning freshness. It was a beautiful day and Jose was looking forward to shooting his photos of Amanda later that morning at the arena. He hoped Claire would be there so he could watch her from a distance.

"Was your wife this way when you married?" He asked innocently.

"No. The first symptoms appeared after we'd been married about five years. It was very rapid after that. Within two years she was very bad and it gets a little worse every year. Although, I don't know that it could get any worse now. I think we've hit bottom."

Jose did some quick math in his head and ascertained they'd been married around ten years. That meant around 2006. Okay, at least she'd mourned him for about five years before moving on. He felt guilty for feeling that way, but dismissed it as human nature. Doesn't everyone want to be missed, at least for a while?

"I'm sorry for all the personal questions. We're supposed to be talking about your daughter. Let's do so. How old is Amanda?"

"She'll be fifteen on April 24th. But she thinks she's twenty-one."

"How long has she been riding?"

"Since she was about five. I think I bought her first horse for her sixth birthday. She's been in love with the sport ever since."

"I know Lauren thinks she's quite a rider. Very graceful, I think were her words."

"That's nice to hear, especially coming from the Wells."

"Do you ride, Brad?"

"Used to, but my knees aren't what they used to be. I don't jump anymore but I like to ride around our farm in Connecticut."

Jose settled back in his chair. "So, what I was thinking for the shot was one of Amanda and Tribute in mid-air as they clear a jump. I'd like to focus on their faces and use streaks of color to convey the motion. Basically, the same angle as the Gabriella work but from the opposite side. You wouldn't want it to look like a copy of the other work."

Jose thought further about the similarities of the two girls. True, Gabriella was older when he painted her on Guida Verde, but the girls did resemble each other. They both had dark complexions and dark hair. They both had beautiful eyes and expressive lips. It sometimes pained him to think about Gabriella. He still carried the guilt of her death with him though everyone tried to convince him otherwise.

He could see the work already in his mind's eye. Moving from right to left on the canvas, to distinguish it from Gabriella's image, he would again use charcoal and oil. Their faces would be close together, maybe even touching. He looked forward to taking the photo and to working on the canvas. He enjoyed painting beauty.

Just as he' done with Gabriella's painting, he wanted to use colors that, in some way were representative of the subjects. For Gabriella he used rich greens, reds, and whites for her Italian heritage.

Jose explained, "Brad, I like to incorporate subtle statements into my work. Visual images that convey other images in the patron's imagination. Tell me a little about Amanda's horse. Where is Tribute from?"

"Lauren found her for us. I believe she was raised in Kentucky. She was eleven when we got her."

The image of the blue grasses of the Lexington country-side came to mind for Jose. Perhaps he would use some deep blue-green mixtures in Tributes features.

"How about your family? Tell me a little about how you met Claire?"

"Actually, it's sort of tragic story, but with a happy ending."

"How so?"

"My wife was killed on 9-11. She worked in the north tower. Cindy didn't come home that day and her body was never recovered."

Distant synapses within Jose's brain began to fire, connecting the name Cindy, the World Trade Center and the name Muller together. Suddenly the image of the attractive research analyst Cindy Muller came into focus. She was in the same class of associates as Jose and they would often share a cream cheese bagel in the morning while reviewing the morning reports from London. She was one of his favorite people at Cambridge and he was suddenly filled with guilt for never having thought of her for all these years. She was, after all, just one of the many faces he'd tried to erase from his memory.

"Your wife was Cindy Muller?" He gasped before thinking.

"Yes. Did you know her?"

Jose recovered quickly. "No. Of course not. I just wanted to make sure I heard the name right."

It was a clumsy recovery but Brad didn't notice. His eyes were welling with moisture at the thought of his first wife. He sniffed and continued. "Anyway, I went to the memorial service every year on the anniversary of 9-11. They were terribly sad occasions for me and I hated to go to them but felt an obligation, especially since Cindy was still there somewhere."

"Wow. That's rough." Jose said sympathetically.

"Yeah, it was. But that's where I met Claire. Ironically, her first husband was also killed on 9-11. In fact, he and Cindy worked together. They were friendly. I remember her mentioning Joey a lot. I like to think that maybe they were helping each other trying to get out of the building, you know, in the stairway or something. It's hard for me to visualize what the end was like for them. I'm sorry." He wiped a small tear drop from his eye.

Jose felt like a piece of shit. He wasn't helping anybody that day. He was sitting across the river watching the whole horrible thing from the safety of a New Jersey park bench. The image of the lovely young Cindy Muller being crushed by concrete and steel made him close his eyes.

Brad saw this and interpreted it as a sign of empathy for his loss. His stories about losing Cindy on 9-11 often elicited a similar response from people. And he appreciated Jose's concern.

"So, although I hated going to those things," he continued, "I kept going. And at the fifth memorial, the one in September 2006, I saw Claire. We'd met once before at some social event for Cindy's company. I can't remember when, but I do remember her making an impression on me, even then."

"Wow. That's quite a story. It's like fate interceded and brought you together." Jose wanted to know more. He wanted to know how and why Claire had been attracted to him. He wanted details that would be inappropriate to ask.

"So, what was the attraction? I mean, what was it about Claire that you were attracted to?"

"I don't know exactly. I remember I was on the opposite side of the memorial service, about a hundred feet from her. She had on a yellow dress that lit her up. She looked beautiful despite all the sadness. It was a sunny day and I remember thinking that I'd stay until Cindy's name was read, then go back to work. I called Claire that night and told her I'd seen her and her daughter standing there. She remembered who I was and said yes when I asked her out. The rest is history. Neither of us ever went back to another memorial service."

"Claire had a daughter? Jose said incredulously.

"Yes. Amanda was only four but she stood there with her mom the whole morning. Why do you seem so surprised?"

Jose shook his head. "I assumed Amanda was your daughter from your first marriage."

"No. Cindy and I had no children."

Jose's mind raced. Brad said Amanda would be fifteen on her next birthday, April 24th. That meant she was born on April 24, 2002. He did a quick calculation and realized that meant she'd been conceived in late July 2001. Claire would have been two months pregnant by early September! How could she not tell him? Or, maybe, she didn't know until after he was gone!

He suddenly felt like he was going to be sick. There was a strangulating pain in his chest forcing him to lean forward in his chair and rest on his elbows. Suddenly all the guilt he carried for all those years, was increased exponentially. He didn't just abandon his wife, he left her with a baby! Now the images of Claire standing over an empty grave included a belly bump and more tears rolling down her face. He left her alone with his unborn baby! The depth of his sin now seemed immeasurable.

Brad noticed his distress. "Are you okay? Do feel faint again?"

"No, I'm okay." He lied. "Just swallowed something down the wrong pipe. You know. I'm okay." He cleared his throat and exaggerated a swallow to prove his condition.

He had to ask specifically, to be sure. He had to know for certain. "So, Amanda was Claire's child from her first husband?"

"Yeah, Joey never got to meet her. He was killed before Claire even knew she was pregnant. In fact, she found out she was pregnant that very day.

Later that morning, Jose sat on a grassy hill on the far side of the main arena. The shock of learning he had a daughter was still overwhelming. He needed to be completely alone.

Brad, Claire and Lauren were seated in the VIP tent directly across from him. From his position, he would be able to get a great shot of Amanda and Tribute as they jumped the fourth hurdle. The mid-day sun would be aligned with the rails so there'd be no glare.

His cell phone hummed in his pocket. It was Lauren. "Hey, you look like a snipper over there." She waved and he waved back. "Listen, do you want to come over for some lunch? They've got a great spread here."

He couldn't bear the thought of facing Claire, even if she couldn't see him. The guilt was crippling. "No thanks."

"You want me to send something over to you? Amanda doesn't ride for another forty-five minutes. She's twenty-third."

"No thanks. I'm okay."

"How about something to drink?"

"No. I'm good, thanks."

While the other junior riders went through their jumps, Jose snapped shots of some as they jumped the fourth hurdle. It helped him line up his shot for when it was Amanda's turn. The lighting was good and his angle was perfect.

It also helped him try to keep his mind off his conversation earlier that morning with Brad. As unbelievable as it was, it all made sense. Amanda had his features and his coloring. She had Claire's green eyes but most else seemed to be from Jose's Puerto Rican heritage. Now that he thought about it, he felt she resembled his mother. She had the same beautiful smile.

For the second time in his life, Jose was confronted by circumstances that left him without a plan. He had no idea what would happen next. Amanda was his daughter but there wasn't a person in the world he could tell, including Amanda. It was as if he had to ignore the fact completely. He needed to pretend he'd never heard the words from Brad Muller.

He assumed lots of men had daughters they left behind in one way or another; divorce, war, …, but there weren't any other good reasons he could imagine for leaving a child behind and moving on. Unless you were forced to do so, who would willingly abandon their own flesh and blood? Only a monster. His self-loathing had found new depths.

Jose used his powerful zoom lens to observe Claire from across the arena. She was smiling and talking to Lauren. It was the first opportunity he had to carefully observe her in fifteen years, years that had been kind to her. Except, of course for her blindness, she'd changed very little. He framed just her face and zoomed in even closer. Tiny crow's feet crept from the corners of her eyes but even those seemed to add beauty to her face in a classic way. She was aging gracefully and at forty-one, was still a knockout, at least to him.

He snapped a shot of Claire. Then another, and another. Suddenly, his phone rang again and once again Lauren's face appeared on the screen.

Hey, are you spying on us? I see you watching us through your camera." She said playfully. "Why don't you come over and say hello. Claire Muller is here and would like to finally meet you. That is, if you can do it without fainting this time!" Again, her tone was playful.

"I'll come by after Amanda rides. I'm trying to get the lighting right." He lied about both.

Twenty minutes later Amanda Muller was announced on the PA and she and Tribute cantered gracefully out into the sunlit arena. As with most Junior events, only a handful of spectators were in the viewing area, mostly friends and relatives of the riders, so the applause was limited.

Now that Jose knew she was his daughter by birth, she looked even more beautiful in her riding jacket and breeches. She didn't notice him on the grassy hill when she rode by. She began her ride well, but on the second jump, Tributes hind hoof clipped a rail and it fell from the cup. The third jump was a double and she kept her focus and cleared it without effort.

Jose had already clicked off a dozen shots but she was now approaching the spot he wanted to shoot for the painting. As she and Tribute cantered toward him, he held down the trigger on his camera and began auto-clicking at ten frames a second. Somewhere in that string of images he would find the perfect shot.

She cleared the fourth jump and finished with only one rail down. Modest applause followed her out of the ring as the next privileged teen entered for her turn. Jose had no intention of joining Lauren in the tent so he lingered on the lawn pretending to be fiddling with his equipment. But, a few minutes later he noticed that Amanda had entered the tent and was approaching her mother. The attraction to be close to her was almost magnetic. He wanted to be near his flesh and blood, if only for a moment and even if it meant confronting Claire.

He slung his camera over his shoulder and headed for the VIP entrance to the large white tent. As he approached the women, he heard Lauren saying something to Amanda about how to look forward.

"Hey, there's the peeping Tom!" Lauren said as she spotted him approaching.

"Amanda, that was a wonderful ride." Jose offered.

"Thank you."

"I was watching over near the fourth jump. Too bad about number three though."

"Oh, she did great. These are bigger jumps than she's used to. She did great." Lauren insisted.

Then, Lauren turned to Claire and said, "Claire, this is my friend, the one you almost met on New Year's Eve. Jose, this is Amanda's mom, Claire Muller."

Claire extended her hand in the direction of Lauren's voice and said, "Very nice to meet you, Jose. I've heard a lot about you."

"*El placer es todo mio.*" He used his most convincing Spanish to say the pleasure was all his. Then he added in accented English, "Your daughter rides like an angel."

Lauren didn't understand the sudden ethnicity but added, "She's jumping professional level jumps and she'd not even fifteen yet."

Jose couldn't take his eyes off Claire. Being so close to her, holding her hand, and yet she couldn't see him. It was a surreal moment. His heart was filled with pity for her and sorrow for himself. For the first time, he had a glimpse of what life might have been like; the life he couldn't imagine fifteen years ago. A life with a family.

"Are you a rider, Jose?" Claire asked, still holding his hand.

"Sadly, no." He looked at her directly. He could see her eyes through her sunglasses. They seemed to be fixed on him, but how could that be?

CHAPTER FORTY-SEVEN

For the next four days, Jose worked tirelessly on the work he came to call his "Amanda". The first four versions were discarded before they were finished. He wasn't satisfied with the way he'd conveyed the motion. The colors weren't right so he kept experimenting with color combinations until he felt it was perfect. No one had been allowed to see the work yet. He'd secluded himself in his home except for the time he spent at the practice ring watching Amanda ride.

Lauren inquired about his seclusion and sudden interest in observing practice sessions but he lied and explained he needed to get more ideas about how she meshed with her horse before finishing his canvas. The truth was he just loved watching her. He was amazed at how one human being can suddenly love another simply because they shared a blood line. He knew so little about her, and yet, he already loved her deeply, as a parent loves a newborn.

He hoped he'd have opportunities in the coming weeks, while they shared a common community, to spend time with Amanda.

He tried to contrive ways in which he and Lauren could be alone with her, without her stepfather and certainly without her mother.

One breezy afternoon, on the fifth day after Amanda's competition, Brad spotted Jose sitting on a bench near the practice ring at the Wells farm. He walked over and sat next to him. Jose looked exhausted.

"How's our little project coming along?" Brad asked.

"Actually, I finished it last night."

"Really?" Brad was very excited. "When can I see it?"

"We can walk over to my studio anytime you like. I am just a few blocks away."

"Excellent. Let's go!"

As they walked down the dusty road, Brad asked, "How did it come? I mean, do you like it? Are you satisfied with it?"

"Yes. I'm very pleased. She is a beautiful subject and it's always a pleasure to paint beauty."

"You know, I'm not going to give it to her until her birthday. At least that was my plan. But now, I don't know if I can wait."

When they arrived at Jose's house, Brad Muller was surprised by its modesty. He knew Jose by reputation. He knew of his renown in equestrian circles. He expected more. When they went inside, he was even more surprised. The living area was lined with stacks of paintings, mostly of riders with and without horses. He guessed there were two hundred in the one room alone. They were mostly on canvas but there were some watercolors as well.

"Come. Amanda is in my studio." Jose led the way through a maze of unfinished works.

Brad spotted several unfinished paintings of his daughter on the floor near the door. "What are these?"

"I wasn't satisfied with the colors on those. I'll reuse the canvases."

The final version of "Amanda" was resting on an easel in the center of the studio. When Brad saw it, he was floored. It was impressive in its bold use of color. But what struck him was the action. The painting conveyed powerful action. Jose had captured the precise moment Amanda and Tribute had leapt from the ground and were starting their ascent. The determination on the faces of both rider and mount screamed off the canvas.

"It's amazing, Jose. Absolutely, amazing! She's going to love it. I love it."

Jose's face beamed with pride as he pointed to the photograph taped to the wall behind him. "I had great subjects."

"You know, we never discussed a price. I guess I lost a lot of negotiating strength when I said I loved it." Brad joked.

"I love it too. Which is why I cannot sell it to you."

Brad suddenly tensed. "What do you mean? I asked you to paint this for me. It's my gift to my daughter. Why won't you sell it to me?" His tone was firm.

"Because it is too beautiful. In my whole life, I have never been more pleased with my own work. And something so beautiful is invaluable. You may have it… as my gift to you, your lovely wife, and your beautiful daughter."

"That's extraordinary. That's too generous of you Jose." Brad searched for the words. "I have to pay you somehow."

"Allow me the pleasure of visiting you in Connecticut someday. I would like to see the home of my work and of the Gabriella." Jose extended his hand to close the deal and hear no more of it.

They shook, but Brad added, "Of course. You're always welcome. But I'll think of something to make it up to you."

"Do you want me to keep it here until her birthday?" Jose offered. "It might be difficult to hide it from her for three months in your home. Unless, of course, you want to show it to your wife first?"

As soon as he said the words, he realized his faux pas. "I'm sorry. That was stupid of me." And it saddened him to think that Claire would never see it.

"Don't worry about it. I do it all the time. You'd be amazed how many times you use the word 'see' in a sentence. I once…." He was distracted by the siren of an ambulance going by Jose's home in the direction from which they'd just walked. Just as the racing ambulance passed, Brad's cell phone rang. It was Lauren Wells.

"Hey Lauren. What's up?"

"Brad, where did you go? I've been looking all over the farm for you. Your car is still in the driveway. Where are you?" She seemed amped.

"I took a walk down to Jose's house with him. I wanted to see…"

"Just get back here right away." Brad could hear the siren coming through the phone now.

Lauren had to shout over the wailing to be heard. "Amanda's had a fall. She's hurt. Get back here quickly. The medics will probably need you."

"I'm on my way." Brad said. Then he looked at Jose and asked, "Can you drive me back to the farm? Amanda's been hurt in a fall."

⊱ ⊰

While her two fathers were walking toward Jose's home, Amanda decided to take one more turn in the ring. Her practice session had gone well and Bret was pleased with the way she was following through on her landings. He saw in her, the same potential that Micah and Lauren had seen.

"I'm going to make one more round," she said from atop Tribute.

"Okay, kid, but keep your heels down when you land those jumps. You were coming up a little on that last one." Bret was a perfectionist, even with a fourteen-year-old.

"Got it." She said as she turned her horse back toward the jumps.

But as she approached the first jump, a fence she and Tribute had cleared a dozen times already that day, she sensed something was wrong. Tribute's canter wasn't smooth. Something was very different.

Had she been a more experienced rider, she would have immediately known to abort the next jump and have her horse checked by Bret. Unfortunately for the teen, her determination to succeed trumped common sense. She continued toward the fence and used her legs to let Tribute know they were about to jump.

But the horse was injured in a way Amanda couldn't sense and at the last moment, refused the jump, sending Amanda flying forward into the top rail. Her left hand was tangled around the reins so she couldn't sail clear of the twelve-hundred-pound horse. Tribute's forward force snapped the rail in half and her momentum carried her down onto the broken wood and Amanda's chest.

Amanda's fragile body hit the ground first, followed by the jagged rail fragment and her horse. Because she was still tethered to Tribute by the reins, the three fell upon each other. The horse's weight alone would have done significant damage to the child, but the force was amplified because Tribute fell onto the rail pushing the rigid object deep into Amada's abdomen.

It all happened within three seconds. Tribute recovered quickly and was now on her feet dragging a limp and unconscious Amanda, still tangled in the reins, with her. To her credit, the horse didn't panic. She walked calmly from the fallen standard toward an oncoming Bret Kennedy.

Bret had seen what happened and was on his feet before Amanda even hit the ground. He opened his pocket knife while running toward the disaster and was able to free Amanda from Tribute as soon as he arrived. He then led the frightened horse away from the child and secured the reins to the fence before returning to attend to Amanda.

"Help!" he screamed. "Help. I need help in the practice ring!"

Bret didn't usually carry a cell phone when he wore breeches but today he had it with him and quickly called 911. "A child's been seriously injured in a riding accident at 12 Appaloosa Trail in Wellington. We need an ambulance quickly. She's unconscious!"

The EMS dispatcher ran through a short series of questions and Bret barked answers into the cell phone as he looked down on the broken child. He could tell she was breathing but her breaths were clouded with gurgling sounds. Blood ran freely from somewhere on her head and her left arm protruded on a disturbingly unnatural angle.

He refrained from moving her at all for fear of making anything worse before medical professionals arrived. "Stay with me kid. I promise, you're going to be okay." He whispered.

Lauren and one of the grooms had been working in the barn, heard Bret's screams, and came running. The groom, an Irish kid named Spencer, had grabbed a first aid kit before leaving the barn. As soon as he saw the puddle of blood pooling near Amanda's head, he opened the plastic box and removed two large rolls of gauze. "Lift her head a bit," he shouted to Lauren.

He began rolling the cotton fabric around Amanda's head, hoping to cover the wound. There was too much blood to know exactly where it was coming from. Within minutes, all but her face was wrapped in gauze which was rapidly turning from white to red.

For the second time in two weeks, an ambulance rolled through the security gates onto the Wells farm. This time, they were definitely taking a patient with them. A police car was right behind them. The EMT's quickly stabilized Amanda's arm and put a plastic collar on her neck before moving her to a backboard and into the ambulance. She was still unconscious and her breathing was labored. Brad rode with them to the hospital and Lauren followed in her car.

Jose and Bret were left standing in the ring staring down at the blood-soaked sand.

"What happened?" Jose asked.

"I don't know for sure. I glanced down at my watch for a second and when I looked up she was already going head over ass into the standard. I think Tribute bowed a tendon but I need to take a careful look. Whatever it was, she refused the jump and the two of them came down hard. I'm afraid Amanda took the full weight of the horse on her when she hit the ground. That's a lot for a little girl who can't weigh more than one-ten herself."

"Where's Micah?"

"He's still in town but I bet Lauren's already called him."

"I think I should…" Jose was cut short by his own cell phone ringing in his back pocket. Lauren's face appeared on the screen. She was calling from the speeding ambulance.

"Hey."

"Jose, can you drive over to the Muller's and bring Claire Muller to the hospital. Brad already called her to fill her in but he didn't tell her how badly Amanda's hurt. She should be there. Can you do that?"

To say anything other than "*Of course*", would be inexplicable. Still, at the moment, the task seemed beyond his ability. Spending time alone with Claire in a car? Driving her to the hospital to be with their daughter? Their daughter who might already be dead! And then to have to pretend he was just another neighbor coming to the aid of a blind friend? It all seemed impossible.

"Of course, I'll do it." He heard himself say. "Which house is it?"

She gave him the address, which was just a few farms away, then added, "Please hurry. She's waiting for you."

CHAPTER FORTY-EIGHT

Claire was waiting on the front steps of their home when Jose pulled in the driveway. On the short drive from the Wells farm, Jose tried to think about how to deal with the needs of a blind person. He realized to his dismay, that he'd need to verbalize to give her the cues she needed to understand what was going on around her. Little things like, "*I'm turning on to Southern Boulevard now*", would be important so she had a sense of where they were. And that meant speaking a lot, something he didn't want to have to do. Surely, if you heard enough of it, you'd recognize the voice of someone you were married to for several years. Even if you believed that someone was dead.

He pulled the white Jeep directly in front of her. "Miss Claire, it's Jose. Let me get the door for you." He used a heavy accent.

She was visibly shaken by the news from her husband. She extended her hand for Jose's assistance.

"I can't tell you how much I appreciate this Jose. I hope this isn't too much of an inconvenience for you." She tried to sound under control but her trembling lip conveyed her concern.

"It's not a problem at all." He helped her into the Jeep and took off down the pebbled driveway.

"Were you there when she fell?"

"No. Actually, I was with Mr. Muller at my house. He was looking at some of my paintings. Lauren called him there and we rushed right over."

"Brad told me he'd asked you to do a painting for us. I hope that's not an imposition. By the way, how are you feeling? Are you alright?"

Under the circumstances, considering what she should be focused on, Jose thought her concern was unusually kind. But that was Claire. She was a very caring person. He was touched by her concern and repulsed by the memory of what he'd put her through.

'Yes, I'm fine. Fit as fiddles, as you say." Again, he laid the accent on heavy.

Mercifully, the short trip to the hospital passed without too much more conversation. As they approached the emergency room entrance, Jose said, "I'm sure your daughter will be fine. This is an excellent hospital. We're just turning into the entrance. I see Lauren's car over there."

He helped her from the car and into the E.R. lobby where they were immediately greeted by Lauren.

"Lauren is here." He said for Claire's benefit.

Lauren rushed toward them. "They've taken her up for an MRI. She hasn't regained consciousness yet. Brad went with them."

"She's unconscious?" Claire stammered.

Lauren hadn't focused on how little detail Brad gave Claire on the phone. She regretted being so stupid. She tried to recover.

"I'm sure she'll be alright. She's a tough kid."

A nurse motioned for them to get out of the busy hallway and pointed to a waiting room just down the hall. Jose took Claire's arm and said, "They want us to wait somewhere else. It's a little busy right here."

Once seated in the waiting room, Claire asked, "What happened?"

Jose motioned for Lauren to do the explaining by pointing directly at her. Then said, "I'm going to get some water. Would anyone like some?"

While he was gone, Lauren explained what she knew. She left out the part about Tribute falling on Amanda but was candid about her head injury and the extensive bleeding. She told Claire about the broken arm but left it at that.

Jose returned with three bottles of water and placed them on the table in front of them. He was thoughtful enough to say, "I brought back water for everyone. Would you like some Claire?"

But when he picked up a magazine from the same table, hoping to pass the time, Lauren shot him a look that screamed, "ASSHOLE! You don't read a magazine in front of someone who's blind!" Of course, she was right.

They made small talk to keep everyone's mind off the obvious. Lauren talked about the upcoming Longines' Championships as if Amanda would be ready for the February event. No one believed that would be the case.

Forty minutes later, Brad appeared in the waiting room door. He gave Claire a prolonged hug. Seeing the two embracing, made Jose feel uneasy. He realized he had no business being there. To them, he wasn't family. At best, to them, he was a newly acquired friend.

After seating Claire again, and while still standing himself, Brad filled everyone in. "They've taken her into surgery to set the broken arm and evaluate the extent of her internal injuries." He looked at Claire and quickly added, "If any."

"What about her head?" Lauren asked.

"Looks like that's just a really bad scrape on the right side of her head. They got her cleaned up and didn't see anything else on her head. It didn't even need stitches. No real damage or anything like that. I think it's just that injuries on your head bleed a lot. That's why there was so much blood." Clearly, Brad was trying to highlight the positives, but Claire sensed his feigned optimism.

"What did they say about internal injuries?"

"All they said was that the bruise on her belly indicted there might be internal bleeding and they wanted to check."

Claire wasn't satisfied. "How do they do that?"

"I don't know for sure. The doctor said they would check while they had her in the O.R. dealing with her arm. Claire..., she's going to be okay."

Four hours later, that didn't seem to be the case. There'd been no word from the O.R. and both Brad and Claire were frantic as their collective imagination dealt with the worst. Jose and Lauren were seated across from Brad and Claire. A small low table, filled with half-empty water bottles and magazines littering the surface, sat between them. They could sense the parent's anxiety and hoped there would soon be some good news.

For Jose, it was the longest four hours of his life. His daughter could be dying. He had to sit and watch her mother's anguish and dreaded being there if the news from the O.R. was bad. After the pain he'd once put Claire through, he couldn't bear watching her told she'd now lost her only child. He would rather face a firing squad then have to be there to witness that.

Once again, his ghosts haunted him. Claire, the woman to whom he'd sworn his perpetual love then deserted, sat before him in tears. He had a vision of the young reporter's mother crying when she heard her daughter had been a 9-11 victim. Then there was Brad's first wife, Cindy and all the other people he worked with that didn't go home that fateful Tuesday. The nightmarish image then shifted to Fiona walking from of her house the morning they took Bert's body out. He knew he'd contributed to the horrible shame on her face that morning. And there was the image of Gabriella Brunelli getting into that car. Now Amanda, his flesh and blood, was lying on an operating table fighting for her life.

And finally, Lonnie Rossetti, someone who loved him for what he was, and he didn't see it. It felt as if any woman he ever got at all close to had been tragically effected by his very existence. To know him was to be hurt by him.

His self-deprecation was interrupted when a nurse came into the room and asked for the parents of Amanda Muller.

"I'm her father." Brad said as he stood. "Is there any news?"

"Doctor Smith sent me down to give you an update." She said, then looked around to be sure it was okay to speak in front of the others.

Brad picked up on her concern and said, "This is her mother, and these are friends."

"The doctor wanted me to tell you they're still in the O.R. They've reset her humorous and ulna. That went fine. Now they're dealing with the internal organs that were damaged. They've stopped the internal bleeding. That's a good thing. But there was a lot of tissue damage, especially to her liver and pancreas. That's what they're doing now."

"Is she going to be okay?" Claire asked frantically.

"I'm sorry, I just don't have enough information to tell you that for certain. I can tell you this, she's in very good hands. Ben Smith is our most experienced abdominal surgeon. If it was my daughter, that's who'd I want."

"How much longer before we know?" Brad asked.

"That's why Dr. Smith asked me to come down here. He said it's going to be at least another four hours. He's called in more surgeons to assist but he told me to tell you it's going to be a while yet."

It was 5:15 in the afternoon. That meant Amanda might not be out of surgery till after nine. There was nothing they could do in the meantime. The four of them agreed that Lauren and Jose should go home. Brad promised to call Lauren the moment they knew anything. Jose could tell Brad wanted to be alone with his wife. Having Lauren and Jose in the room made it difficult for him to give her the comfort she so desperately needed.

On the way back to the Wells farm, Lauren was silent. Jose tried to make relevant small talk but she just stared out the window. Finally, as they turned on to Appaloosa Trail approaching the Wells farm, she said, "I can't imagine what I would do if that were one of my girls. I mean, if God forbid she doesn't make it. If it was Katie or Liz, I'd have to kill myself. I couldn't live with that heart-ache. It would be too much to bear."

"But you'd still need to be there for the others; your other daughter would need you desperately. It would be selfish to take the easy way out. Others need you around." Jose offered without much conviction.

"I don't think I could do it. I mean I don't think I could go on. Not after losing a daughter."

"You would because you'd need to be there for your other daughter."

"Maybe. I don't know. But what about poor Claire? She doesn't have another daughter."

CHAPTER FORTY-NINE

Jose stared at the half empty bottle resting on his kitchen table. Usually, the Chivas only came out when a guest asked for scotch, but tonight, he was determined to escape the ghosts. He needed more than wine and had been draining the pear-shaped bottle for nearly an hour.

It was after eleven and he'd had no word from anyone about Amanda. He was alone, drunk and depressed. He no longer wanted to deal with all the feelings of self-loathing. He needed to forget, at least for a few hours, that his daughter might die before he even got to know her. Perhaps that was to be his punishment for his sins; discovering something to love, only to have it snatched from your grasp just as you become aware of it.

He staggered to his bed with the Chivas in his hand and fell asleep fully clothed, the remaining liquid pouring onto the floor. But sleep provided no sanctuary from his ghosts. His night was filled with fretful nightmares.

First, there was a dream in which he and Amanda were sitting and talking at his desk at Cambridge. She was much younger, probably not more than five. Suddenly the floor beneath them gave out and they were falling a great distance. Amanda was screaming and falling away from him, her hand outstretched and yelling "Daddy, save me!".

Then he had a nightmare about Fiona. He and Fiona were cooking something black on his stove while Bert Wells looked on from outside his window. Bert was screaming something in another language and holding a gun. There was a knock at the door and Micah and Lauren were there asking if anyone had seen Bert. He'd been missing all day.

He had a dream about he and Lonnie making love on a beach. There was a decrepit peer in the distance that appeared to be on fire. Lonnie was trying to warn him about the fire but he ignored her. As they rolled around on the sand, Lonnie was bitten by hundreds of tiny red ants which she tried desperately to brush off herself with a canvas painting. When she succumbed to the bites and fell to the ground, the painting fell face up. It was the Gabriella work.

Finally, just before awakening, he dreamt about Claire. She was standing over a huge hole in the snow-covered ground. She was alone, peering into the hole. Joey came up behind her, stood at her side for a few minutes, then pushed her into the hole and began shoveling snow into the hole. As he looked down to see if he'd properly buried Claire he noticed she was talking to two other women. At first, he couldn't see who they were so he kept shoveling snow on top of them. But when they all looked up at him he could see it was Claire, Sarah Bideaux, and Megan Minnick. Suddenly, on the other side of the hole, starring at him were his parents.

He awoke at seven in a terrible sweat. The room smelled of scotch whisky. His head pounded.

The sun had just crept over the palm trees lining his yard. Its glare sent a knife through his eyes. In the distance, he heard someone pounding on wood. It took a moment for him to realize someone was pounding on his door.

Still in the previous day's cloths, he staggered to the door.

"What the hell happened to you?" Lauren wanted to know. "You look like shit!"

The best he could muster was a low groan as he shook his head.

"I've been trying to call you for an hour. Your phone keeps going to voicemail."

Jose looked around as if to say, "I don't know where it is."

"Are you drunk? You smell like you slept in the Bowery."

Jose ran his hand through his hair in an attempt to tidy himself and reassure himself his head was still there. The rubber band that usually kept his hair out of his face was long gone.

"Come in," he whispered. "But please stop yelling at me. My head is going to explode."

"Sit down asshole. I'll make you some coffee." She pushed him toward the kitchen.

He found a rubber band on the table and slipped it around his long black mane. It helped in appearance only. He still felt like his skull was in a vice. Lauren filled a cup with water and tossed it in the microwave. She stood starring at him in silence for the requisite three minutes, then threw two spoonfuls of instant coffee into the cup and handed it to Jose. "Drink this, moron."

"Thanks."

"Where have you been? I tried calling you last night."

"I was here." He pointed at his living room sofa. "I guess I had too much to drink."

"You think?"

"So, why were you calling me?"

"Do you remember anything about yesterday?" Her question dripped with sarcasm.

It came rushing back to him. He rested his head on his palms. "Oh, shit. Please tell me she's okay."

"She got out of surgery at 11:30 last night. Brad called us around midnight and I tried to call you but…"

He looked at her as if to say, "Please have mercy on me and just tell me she's okay."

"She regained consciousness, at least for a while. That's a good thing. But that's about the only good news. The doctor says her liver and pancreas are severely damaged. Apparently both organs were completely crushed by the weight of Tribute falling on her. Actually, it was probably the rail pushing into Amanda and Tribute pushing down on the rail. I guess the hard wooden rail is what did the damage. One of her kidneys was removed last night. The other one's okay and you can get by with one kidney. They were able to repair a bunch of tears in her stomach but the big problem is the liver. And she lost a lot of blood."

It took him a moment to process the information. His brain was working, but slowly. "So, is she going to be okay?"

"We'll know more today after Brad talks to a liver specialist from NYU. Nobody can live very long without a liver and they think hers is irreparable. So, unless this big shot liver doctor from New York can come up with a way to fix hers, a transplant would be her only option, and it would have to be really soon."

"A liver transplant? They do that?"

"Yeah. According to the doctor Brad spoke with last night, liver transplants are not uncommon. The problem is finding a healthy liver to transplant. It's like heart transplants, you can only get one from someone who doesn't need theirs anymore, someone dead."

"That's horrible. The poor kid." He held his head in his hands.

"Yeah, Brad and Claire are a mess. I feel so bad for them."

"So, what's next?"

"What do you mean?"

"I mean, do they take her to some big hospital? Is Wellington really the best place for her? I mean, her parents have money. They can afford the best doctors. What are they doing?"

"I told you. Brad is meeting with a liver specialist who arrives at PBI at ten. I guess we'll know more after this big shot specialist sees her."

"And what if he can't help? What if she needs a transplant? How do you go about finding a donor?"

"I don't know. I assume there's some sort of waiting list you get on. But I don't really know."

"Well, they've got money. Maybe that will get Amanda to the top of the list."

"I don't think it works that way. I don't think you can bribe your way to the front of the line. But I really don't know how it works." She was straightening out his kitchen as she spoke. "Hey, asshole, here's your phone. It's off." She had uncovered the phone from under a pile of magazines on the counter.

"I don't remember turning it off."

"Yeah, I'm sure you remember everything about last night." She said sarcastically. "Listen, take a shower, pull yourself together, then come over around noon for lunch. By then maybe we'll know something. I've got to take Liz for her swimming lessons in ten minutes. I have to run."

Jose nodded weakly. "Noon," he said as Lauren went through the door. He was glad she'd invited him over. He didn't want to wait this out alone.

After a shower and another two hours of dreamless sleep he felt a lot better. He turned on his phone noticing all the missed calls from Lauren. He plugged it into the charger and retreated to the solitude of his studio. Resting on an easel in the center of the room was the canvas of Amanda and Tribute. Jose sat on the edge of his desk staring at the work he was so proud of and focusing on Amanda's face. She was so beautiful and young. He hoped she'd one day get to see it.

Seeing her face on the canvas reminded him of one of his nightmares, the one where he was sitting at his desk talking to a very young version of Amanda. He didn't recall what they were talking about but it seemed she was very interested in what he had to say. There were a lot of other people around but she was focused completely on him. Then suddenly the floor beneath them gave way and everything was falling. As she reached out screaming for him he reached back but she was already too far away.

Jose buried his palms into his eyes. "Please don't let her die," he said to no one in particular. He wasn't much a believer in god and hadn't prayed in a long time, but he needed someone to talk to. He needed someone to tell him this wasn't his fault, that he had nothing to do with her accident. Intellectually, he knew that was true, but he also knew that if he hadn't run out on her mother fifteen years ago, she wouldn't have been in Wellington in the first place.

He paced his studio for almost an hour, stuck in a limbo between self-loathing and self-pity, until he heard his phone ringing in the kitchen. It was Lauren.

"Hey, are you coming over for lunch?"

He hadn't realized so much time had gone by. "Yes, yes. I'll be right there."

When he arrived at the Wells farm, there were several cars already parked in the circular driveway. He recognized Micah's, Lauren's, and Bret's, but there was also a black Mercedes with Florida plates he'd not seen before.

Micah greeted him at the door. "Oh, good, you're here. Brad Muller was just about to fill us in on what the specialist had to say. He just got here. Come in."

Inside the great room, six adults stood around the granite-topped center island. Liz and Kate were in the lanai watching television. Jose immediately notice Claire seated at the counter, her husband standing next to her. Bret and Terry Kennedy stood next to them with Micah and Lauren on the opposite side. Jose took a position next to Lauren.

Brad was the first to speak. "So, as I started to say, we only have a few minutes. Claire and I just came home to change our cloths and shower. We're going right back to the hospital." He paused for a second, then continued. "Doctor Vartebedian flew in this morning and went straight to the hospital. By the time I met him there he'd already seen Amanda and Doctor Smith. He reviewed all Smith's surgical notes and the MRI's that were done yesterday. Unfortunately, he doesn't think the liver can be repaired. Smith had said he thought maybe they could remove about seventy-five percent of the damaged liver, and hope she could get by on the remaining tissue until an acceptable organ donor could be found. Vartebedian didn't agree. He said sometimes that can work but in Amanda's case, the vital part of the liver, the part you can't live without, is the part that was completely crushed."

Brad cleared this throat and looked over at his wife to see how she was handling all this.

Lauren asked, "So is a liver transplant the only option?"

"In Vartebedian's opinion, yes. And it would have to be a complete liver, meaning it must come from someone dead. Sometimes they can take part of a healthy liver from a living donor and sew it on to a damaged liver. But in Amanda's case, there was just too much damage. Before the accident, Amanda was an otherwise healthy and strong teenager and would have been an excellent candidate for a transplant. But there are two problems."

At this point Claire reached out for her husband's hand. He grasped it and held on.

"The first problem is that Amanda went through seven hours of surgery yesterday to repair her spleen, pancreas and stomach. Although she came through all that well, she's in a very weakened state. She's not what he called an ideal candidate for another major surgery. Transplanting a liver is another twelve hours of surgery. Nonetheless, he sees a transplant as the only solution and is willing to do the surgery assuming a viable donor can be found…" He hesitated, then finished the sentence, "…in time."

An uncomfortable silence filled the room. Then Micah asked, "Brad, you said there were two problems. What else?"

"Yes, well the other issue is finding a suitable donor. Because of her age, Amanda would be on a fast-track for a donor. That's about the only good news. And there are over six thousand liver transplants done each year. The bad news is she has a rare blood type, AB negative. Apparently, it's the rarest type of human blood and we need to find a liver from someone else who has the same rare blood type. That's going to really limit the population of potential donors." He said somberly.

Claire now spoke for the first time. Her voice was surprisingly solid. "So, we need to find a donor with type AB negative blood, a blood type that only one in a hundred and eighty people have, and we need to do so in the next few days. Doctor Smith said, they can only filter Amanda's blood artificially for a few days. After that…, after that, there's too much of something, I forget what it's called, that builds up and could cause clots." Her voice trailed off.

Brad took over. "So, because she has this rare blood type, we need to do more than just get on the waiting list. It sounds horrible but we need to find someone who dies traumatically in the next few days that has AB negative blood and an otherwise healthy liver. Oh, and their family needs to be willing to donate the organ. Doctor Vartebedian is connected to all the right organizations and they have a sophisticated computer network all over the country that will search E.R. admissions for what we need. He claims, if there's a viable match out there, his network will find it. The problem is, we have so little time. The longer it takes to find a donor, the less likely Amanda will be able to survive the transplant surgery. We need to find a donor right away."

"Is there anything we can do?" Lauren asked.

"Yes, as a matter of fact you can be very helpful. You see, Doctor Vartebedian's network only covers hospitals in the United States and Canada. I know that you and Micah have many relationships in Europe. It would be most helpful if you could make contact with them and..."

Jose was no longer listening. He recalled from his brief stay at Wellington Regional Medical Center, a young doctor telling him that he had the rarest type of human blood.

He knew immediately, what he had to do.

CHAPTER FIFTY

Jose drove home still unable to shake the headache he'd brought on with the Chivas. When he got there, he went straight to his bathroom, took three aspirin, then made two phone calls. The first was to Wellington Regional Medical Center. He had to find out if his recollection from so many years ago was correct.

As expected, the hospital would not release any information over the phone so he agreed to stop by in person. "I'll come by in about a half hour. I need to go into Palm beach anyway and it's on my way."

The second call was to Larry Finch, his lawyer. When he first started selling his art, Bert Wells had referred Jose to Larry so he could set up an LLC and copyright any prints he produced. Larry had since helped Jose with his house purchase, a will, and, in 2014, represented him in traffic court after Jose was clocked doing seventy-seven in a fifty.

"Larry, it's Jose Martinez. How are you man?"

"Never too busy for you, my friend. What can I do for you? Another speeding violation?"

"No, I learned my lesson. I just need an hour of your time this afternoon."

"I'm around all day. What's up?"

"I'll fill you in when I get there. I can be in your office at three. Does that work?"

"See you then."

On his drive to the hospital, he thought about Amanda, the daughter he never knew existed until a few days ago; the unborn baby he'd abandoned fifteen years ago. He thought about her lying in a hospital bed, connected to a dozen tubes and machines. Then he thought about Claire lying in the hospital holding her newborn in her arms and crying for the husband she'd never see again; the perfect family they'd never be.

It didn't take long at the hospital to confirm what he thought; he was type AB negative. From the emergency room, he went up to the pediatric recovery floor and asked to see Amanda Muller. The receptionist greeted him kindly but said, "I'm sorry, she's in ICU and only immediate family is allowed to visit."

"But I'm..." He hesitated. What good could possibly come from exposing himself now? He wanted to scream that he was her father! But that would only cause Claire and so many others even more pain. He didn't have the right to do that.

He noticed that the nurse's station at which he stood was in front of a long wall of glass. He assumed the ICU patients were behind the glass. "Would it be possible for me to see her from out here, I mean from behind the glass? I've traveled a long way and probably won't get another chance to see her before I must leave. Please..., she's like a daughter to me."

"You can look from here." The portly nurse pointed directly behind her to the small window. "You definitely can't go in there. But you can see her through the glass if you come over here." She got up from her desk and showed him where to stand to catch a glimpse of Amanda.

He could see her through the window. Just as he'd imagined, she was connected to several machines that were breathing for her, feeding her, and circulating her blood through a large device to her left filled with blinking blue lights. It had the letters MARS on it. She looked barely alive. Her olive complexion was blanched and she wore a massive bandage around her head.

Yet, she was the most beautiful young woman he'd ever seen. He put his hand on the glass as if to touch her face. "We're going to help you get better Amanda. You're going to be okay. I promise. I love you and I'm so…, so very sorry."

Jose drove into Palm beach for his meeting with Larry Finch. The process took very little time and he was back on the road to Wellington by four thirty. It was a beautiful January afternoon and the sun hung low over Southern Boulevard as he drove west. When he passed the hospital, he whispered, "It's going to be alright Sweetie."

He was reminded of his first day in Wellington when he walked from the hospital toward a life he couldn't imagine. He could see himself walking on the side of the road. He'd been so fortunate to find Alex McCurry and, through him, Micah and Lauren Wells. They'd become his family. They'd been so wonderfully kind to him. So many people had.

When he arrived home, he spent the next two hours doing research on Google. He needed to be sure his plan was viable. When he was certain, he looked at the clock in his kitchen. It was 7:44 P.M., about twenty-seven hours since Amanda's accident.

He wasn't frightened. He was resolved. He was at peace.

Jose took out a pad of paper and wrote two brief notes each on a separate piece of paper. Then he took a small piece of tape and secured it to the top of one of the notes and placed it on the kitchen counter. He took the other note and put it in an envelope, sealed the envelope, and wrote a name on the outside. He placed the envelope next to the first note.

He walked into his bedroom, removed his shirt and retrieved from his closet, a small box. The took the box into the kitchen and placed in on the counter. He opened the box and saw the cold silvery steel. He checked to make sure Bert Wells' gun was loaded then tucked it into his belt. He walked slowly to his front door, opened it and left it ajar. He then pulled a kitchen chair near the counter with the two notes and sat, facing the front door. He took the note with the tape and taped it to his right leg.

He pulled his cell phone from his pocket and made his last call.

"911, what's your emergency?" A female voice asked.

"A man had a heart attack. CPR is in progress. We need an ambulance quickly at 66 East Appaloosa Trail in Wellington. Please come quickly." Then he placed the phone on the counter leaving the line open. He could hear the dispatcher asking questions for which she got no answers.

Then he waited. While he waited, he conjured an image of Amanda once again riding a horse. She was riding through a field of long grass, the wind gently pushing the grass to and fro as she galloped and smiled. It was early morning; the sun was just over the horizon and leaving long shadows on everything it touched. Amanda seemed happy and carefree; as a child should be.

In the distance, he could hear the siren. He waited until the wailing was just a few blocks away. Then he pulled the gun from his belt, put it under his chin and whispered, "I'm so sorry."

Then he pulled the trigger.

EPILOG

Friday, March 3, 2017

As she'd done every day for the last few weeks, Lauren Wells walked the few blocks to what used to be Jose's house and checked his mail. She'd taken it upon herself to make sure his bills were paid and started to keep track of monthly statements mailed to him from banks, brokerage accounts and mutual fund companies in which Jose had invested. She was surprised at the significant balances he held. But upon reflection, she realized he spent very little money. He took no vacations other than the travel he'd done with them. And, other than painting, he had no hobbies or indulgences she was aware of.

Today there were just two pieces of mail, both letters, hand addressed to Jose. She carried them into the deserted house. As she passed through the door she was reminded of that horrible day six weeks earlier.

Terry Kennedy had alerted her to the commotion at Jose's after passing by on her way back from the equestrian center. Lauren ran from her home and arrived just as the medics were carrying Jose from the house to the ambulance. His head was covered by a blood-soaked towel.

A policeman was standing by the front door. Lauren recognized him as the assistant coach of Liz's soccer team. "Jerry! What happened? Was that my friend Jose they just took away?" She was near hysteria.

"I'm afraid so Lauren. Looks like he took his own life. It still qualifies as a crime scene, so I need to stick around till the detectives get here."

"I don't understand. He wouldn't do that. That can't be right."

"Look, I'm sure I'm not supposed to show this to anyone yet but the EMT's gave it to me and I'm holding it for the homicide guys." He handed her the note that had been taped to Jose's leg. Lauren read it out loud in disbelief.

"I am Jose Martinez. I am blood type AB negative and wish to donate my organs to Amanda Muller who is a patient at Wellington Regional Medical Center and awaiting a liver transplant. Please take my body there immediately and notify the hospital that Dr. Vartebedian should be alerted that a liver donor has been found for Amanda Muller. Time is of the essence."

It was signed by Jose. She recognized his decorative signature immediately.

Today, the house was quiet. The crime scene tape had been taken down after a few days. Lauren had arranged for all Jose's clothing to be donated to the local homeless shelter. She didn't dare do more without some sort of authorization. His car, furniture and paintings would all be covered in his will, which she knew was one of today's two pieces of mail. Larry Finch had called Micah a few days after learning of Jose's suicide to tell him about the will Jose executed on the day he took his life. It had been duly signed and witnessed at Larry's office that afternoon. He told Micah he couldn't discuss the wills contents but promised to send a duplicate to Jose's home, something his clerk would have normally done anyway.

Lauren opened the legal-size envelope and read the short document. Lauren was appointed executor of his estate. His property was allocated as follows;

- The painting of Amanda Muller was left to Amanda Muller
- The paintings bearing the image of Lonnie Rossetti were left to Lonnie Rossetti
- All other artwork was left to Lauren to be disposed of as she saw fit
- All his household furnishings were to be donated to charities to be named by the executor.
- His home in Woodfield was left to Micah since the land had originally come from his farm.
- All residual property, including his home in Wellington and all financial assets which totaled nearly three million dollars, was left to Alex and Erica McCurry.

It seemed like a pathetically simple disposal of a man's life. As she'd done many times in the last few weeks, Lauren began to cry. She wasn't sure if she was weeping out of sorrow for her friend or from regret that she knew so little about him. His incredibly magnanimous gift to the Mullers made no sense to her. His entire life and death now made no sense to her. She was left with so many questions; questions she'd hoped the will would answer. It didn't. It only confused her more.

She wiped away the tears and looked at the second piece of mail, addressed simply to Jose. No last name. It was a handwritten letter from Lonnie Rossetti, the woman mentioned in the will. Her hands trembled as she read it:

"Dear Jose,
When we last spoke, I said being with you would always be a painful reminder of my friend who was killed on 9-11. I never got

to fully understand my feelings for Joey because he was killed before we had a chance to see what we might have become.

But I now realize I was wrong. Since our night on the beach all I can think about is you. Not because you remind me of someone else, but because you are someone I want to get to know. Not giving us the chance was a huge mistake on my part and I'm sorry it's taken me six months to realize that.

If you're still interested, I would love to get to know you better. I don't have a phone number for you or even a last name but this address was on your brochure (one I took from your booth at the Hampton Classic) and I hope this letter finds its way to you.

I hope it's not too late to try.

Lonnie"

Later that afternoon, Amanda Muller walked out of the Wellington Regional Medical Center with her mother and father at her side.

ABOUT THE AUTHOR

Stephen F. Medici lives in Huntington, New York. He is an adjunct professor at Molloy College and former CEO of the Black Mountain Group of companies. He is a firefighter and EMT in the Halesite Fire Department and has written three other novels: "The Girls in Pleated Skirts", "A Walk Around Cold Spring Pond" and "Adverse Selection".

Made in the USA
Middletown, DE
09 August 2017